THE MANY LIVES OF IVY WELLS

THE COMPLETE COLLECTION

MICHELLE FILES

Edited by
CECILY BROOKES

PUBLISHED BY BOOKLOVERS.PUB

INTRODUCTION

What would you do if a serial killer was tracking you through time?

Ivy Wells never wanted to die. When she does, she thinks it is all over. It isn't.

When the 30 year old mother of two wakes up as a 12 year old, she has to navigate her life all over again. And she remembers everything. Including the serial killer who is terrorizing her small town.

Can she stop him in time to save her friends? Can she somehow get back to her old life, with her children?

Get your copy of this gripping time travel serial.

Novels by Michelle Files:

TYLER MYSTERY SERIES:
Girl Lost - Book 1
A Reckless Life - Book 2

WILDFLOWER MYSTERY SERIES:
Secrets of Wildflower Island - Book 1
Desperation on Wildflower Island - Book 2
Storm on Wildflower Island - Book 3
Thorns On Wildflower Island - Book 4

THE MANY LIVES OF IVY WELLS
5 Part Time Travel Serial

For information on any of Michelle's books:
www.MichelleFiles.com

PART 1

CHAPTER 1

With the radio belting out some great '70s dance tunes, I swung my hips to the music, singing my favorite old songs, my long red hair swaying along in perfect rhythm. I knew every word to almost every song, and I was in the zone. The never ending chore of preparing dinner was always more fun to do while dancing.

My kids were sitting on a nearby couch playing a video game. The constant ratta tat tat of the machine gun on the video game grated on my nerves and I raised my voice in protest, singing louder than that damn game.

Hunter and Courtney turned to see what all the commotion was. The pair rolled their eyes in unison at the sight of their mother having the time of her life, while chopping carrots for dinner. My voice could rival any chainsaw, and I knew it. That was okay though. I knew singing was not my strong suit. It didn't matter, I loved it anyway.

"Mom, you are way too old for that," Hunter announced without taking his eyes off the game. "Whoa! Did you see that?!" he asked his little sister, excitedly pointing at the figure on the screen that just had his arm blown off. He had already forgotten me and my singing. Nine year olds didn't have much of an attention span.

I didn't bother responding to my son. He had already moved on. I shrugged my shoulders. Hunter's comment made me think about our lives. I was no longer with their father. That was by choice. I had just turned 30. That was not by choice. But I really did want to find a nice man and settle down. Maybe have more kids. I looked over at the two loves of my life sitting on the couch, engrossed in the bloody video game, and smiled. A couple more wouldn't be so bad, I thought.

If I did choose to have more children, it certainly wouldn't be with Hunter and Courtney's dad. That ship could sail right off the edge of the world, as far as I was concerned.

"Have you two done your homework yet?"

Not a peep came from either child.

"Hey! Did you two hear me? Get your butts up off that couch and get your homework done!" I wasn't really angry, but with the two of them it was often necessary to yell just to get my point across.

Seven year old Courtney jumped up first. She was more afraid of me than Hunter was. I stared daggers into the back of my son's head until he reluctantly got up, turned off the TV, and climbed the stairs to his room. I smiled when I heard both of their bedroom doors slam. A couple of minutes later, both children emerged from their rooms carrying books and paper down the stairs, to the dining room table. It was where they always did their homework, as I supervised. They both started on their homework as I continued making dinner.

As I started scooping up the sliced carrots and dropping them into the boiling water on the stove, a news story came on. I was instantly immobilized when I realized they were talking about my hometown.

The news announcer said that the bodies of three missing teenagers, all girls, had been found near Red Lake. Because of this, the local sheriff had decided to re-open an old cold case from 15 years ago, where two teen girls had gone missing, and were found a short time later in the same area. The sheriff wanted to caution that this may just be a coincidence, or even a copycat. It wasn't entirely clear at this point. There was no proof yet that this was the same killer from the previous homicides.

I remembered the original case well, because I knew both victims from 15 years ago, when I was just a teenager myself. The killer had never been caught, and he left the entire town with a serious case of the jitters.

Red Lake previously had been one of those places where no one locked their doors at night. That changed 15 years ago. Once the sun went down, the town closed its shutters and no one ventured out until daylight. In the daytime, people were more relaxed, safety no longer in the forefront of their minds. Even so, those two young girls, who had been brutally murdered, were never forgotten. And the killer had never been apprehended.

The announcer continued with the story as I listened intently, forgetting all about dinner.

"Fifteen years ago, Bernadette James went missing. She is believed to be the first victim of the Red Lake Slasher."

Ah, geez, I thought. Just what that town needed. A nickname like that will stick in everyone's minds forever. As if the name Red Lake for a town wasn't bad enough.

"Several months after Bernadette's untimely death, the second victim of the Red Lake Slasher was..."

The phone rang just at the moment that the news was about to name the second victim. I didn't hear the name as the phone drowned it out. It didn't matter anyway. I knew the name. I knew it well. I turned the radio down and continued chopping vegetables as I propped the phone between my left shoulder and ear.

"Hello?"

That was the only word I said into the phone that day. Listening to the voice on the other end of the line, I was rendered

THE MANY LIVES OF IVY WELLS

speechless. My face blanched and I dropped the phone, scattering vegetables everywhere. It didn't matter.

Dropping the knife onto the kitchen counter, I began yelling to my kids. "He's found us! Code red, code red!" That was all I needed to say to them. I had prepared my kids well.

Without a word, Hunter and Courtney jumped up out of their chairs, ran to the hall closet, and grabbed their pre-packed back-packs. Hunter grabbed my backpack also, as he had been previously instructed to do. Those packs had been sitting in the closet, untouched, for two years. I was relieved that I had been smart enough to pack them back then, hoping beyond hope that we would never need them.

With the lights on, and dinner still simmering on the stove, the three of us convened at the front door in less than one minute from the time I picked up the phone. Hunter handed my backpack to me and we headed out, no conversation necessary.

As I pulled the front door open, I gasped. There he was, right in front of me. His dark hair was shorter than I remembered. But those eyes. Those steel gray eyes. Those would never change. A shudder ran up my spine as I stared back into those eyes.

"Hi Ivy, Baby. Happy to see me?"

He was smiling at me and it was the creepiest thing I had ever seen. If Freddy Krueger himself had been standing there, it would not have been so chilling. Simon was a whole other monster.

He stood there, holding my gaze, for what seemed like an eternity. I dared not look away, for fear that he would get to me in that briefest of moments when my attention was temporarily elsewhere.

As he started to look down at the children, I needed to take action.

"Kids! Go upstairs right now to Hunter's room. Lock the door and stay together!"

Both of the kids hesitated as they looked at the man standing before them.

That was something I could understand. They had not seen him in two years. Memories faded over time, especially for children. I could see that they were hesitant to leave, both instinctively wanted to engage with him.

It broke my heart, but I just couldn't let that happen. He was evil. He was not going to get his hands on my children. I would die before I let that happen.

With everything I had, I tried to slam the door in his face and began yelling at the children.

"Go upstairs now!" I screamed as he shoved the door hard, causing me to slam into the wall next to the door. Stars floated around my vision. Luckily I was only stunned for a moment though. I shook the cobwebs from my mind, because I knew that I needed to act fast.

"Go!" I yelled again.

Hunter grabbed his little sister's hand and the two of them ran up the stairs as fast as they could. I didn't have time to confirm that they had reached their destination. I had to attend to the man standing in front of me.

CHAPTER 2

That's when Simon grabbed me by the throat with one hand. He yanked me away from the wall and toward the kitchen, holding me up high, so that my feet barely touched the floor. Thankfully, Simon was not squeezing the air out of me as he did so, because I was no match for his strength. He had biceps that I didn't remember him having. The man had been busy while we were away.

I knew that I needed to do something to get out of the impossible situation that I had found myself in. If I didn't act quickly, I was going to die. That was inevitable. Simon would have no qualms about killing me right then and there. He had two years of hatred to make up for.

I reached up and grabbed a handful of his hair. Then with everything I had, I twisted his head at an almost impossible angle, causing Simon to yell out in pain and briefly release his hold on my throat. Gasping for air, it was just enough for me to get away, and I released my hold on his hair. Just as we reached the kitchen, I tried to bolt, but didn't get far. Simon lunged at me from behind and grabbed me around the waist. He managed to pin my arms to my sides, knocking the wind out of me as he did so. With my back to him, he held tight so that I couldn't move. Barely able to breathe, my breath escaped in shuddering gasps.

"Really, Sweetheart, is all of this fuss necessary? What kind of way is this to treat your husband?" he asked calmly, as he gently nuzzled the back of my neck.

I stiffened. His voice gave me the chills.

"Ex-husband," I reminded him.

"Not really, no. I'm still legally your husband. You didn't forget that, did you?"

"What do you want?" I gasped out as I tried to calm down and catch my breath.

"I just want to see you. And the kids. I miss all of you." Simon almost sounded human to me when he said that.

"Well we don't miss you. Can't you just leave us the hell alone! We have been doing just fine here without you," I told him bluntly.

Simon spun me around so that I was facing him and released my arms. He held onto my waist so tightly that I had to struggle to breathe. But, I knew that he wasn't about to give me the maneuverability that I needed to escape his embrace.

"Come on Sweetheart, don't be like that. I want you back. We can be a family again."

Simon leaned in and kissed me passionately on the lips. It was all that I could do not to gag. The man was revolting and I wanted nothing to do with him. Not now. Not ever. Without thinking it through, I reared my head back and threw it forward as hard as I could muster into a near skull cracking head butt.

Simon was so caught off guard that he released me at once, and I took a couple of steps back. I immediately regretted the head butt. It gave me an instant, piercing headache. Why that possibility didn't occur to me, was beyond my comprehension at the moment. Instinctively, I reached up and touched my forehead, to make sure it wasn't cracked. Miraculously, it seemed okay.

"You bitch!" he screamed as he held his left palm up to his

forehead and pulled it down to look at it. No blood. "I'm gonna fucking kill you!"

As he stepped toward me, I had to do something, and I had to do it fast. I reached my right hand over to the counter next to where we were standing and felt around for the knife that I knew was there. I made sure that my eyes never left his. It was working. He didn't realize what I was doing, until it was too late. As he reached me, I swung the knife in his direction. But I was no match for him in height or strength and he was easily able to grab my arm and stop the forward motion of the knife toward him.

"Drop the knife," he ordered.

I wasn't about to give in though. My life, and my kids' lives were at stake. I yanked my arm back and we struggled, neither one wanting to let go. At one point, our commingling sweat caused Simon to momentarily lose his grip on my knife wielding arm. As his grip slipped, I mustered all the courage I could and stabbed him in the stomach.

It momentarily surprised me at how easily the knife went in. In shock and disbelief, I couldn't believe I had done that. I instinctively pulled the knife back out, but held onto it for dear life. It might mean the difference between living and dying today.

He cried out in pain and his right hand immediately dropped to cover the wound, gushing with blood.

"What the hell? You actually stabbed me?"

Simon was calmer than I had expected and looked at me with incredulous eyes. No matter what he had done to me, he couldn't believe that I would ever stab him. I had always been the submissive one, and the last person he would ever expect to fight back. I was not the same person as I was two years ago. Things had changed. I had changed. I was a stronger, more self-assured, person. I wasn't backing down. I wasn't about to let him get to me and my children.

Before I had a chance to turn and run, he found some new strength, deep down in his core somewhere, and attacked. Simon reared back his bloodied right hand and punched me squarely in the left cheek. I felt the bones crunch and my head started spinning. I had no choice but to drop the knife that I had been holding onto so tightly, and put both hands on the kitchen counter to steady myself. If I didn't do that, I would surely have hit the ground. I began shaking my head, trying to get my wits about me, as I adjusted to the blinding pain in my face. I knew that losing consciousness could be deadly.

About three seconds later, I felt like I was being punched in the back. It didn't really hurt though. It was such an odd feeling and I was temporarily confused, as I looked up at Simon to confirm what I felt. That's when I realized that Simon was holding the bloody knife. The very one that I had just dropped moments ago. Suddenly, I could feel the warm liquid gushing out of my back. Oh my god, he had stabbed me. Momentarily, I was surprised that I didn't feel any pain.

With everything I had, I bolted for the front door. I had to get help. In that moment, I actually hoped that Simon would follow me out. I didn't want to leave him alone with Hunter and Courtney. But even if he didn't follow me, I knew in my heart that he would never harm his own children. Even with everything that was going on right then, that was something he would never do. It was only me that he was after. Regardless of the man he had turned out to be, I knew that he loved his kids. He would not hurt them.

He did follow me out and caught up to me on the front lawn, where we continued our fight for survival. I didn't know how much longer I could last, because I was beginning to feel light headed and dizzy. The pain of the broken bones in my face, and most certainly the blood loss, were starting to get to me. I wondered why it took so long. Maybe it was the adrenaline. Maybe it was the thought of giving up and leaving my children to this horrible man in front of me. I still don't know, but I was not going to go down without using the last tiny bit of momma bear strength I could draw upon.

As the sun was dipping below the horizon, Simon stabbed me twice more in the stomach before I just couldn't fight anymore. I finally gave into the inevitable, and felt a sudden peace wash over me. Somehow, though I don't know how it was possible, I was still on my feet.

That's when Simon suddenly fell to the ground. His once blue shirt was soaked in a dark red stain and a large puddle of blood formed around him. I didn't have time to worry about him. I kicked the knife as hard as I could. It landed in the bougainvillea bushes I had planted the previous spring.

As I turned to run back into the house, toward my waiting and frightened children, my head began to spin. Before I had time to react, my vision grew increasingly darker and darker. I landed hard on the ground next to my husband.

Three things happened as I laid there in a pool of my own blood, the life draining from my body. The first was that I could hear the radio in the kitchen playing one of my favorite songs. It actually made me smile as my life faded away. The second thing was that I could smell the dinner that I had been preparing. It was now burning on the stove, and I thought of my kids hiding in a burning house. The third was the earthquake I felt at exactly 6:59 pm as I took my last breath.

CHAPTER 3

As I slowly returned to consciousness, something was amiss. The ground underneath me was damp and there was a cool breeze around the rest of me, giving rise to goosebumps on my arms. For just a second, I was confused. Then a moment later, I realized I was outside, lying in damp grass, before even opening my eyes. The grass was tickling my nose, causing me to instinctively raise my right hand to rub away the itch. When I opened my eyes and sat up, I took in my surroundings, looking up when a dog barked in the distance.

The first thing I noticed was that I was no longer lying in my own front yard, and Simon was not lying next to me, as expected. This brought about instant panic, as I wondered where he had gone. Was it possible that he had survived our fight and gotten away? I had no idea how that could have happened. He had been severely injured. So was I, yet here I was. Alive and well. But where was I?

Looking around, I could see that I was in the backyard of someone's house. Whose house? I perused the beige walls and white trim of the huge house. Mansion really. Even the back patio was enormous. It had some of those huge planters on the patio with trees in them. You know, the kind you see in malls, and sometimes in parking lots of upscale shopping centers. It would take a forklift to move those things.

The whole scene in front of me was all very familiar. I had been here before. But when? I turned to look out into the yard, hoping to shake something loose in my head. And that did it. There was the lake. Red Lake. The very one that my hometown had been named for. Instantly I knew exactly where I was. In the backyard of Bernadette James' house. I had spent many summer days playing in the backyard, and swimming in the lake right near where I was sitting.

I hadn't been in this backyard for many years though, ever since Bernadette decided she no longer wanted to be my friend. But that was a story for another time. At the moment, I needed to figure out how I managed to get here, from the town that I currently lived in.

That's when a cool breeze hit me and my body shuddered in response. I wrapped my bare arms around my chest, in an attempt to push back the chill coming off the nearby lake. I was only wearing a pair of shorts and a t-shirt. No shoes and no sweatshirt. I could have used both of them at the moment. How did I get into these clothes?

Standing up, I realized that I felt no pain. I had been stabbed multiple times in my back, and in my stomach, yet when I looked down, there was no blood. I reached around behind and felt my back. No blood there either. What in the hell was going on? This was completely impossible. I lifted the front of my shirt to double check. No stab wounds. Not even a scratch. Geez, look how skinny my belly is. Did I lose weight while I was unconscious?

Lost, cold, and scared, the fear started showing itself in my chin, and worked its way up to my trembling lips, as I began to cry. I couldn't help myself. It all just came blubbering out.

Once I calmed down a bit, I looked over at the house and wondered if I should knock on the back door or run around to the side and let myself out the front gate, hoping no one would see me. Then where would I go? Nothing like this had ever happened before and I began wondering if I had sleep walked here. What other explanation was there?

If sleepwalking was the answer, where was I sleeping in the first place? I couldn't possibly have walked several states over, from my own home to Red Lake.

Even if somehow I had sleepwalked, and just didn't remember being in town, that doesn't explain the lack of blood or wounds on my body.

I was beginning to feel a bit overwhelmed and walked over to sit at the patio table. I needed a bit of time, just long enough to gather my wits about me. I looked around for anything else that might be familiar in the yard. When I noticed the red water tower off in the distance, I was paralyzed.

"What the...No way. Where did that come from?" I was talking out loud, something I did a lot anyway, when I realized that my voice sounded strange.

That's when I looked down at my body. Really looked at it. I no longer had the body of a 30 year old woman, but looked like a young child. My bare legs were skinny. I caressed my smooth, thin arms. My skin was tight and firm, something that I was starting to lose at 30 years old.

I looked up into the sliding glass door of the house and caught sight of myself for the first time, and gasped at at my reflection. I looked like I was 11 or 12 years old. What the hell is going on? I jumped up in a panic, temporarily forgetting how chilly the afternoon air was.

Looking over again at the sliding glass door, I saw a woman sitting at her dining room table, looking at her computer, and drinking something. She must have heard me, or caught a glimpse of me moving around in her backyard, because she looked up then and our eyes met. Cautiously, she got up and walked to the glass sliding door to peer out. I'm sure that I was the last thing she ever expected to find in her backyard. A cat brushed my leg and I looked down.

"Matilda, come here. Kitty kitty," the woman called. Matilda complied, darting in through the small opening of the sliding door.

"Ivy, are you all right?" she asked, walking out into the backyard. "What are you doing here?"

I recognized Mrs. James as soon as she walked out. Her daughter and I had been good friends once. I ran to her, grabbing her tightly around the waist and holding on while I slowly calmed down enough to speak. Mrs. James wrapped her arms around my shoulders and just let me cry.

"How di-did I g-get here?" I stuttered between sobs.

"I don't know. I was just about to ask you the same thing. You are at least a couple miles from your house."

"I w-was having a fight with my husband, and then I woke up here. I d-don't remember anything else." I was still blubbering.

"You were what?" Mrs. James pulled back from my embrace and gave me questioning eyes.

That's when I realized what I had just said and how it must have sounded to her. I was a young child after all.

"I, I..mean, I fell asleep and then I woke up here. Do you think I was sleepwalking?" Nice cover, I thought.

"What are you doing in my backyard?"

We both turned toward the snarky voice. I recognized the girl immediately and stared in disbelief. It was Mrs. James' daughter, Bernadette. The first victim of the Red Lake Slasher. My jaw dropped open. My entire body began to shake in response.

"Bernadette?" That was all I could get out. "Oh my god. Is that you?"

"Yeah, who else would it be? You are in my backyard."

Bernadette stood in the doorway with her arms crossed, looking quite annoyed with me. She hadn't changed a bit. She was still that hateful, privileged, girl that I remembered.

CHAPTER 4

It had been 15 years since I saw Bernadette last, and we had both been 15 years old at that time. Now, we both were obviously younger than that. This is crazy, I thought. I had to be dreaming. Or was I actually dead from my stab wounds, and this was heaven?

"Hey, let's go inside and get you a blanket to warm up. You're barefoot and must be freezing out here. I'll make you a hot chocolate before I take you home. Okay with you?" Mrs. James asked me.

"Y-yes." I was trying very hard to calm down, but was still upset and in shock from everything that had transpired in the last few minutes.

Bernadette reluctantly stepped aside to allow her mother and me to enter the house. She followed us into the kitchen.

As we sat at the kitchen table drinking hot chocolate, I could not keep my eyes off of Bernadette.

"Why are you staring at me? What is your problem?" Bernadette asked me, disdain dripping from her voice.

"I don't know. Sorry." It was the only thing that I could think of to say, lowering my eyes and staring into my mug.

"Bernie, shut up. Can't you see that she is upset?" Mrs. James scolded her daughter.

Bernadette shrugged her shoulders and ignored her mother. She shook her head in a familiar backward motion to get her long straight hair out of her face. It reminded me of years ago, when I was very jealous of that straight blonde hair. My own red hair was curly and often unruly. It was the bane of my existence as a teenager. By the time I was grown though, with kids of my own, I had learned to love my red hair and wore it with pride.

I needed to get some answers, and wondered what the best way was to go about that. Do I just blurt out my questions, making me look like a crazy person? No, that's a bad idea. I needed to work them into a casual conversation, not making them sound so obvious. Okay, here goes.

"Um, how old are you?" Oh great, that was not casual at all. I sounded like an idiot.

Bernadette narrowed her eyes. "That's a stupid question. We are both 12. You know that. Did you hit your head on something in the backyard?"

"Bernadette!" her mother snapped.

Even with all of the evidence in front of me, such as my young, skinny body, my reflection in the sliding glass doors, the water tower, the fact that Bernadette was alive once again, and even now with Bernadette confirming that she was 12 years old, I still couldn't believe what I was hearing.

Was I dead? Is that why I turned up at Bernadette's house at only 12 years old? How was that even possible? And, I remembered everything from my actual life. I have two children and had been on the run from Simon. Was I reliving my life? If so, where are my children? Do they exist somewhere else? Did they never exist at all now that I'm a kid again? Was I maybe hallucinating all of it? It all hurt my brain to try making sense of it all.

"I asked you a question." Bernadette's voice pierced through my daydream and snapped me out of it.

"You did? What question?"

"Ugh, never mind." Bernadette had finished her hot chocolate and got up to leave the kitchen. She didn't bother to put her cup in the sink.

About 20 minutes later, Mrs. James and I walked into my house together.

"Oh my god, Ivy!" My mother ran across the room and dropped to her knees to hug me. I was still wrapped up in the green blanket with pink embroidered flowers that Mrs. James had given me. "Are you okay?"

I couldn't even answer and started crying all over again. The experience was clearly very traumatic. Why wouldn't it be? Besides, seeing my parents again was overwhelming. I hadn't seen them or talked to them in over two years. They were obviously a lot younger than the last time I had seen them.

My father walked out of the kitchen about 30 seconds later and saw us there, still hugging. I was trying to squirm out of my mother's arms, but she was holding on tight. The look on my father's face was relief at the sight of me. He looked like he was struggling to find the right words, and just ended up standing there, speechless. Once my mother loosened her grip, he walked over quietly and gave me a strong, reassuring hug.

As my mother got back up to her feet, she turned to Mrs. James, who had been standing there silently while the family reunited.

"Ivy's been missing for hours," she began. "How did she end up with you? Where did you find her?" my mother asked.

"Well actually, Ellen, I found her in my backyard. She was just sitting there all by herself, crying."

"What? You live miles from here. How do you think she got there?" My mother asked her, a bit suspiciously.

"Why are you looking at me like that? I have no idea. I asked Ivy and she said she doesn't know. She said she just woke up there," Mrs. James replied, opening her mouth again to make a smart comment, but thought better of it, and closed it tight.

"Just woke up there?" My mother turned to me then. "Ivy, what is going on? How did you get to Mrs. James' house?"

"I don't know, Mom. I just woke up in her backyard. I don't know how." The problem was that I really didn't know. I had no idea where I was before I woke up in the backyard. The only thing I remembered was being at my own house, at 30 years old, fighting with Simon.

"So you just showed up there? You didn't walk over with someone? No one gave you a ride? Are you sure, Ivy?" My father, Walter, grilled me.

My mother seemed to notice my feet for the first time. "And why are you barefoot?" she asked as she looked back up at me. "It's chilly out there."

"I said I don't know!" I yelled back. I had no idea why I did that. It just came out. I did remember being a bit of a brat as a child.

"Well, I should go." Mrs. James was crossing and uncrossing her arms, and looking around the room, clearly uncomfortable being in the middle of a private family matter.

Once the woman was gone, my parents sat me down to have a talk with me. Oh great, I'm 30 years old and getting chastised by my parents. This is going to be a lot of fun.

"Ivy, your story is really hard to believe. There's no way you could walk across town, alone, and not remember it. Come on, what's really going on here?" My father asked me again.

I just sat back in the chair and crossed my arms over my chest defiantly. I needed some time to figure out what was going on, and to come up with a plausible explanation for landing in Bernadette's backyard. At the moment, I had nothing.

"Well, that's just fine. You are grounded young lady, until you can tell us the truth," my mother announced. "Now go up to your room." She pointed toward the staircase.

"I don't care if you don't believe me!" I screamed as I got up from the chair and headed up the staircase.

Wow, I thought. It must be the hormones. Did I actually treat my parents like that back then? I honestly couldn't remember. Twelve years old was a long time ago.

I stopped just around the corner at the top of the stairs, eavesdropping on my parents.

"Can you imagine what she's going to be like when she's a teenager?" my mother asked. I doubted that she expected an answer to that question.

"Do you think she sleepwalked?" my father responded.

"I don't know. Is it even possible for a 12 year old to sleepwalk, in the middle of the day, across town? She would have to cross several streets on her way without getting hit by a car. Then she ended up at the house of someone we know. Could she do that?" my mother replied. "And I don't think she's even been to the James' house in years, ever since she and Bernadette had that falling out. So, I wonder why she would go there?" My mother had a lot of questions.

"She does get into a lot of trouble for her age. She probably just walked over there because she didn't want to do her chores. I don't see any other explanation that makes sense." My father had always been the more reasonable one of the two. "Besides, she does know Bernadette. Maybe she walked over to see her."

CHAPTER 5

Reaching my bedroom, I walked immediately over to my dresser mirror. I needed to get a better look at myself. It was the first good look I had gotten ever since this ordeal began. Looking at my medium length red hair, that was always a bit wild when I was this age, I tried to smooth it down, to no avail. When I got older, I was able to tame it to make it a bit more manageable.

Leaning in to the mirror, I looked closely at my young face. No crows feet around my eyes. I liked that. There were definitely benefits to waking up so young. My skinny body was 12, but my mind was still 30. That was an odd problem to have. And maybe a blessing. I knew way more about life than any other 12 year old on the planet could possibly know.

Plopping down on my lavender bedspread, I pulled a blanket up over me, in an attempt to warm up. I was still only wearing a t-shirt and shorts and was still chilled. I thought about the situation that I had found myself in. How could this have happened? I remembered feeling an earthquake just as my mind faded to black in the front yard of my house. Was there really an earthquake? I suddenly wasn't sure. So much was going on at that moment, and in the last few minutes of my life, I just couldn't be sure.

Did I actually die? No, I couldn't have. Here I am, sitting in my bedroom, definitely alive. It had to be something else. I'm sure people didn't die and just come back to life as their younger selves. The world would be in chaos if that really happened on a regular basis. Can you imagine a bunch of 12 year olds acting like they were 50? Trying to run companies. Trying to drive. Wanting to get married. I just laughed at the absurdity of it all.

And if there was an earthquake, I wondered if it had something to do with me coming back? No, that was ridiculous. Earthquakes don't cause people to come back to life.

Do they?

"Ivy! It's time for dinner!" my mother yelled up from the bottom of the stairs.

"Okay, I'll be right down!" That's when I realized that I was famished. It had been 12 years since I had my last meal. No wonder I was so skinny. The thought made me smile.

As we ate dinner that evening, I didn't talk much. I had to be very careful about what I said. Blurting out something that had happened, or would happen, I guess, in my future, could be disastrous. I so very badly wanted to talk to my parents about my children. Hunter and Courtney were in the forefront of my thoughts. My parents had loved them so much. But since my children didn't actually exist in this timeline, not yet anyway, I obviously couldn't talk about them.

My brother, Parker, three years older than I was, did most of the talking, which was fine with me. I felt that keeping my mouth mostly shut was the best thing for the time being.

"Ives, why are you so quiet all of a sudden?" Parker asked me. "Usually your mouth is going a million miles a minute."

I narrowed my eyes at him. "Ha ha, very funny. I just don't have much to talk about tonight, I guess."

His use of that nickname for me made me smile. Since I had been on the run from my husband, Simon, I hadn't spoken to Parker much, and rarely heard the nickname anymore. The name used to annoy me as a child, but I decided that I now liked it. Parker was the only one that was allowed to called me that.

Parker looked so young at 15 years old. I took in the unruly mop of hair on his head, that was the same shade of red as mine. And that pale skin of his. Somehow he ended up much paler than I did. I was thankful for that. His skin blistered if he spent any length of time in the sun. Mine seemed to tan nicely.

Still...he was different this time. It took me a minute to figure out what that was, since I hadn't seen him at this age in 18 years. He wasn't the awkward, gawky, teenager that I remembered. He seemed more self-assured. A bit cocky, maybe. He had been working out. I liked the new Parker. It suited him.

This was the first thing I noticed that was different this time around, and I wondered why it was different. In my non-existent knowledge of time travel, it seemed to me that things would be the same each time, unless I maybe caused it to be different. But I hadn't been in this lifetime very long yet. Certainly not long enough to change anything.

Perhaps I would find out before I returned to my usual life. I certainly hoped that would happen soon. I had no desire to remain 12 years old for any length of time.

I had especially missed my parents. Ever since I went on the run, I was afraid to contact them or let them know where I was, afraid that Simon would find out. He had a way of making people talk. My parents might have mentioned my whereabouts to him, in casual conversation, without even realizing it. So I had to make the heart wrenching decision to have no communication with them at all, so they could stay safe. And so my children and I could stay safe. My parents knew why I left. I felt badly that they hadn't seen their grandchildren in two years. Knowing that I didn't have to worry about Parker, we kept in semi-regular contact. I knew that Simon would never get anything out of him.

Why did this thing have to happened to me? If I was going to come back to life, why did it happen when I was 12 years old?

There must be some reason, but I had no idea what that could possibly be. Maybe if I went to sleep, I would wake back up in my own bed, with my children in their rooms. Though my life was chaotic, having to be on alert for Simon always, I desperately wanted to be back there with Hunter and Courtney. Was that possible? The thought gave me hope. Maybe I would wake up and realize what I was currently experiencing was just a dream.

I never left the safety of my bedroom that night. Not long after dinner, as I laid on my bed thinking about my new life, I drifted off, hoping and praying that things would be different in the morning.

"Ivy! The phone's for you, as usual!" My eyes flew open when I heard my brother yelling from downstairs.

For just a moment, I was confused. Lying in bed, I took in my surroundings. The bedroom was awash with morning light, giving the lavender walls a bright glow. It all came back to me. I was 12 and living at home with my parents again. It wasn't all a dream. I did not wake up in my own home, with my kids nearby. Pulling the blankets over my head, it was almost more than I could bear.

"Ivy! I'm gonna hang up the phone if you don't come get it right now!" It was Parker's voice again.

"Okay, okay, I'm coming!" I yelled back.

There was no point in lamenting over my circumstances. It was what it was. And until I could figure out a way to make everything right in the world, it was my current reality. In fact, unless I could find a time portal somewhere that would magically swoop me back to my future self, then I was stuck here. And, unless that magic time portal was in Bernadette's backyard, I wouldn't even have a clue where to start to find it.

I jumped up out of bed and wrapped my robe around myself.

That's when I realized that I was still wearing the same t-shirt and shorts from the previous day. I really needed a shower and change of clothes.

"Hello?" I said into the living room phone, wondering who in the world it could possibly be. Who would be calling my 12 year old self?

"Hey. What are you wearing to school today?" the voice on the other end of the line asked.

"What? Who is thi....." I never finished the sentence and dropped the phone as my hands shook and I lost my grip on the receiver.

Josephine. I hadn't heard Josephine's voice in 15 years. My mother walked into the room just as I burst out sobbing.

"Ivy, Honey, what's wrong?" my mother asked, taking me into her arms.

"It's...it's...Josephine. On the...phone," I stuttered out between sobs.

"Did something happen? Is she all right?" My mother had that look of concern on her face that mothers get. I remembered that look well.

"Yes, she's supposed to be..." I paused to think over what I was about to say. "Oh, no I guess not. I just...I don't know." That was all I could get out as I continued sobbing into my mother's shoulder.

My mother stepped back from my embrace, holding me at arm's length and looked me in the eyes. "Sweetheart, are you all right?" she asked with a wrinkled brow.

I could see the worry on her face. "I'm okay. I need to get back on the phone. Really, I'm okay." I took a deep breath, trying to compose myself.

"Well all right. We can talk later if you like." With that, she walked out of the room.

I picked up the receiver from the floor. "Josie?"

CHAPTER 6

"What happened to you? I could hear you crying. Did something happen?" It really was Josephine on the line. It was still hard to believe.

"Um, no...I stubbed my toe hard on the table. Sorry about that." It was the first thing that came to my mind.

"Oh, okay. So what are you wearing to school today?" Funny how young girls can just jump from topic to topic without a second thought.

"School? We have school today?" Oh my god, I have to go to school?

"Yes, dummy, it's Monday. Are you sure you're okay?" Josephine asked again.

"Yeah, I'm fine. I don't know what I'm wearing. I just woke up."

"I'll be there in 20 minutes, so hurry and get ready." Josephine hung up.

"Oh crap, I have to go to school," I said out loud. "What grade am I even in? Sixth grade? Yes, that must be it. Elementary school. Just great."

"You are losing your mind, Ives," Parker said casually as he walked past me and out the front door.

"Yeah, I guess I am," I replied back to no one.

I ran upstairs to shower and change before Josephine arrived. I didn't have much time. I had no idea what to wear, as it had been a lot of years since I was last 12 years old. I chose a pair of jeans and a pink t-shirt. They would have to do. The items were in my closet, so I figured they would work. I found matching pink tennis shoes and put them on just as I heard the front door open. I ran down the stairs without taking the time to tie my shoes.

Josephine walked in the front door precisely 22 minutes after our call. No knocking necessary. I leapt into her arms and started sobbing. Again.

"What is the matter with you?" Josephine asked as she just stood there letting me hug her and cry.

I quickly collected myself. "Oh nothing. Sorry. I'm just in a weird mood today. Wow, you look so great."

"Thanks," Josephine replied, spinning around to show off her new outfit to me.

The two of us walked to school together. Though Josephine had no trouble keeping the conversation going all on her own, I tried to participate. I had to make a concerted effort to speak like a 12 year old would, and not a 30 year old, with life experiences.

The whole thing was difficult though. I still couldn't believe that I was actually walking with, and talking to, Josephine again after all these years.

I thought back to the day before when I was making dinner for the kids and the radio was talking about the Red Lake Slasher. He spoke about Bernadette being the first victim. Just as he was about to announce the second victim, was the moment that the phone rang and Simon was on the other end. In all the confusion of the next few minutes, I had forgotten the news that I had been listening to. I knew who the second victim was though. He didn't need to tell me. It was Josephine. My very best friend, and the girl that I was currently walking next to. It took everything I had not to break down blubbering, once again.

Still in a state of shock over everything that had transpired recently, I hadn't even thought about what I was going to do once we reached school. As we walked onto the school grounds, a flood of memories hit me. It was almost as if the last 18 years had not happened. I was no longer a 30 year old woman, but now a 12 year old little girl.

The elementary school was exactly as I remembered it. Light green walls with dark green trim. It was really ugly actually. I wondered who in the world came up with that color scheme. And then, who green-lit it? Pun intended.

Boy, what a crazy day this is going to be, I thought. I remembered that I had the same sixth grade class as Josephine, thankfully, and followed her to our classroom, sitting down in the desk next to my friend. I looked around at our classmates. Many of them I remembered, but many I didn't. Funny how people float in and out of our lives.

When my eyes landed on Bernadette, I froze. The two of us were not friends. In fact, I remember avoiding her at all costs. Bernadette was the rich kid in school and was spoiled and snotty. She had her core group of friends, and many others that wanted to be her friend. I was not one of them. We had actually been best buddies in school when we were younger, until we hit fourth grade. That's when Bernadette realized that her family had money, and started acting as if she was better than anyone else.

My family was not well off, though we did just fine. But we were not good enough for the new, enlightened Bernadette. She lived in the big, fancy house on the lake. We did not. We had hardly spoken in the subsequent years, until Bernadette's untimely death at the age of 15.

Though all day long I felt like I was going to jump out of my skin, I somehow got through the first half of the school day. As Josephine and I headed for lunch, I realized that I hadn't brought anything to eat and didn't have any money on me for the cafeteria. Josephine came to my rescue. Then, as luck would have it,

Bernadette bumped into me on purpose just as Josephine was handing me some money to buy lunch. The coins went flying everywhere and Bernadette laughed as I scrambled to pick them up off the floor. It was quite the sight as I dodged around all the students shuffling in to the cafeteria, listening to all the snickers aimed in my direction. I told myself to just let it go. It was my first day back from the future after all. I needed time to get the lay of the land.

Bernadette and her friends sat down at the same table we were at. Of course they did. My transition to a young girl couldn't be easy, could it? I tried my best to ignore their snide, off handed comments about Josephine and me. I really didn't want any trouble. I wanted to lay low, taking in the atmosphere of sixth grade all over again.

Unfortunately for Bernadette, I was no longer a scared 12 year old that could be easily intimidated. Regardless of my outer appearance, I was a 30 year old woman that had learned over the years to not take crap from anyone.

"So, Ivy," Bernadette said quite a bit louder than I would have preferred. "Do you make it a habit of sneaking into people's backyards and taking a nap on their lawn?" Bernadette's friends all cackled with laughter.

I did not respond, and refused to look Bernadette's way. Just let it go, I told myself. Just let it go.

"Loser," Bernadette continued.

That time, quite a few more students in the cafeteria started laughing. They were at the perfect age that made it a lot easier to join in with a bully, than with the bullied. I was on my own. Even Josephine sat quietly, her eyes downcast.

"You better just shut the hell up," I replied, my eyes deadlocked with Bernadette's.

Bernadette did not respond. I think she was in a bit of shock that I back talked her. That was completely new territory for her.

"Are you going to let her talk to you like that?" One of her friends goaded Bernadette.

"Listen, Bernadette," I said louder than I meant to. "I'm not going to put up with your bullshit. Got it?"

"What are you going to do about it?" Bernadette smirked at me.

That was it. There was no way I could let Bernadette's comment go unchallenged. I knew that the best way to beat a bully was to not back down. Once you backed down, it was all over. You would be their target for the rest of time. Those were the unfortunate politics of the sixth grade.

That's when I stood up and walked over to where she was sitting. Bernadette just looked up at me with a crooked smile. I don't think she had any inkling of what I was about to do. Before she realized what I was doing, I reached down, slid my hand under Bernadette's food tray, and flipped it up into the air, showering Bernadette with beans, rice, and tacos, the specialty of the day. Bernadette immediately jumped up in horror.

"There, that's what I'm going to do about it. Bother me or my friend again, and there will be more where that came from. And if you call me a loser again, I'll knock the shit out of you."

I stood staring right into Bernadette's eyes, refusing to be the one that backed down first. Neither one of us dared to look around the dead quiet room. We knew all eyes were on us.

Bernadette turned and ran for the bathroom, her posse trailing close behind. I felt just a ping of guilt. Twelve year old Bernadette was no match for a grown woman.

"Come on Josie, let's go." Josephine dutifully followed me out of the cafeteria, while every other student gaped.

An hour later, Bernadette and I were sitting in the principal's office. Bernadette's hair was hanging limp after she had to rinse it out in the school's bathroom sink. She glared at me, but didn't say a word. Both of us got a stern talking to, but neither were suspended.

All in all, I felt that my first day of school in so many years was a raging success.

CHAPTER 7

Josephine had a dentist appointment that afternoon, so her mother picked her up from school, leaving me to walk home alone. That was all right with me. I needed some time to think anyway. During the walk, I thought about the incident in the cafeteria and regretted it. Twelve year old Bernadette was no match for me. I was an adult, with adult experiences, regardless of what I looked like. I could easily outsmart a 12 year old any day of the week.

I also felt a duty to try to save Bernadette from the serial killer in town. The Red Lake Slasher, as he would be known many years in the future. No one had died yet, but it was coming, and I was the only one that knew that. Wow, what a burden to put on a young girl, such as myself.

I figured that the only way to save Bernadette was to befriend her, as repulsive as that thought was. Besides, what if I came back to life just to save her? I couldn't just let Bernadette die, knowing that I might actually be there to help her. We had been friends once. I couldn't let myself forget that.

Of course, Josephine was also a victim of the Slasher, but that would be months after Bernadette's death. I couldn't focus on

Josephine just yet. There was no need to. There was nothing I could do at the moment to help Josephine anyway. She could wait.

Bernadette was the first victim. But even Bernadette wasn't going to be killed for another three years. Would I even still be around then? I fully expected to wake up any day now, back in my normal life, at 30 years old. And with my children.

With that thought, a single tear made its way down my cheek and landed on the math textbook that I had been carrying. I wiped it away, smiling. Yes, I missed my children desperately, but they were a good memory. I couldn't be sad when I thought of them. I wondered if they were okay. Then I realized that they hadn't even been born yet. So I was mourning children that didn't exist in this world of mine. Or this reality of mine. Or whatever the hell it really was.

Turning the corner to the street that I lived on, I had walked home, almost automatically. It was a well worn path in my memory. Something I had done almost every day for many years. Reaching my house, I turned up the walkway and headed toward the front door of the gray house with red shutters.

"Hey, how was school?"

I turned toward the voice, and smiled.

It was Carter, my first childhood best friend. Josephine and I were recent best friends, but Carter and I had been inseparable since we were 9 years old when he moved in next door to me. It had been so long and I couldn't believe I was seeing that wonderful face of his.

I dropped my school books on my front porch and walked over to his house. I hadn't realized how much I had missed him over the past few years. We hadn't seen each other since our high school graduation. Simon and I were together by then. So my relationship with Carter had just kind of drifted away at that point.

I hugged Carter tightly. His eyes widened in response. I know he didn't expect such a vigorous greeting from the girl next door, but it didn't matter. I had missed him so much.

"I'll tell you about school later. I didn't see you. Were you there today?" I asked him as I sat down on the front porch step next to him. I picked up the soda can he had been drinking out of and took a long swig. He didn't mind. It was like no time had passed at all between us.

I smiled as I looked at Carter. He was still the same pudgy kid with the big brown eyes and shaggy brown hair that I remembered. I never asked, but was pretty sure that his aunt cut Carter's hair herself. And she wasn't very good at it.

Carter never had many friends. I was really the only one. And I became his friend by default, since he lived right next door to me. I remembered him as a bit of an odd duck, but that was okay with me. I never really was the sort that worried about what others thought, and liked Carter despite his oddities.

The day we met came flooding back to me. I was a skinny little 9 year old and was sitting on my front porch that hot July day, reading Nancy Drew. I had heard that the lady next door had a child about my age coming to live with her. That was all she said. There weren't many children in my neighborhood, and I couldn't wait to see who showed up.

When the avocado green station wagon pulled into the driveway that day, and a boy climbed out, I was disappointed. I really wanted a nice girl my age to move in. But that's not what I got.

I pretended to be focusing on the book in my lap, but I kept sneaking peeks at the boy. A woman, dressed in a brown skirt, white blouse, and high heels, got out of the station wagon and opened the very back door of the car. The two of them didn't look like they belonged together. They didn't speak, and he never once looked her in the eyes. I found out later that the woman was a social worker and it was her job to deposit him with his aunt. She never even went to the front door.

The social worker looked tired and exasperated with the entire process. It was something she had probably done dozens, or maybe even hundreds, of times during her career. I would be willing to bet that she forgot the kid's name the second she pulled out of the driveway.

I continued watching while the boy dragged his suitcase up the walkway toward the front door. He wasn't very big and appeared to be struggling quite a bit with it. I dropped my book on the front porch and ran over to help him.

"Hi. I can help," I told him, reaching down and lifting up the bottom of the worn brown suitcase.

The boy didn't reply.

"My name's Ivy. What's yours?"

"Carter."

The two of us hauled his suitcase up the steps, just as his aunt opened the front door. Carter dropped his end, causing me to lose my grip, and drop the other end. It thunked as it hit the concrete porch.

"Oh hi, Ivy," his aunt said to me. "I can take care of this now. Thanks for your help."

I took that as my cue to leave. I started back toward my house, but turned back when I reached the lawn.

"Carter, come over anytime. I live right there."

I pointed to my house and all three of us looked over at it. He just nodded back to me.

Though our first meeting was not that extraordinary, and Carter had barely said one word to me, at the strongly suggested request of his aunt, he took me up on my offer the very next day. We were inseparable after that.

And this was the first time I was meeting him all over again, after we had grown up and gone our separate ways. I so badly wanted to tell him about my kids. Once again, I knew that would just be stupid.

"I didn't feel good this morning, so Aunt Jean told me to stay home. But I'm feeling better now," he told me.

For a moment I actually debated telling my best friend that I had lived this life before, but thought better of it. No need for everyone to think I'm a complete freak.

CHAPTER 8

The next two and a half years flew by in a whirlwind of school, homework, and friends. I had long ago accepted the fact that I was not going to wake up at any moment and go back to my previous life. So, I figured that I would embrace this new existence of mine. It didn't take long for me to get back into the swing of being a teenager, and actually enjoyed the experience. And I have to say that it was much more fun the second time around.

It certainly helped that my popularity was at an all-time high. During my first life, I was quite timid, never knowing how to act or what to say to people. Especially kids my own age. Of course, this was a common affliction among young teens, but it still made for a tough go of it.

This time was different. I had the real world experiences of going through puberty, middle school, high school, boyfriends, a husband, sex, and even having children. Some of those were things that my friends were just now experiencing, and it was quite difficult and awkward for them. Not for me though. I had already dealt with all the fear and floundering that went along with those experiences. It was fantastic getting the chance to re-do everything. I'm sure that I was quite unique in that respect.

I found myself to be confident and outgoing. When a boy was interested in me, I knew exactly what to say to encourage him. Or discourage him, if that was my goal. And it usually was. I didn't want to waste my time with a bunch of young kids when I knew those relationships were going nowhere. My friends all thought I was crazy when I turned down some of the cutest boys in school. But they were just that...boys. I was a grown woman. Sort of. And it was a bit weird to go out with young teen boys, though I had to once in a while. If I didn't, that could be detrimental to my school health. When I did go out with them, I always made sure we were with a group of friends, and I kept them at arm's length. What else could I do? I really was much too young to be dating anyway. I wasn't even 15 yet.

After the cafeteria incident on my first day back, Bernadette never gave me anymore trouble. She also rarely talked to me, avoiding me as much as possible. I was the plague as far as she was concerned. I had let it go for a while, since there was no need to befriend her quite yet. But the time of the Red Lake Slasher was drawing near and I needed to do something about Bernadette.

I knew that Bernadette had disappeared, the first time anyway, on my 15th birthday. Halloween. I loved the fact that my birthday fell on Halloween. And it was coming up soon. I had no idea if the circumstances would be the same this time. But one thing I did know was that things could change. I certainly had different experiences this second time around. I had some new friends, people that never gave me the time of day the first time. My grades were better, and just a long list of things that were different.

So, did that mean that maybe Bernadette was not destined to be killed this time? That was a good question. It was entirely possible. I mean, what if I knew the Slasher and unknowingly had done something in this life to stop his killing spree? Or worse yet, maybe I had done something to anger him and he went on a killing rampage, slaughtering half the town. I could have done either without even knowing it.

THE MANY LIVES OF IVY WELLS

Obviously, that was not a chance I could take. It was important that I do my best to keep an eye on her, to keep her away from the killer. I would never forgive myself if I didn't. I was probably the only person on the planet that knew the future, and all of the horror that came with it.

The problem was that I had no earthly idea who the killer was. The only person I knew that maybe, sort of, could be considered a killer, was Simon. My husband. He had killed me after all. Though that was in the heat of the moment. I'm not sure that even I could make the leap from our fight to him being a serial killer.

I had made some half-hearted attempts over the years to befriend Bernadette, but to no avail. Bernadette wanted nothing to do with me, and I couldn't really fault her for that. Who would want to be friends with someone that dumped a tray of food over your head in front of the entire school? Not Bernadette, that's for sure. Her memory was long, and her hatred of me, even longer. I certainly had my work cut out for me.

Halloween was fast approaching and I needed to figure out a way to get Bernadette to talk to me and trust me. I thought about it and came up with the perfect plan. At least I hoped so. I knew that Bernadette had a crush on my brother, Parker. The few times that Bernadette actually did talk to me, it was to ask about him. She always tried to make it sound like casual conversation where he just came up, but I was no fool.

The conversation usually went something like this:

"So, who's at home right now?" she would ask, knowing full well that my parents were at work.

"No one. Why do you ask?" I would say.

"Oh, no reason. Just making conversation."

Yeah right. Nice try.

Now I could use that knowledge to get Bernadette to my house on Halloween where I could keep an eye on her. As far as I knew, Parker never gave Bernadette the time of day. She was just a little kid to him. The age gap from 15 to 18 was quite large to him. He liked girls his own age. College girls.

I did remember that originally Bernadette had disappeared while she was out walking on Halloween alone after she left the house of one of her friends that night. It wasn't my house, because I didn't have a Halloween party the first time around.

It was assumed that she was grabbed somewhere between her friend's house and hers. No one knows for sure. She may have met up with someone and things may have gotten out of hand. Maybe a fight ensued and went too far. We just don't know for sure.

By all accounts Bernadette was intoxicated and should never have been out walking alone late at night in the first place. From what I understand, she had a fight with one of her friends over a boy and stormed out.

Unfortunately, many of her friends had also been drinking, which means none of them had the wherewithal to stop her. Besides, we lived in a small town where crime rarely happened. So no one really thought there would be an issue. Then it happened. She just disappeared that night. When her body turned up later, it was clear she had been murdered.

"Hello?" Bernadette answered the phone on the first ring.

"Hi Bernadette. This is Ivy. Can you talk?"

There was a pause on the other end of the line.

"Bernadette? Are you there?"

"Why are you calling me?"

Though I couldn't see her, I could hear her speaking through clenched teeth. The irritation in her voice came through, loud and clear. I decided that idle chitchat was not going to work. So, I got right to the point.

"I wanted to invite you to my Halloween party. It's at my house. I know we aren't really friends anymore, but I would like to change that. It's my birthday, so will you?" I did my best to sound sincere.

Another pause, longer this time.

"Bernadette? Are you still there?"

"Yes, I'm here. I was just thinking. I don't know. I mean, why would I want to come to your party? We don't like each other. Especially after what you did to me."

I knew exactly what she was referring to. "I know. I'm sorry for dumping the food tray on you, but that was years ago. Come on, we were 12. Can we move on? Please come to my party. It will be fun. You can bring some of your friends if you like." Then I quickly added, "Parker will be there."

"Well, okay. We were just going to walk around the town anyway."

"Great! It starts at eight. Costumes are optional. No presents necessary. See you then."

I hung up the phone without waiting for Bernadette to respond. I knew that adding Parker in would tip the scales in my favor. Bernadette didn't need to know that Parker was not invited.

Phase one complete.

Josephine and I kept busy over the next few days with party planning. The girl had a knack for it. She was the perfect blend of someone with a 'take charge' attitude, along with easily being a team player. We worked together very well.

I somehow convinced my parents to go out that evening, promising them that my brother, Parker, would supervise. He had agreed that he would tell our parents he would be there the entire time. He had also agreed when I told him not to be there. Some cash was involved. He and his girlfriend had made other plans anyway.

Halloween landed on a Saturday night, which was perfect. A lot of people showed up, which was a good thing. Having a sparsely populated party would have sent the few people that did attend scurrying for more lively entertainment. Bernadette and her posse, as I liked to call them, arrived fashionably late, at 9 p.m. They had clearly started the celebration early and were intoxicated. When they arrived, I walked up and welcomed them.

"I'm really glad you could all make it," I told them.

"Oh, Ivy, I want you to meet my new friend." Bernadette smiled and turned to take the arm of the guy that had walked in

44

behind her. She pulled him forward until he was standing next to her.

I looked up at him and froze, the hair lifting on the nape of my neck and arms.

"Hi, I'm Simon. Nice to meet you."

Simon reached out to shake my hand. It was an odd gesture for a teenager. They rarely shook each other's hands. That was a very adult thing to do.

My eyes were deadlocked into his. Those gray eyes. Those unmistakable, steel gray eyes. His hair was almost shoulder length, just like he had worn in high school the first time around.

I began trembling and couldn't move, leaving Simon's arm hanging there in the air.

"Well, okay," he said as he lowered his right arm to his side, and looked around a bit uncomfortably.

"Ivy, that was rude," Bernadette told me. "He's new in school." Then she leaned over to me and whispered in my ear. "Isn't he cute?"

"Um, yeah, I guess," I whispered back, trying desperately not to give myself away. I needed to act like absolutely nothing was wrong. That was so far from the truth.

Then to Simon as I reached out my hand, "I'm sorry for being rude. You just remind me of someone and I was surprised. No hard feelings?"

He took my hand and gently shook it. "That's okay. Do you have something to drink around here?"

"Um, yes, there's some punch over there." I tilted my head in the direction of the kitchen, not taking my eyes off of him.

I wasn't stupid enough to provide alcohol to a bunch of underage teens, but many of the party goers had brought their own. It was flowing freely.

"Where's Parker?" Bernadette asked me when Simon headed for the kitchen and was out of earshot.

"He's not here." I did a half shrug and gave her the 'I'm sorry, but I tried' look.

Bernadette glared at me. I'm pretty sure she was on to me, and realized that Parker had never intended on attending the party ever.

"Fine. Whatever." Bernadette followed Simon into the kitchen.

"What, are you friends with her now?"

I turned to see Carter standing next to me. I hadn't even seen him come in. I had invited him, of course, but really didn't expect him to show. This wasn't his type of crowd. Actually, no crowd was his type of crowd. He was the type that liked hanging out with only one person at a time. Groups of people made him nervous.

He was wearing baggy jeans and a sweatshirt. Not really party wear, but exactly what I would expect from him. I wasn't sure if he dressed that way because he didn't care at all what people thought, or because he just had no clue about the ways of the modern teenager. My guess was that it was the latter.

"No, I'm not friends with her. Not really. I just thought I would try to repair the rift between us. It's been way too long, you know?" I tried to explain it to him.

"No, I don't know. She has always been horrible to you and you want to be nice to her now? She's a bitch and you know it. You should just stay away from her."

Carter sounded angry. He almost looked like he was baring his teeth at me and I took a step back.

"Don't tell me what to do. I can be friends with anyone I want."

With that, I stormed off toward the kitchen. I could feel the heat in my face as I walked. I left him standing there by the front door alone. Without turning around, I was positive that he was watching me walk away.

I hesitated at the doorway to the kitchen before entering, and took a deep breath. In the almost three years since I had returned to this life, I had just about forgotten about Simon.

Now, I was about to have a conversation with the person who killed me. For a brief moment I wondered if any person that had ever lived had been able to say that. I wondered if I was the only one.

I willed my feet to move. They refused to do it on their own. In to the kitchen I went, a smile plastered on my face.

"So, how did you two meet?" I asked Bernadette and Simon, who were standing in the kitchen pouring vodka into their cups of cherry punch.

It was all I could do to not turn and run. I kept my eyes on Bernadette, not wanting to make eye contact with Simon. The man, or boy actually, standing in front of me, had stabbed me to death. He was the reason I was in the living hell of being a teenager all over again, and the reason I no longer had my beautiful children. I had mostly put him out of my mind over the last three years since I had returned from the dead. And I certainly wasn't expecting him to show up at my house on this very night. In my first life, I didn't have a Halloween party on my 15th birthday, so this was all new to me.

I couldn't help but notice Simon taking me all in from head to toe. He took his time too, as if nothing else in the world was more important at that very moment. It gave me the creeps and I crossed my arms in front of my chest for just a bit of protection from his leering gaze.

Bernadette noticed it too and stepped up a little closer, to partially block his view of me. I was actually thankful for her jealousy right about then.

She smiled and shook her head, shaking her straight blonde hair from her face, as she began to speak. It was a flirty move that I knew all too well. I had seen her use that signature move many times in the presence of adolescent boys over the years. They seemed to appreciate it quite a bit.

"He was in the school office yesterday asking how to get to his first class and I was there anyway, so I offered to show him. And now here we are," Bernadette explained. She wrapped her arms around his left arm, marking her territory, so to speak.

"Are you two dating?" I asked. I was genuinely curious, because in my first life, Bernadette and Simon never knew each other. Or barely knew each other maybe. She was killed right after he transferred to our school.

"Yes. We are on a date right now," Bernadette blurted out before Simon had the chance to answer.

Both of us looked at him and Simon just shrugged.

"We just met. We're friends," Simon replied, smiling at me and wiggling out of Bernadette's grasp.

I heard her huff as she reluctantly released her hold on him. Simon then moved toward me, which was a little too close for my comfort.

This did not go unnoticed by Bernadette.

It did not go unnoticed by me either, and I quickly looked over at Bernadette to gauge her reaction.

I could almost see the steam rising from the girl. Bernadette's expression became tight and her eyes narrowed. Her hands instinctively twisted her straight blonde hair.

"You know," I began, "I really should go talk to some of my other party guests. I don't want to be a bad host."

"I'll go with you. I need to meet more people anyway," Simon told me, as he followed me out of the room.

Once out of the kitchen, I turned and put my palm up toward Simon. "No, really, that's not necessary. Why don't you stay here and talk to your date."

"She's not my date. I just met her. I was actually hoping that you might want to go out with me sometime?" He smiled that handsome smile that I knew all too well.

"What the hell?" Bernadette walked out of the kitchen just in time to hear the last part of our exchange.

"Oh hey, Bernadette, don't be mad," I jumped in. "I'm not interested in him. I mean, seriously not interested."

Against my better judgment, I turned and gave Simon an apologetic look. I knew that this Simon was not the same guy that had stabbed me in that other lifetime. Or was he? Could this one be a lot different? It was all very confusing. Regardless, I didn't want to find out. But, at this point in time, this Simon had done nothing to me but be nice. So, I felt a bit of a duty to at least seem as if I were sorry for what I said.

Simon just shrugged his shoulders at her. He seemed to do that a lot.

"Whatever. You two deserve each other," Bernadette snarled.

Bernadette tilted her head back and downed the drink that was in her hand. Then she reached over, yanked the drink out of Simon's hand and downed that one too.

"The hell with both of you. I'm going home." She stormed her way toward the front door.

"Wait, no. Please don't go." I was in hot pursuit. I couldn't let Bernadette leave on her own. That was the worst thing that could happen.

"Hey," Simon grabbed my hand and spun me around. "Don't worry about her. Now we can hang out."

Simon pulled me toward him. He wrapped his arms around my waist and leaned in for a kiss. He was rewarded with a nice hard slap to his left cheek.

Simon released his grip on me immediately. "Dammit! Why did you do that? I was just trying to be friendly." Simon put his left hand up to his cheek where it was stinging. "Did you really need to hit me?"

"Yes, I really did. Don't ever touch me again." I said it calmly and evenly.

"What's going on here?" Carter interrupted our conversation.

"Nothing," I responded. "I've got it all under control."

I looked over at Simon, who was still holding the side of his face. God, what a baby, I thought. I didn't even hit him that hard.

"It didn't sound like nothing," Carter replied, pushing his shaggy brown hair from his face.

I was surprised at Carter's willingness to get in the middle of things. He was more of the slink into the shadows type. He never caused problems with anyone.

"No, no, it's fine. Simon and I were just talking. Don't worry about it. Can you just leave us alone please?" My words to Carter sounded harsher than I meant them to.

"I just came over to wish you a happy birthday. But Fine. Do what you want. I'm outta here."

Carter stormed off. I certainly was not making any friends that night. Well, I would go over and make up with Carter tomorrow. Tonight I had more important things to deal with.

"I'm leaving too. I'm going to try to catch up with Bernadette. At least she wants to be with me," Simon told me.

"Wait, I'll go with you. She's drunk and you might need my help." I began following him.

Simon stopped and turned to me. "No, you stay here at your party. I'll find her and make sure she gets home okay."

Simon didn't wait for a response. He turned and walked out the door. I figured Simon could take care of Bernadette and himself. I needed to stay at the party.

That was a big mistake.

CHAPTER 10

Within minutes I regretted letting Simon go after Bernadette without me. I wondered if Simon could be the killer. No, I didn't think so. He was a jerk, with a really long list of bad qualities, but I didn't really think he was a killer. Not this Simon anyway. On the other hand, I knew that I could be terribly wrong, since he did kill me. Though I'm not entirely sure that was his intent when he showed up at my house and we fought over the knife. Both of us getting stabbed could have just been in the heat of the moment and may never have happened at all if I hadn't picked up that knife.

Did that make me responsible for my own death? Interesting question. Had I not grabbed the knife and used it first, I may have gotten out of the incident just a bit bruised up. In fact, if I had just let Simon in, we might have had a chat and sorted everything through. Like adults…Yeah right. I knew Simon way better than that. He would not have just let me walk out of there without a scratch. That's why he called me in the first place. He did it for one reason only. To torment me. That was his style.

"Ivy, we need more punch," Josephine called from the kitchen.

That snapped me back to reality. "Okay, I'll get some," I yelled back over the noise of the party.

I headed out the front door and toward the garage, where the extra party supplies were kept. When I returned a couple of minutes later, Josephine pulled me aside.

"What was all that about with Bernadette and that cute boy she brought with her?" Josephine whispered.

"Simon?"

"Is that his name? Yeah, Simon. What happened?" she asked again.

"Oh nothing. You know how Bernadette is. Drama all the time. That's her motto." I tried to make it sound like it was just dumb teenage stuff. It seemed to convince Josephine.

"I don't know why you invited her anyway. You don't want to be friends with her, do you?" Josephine sounded a bit concerned that I might be trying to replace her with a new best friend. Was that jealousy I saw in her face?

"No, not really. I just thought it was time that we all tried to get along. I don't like that new boyfriend of hers though. He seems creepy." Just in case this Simon did turn out to be dangerous, I didn't want Josephine to get to know him.

"You know, it looks like we are low on cups too. I'm going to go get some," I added.

I headed back outside, but cups were not what I was after. I walked directly over to Carter's house next door.

"Hi," I said to Carter's aunt, who answered the door. "Is Carter home?"

She tilted her head at me. "Well, no. I thought he was at your party."

"Oh." I wasn't sure how to respond. I didn't want to get him into trouble with his aunt. "Um, well, maybe he is over in the backyard. I saw him not long ago. I'm sure he's around. I'll go back over and look."

I took off without waiting for Carter's aunt to ask me any questions.

Now this is weird, I thought. We did have a bit of a disagreement, and I fully expected Carter to leave, but where would he have gone, other than home?

About an hour later, I called Bernadette's house. Her mother said she had not arrived home yet. Oh no. She then let me know that she didn't expect Bernadette until late, since she was out with friends. They didn't keep a tight leash on her. Mrs. James then asked me politely, but firmly, not to call the house so late again. I agreed, knowing that it probably wouldn't be the last time I called outside of normal operating hours.

That's when I couldn't take it any longer and left my own party to go look for Bernadette, Simon, and Carter. I had been getting increasingly worried and needed to know what was going on and that Bernadette was okay. I feared that letting Simon go after her would turn out to be the biggest mistake I could possibly make.

As I walked down her street, I looked around nervously, through the little clouds of breath condensing in the still, frigid air. It was long after the last Halloween hangers on had finally given up and gone home, the night's spoils in tow.

I pulled my jacket tightly around my body, as I walked toward town. Not so much due to the cold, but because it made me feel more protected. Dumb, I know. But I felt better anyway.

There was no moon out that night. The neighborhood had widely spaced street lights, probably to save money, and I was having a hard time seeing around me. A house here and there had their porch light on, but I suspect that most had turned them off to warn away potential treat seekers. Once the candy was gone, the lights went out. I walked right down the middle of the street, figuring that it would be tougher for someone to jump out from the bushes to grab me. I could get out of the way of an oncoming car easily enough.

A cat screeched nearby, causing me to jump and spin around, full circle, searching for danger in the shadows. With regret spreading over me, I wished I had brought Josephine along. Not that she would be much protection. But at least two people were less likely to get accosted than one lone, idiot teenager, out walking late at night, without regard for her own safety. This is exactly how Bernadette was grabbed the last time. And here I was, stupidly doing the same thing.

Just as I was about to turn back to go get her, I saw a figure approaching. Fast. He was coming right at me. Having nowhere to run, I stopped in the middle of the street and didn't move. I couldn't move. It was as if my feet were glued to the asphalt below me. I began shaking, and just as I thought I might pass out from fear, I recognized him.

It was Carter jogging toward me. I let out the breath of air that I hadn't realized I was holding.

"Where the hell have you been?" I demanded, as he slowed down to a stop in front of me.

"Wait." He put his palm up toward me as he bent over, trying to catch his breath. Even on this chilly night, he was drenched in sweat.

"Carter, I need to know what's going on. Have you seen Bernadette?" I demanded.

"Um, no. Why would you ask me that? You know I can't stand her. It's not like we hang out or anything." Carter began fiddling with his shoe. He pulled off the right one and inspected it for pebbles.

Bright headlights turned a corner and headed straight for us. We both moved to the safety of the sidewalk, Carter hobbling as he carried one of his shoes.

"What are you doing out here at this time of night jogging anyway? You don't jog."

It was true, he didn't jog. He was pudgy and worked hard at keeping it that way.

"I, um, I just needed to be alone," he responded. "Why do you care anyway? Aren't you and Bernadette like best friends now?" It sounded almost like an accusation.

I narrowed my eyes at him.

"Ugh, no. I told you I was just trying to be nice. Why do you have a problem with that?"

I confronted him, as I reached up and tried to smooth down my hair. It had frizzed out in the moist night air. I wondered if I looked like some crazy frizzy redheaded clown right about then. Carter didn't seem to notice.

Carter walked past me toward his house. "You know what? Whatever. It doesn't matter anymore anyway," he said without turning to look back at me.

"What is that supposed to mean?" I followed him up the road.

"Nothing. It doesn't mean anything. I just don't care anymore. Okay?" Carter almost spat out.

Carter was picking up speed, trying to lose me, but I was right on his heels. Unfortunately for him, I was in much better shape and had no trouble catching up to him.

I passed him up and stopped in front of him, forcing him to stop. He was wheezing as he tried to catch his breath once more.

"Are you mad at me?" I looked at his sweat soaked clothing as I spoke.

"Yeah, I guess. I just thought we were friends. I don't know why you felt it necessary to be friends with that witch, Bernadette." The wheezing slowed as he stood there, taking in deep breaths.

"What, I can't have more than one friend?" I asked, with a look of determination on my face.

"No, that's not it. Well, maybe that's it. I just don't like her. We are all better off without her," he told me.

"What is that supposed to mean?" I asked, considering what night it was and what had happened to Bernadette the last time this date rolled around.

Carter just looked at me without responding.

"Have you seen Simon?" I tried to change the subject.

"Who's Simon?" He looked up trying to recall the boy. "Oh, you mean that guy you and Bernadette were arguing over? No. I haven't seen him. I haven't seen anyone!" Carter looked around. "I'm going in. It's cold out here."

That time I didn't try to follow him.

CHAPTER 11

I walked into town to continue my search for Bernadette. I was getting a bad feeling. I knew that I had royally screwed up when I let Bernadette leave my sight that night. How could I be so stupid? It was my one and only chance to save Bernadette and I wouldn't get another chance. If the Slasher got to her, it would be all my fault. I've had almost three years to prepare for this night, and there I was, probably too late to save her. I had to keep trying though, just in case there was still a chance.

I headed to the burger place that was a big hangout for the teenagers in town. As I looked around the restaurant, I saw a few familiar faces, but not many. Most of the people I knew were either at my house, enjoying my party, that I wasn't even at, or they had gone home for the evening.

"Hey, what are you doing here? Don't you have a party to attend to?"

I turned to see Simon standing behind me and it made me jump involuntarily.

"Why are you so jumpy?" he asked, smiling.

"I'm not jumpy. Why are you here?" I asked as I took in Simon. "Why is your hair wet? It's freezing out there."

"I..well..um.. I just took a shower."

There was no way that I could miss the fact that he was a bit disheveled, and thought it was strange that he was stuttering over his words. I had never known Simon to be nervous about anything. He was the epitome of a cool customer, and it took a lot to rattle him. I wondered what in the world he was up to. I narrowed my eyes at him.

"And you left your house with wet hair? In this weather?" I asked him. I'm sure that he could tell by the look on my face that I didn't believe him.

"What? I was working out in my garage and got sweaty. Don't you take a shower after you workout?"

I noticed that he was looking around the room, and seemed to be nervous about something. In fact, he was looking around at every object, and every person in the room, except for right at me. That was interesting, I thought.

"Yeah, I guess," I replied, reluctantly.

"Hey, did you make sure to get Bernadette home, like you promised?" I lifted my eyebrows in anticipation of his response.

"Well...no. I couldn't find her after I left your house. She was nowhere to be found." He looked down at his feet as he answered me.

I found that to be highly unlikely. He had left only a few minutes after Bernadette. Though it could have been enough time for her to get a couple blocks away. Apparently I would have to give Simon the benefit of the doubt.

"So...you left the party to look for Bernadette, spent a couple minutes on the task, then went home to work out? Even after you had been drinking? Is that your story?" I asked him point blank.

Simon shrugged his shoulders. "Yeah, I guess. What difference does it make anyway? She's probably home, dead to the world by now."

Oh boy. I grimaced at his unfortunate use of words.

I took a deep breath then, already regretting what I was about to say, but I was starting to feel desperate. "Can you please help me find Bernadette? I'm really worried about her."

"Sure," he smiled. "Where do you want to start?"

"I'm not sure where to start really," I replied. "I guess we could just walk around town and talk to people. Do you think we should let her parents know she's missing?" I asked him.

"Why do you think she's missing? Have you checked her house?" he asked me.

"Of course I checked her house. Do I look stupid to you? She's not at home and no one has seen her." I said that in the nicest way possible. "Her mother wasn't too happy that I called so late. So maybe I shouldn't call again right now."

"Mmm hmm," he mumbled, setting his lips in a tight straight line. He looked almost like he was trying really hard not to say something that he might regret later. "Well, she's not really missing yet, is she?" Simon asked. "It hasn't been that long."

"You don't understand. Tonight is the night that she…" I halted in the middle of my sentence.

"The night that she what?" He was looking right through me with those creepy gray eyes of his. It was unnerving.

"Oh…I just mean that she was drunk when she left my house and she might get hurt, or in trouble. I feel responsible."

Simon waved his hand in the air dismissively. "I'm sure she's fine. Bernadette's not your responsibility." He looked up at the menu board behind the counter. "Do you want to get a burger, since we are here? I'm starving."

"What?" I gave him an incredulous stare. "No, I don't want to get a burger. I'm worried about Bernadette. Are you going to help me or not?"

"Okay fine. I'll help." Simon had a look of disappointment on his face as he followed me out the door of the burger place. "I really could use something to eat," he mumbled behind me.

I ignored him. We had a more pressing matter at the moment.

The two of us spent the next few hours scouring the town of

Red Lake. Simon was actually a lot more helpful than I had expected. And I was grateful that he didn't try any funny business with me at all. He could probably see how determined I was. Being laser focused on a task left very little time for anything else.

It was a night I never wanted to end. Having it end, meant the reality of what I was sure was already done. I prayed that I was wrong. Terribly wrong.

By the time we arrived back at my house, sans Bernadette, I was terrified. I had that awful, deep in the pit of my stomach feeling, that I had blown it. The party had dispersed by then, leaving me to clean everything up alone. Fantastic. It would have to wait though. I had more important things to deal with.

"Do you want some help cleaning up?" Simon asked, as he took in the scene.

The house was a colossal mess and would take hours to clean, even with help. My parents would be back long before it was done. There was nothing I could do about that. I would worry about it, and them, later.

"No, it's fine. I'll take care of it. Thanks though." I walked to the front door and opened it for Simon, hoping he would take the hint.

He did.

"Well, okay. If you're sure. I really don't mind helping though."

He said it with lifted brows. I could see the hope in his face. He wanted to spend more time with me. That was clear. No freaking way, I thought.

"No, really, it's fine. Thanks for your help tonight. See you at school."

I closed the door before he had a chance to respond. I stuck my eye up to the peephole in the front door and watched him walked down the steps. He turned back one last time and looked toward the door before he disappeared around the corner, toward his house.

"Okay then, that's done," I said to myself, turning toward the phone.

I promptly called Bernadette's house, once again waking her mother, to ask if Bernadette was home. I knew she wouldn't like it, but it had to be done. Her mother sounded irritated as she put the phone down gently and checked her daughter's bedroom. At least that's what I assumed she did.

I grabbed a trash bag and began disposing of cups, paper plates, and especially the beer bottles while I waited. Having my parents come home and finding the remnants of a party was bad enough. But I could handle that. Having them find empty beer and vodka bottles was something I couldn't handle. I certainly didn't need that grief on this night of all nights.

When Mrs. James returned to the phone, it was bad news.

"Ivy, she's not in her room." Mrs. James sounded worried, as expected. "What's going on?" she asked me. "Why do you keep calling here looking for her? Is something wrong?"

"Well..." I had no choice but to tell her the truth about her daughter. A truth that could be shared anyway. A truth that didn't make me sound like a raving lunatic.

"Bernadette was at my house for a Halloween party that I threw. She came with her friends, and a boy that I had never met before," I told her.

"What boy?" Mrs. James interrupted.

"Um, his name is Simon. He helped me look for her," I explained.

"You went looking for her?" she asked. Her voice sounding a bit more worried.

"Yes. Anyway, she got drunk at my party and left. Alone." I grimaced, fully expecting to be yelled at.

"You had alcohol at your party? You are all underage! What were you thinking? And where were your parents!" Yep, there it was.

"No, Mrs. James, I didn't have alcohol at my party. But people brought it anyway. I tried to stop them, but they wouldn't listen to me." Oh boy, this was not going well. "My parents went out for the night. I'm pretty responsible, though I know this didn't go very well." I tried to defend myself, but ended up sounding like an idiotic teenager just making up excuses for her poor judgment.

"I see." Her voice was eerily calm.

"So, as I was saying," I continued, "Bernadette was drunk and stormed out of my party alone. Simon went after her."

"Simon? The boy she went to the party with?" she asked.

Thankfully she couldn't see me rolling my eyes. This conversation was going to last all night if she didn't stop interrupting me to ask questions. It took all I had not to sound exasperated.

"Yes, the boy she came with," I answered. "Anyway, when Simon couldn't find her, he and I went looking together. We didn't have any better luck. That's why I am calling you. I'm worried about her and I think it's time to call the sheriff." I took a deep breath once I had finished.

Twenty minutes later, Sheriff Hayes arrived at Bernadette's house. Simon and I arrived only two minutes before he did. We answered all of his questions, and all of Mrs. James' questions, which seemed to go on forever. But it had to be done. Maybe, just maybe, I was wrong, and Bernadette was holed up somewhere, with some boy or other, and would be just fine. I didn't believe it, even as I prayed it was true.

The next morning, a full scale search began.

Two weeks later, after everyone Bernadette knew had been questioned, and the entire town had been searched, and the lake had been dragged for her body, the sheriff concluded that she was a runaway. He did not close the case, but explained to her parents that they would no longer waste their resources on a girl that had run away.

I knew he was wrong. Dead wrong. But, I couldn't tell that to the sheriff. How would I explain that I knew Bernadette was dead? What could I possibly say that wouldn't land me on the wrong side of the looney bin?

I did know where Bernadette's body probably was though. Or at least where it was the first time. It was entirely possible that the killer didn't use the same disposal method this time. Many things had been different in my current life than they were in my former life.

I wrestled with the idea of telling the sheriff where I thought the body was. I even considered going to the spot and looking for her myself. I had avoided the latter so far, because i was afraid of accidentally tampering with the evidence, or leaving some of my own evidence behind. Such as hair or footprints. If I went to the dumpsite and then left evidence behind, then told the sheriff about it, I could end up as a suspect.

In the end, I kept my mouth shut. Was that the wisest thing to do? I didn't know, but I didn't want to find out the hard way.

CHAPTER 12

Devastation hit me like a hammer after Bernadette's death. I hadn't been able to save her and lamented over the fact that perhaps I hadn't tried hard enough. Since Bernadette's body had not yet been found, I couldn't tell people that the girl was dead. I had to go along with the theory that she was just missing and had probably run away. I was the only one that knew the truth. For the time being anyway.

"Why are you at my house?" I asked Simon when I opened my front door and found him standing there.

He didn't seem to notice the snark in my voice.

"I just wanted to see how you were doing? Since Bernadette is still missing and all." He sounded sincere, but it was still Simon. I didn't think I could ever trust him fully.

"She's not missing, she's..." I stopped mid-sentence and looked around uncomfortably. I would need to be more careful about what I said.

Simon just looked at me with a head tilt, but didn't ask me what I meant.

"Come on. Come sit out here with me on the front porch and we can talk."

Simon offered me his hand and for some reason that I can't explain, I took it. Perhaps I just needed a friend at that moment. I just don't know for sure.

As the two of us sat on the front steps, in the middle of the day, which was the only time I would ever contemplate doing that with Simon, he tried to comfort me.

"You know, she'll turn up," Simon told me. "I didn't know her well, but she struck me as the kind of person that could take care of herself. Kind of like you."

He said it with sincerity, causing me to smile at that last comment, unable to stop myself. The compliment, and my reaction, surprised me. Maybe *this* Simon wasn't so bad. Maybe he wasn't at all like the other Simon, in that other life of mine. It was possible.

Simon reached his arm out and wrapped it around my shoulders. I responded by laying my head on his shoulder. I had actually loved him once. That seemed like another lifetime ago. Wait…it was.

Just at that moment, a car drove slowly up the road. I recognized it as the car belonging to Carter's Aunt Jean. I saw Carter glaring at the two of us sitting together and looking very comfortable. He got out of the car, watching us the entire way. It felt creepy and more than a little bit uncomfortable, as if his eyes were boring holes into us. I just stared back. I could see the unmistakable hatred in his eyes. As he followed his aunt into the house, the door slammed behind him. He never said a word to us.

Simon and I sat on the steps for another half hour talking about Bernadette and the investigation that had been stalled. When Simon decided it was time to leave, he got up and turned to me.

"This was really nice," he told me.

I nodded. I hated to admit it, but I actually enjoyed his company. It was nice having someone to talk to.

"Would you like to go out to a movie on Friday?" He looked a bit restless as he waited for an answer, his feet shuffling from left to right, and back again.

As much as I had liked talking with Simon that afternoon, and as nice as he had been, I just couldn't get the images out of my mind of the two of us stabbing each other. And I didn't think that was ever going to happen. Those images were permanently glued to my brain. How could I go out with someone that I still wouldn't be alone in the house with? Sitting on the front steps with him, in broad daylight, was completely different. I felt relatively safe doing that.

"You know...I don't..." I hesitated as I spoke.

Simon threw his palm up in front of him. "Never mind. Maybe now's not a good time."

With his lips pressed tightly together, I could see the disappointment written all over his face. Simon turned his back to me and walked away. I let him go.

As Simon disappeared from view, I looked toward Carter's house, and contemplated going over to confront him about his behavior. I knew why he had been glaring at the two of us. Carter had a big crush on me. I had known it since the first day we met. I knew it in my first life, and I knew it in this life.

"Hey Ives, Mom said it's time for dinner." Parker startled me. I had been so engrossed in my thoughts, that I hadn't heard him open the front door.

"Okay, I'll be right there."

The next day, after school, Josephine and I were walking to my house to work on a term paper that was due in a few days. There was a topic I wanted to approach Josephine about, but had been hesitant to do so. Something I had wanted to say since I woke from the dead three years prior.

It took some time, but I eventually summoned up the courage to speak.

"Josie."

"Yeah?"

"I want to tell you something. I know it will sound crazy. I mean really crazy. But, please let me finish before you respond." I kept my gaze straight ahead as we walked, not daring to look Josephine in the eyes.

"What are you talking about?" Josephine looked over at me with a tilt of her head. I saw her out of the corner of my eye.

"Okay...Well, you know how you said I've been acting strangely since Bernadette went missing?" I began.

"Yeah?"

"There's a reason for that. I know that she was murdered," I blurted out, and turned to look at her. I wanted to gauge her response to my declaration.

"What? You do not. Why would you say that?" Josephine asked.

"Please, let me finish."

Flicking her wrist in the air, she answered. "Okay fine. Go ahead."

I continued. "Okay, here's the crazy part. This is the second time that I've lived my life." I looked over at my friend quickly, as we kept walking, to gauge her reaction once again.

Josephine said nothing.

"What? No reaction? You don't think that's crazy?" I asked her.

"Yeah, I think it's completely crazy. But you told me to let you finish. So that's what I'm doing," Josephine said calmly.

"Oh, okay." I took a deep breath, waiting for courage to leap upon me. "In my first life, I was married to Simon and he stabbed me to death." I paused to think about it for a moment. "Um, actually, we stabbed each other to death. I think. I don't actually know if he died or not. Hell...I don't even know if I died or not."

Josephine came to a sudden stop and I held my breath as I stopped walking also.

"What the hell are you talking about? You were married to Simon? I thought you didn't want to have anything to do with him?" Her mouth hung open when she finished speaking.

I could feel my heart beginning to pound in my chest. This wasn't going to go well. I just knew it.

"Yeah, that's why! Because he killed me!" I shouted, looking around quickly to make sure no one heard me. "Oh sorry. I didn't mean to yell."

"Did you hit your head or something?" Josephine was serious.

"No. I know it sounds crazy. I just don't know what I can say to make you believe me." I was at a loss, knowing that she would either believe me or not. It wasn't something that she could sort of believe in. What could I say to convince her?

"So…if this is true, and I'm not saying I believe you, why are you telling me now? I mean, you've had years to tell me." Josephine's voice was hesitant. It was as if she wanted to believe me, but couldn't bring herself to.

"Because I need to tell someone about Bernadette," I answered.

"What about her?" Josephine was genuinely curious by then. "Do you know where she is?"

"Yes. I mean, I think so. I know where she was put in my first life."

"Put? Oh…you don't mean…" Josephine's voice trailed off.

"Yes, she was killed. And, I'm sure she was killed this time too. I just don't know by who," I explained.

"Why don't you tell someone?" It was a valid question.

"I am. I'm telling you," I responded.

"No, I mean the cops."

"I thought about it. I just don't think they'll believe me," I confessed. "Besides, what if he didn't put her in the same place this time? If I tell the cops about it, and then they can't find her, they'll never believe anything I tell them again."

"There's only one way to find out." Josephine gave me a small, crooked smile.

THE MANY LIVES OF IVY WELLS

My eyes widened. "You believe me?"

"I didn't say that. I mean, that story is ridiculous."

Yeah, she had a point.

"Hey girls. What's shakin'?"

We both turned to see Simon walk up from behind. He was wearing all black, from head to toe. With his dark hair and gray eyes, it suited him.

He worked his way in between the two of us and put an arm around the shoulder of each of us. Josephine gave me a look that said 'Holy cow. Did this guy really kill you?' I didn't have to read her mind to know that was what she was thinking.

I reached up my left hand, took Simon's hand in mine, and flung his arm off of my shoulder. Simon gave me a pouty look and pulled his arm from around Josephine's shoulder also.

"So, what story is ridiculous?" Simon looked left and right at each of us.

"Were you eavesdropping?" I asked him.

"No, not really. I just heard that last part when I walked up."

"Oh Simon, you're gonna love this," Josephine began. "Ivy just told me that you and she…"

"Josie! Shut up!" I yelled before Josephine could finish her sentence.

"Me and Ivy what?" Simon asked her, with a silly grin on his face. He looked from Josephine over to me.

"Nothing!" I felt like I was going to hyperventilate and stopped walking to catch my breath.

"Are you okay?" Josephine asked me.

"Yes. Just give me a minute." I took a few deep breaths in an attempt to slow my rapidly beating heart.

Neither Simon nor Josephine said a word while they waited for me to regain my composure.

"Simon, we need to get our paper done. So we need to go, okay?" I told him. I then tilted my head toward my house at Josephine, who dutifully followed me.

"Hey, we should hang out later!" Simon called after us, but neither answered him. He turned and walked back the way he had come.

Once Simon was out of earshot, I laid into Josephine. "Why did you do that? Why did you almost tell Simon what I told you about the two of us?" I asked, trying desperately to mask the anger in my voice. I didn't want to alienate her just when she might be coming around to believing my story.

"What? Are you mad?" Josephine asked. "It was just a joke. Like he would actually believe that crazy story of yours."

"I thought you believed me?" I felt a bit hurt.

"You usually don't lie to me, so I don't know." She shrugged her shoulders.

"I know it sounds crazy. Really I do. But try to give me the benefit of the doubt, okay?" I pleaded.

"Yeah, okay. Do you really know where Bernadette's body is?" Josephine whispered, looking behind me to make sure Simon hadn't sneaked up on us once again.

"Yes. Like I said before, I think so."

"Let's go see if she's there. Is it around here?" Josephine asked, looking around, as if she was going to see Bernadette in the bushes.

"It's not far. It's in the woods. Let's go do our paper, then we can go take a look," I told her.

CHAPTER 13

An hour later, I told my mother that Josephine and I were going to go over and hang out with Carter for a while. Carter had been a constant in my life for years by then, so my mother didn't give it a second thought.

We had no intention of going to see Carter.

The town of Red Lake circled the actual lake, and was surrounded by a dense pine forest. Sometimes it seemed like we were our own little island, because the forest gave us the feeling of being cut off from the rest of the world. So isolated.

Deep in the forest, there was a huge sinkhole, which had formed many, many years prior. No one knows exactly when. It was just there one day. It's a bit of a hike to get to the sinkhole, so it may have been there for hundreds of years before it was discovered. Of course, once it was discovered, then everyone had to go see it. The sinkhole became a local mystery and everyone in town had hiked into the forest to see it at one time or another.

The sinkhole was quite deep, as far as anyone could tell, and there were 'No Trespassing' signs posted everywhere. Regardless, it was a favorite hangout for the local teenagers.

Once, about 25 years ago, a 12 year old boy and his friends

were goofing off around the sinkhole, when the boy fell in. Search and Rescue teams were called in, but his body was never recovered. After that heart wrenching incident, officials had the hole filled with large rocks and dirt, to no avail. Those sunk down even further. It was as if it was a vast, bottomless pit.

Because of this, many theorized that there was a large cave underneath, with running water, maybe even an underground river, that could carry debris away. But, the ground surrounding the sinkhole was so unstable, constantly caving in, and making the hole wider, that no one wanted to get too close to study it. Therefore, it was left untouched for many years. Parents warned their children to stay far away, and most did.

Josephine and I trudged through the forest, staying very close together. The forest was quite dense with trees, blocking out much of the sunlight. This made it difficult to navigate our way there. Between the two of us, we were a bundle of nerves. Neither of us spoke a word as we carefully navigated our way through. Years ago, someone had tied powder blue ribbons around some of the trees, in an attempt to help navigate the way to the sinkhole. It was very helpful as the path was hard to find in some spots. We followed the blue ribbons dutifully.

When we reached the sinkhole, we were both terrified of getting too close, for fear of falling in. It didn't take long for us to realize that we were not going to ever be able to see a body down in that black abyss. I sat down on a rock and began to cry.

"What's the matter?" Josephine asked me, as she sat down on the rock next to me. She put her arm around my shoulders in an effort to comfort me.

"I feel like this is all my fault. I knew Bernadette was going to be killed on Halloween. I've know it since I returned." I used the back of my hand to wipe away tears as I spoke.

"What do you mean 'returned'?" Josephine tilted her head at me and removed her arm from around my shoulders.

"After I died when I was 30, I woke up here when I was 12 years old." I sniffled as I spoke.

"I don't understand. You weren't born again?" Josephine was struggling with the whole concept. "How could you start your life over at 12?"

"I'm not positive how it works, but I've thought a lot about this," I tried to explain. "I was actually born again. But for some reason, after I died, I wasn't aware of my next life until I woke up in Bernadette's backyard at 12 years old. Does that make sense?"

"Not really."

"It doesn't really to me either. But, that's what happened," I told her. "It was as if my current mind, or soul, or whatever, was just plopped into this body at 12 years old. That's the best explanation I have for this whole thing."

"You remember your life from before, and this one started at 12? Why are you just now telling me this? Why not three years ago?" It was a fair question for Josephine to ask.

"I didn't think you would believe me. I thought you would think I was nuts. I'm only telling you now because Bernadette has been killed and I need help figuring out what to do about it," I told her.

"How do you know you died? I mean, what did it feel like? What do you remember?" Josephine was starting to ask a lot of questions. Maybe that meant she was beginning to believe me. I could only hope.

"Um.." I thought for a moment, back to the time when Simon and I were in a life and death struggle. "I remember that I was stabbed and bleeding a lot. Simon looked like he was dead and I turned to go back into the house to get my kids…"

"Kids! You had kids?" Josephine interrupted, her mouth hanging open.

"Oh yeah, I didn't tell you that part," I smiled. "They were the best. I miss them every day. Their names are…were, I guess… Hunter and Courtney. I'll tell you all about them later, okay?"

Josephine nodded her head. "Okay."

"So," I continued, "when I turned to go back into the house, I started getting lightheaded, and I fell. I don't think I passed out though, because I remember some things. I remember the radio playing…oh, and I remember the dinner I was making smelled like it was burning. Then, just as I died, there was an earthquake. Weird timing, huh?"

Josephine's eyes lit up. "Maybe that was it. The earthquake. If it happened exactly at the time you died, could that have been what caused you to come back at 12 years old?" Josephine was starting to get into my story.

I shook my head. "I doubt it. Earthquakes happen all the time and people don't start their lives over. At least as far as I know, they don't. I've never actually asked anyone." I laughed at the absurdity of it all, wondering how a conversation like that would go.

"Maybe if they were dying at that exact moment, they do," Josephine added. "Who knows, maybe there are thousands of people out there just like you."

I shrugged my shoulders. I was pretty sure I was that one anomaly in the world. If there were others, someone would have talked. That would have been big news. No, I was the only one. I was sure of it. Maybe.

"Sooo….." Josephine began. "Why did Simon stab you to death?" That was an odd question. One I'm sure that Josephine never expected to ever ask someone.

"Oh Josie, he was horrible to me. He had a terrible temper and sometimes knocked me around. After the kids were old enough, I took them and ran. We were in hiding, in another town, for about two years. My parents didn't even know where we were. Only Parker knew. He would never say a word to anyone. I was sure of it. And as far as I know, he never did."

I paused for a moment, thinking back to that day.

"Then, when Simon found us he was so angry and he attacked

me. When we fought, I grabbed the knife first. It was kill or be killed."

I let out a deep breath and started sobbing. I had wanted to tell someone for years. Josephine comforted me the best she could.

"Oh. Now I understand why you won't go out with him. I don't blame you. It's weird though, because he seems so nice."

I could see the sincerity in her eyes. I tried to calm down, taking in slow, concentrated breaths.

"I know. And it might be entirely possible that *this* Simon is a nice guy," I admitted. "He might not be the horrible person I knew at all. Not everything is the same this time around. But, I can't take that chance, you know?"

"I know. And I don't blame you at all. With all of that happening, I doubt that I would go out with him either," she told me. "Even if he does seem like a really nice guy," she added.

That's when both of us heard a cracking noise in the trees and turned our attention in that direction. I jumped up off the rock we had been sitting on and watched the dark forest intently, listening for even the slightest sound.

"What was that?" I whispered, not taking my eyes off of the trees.

"I don't know," Josephine replied, whispering back. "Are there bears out here?"

"Sometimes, yes. But, it's winter right now. I doubt that was a bear. I have a really bad feeling. We should go."

I grabbed Josephine's hand and we walked swiftly toward the road, following the powder blue ribbons in the opposite direction from earlier.

As we passed through the dense forest, our feet crunched over the well worn dirt path that led from the road through the forest. Both of us kept looking back to make sure nothing was stalking us. Suddenly the forest seemed to go dark, and the temperature felt as if it had dropped 10 degrees in a matter of seconds. Both of us instinctively pulled our sweaters tighter around us, in an attempt to ward off the sudden chill.

We both snapped our heads around when we heard a sound to our left. I can't describe it. It didn't quite sound like footsteps, but something was definitely there, and we quickened our pace. Neither of us said a word, terror gripping our souls. I began to shiver, unable to distinguish my fright from the cold. The shivering could have been from either one. Or probably from both.

A minute later it sounded as if someone, or something, was following us at a distance. That time it was more obvious. It definitely sounded like footsteps, and without discussion, we both started running. It may well have been our imaginations getting the best of us, but when we reached the road, both of us let out a huge sigh of relief.

We covered the short distance to the burger hangout in minutes. None of our friends were there though, so we sat in a corner booth and ordered some food. I got a chicken sandwich and Josephine ordered a veggie burger. We both wanted hot chocolate, to calm our nerves, and to warm us up. I could really have used something much stronger. But in this lifetime, I wasn't even close to being old enough. That would have to wait a few more years.

As we waited for our meals, Simon walked up and sat down in the booth next to me, without waiting for an invitation. I scooted over to give him some room.

Josephine and I gave each other a knowing look.

Simon must have noticed it, because he looked back and forth between Josephine and me. "What was that all about?" he asked.

"What was what?" Josephine asked in response.

She tilted her head at him and played dumb. It made me smile.

"That look the two of you gave each other when I sat down? Is something up that I should know about? And why are you smiling?" He turned and was staring straight at me when he spoke.

THE MANY LIVES OF IVY WELLS

"It's nothing. Nothing about you anyway. We were just talking," Josephine responded.

Simon shrugged his shoulders in response and motioned for the waitress. Once she took his order and left us alone, I couldn't help but ask Simon the question that had been burning through me ever since we got out of that forest.

"Are you following us?" I asked him, point blank. "Was that you in the forest?"

"What? Me?" Simon pointed at his chest as he answered me. "I don't know what you're talking about," he replied.

The smile that Simon gave me then was him trying to be cute, with a bit of satisfaction mixed in. It gave me the creeps. Though I knew this was not the same Simon, and this guy gave me no concrete reason to dislike him, I still didn't trust him. Same Simon or not, he was still Simon.

"I still think you should go out with me," he said directly to me. "I'm not a bad catch."

This Simon wasn't all that different, I thought. At least not in the self-assured way that he acted.

"Look, this just isn't going to happen. You and me. I'm not interested." I saw no other choice than to be brutally honest with him.

His hand flew to his heart and he feigned being hurt by my comment. It almost made me smile. Did nothing rattle him?

"Oh, you just don't know me well enough yet. I'll wear you down." Confidence exuded from his pores.

"No, really, you won't," I told him.

The waitress arrived at our table then with our meals. Simon had ordered a burger. He obviously was not deterred by my bluntness.

CHAPTER 14

Later that same evening, Josephine called me to talk about our experience in the forest. We hadn't been able to have a conversation about it in the burger place because Simon had shown up out of the blue. We hadn't invited him there, but that didn't stop him.

"You know, I think maybe we should go back out to the sinkhole," I told my friend as I laid on my bed, staring up at the ceiling.

"No way. It is way too creepy out there. And that noise freaked me out. We still don't know if it was a bear or a person watching us." I could hear the quakiness in Josephine's voice as she shuddered in response.

"Oh, I'm sure it was nothing. Probably just a squirrel." I tried to ease Josephine's nerves.

"That was no squirrel. I think someone was watching us, and there's no way I'm going back out there." Josephine was adamant, and I knew that it would be an uphill battle to get her to change her mind.

"Okay fine. Do what you want, but I'm going. I need to find out if Bernadette is in there. Maybe there's another entrance to get in. I've heard people say that the sinkhole is probably an underground cave that collapsed." I knew it was probably just wishful thinking, but I had to try. "I would be really grateful if you came with me."

I was begging a bit. I didn't like the idea of going out there alone, but felt that I had no choice. I needed to find out. If I had to go alone, then so be it.

"I don't think that's a very good idea. Ivy, you shouldn't go out there alone. It's dangerous," Josephine told me quietly.

"I wouldn't be alone, if you would go with me…pleeeeeease."

"I'm really sorry, but I can't do that." Yep, she wasn't going to change her mind.

"Whatever, suit yourself…"

I heard a thump coming from my closet and stopped mid-sentence, looking in the direction of my closet.

"What was that?" I said out loud.

"What?" Josephine asked me.

"Um, I gotta go." I hung up before Josephine had a chance to respond.

As I got slowly off my bed, I picked up my brother's baseball bat that was propped against the wall next to my bed. I had been sleeping with it there since not long after I woke from the dead three years prior. Parker said it was fine with him. He would just need it when he had practice anyway.

I lifted the baseball bat high above my right shoulder, creeping quietly across the carpeted floor of my room. With my left hand I reached out and yanked hard on the closet door, and it flew open.

"What the hell are you doing in there?" I asked as I lowered the top end of the bat down to the ground.

"Oh, hi. I'm not doing anything." My brother, Parker, then walked out of my room without another word.

"Okay, that was weird," I said out loud.

But it was not completely out of character. I had caught my brother in my closet a few times over the years. He was just odd and was usually asleep when I found him. He liked to eavesdrop on my conversations. I wondered how much of the conversation with Josephine he had overheard. No need to wonder though. He had heard all of it. That was something I was sure of.

The next morning was a Saturday. I got up just as the sun was peeking over the horizon. Much too early for the rest of the family to be up. After I quickly got dressed, throwing my unruly bedhead hair into a ponytail, I grabbed my backpack and some water, and walked quietly out the front door. When I reached the garage, I stuffed a small gardening shovel into my backpack, though I had no idea what I was going to do with it. Plant carrots in the forest? Probably not. It just seemed like something I should take. I also took a flashlight from my father's workbench.

Forty-five minutes later, I reached the sinkhole. Though I was afraid of what secrets the dark, creepy forest might hold, I had braved my way through the trees, and made it to my destination alive.

When I heard a twig snap nearby, I instantly regretted going out there alone. I was pretty sure that time it really was a squirrel though and took a deep breath of courage.

I spent several minutes walking around the perimeter of the sinkhole, surveying it for obvious damage, such as footprints near the edge. I also tried to look over the edge, into the hole, but each time I got near it, the dirt on the ledge began to give way. I jumped several feet back and realized that getting a good look inside, from the top, was not going to happen.

Now what?

I spent an hour walking around in the forest, hoping to find a cave entrance. I used the flashlight to look behind every low hanging tree branch and under as many rocks as I could lift. I even used the small shovel I had brought to do a bit of digging under some rocks. Nothing. If there was another way into the cave, I couldn't find it. Besides, that sinkhole had been there for

THE MANY LIVES OF IVY WELLS

more years than any of us knew, and no one had ever reported finding a cave entrance nearby. It was just speculation that there even was a cave down in that hole. Even so, that didn't mean that there was an entrance anywhere.

Snap!

I had been kneeling next to the rock I had just turned over when I heard the noise. Jumping to my feet, I spun around, toward the sound.

I couldn't see a thing. The sun was right where I was looking, and had risen just high enough that I had to squint to look into that part of the forest. So I walked a few feet closer. Still, I couldn't see very well through my squinty lids. A few feet closer. I stopped to listen. Nothing more.

It was probably just some critter looking for breakfast, I thought, and felt stupid for being so jumpy. No one was out there that early in the morning watching me. I wasn't that interesting. I smiled to myself for acting like a dumb teenager. I needed to get back to my search so I could get home before my family woke up. The barrage of questions that would inevitably come if they found me gone at the crack of dawn was not something I wanted to deal with.

Just as I turned to head back toward the sinkhole, someone grabbed me from behind. I hadn't even heard them coming. My scream was cut off by an arm wrapping around my neck and squeezing. I reached up to pull his arm away so I could breathe, but he was much too strong for me. Due to my struggling and his ever tightening grip on my neck, I started seeing stars and my vision began fading.

My arms and legs flailed wildly in a desperate attempt to free myself, before I passed out. Unfortunately it wasn't working. The man had a solid grip on me and there was no wiggle room. I was no match for his strength and I wasn't going anywhere. The arm around my neck prevented me from trying to speak to him. For just a moment, I thought that if I could reason with him...

That's when I felt it. That exact feeling of being punched in the back. A feeling I knew all too well. I knew immediately that I hadn't been punched though. I had been stabbed...then stabbed again...and again. I fell to the ground, face first, as I felt the life draining from my body. Once again.

I couldn't move as I watched white shoes running away. That's all I could see, the shoes, and nothing else, as my eyes closed and everything went black.

PART 2

CHAPTER 1

I felt like I was falling. The feeling was unmistakable. Almost like a dream...but it wasn't a dream. Just before I hit the ground, I woke with a jolt and my eyes popped open. I immediately, and involuntarily, squeezed them shut again, as the bright sunlight stung them. My hands instinctively flew up to cover my closed eyelids. It helped to block out the still strong sunlight.

While I laid there with my eyes closed, though it was only for a few seconds, I could feel the heat on my body. It was a sweaty, sticky heat.

I carefully opened my eyes, still holding my hands up to shield them from the sun. The sun was blinding. I sat up as my eyes slowly adjusted to the bright light. I looked around and realized that I had been lying on a beach, in a bikini, and my skin was turning a bright shade of pink.

"What is going..." I paused, my mind reeling, as it all came flooding back. "Oh my god. Not again."

I looked around at the people on the beach. No one paid me any attention. As the events of my previous two lives swam around in my head, I watched several children on the beach run in and out of the water as it chased them back onto the shore. They squealed with delight and I couldn't help but smile at their innocence.

My skin felt like it was on fire and I looked around for my clothes. I found a beach bag stuffed under the lounge chair I had been lying on. In it I found shorts, a tank top, and some sandals. I quickly threw the clothes on over my purple bikini. There was another lounge chair next to mine, with a beach towel spread out over it, but no one occupied the chair. There were actually several in a row. Some had people in them, some didn't, and I didn't recognize any of them.

Now what? I thought.

By my height and the clothes I had just put on, I guessed that I was about 15 or 16 years old, the same age I had been when I was killed the last time.

Was I killed? Yes, this time I was sure of it. The first time it happened, when Simon stabbed me at my house, with my kids upstairs, I wasn't positive that I had died. This time I was. I had been stabbed and left for dead in the forest, and the killer had run off as I laid there, fading to black. There was no one around to find me. No one to save me from my inevitable fate. So yes, I had died. There was no doubt in my mind this time.

But the question is, why would I wake back up at the same age as before? For a split second I wondered if maybe I had just blacked out and someone saved me. But, that wouldn't explain how I wound up on the beach, alone, a long way from home. I didn't know exactly where I was, but it certainly wasn't Red Lake.

"Um, excuse me." I called out to a young couple that was walking past me. They stopped. "What beach is this?" I asked, knowing how the question must have sounded to them.

The couple glanced at each other, and it was the young man that spoke up. "Summer's Bend."

"What? How the hell did I wind up here?" I meant to say that in my head.

"Are you all right?" the man asked me as he tilted his head to one side.

It wasn't a stupid question. I was positive that they thought I had lost my mind. How could I be out enjoying the beach, in a bikini, and have no idea where I was?

"Um, yeah, I'm fine. Just out in the sun too long, I guess." I smiled reassuringly at the couple. "Thank you, and sorry for bothering you."

They both nodded my way and continued toward their destination.

I knew that I had another question, several questions actually, but wasn't about to ask the same people. A little concern from strangers was one thing, but acting completely looney was entirely different. It was best to act a little odd to different sets of people. Oh boy, I thought, maybe I really am losing it.

I picked up the beach bag and the sandals and headed away from the water, leaving the beach chair behind. Reaching into the bag to see what was left inside, I found a bottle of water and drank it all. Dying and coming back to life was thirsty work.

"Now what am I going to do?" I said out loud. "Well at least I'm not 12 years old again. That sucked. And getting stabbed two different times sucked. Let's try to not let that happen again."

Stopping right before I left the sand and reached the pavement, I sat on the beach retaining wall and slipped on my sandals. Then I took a couple of minutes to apply some sunscreen that I had also found in the beach bag. At least I came prepared, I thought. Even with the sunscreen on, I needed to get out of the sun and find a nice shady spot to contemplate my next move... such as how I was going to get home.

I wandered around the main street of Summer's Bend for a little while, trying to decide what to do. I only had ten dollars in the beach bag and was probably 100 miles from home. Alone. I couldn't figure out why I was at the beach alone, so far from home.

"Oh my god, Ivy, there you are!"

I turned to see Josephine walking swiftly toward me and let out a sigh of relief.

"Where have you been? I went to the bathroom and you were gone when I returned." Josephine had a pained look on her face.

"Oh, sorry. I must have fallen asleep," I responded. "When I woke up I couldn't find you. I'm sorry if I worried you."

Josephine readily accepted my explanation. "Okay. Do you want to go get lunch? I'm starving."

Just then I realized how hungry I was also. I had no idea how long it had been since I had eaten.

"Yeah, let's go." I figured that I could work on Josephine for answers as we ate lunch.

Fifteen minutes later, we were eating sandwiches from the deli just up the road. The restaurant sat right on the sand. It had an outdoor seating area and it was fairly busy that day. Tons of people wandered around the deli and beach in various stages of dress. Or undress, as the case usually was. There was everything from small children in just their diapers, to teen girls in bikinis, to old men wearing knee length khaki shorts and black socks with their sandals. It was quite a sight as we people watched, while eating lunch.

"How did we get here?" I asked my friend. I knew how it would sound, but had to ask anyway.

"What do you mean?" Josephine took a huge bite of her turkey sandwich.

"I mean, did we take the bus here?" I couldn't look her in the eyes as I asked a question that had to sound crazy. Why wouldn't I know how we got to the beach?

"Seriously Ivy, I think you were out in the sun too long. You know that your brother, Parker, drove us. Don't you?"

"Oh yeah, that's right." I took a quick sip of my soda and looked down at my food. "So where is he?"

"He went to meet up with some friends that live nearby. Ivy

are you okay?" Josephine drew her eyebrows together as she looked at me.

"Yes, I'm fine. I just have a really bad headache. I guess it's affecting my memory," I lied. Well, sort of. My memory was definitely affected by something.

"Oh. Maybe you'll feel better now that you are eating and out of the sun." Josephine reached up and tucked her short brown hair under the cute baseball type cap she was wearing. It wasn't really a team cap. It was one of those types they make for girls, pink with fake diamonds glued on it. I liked it.

I still had that other question that I needed to ask, and was contemplating how to go about it without sounding even loonier than I already sounded. I couldn't figure out how to get the date without just coming out with the question.

"Hey, what's the date today?" I asked, biting my lower lip.

Josephine had just taken a drink of her soda and almost spat it out when I asked the question.

"What? How can you forget your birthday. What is going on with you?" Josephine had a concerned look on her face.

"My birthday! You're right, how could I forget that? I'm so stupid." I gave my friend a cheesy grin, to lighten the mood. "So, how old am I today?"

I tried to make the question sound casual. But really, there was no way to sound casual when asking someone how old you are on your own birthday.

"Okay, now I know something is wrong with you. You don't even know how old you are. You are 15 today. Ivy, I'm really worried about you."

Josephine stopped eating as she spoke. She was rightfully concerned. My questions were very strange. I couldn't blame her for wondering what was wrong with me.

"Oh my god," I said as realization dawned on me.

It was my 15th birthday. The day that Bernadette is supposed to die. And I'm 100 miles from home.

"What?" Josephine asked me.

"We need to go. Right now."

I jumped up, grabbing my beach bag and leaving my half eaten tuna sandwich on the table. As I ran out the door of the cafe, Josephine followed me. I barely noticed that she was having trouble keeping up. I was on a mission to get us home as quickly as possible.

When she caught up to me, Josephine reached out and grabbed my right shoulder, spinning me around to face her. "Ivy, please tell me what is going on."

"We need to get home. When is Parker supposed to pick us up?"

I looked around the street frantically. What if it was hours before he showed? We would be too late then. I couldn't bear to go through another lifetime without saving Bernadette.

"Do you know if there is a bus that runs between here and Red Lake?" I asked her before she had a chance to answer my previous question.

"I have no idea. Why would we take the bus? Parker is supposed to pick us up around two, which it almost is," Josephine told me, glancing at her wrist watch. She looked up the sidewalk. "See, there he is now."

I turned to see my brother pulling his car into a parking space about 20 feet from where we were standing.

"Come on, let's go."

I didn't wait for Josephine. I ran to the car, and jumped into the front passenger seat, next to my brother.

"We need to go. I have to get home right now," I told Parker. I was starting to sound a bit frantic.

"Um, can we wait for Josephine to get in first?" he asked me as he looked toward the sidewalk.

I rolled down my window and called out. "Josie! Come on!"

Josephine hurried to the car and climbed into the backseat. "What is the big rush?"

"I…need to talk to Bernadette," I stammered out.

"Why? You hate her," Josephine announced.

"I do not. Why would you think that?" I guess we weren't friends in this life either. Some things never seem to change.

"Because of that huge fight you had with her this morning," Parker answered before Josephine did.

"What fight?" I asked.

"Are you serious?" Josephine asked. "Did the sun fry your brain today?"

"I don't know. I just don't remember. It must be this headache I have." I reached up and rubbed my temples for emphasis.

"You two were fighting over Simon. She's been flirting with him and it pisses you off," Josephine explained. "You got in a big fight over it. Parker and I both saw it. A bunch of people saw it. Really, you don't remember any of that?" Josephine furrowed her brows when I turned to look at her in the seat behind me.

I then looked over at Parker, sitting next to me. "Oh yeah, I guess I do remember that."

I was trying to play along. I didn't remember anything from before I 'woke up' on the beach that afternoon.

"So, why do you need to talk to her so badly now?" Josephine asked me.

"Well, I don't hate her anymore. I'm over the fight from this morning. Besides, I just need to talk to her. We don't have to be best friends to talk. Do we?" I spun around in my seat to look Josephine in the eyes.

Josephine shrugged her shoulders in response.

"Come on Ives, tell us what you need to talk to her about," Parker asked, as he turned onto the highway.

"Nothing. It's private."

"It sounds like life or death to me, by the way you're acting." Parker looked sideways at me, as he attempted to keep his eyes on the road at the same time.

"Yeah, well, it sorta is. Just drive. I can't tell you what it is, so don't ask."

CHAPTER 2

The rest of the drive home was done in silence, save for one bathroom break instigated by Josephine. I was furious that we had to pull over. It was lost time. I kept my opinions to myself though.

My mind was reeling as I went over the events of my last life, and my failure to save Bernadette. I knew in advance when Bernadette was going to be killed, and I still failed. I couldn't let that happen again, no matter what. I wouldn't be able to live with the fact that I failed once again. I was going to save Bernadette this time, even if it killed me. And, I knew that could actually happen. Would likely happen. It didn't matter. I had to try.

I thought about Simon. The first one, and the second one. The first one had killed me during our knock down, drag out fight in the front yard of my house when I was 30 years old.

The second Simon seemed like a nice guy, and I was sort of friends with him, despite my effort to keep him at arm's length. I never accepted a date with him, no matter how hard he tried, but he pursued me nonetheless.

Then he killed me. Again. He killed Bernadette, then he killed me. I was sure of it. He was always around and I knew he was capable. Besides, who else could it be? I shuddered at the thought of allowing Simon to comfort me after the second death of Bernadette.

"You okay?" Parker asked me, as he took the highway offramp into town.

"Yeah, thanks. I'll be fine. Can you drop us off at Bernadette's house?" I asked him.

"Sure." He turned left, toward her house.

"I don't want to go to Bernadette's house," Josephine called from the back seat.

"It won't take long, I promise," I replied.

Josephine crossed her arms and let out a huff, as she leaned back and stared out the window of the car. She didn't say another word to me.

Ten minutes later, I jumped out of Parker's car before it had even rolled to a complete stop. I didn't bother to close the passenger door.

"Hey! Can you at least close the door?" he yelled out his window after me. I ignored him.

"I'll get it." Josephine closed her own car door and walked over and closed mine. "Thanks for the ride," she told him, leaning into the passenger door window.

"See if you can calm her down. She's really wound up," Parker requested. Even though I was almost to Bernadette's front door, I could still hear them talking.

"I will. See you later," Josephine responded.

Parker sped off as Josephine walked up the path toward the house. She arrived just as Bernadette's mother answered the door. It was late in the afternoon by then and I was shuffling back-and-forth between my feet as I started speaking to Bernadette's mother. Josephine walked up the steps and stood next to me.

"Um, hi. We were wondering if Bernadette was home?" I did all the talking.

"No girls, I'm sorry, she's out with friends today. Can I give her a message?" Mrs. James replied.

"Do you know where she is? Or when she will be back home?" I continued.

"They went into town to do some shopping, I guess. She said she'll be back after dinner."

"Okay thanks. Come on Josie, let's go."

I grabbed Josephine's hand and pulled her down the steps and onto the sidewalk toward the street. We were both still in our bikinis, with shorts and tank tops over them. The sandals we were wearing made it difficult to run. I gave up that thought and continued swiftly down the road. We had left our beach bags in the car, thankfully. I didn't want to have to deal with dragging those around.

Josephine was having a hard time keeping up and I was pretty much dragging her along with me. We made a right turn on the sidewalk, toward the town. Josephine yanked her hand away from me and frowned.

"Would you stop dragging me everywhere? What is all of this about? I'm not really in the mood to see Bernadette and I want to go home," Josephine told me.

"Suit yourself. I'm going to look for Bernadette. She's in danger." I kept walking as I spoke. There was no time to waste, standing around chatting about it all.

"Why would you say that? How would you even know if she is in danger?" Josephine questioned. She was starting to breathe heavier, from our fast pace, and laboring to get the words out. "Would you...slow down...please?"

I hesitated. "Okay, I'll tell you, but please try to have an open mind. Can we keep walking while I try to explain this to you?"

"Sure."

For the second time in my life, or lives rather, I explained to Josephine about how I have died and woke back up, twice now. I told her all about Bernadette being killed by a serial killer and how I felt it was my responsibility to try to save Bernadette. I thought that it was likely Josephine would have an open mind, like she did before. It didn't take much convincing the last time I explained everything to Josephine. This time, was another story though.

"Are you out of your mind?" Josephine asked me when I was done relating my ridiculous story.

"No, I'm not," I replied. "It's true. Every word of it." I turned another corner. This time Josephine did not follow.

"Yeah right. I'm going home." Josephine turned and started walking in the opposite direction.

"You have a doll, named CeeCee, that your grandmother gave you when you were four years old. You keep it in a pink box in the top of your closet," I called after her.

Josephine stopped dead in her tracks, and turned to me.

"How could you know that? I've never told you about that."

I walked toward my friend and stood in front of her. I wanted her to see the sincerity on my face as I explained.

"Maybe not in this life, but you did in my first life. You even showed her to me once. She has purple and yellow butterflies on her dress. And red hair, that you said looks like my hair."

Josephine's jaw dropped open. I got no satisfaction out of showing up my friend. But I just knew that this was the one thing that would convince Josephine that I was telling the truth. There was no way I could have known about that doll, unless Josephine had told me about it.

"You went through my closet? You had no right!"

Josephine had always been someone that talked with her hands, but this time was different. She was flailing her arms around as she yelled at me. I stepped back a couple of feet to make sure that I didn't get hit by one of Josephine's wayward arms. I couldn't believe the doll thing blew up in my face like that. I was so sure it would be the one thing that finally convinced her I was telling the truth.

"No, that's not what happened. I would never go through your things. I'm telling the truth. I've lived this life before." I did my best to convince Josephine of my sincerity, but it wasn't working.

Josephine rolled her eyes heavenward and spun around on her heels and stormed off. I did not follow her. I resigned myself to Josephine not believing me in this life. I would just have to do what I needed to do without my friend at my side.

Thirty minutes later I found Bernadette's friends at the burger place.

"Hey guys," I said as I walked up to their table. "Where's Bernadette?"

"What, are we her keepers now?" a plain looking girl that I didn't know very well answered.

I took a deep breath. Getting into an argument with any of them was not going to help me find Bernadette.

"No, of course not," I responded. "I just need to talk to her. It's really important. Please, do any of you know where she is?"

I did my best not to sound desperate, but that was exactly how I felt.

"She said she was meeting someone. He was going to pick her up around the block," Bernadette's friend told me.

"A guy? She was meeting a guy? Who is it? This is really important. I need to find her." There was that desperation shining through.

"We don't know who it was. She was being really secretive about it."

The girl who spoke was Bernadette's best friend. She didn't act a bit worried or surprised at Bernadette's actions. Bernadette was known for jumping into things without thinking them through. That was the part that worried me.

"Are you sure you don't know who it is?" I asked. "It's really important."

I looked around the table at the girls and all of them shook their heads at me.

"We just told you we don't know where she is. Get a hint already." It was the same plain girl that smarted off when I first asked the question.

I turned and walked out the door of the burger place without responding to the girls.

CHAPTER 3

I had no idea where else to go to find Bernadette, and ended up walking home alone, defeated. Her friends certainly weren't going to be of any help. They had no desire whatsoever to help me. I couldn't blame them, really. They had no idea that Bernadette was in any danger. Only I knew that. And, I couldn't tell them, of course. That would be an awkward and fruitless conversation.

I wondered what else I could possibly do. Go to the police perhaps? They wouldn't believe me. I had no qualms about that. Why would they? No one had died at this point. I would just sound like a crazy teenager making up stories.

On the other hand, maybe I should go talk to them. Maybe, just maybe, they would send someone out to look for her, just to make sure she was all right. I could tell them that no one had heard from her, and I was worried. Would they take me seriously? Would they tell me that they had to wait 24 hours before beginning any sort of search? Would they tell me that her parents had to report her missing before they could do anything?

It was something I felt the need to think about a bit longer.

The sun had gone down and it was starting to get chilly. It was

THE MANY LIVES OF IVY WELLS

the end of October, after all. Even in our temperate climate, it did get pretty cold at night this time of year.

That's when I realized that I was still wearing the purple bikini, with shorts and a tank top over it. The sandals certainly weren't helping to keep me warm either. Because I was so worried about finding Bernadette, I hadn't taken the time to go home and change into something warmer. I picked up my pace toward home.

This was the time in my previous life that I had thrown the Halloween party, in an attempt at keeping my eyes on Bernadette. However, in this lifetime, I had awakened much too late, and too far away, to plan anything. That left me super nervous and desperate to find Bernadette's whereabouts. But I had no idea where else to look. I had exhausted all the usual places, such as her house and the burger joint, as well as other shops around town. I had even talked to her friends. No one had a clue where she was.

Instead of going to my own house, I walked next-door to talk to Carter. Maybe he would be willing to help me look for Bernadette. I wasn't ready to give up quite yet.

"Hi. Is Carter home?" I asked his Aunt Jean when she opened the door.

"No, Ivy, I'm sorry, but he's out," she replied, looking at me from head to toe. "Aren't you freezing, dear? You are way under-dressed for this weather." She looked up and out into the night, as if she were gauging the temperature just by looking at the darkness around us.

I looked down at my sparse clothing in response. "Oh, I'm fine. Yes, it is cold out here. I was at the beach today and was just heading home to change. I wanted to talk to Carter first though," I tried to explain. "Do you know where he is?"

"Well, no. He just said he was going to see some friends. It's been a while now. He should be home soon. Do you want me to send him over to your house when he gets back?" she asked me.

"No, that's okay. I need to go get a shower and dinner anyway,"

I told her. "Please just let him know I stopped by and will call him later. Okay?" I asked over my shoulder as I walked down her porch steps toward home.

"I will," she called after me. I heard her close the door behind me.

Carter not being home at night was very odd. He didn't really have any friends, other than me, and was rarely out on his own. At least that was the case in my last two lives. Was that still the case? I had no idea, since I hadn't had any contact with him this time. Maybe he was now the cool guy in town. The one that everyone loved and wanted to be. No...that was pretty unlikely. I couldn't see him changing that much in this reality. He was what he was. Just a small town boy that no one really paid attention to. The quiet one. The strange one.

I hoped that we were still best friends in this lifetime. His Aunt Jean didn't seem surprised to see me on her doorstep. That was a good sign. It probably meant that there had been no falling out between us.

I gave up for the time being and decided to go home to take a shower. I had a sudden urge to wash all of the day's grime off of me. Besides, a hot shower would be heavenly. I was freezing. First there was the sweat and sand from the beach. Then there was the time I spent running through the town looking for Bernadette. With the worry and perspiration washing over me, I just felt unclean. Fifteen minutes later, as I stepped out of the shower and was toweling off, the doorbell rang.

"Ivy! Simon's here!" my mother called out.

"I'll be there in a minute!"

I wondered why Simon was at my house. Previously, I had only met him on Halloween, which was today. That was because he had just moved to town and started school a few days prior, and Bernadette had been the one to introduce us. Had she introduced us earlier this time, I wondered? And if we barely knew each other, why was he here to see me? Why wasn't he out with Bernadette?

I quickly dressed in a clean pair of jeans and a nice warm sweater. As almost an afterthought, I put on my socks and shoes. I figured that I would be outside talking to Simon, so I needed to be fully dressed for that. It was cold out there.

When I walked downstairs, I found Simon out on the front porch, waiting for me. He was wearing a long, black overcoat. It seemed that black was his color this time around. It suited him. He seemed very polished. His jet black hair was slicked back and he was smiling at me with those steel gray eyes of his as I closed the front door behind me. It didn't seem quite cold enough for an overcoat, so I didn't know what was up with that.

"What are you doing here?" I hadn't meant to sound so accusatory. It was the first time I was seeing him in this life and needed to find out what this Simon was like.

"What? Can't I come see my girlfriend without getting yelled at?" Simon smiled innocently at me, as he bent over, wrapped his left arm around my waist, and kissed me passionately on the lips. All in one swift move.

My eyes lit up in surprise. Oh no. We are dating? Just great.

When he let go, I backed up to get a better look at my new boyfriend. This one already seemed somewhat different than before. I couldn't quite put my finger on it though.

"How did you get those scratches on your face?" I asked, reaching up my right hand to trace the path from his left cheek, down to his chin. The scratches were fresh. And deep. "You should put some bandages over them. They look terrible," I admitted.

He reached up and took my hand, removing it from his cheek. He then touched his own cheek as he spoke.

"Oh this? It's nothing. My cat got spooked and flipped out on me. Don't worry about it."

His story didn't sound all that convincing. "Your cat? You have a cat?"

I realized after I said it that I probably shouldn't have sounded so surprised. Maybe I had been to his house many times in this life, and knew full well that he had a cat.

"Yeah, well, the neighbor's cat actually. Whatever, it doesn't matter." He grabbed me around the waist and lowered his head to kiss me once again.

At that moment, I spotted Carter walking up the street, toward our houses. It was dark outside, but I could still tell it was him. Relief washed over me.

"Hey, there's Carter," I announced.

I squirmed out of Simon's embrace and walked around him and out toward the street to greet Carter. "Hi, where ya been?"

"Um, just...out walking. Why?" Carter replied.

He seemed a bit disheveled, but really not that different than his usual scruffy look.

"Oh, just wondering. You are usually home. I went over to see you, and your aunt said that you were out with some friends." I didn't ask him what friends, for fear of putting him on the spot. I wasn't sure how close we actually were this time.

"You came to my house looking for me? Why?" Carter asked me.

"I just wanted to talk to you," I told him, glancing back at Simon.

"About what?" Carter squinted his eyes at me and ran his fingers through his unruly mop of hair. He seemed a bit nervous, but that could have just been the way he was. It wasn't out of character at all. At least from my previous experiences with him, it wasn't.

Carter glanced up at Simon still standing on the front steps, watching us.

"What is he doing here?" Carter asked. His attempt at

sounding casual with the question, wasn't working. Carter didn't care for Simon and it showed, loud and clear.

"I'm her boyfriend. That's what I'm doing here," Simon answered for me.

I guess that was all the standing off in the shadows that Simon was willing to do. He walked over and stood next to me, wrapping his right arm around my waist in the process. The possessive nature of that gesture was not lost on me. Or Carter.

"Is that blood on your pants?" Simon asked Carter as he looked down at the dark stains on Carter's jeans.

Carter and I both looked too.

"Uh, no, it's not," Carter stammered. "I spilled sauce on my pants earlier. I was just going in to change."

"Wow, that's even worse. You spilled something all over your pants, then you went out like that. Seriously, what a loser," Simon blurted out, rolling his eyes in the process.

I glared at Simon. "Don't talk to my friend like that." Then, without hesitation, I continued. "You know what? You're a jerk. Why am I even dating you? Especially after the way you treated me when we were married! Ugh."

I pulled away from his hold on me and folded my arms as I stared at him.

"What the hell are you talking about?" Simon asked me. "Married? Yeah, I don't think so."

That's when I realized what I had just said. Oh crap, I thought. I looked over at Carter who was also looking at me strangely. Everyone forgot all about the stains on his blue jeans.

"Oh...sorry. That's not what I meant." I had to do some serious backpedaling to get out of sounding like a total crazy person. "I think I spent too much time in the sun today at the beach. Just ignore what I said." I smiled at Simon to try to diffuse the situation.

"Are you okay?" Carter asked me.

"I'm fine. Really." That's when I remembered my task. "Hey, have either of you seen Bernadette? I really need to talk to her."

Both of the boys said that they had not seen her that day.

"Come on, Baby, let's go." Simon wrapped his arm around my waist again and led me down the sidewalk, toward town.

I looked over my shoulder to see Carter standing on the sidewalk watching us. I couldn't quite read the look on his face. It appeared to be a cross between hatred and anguish.

CHAPTER 4

"I don't know why you are friends with that freak," Simon bluntly told me as we continued down the street toward town.

I pulled out of his grasp. "He's not a freak. Don't call him that."

"Yes he is. And I don't want you seeing him anymore," Simon proclaimed.

"Whoa!" I stopped in my tracks and looked Simon right in the eyes. "You don't get to tell me who I can and can't be friends with. Got it?"

I couldn't believe his nerve and that I was letting Simon manipulate me like that. At least I apparently was before I 'woke up' in this life. I had already decided that there was no way I was going to let that happen again. But here I was, walking arm and arm down the street with him.

"Hey, Baby. Come on, I'm just trying to help you out." Simon wrapped his arms around me and leaned in for a kiss. "You clearly have a soft spot for that guy."

"Ugh, get off me!" I squirmed out of his grasp. "And I'm not your baby."

"What the hell is your problem?" Simon was perplexed at my about-face. I didn't care.

"Look, I remember how you manipulated me into doing and acting like you wanted. And how you isolated me from my family and friends. I didn't even see it coming. I'm not going to let you do that to me again."

I knew that I was yelling at him about things that this Simon hadn't actually done. It didn't matter. I needed to make sure that he knew I wasn't going to put up with any of it this time. Maybe letting him know how things were going to be, he would act differently. Of course, I had no idea if any of it would work or not.

"What are you talking about? I haven't done any of those things." Simon couldn't believe what he was hearing. "We've barely started seeing each other."

The confused look on his face said it all.

"Well, maybe not yet. But you will." I didn't even try to hide the fact that I was talking about another lifetime and Simon had no way of knowing that.

Then I paused for just a moment, thinking about my next step. Yeah, it was time. "You know what? We are done."

I turned and started walking back toward my house.

I didn't need Simon in my life. Not now. Not ever. Since we had just started dating, it was a good time to end it. I needed to call it quits before we got too serious, and before Simon turned into the man that I had grown to loathe.

"Oh, come on Baby...oops, I mean Ivy. Come on, don't do me like that."

He sounded so pathetic as I walked away. But what else could I do? I needed to get away from him. And fast. The best way I could think of was to just ignore him. I could clearly see that he was the same old Simon from before. What was that saying? A leopard never changes his spots? That certainly seemed to fit Simon.

Thankfully, Simon didn't follow me home. I dared to turn back only once, and saw him standing there, watching me walk away. Once I saw the look on his face, I wished I had been a bit more gentle with him. This guy hadn't done anything to me yet, and probably didn't deserve me being so harsh with him. I would have to apologize to him later. After things calmed down a bit.

I looked up the road and saw Carter still standing on the sidewalk, pacing and watching us. I wasn't entirely sure how that made me feel. Was he just concerned for me, based on Simon's recent behavior? Or was he watching us in some sort of stalkery way? I sometimes had doubts about his sincerity.

Carter stopped pacing and smiled as I walked up. "You came back."

"Yeah, Simon's a jerk. I have no idea why I went out with him in the first place. I'm done though, and want nothing more to do with him. You can rest easy about that."

"I could have told you he was a jerk...Wait, I did tell you that. You wouldn't listen to me," Carter smiled, trying to lighten the conversation.

"Yeah, I know. Sometimes you just gotta figure things out on your own, I guess. Sorry if I was a jerk," I told him.

"You weren't," he told me. "And even if you were, I will always forgive you. You're my best friend."

Carter leaned over and hugged me. It was nice. I had forgotten how close Carter and I used to be. I would have to make more of an effort this time to keep that friendship going. He was such a sweet guy, even if no one else saw his potential.

When he released me, I looked down at my jeans. Apparently the sauce Carter had spilled on himself had transferred to me.

"Are you sure that isn't blood on your pants?" I asked him, a knot forming in my belly.

"Yeah...of course," Carter answered too quickly for my satisfaction. "Why would I have blood on me? And if I did, that would be really gross."

"Ivy! Phone!" It was my mother again.

Sheesh, I never got this many phone calls last time.

"Can you wait a minute for me? I want you to help me look for Bernadette," I asked Carter.

I didn't wait for an answer from Carter and ran up the sidewalk toward my house. I made a quick detour through the kitchen to grab a hand towel off of the counter and wet it down at the sink. I scrubbed the red stuff off of my pants on the way to the living room phone.

"Did you hear?" It was Josephine on the other end of the line. Her voice was high pitched and rushed. Not like Josephine's normally calm demeanor at all.

"Hear what?" I continued scrubbing at my jeans.

"Bernadette. They found her body in the woods. She's dead!" Josephine let out a small shriek.

"What?" I whispered as I dropped the wet towel I had been holding and involuntarily slumped to the carpet. I didn't need to hear the answer. I knew it was true. It was Halloween, and my birthday. The same day Bernadette died every time.

Before Josephine answered me, I spoke. "I've gotta go." I hung up the phone.

I curled up on the floor in my living room, sobbing. I couldn't believe that I had failed Bernadette once again. How could I let that happen? I was the only one in the world that knew it was going to happen, besides the killer, and I couldn't stop it.

It was a full ten minutes of me lying there, distraught, before Carter walked in. I had completely forgotten that I left him waiting for me outside on the sidewalk. When he found me curled up on the floor, head in my hands and tears running down my face, he sat down next to me. He didn't even ask me what the problem was. He just pulled me up into a sitting position next to him and put his arm around me. I cried on his shoulder. He stroked my hair gently and never said a word.

When I finally calmed down enough to speak, I turned to Carter.

"Don't you want to know what happened?" I asked him, sniffling as I spoke.

"I figured you would tell me when you were ready. Right?" he responded.

"Right." I nodded.

During my meltdown, Carter had reached over to the tissue box on the end table, picked it up and had set it down in front of us. He pulled three tissues out of the box and handed them to me. I took them gratefully.

I wiped down my tear streaked face and blew my nose. If Carter was any other boy, and not my best friend, I would never have blown my nose in front of him. Girls just didn't do that. But, he was Carter. Since we were 9 years old, he had seen my best, and my worst. This one was the latter.

"Bernadette's...d..d..dead," I stuttered as I tried to reign in my sobs.

Carter gave no indication of a reaction. He just pulled me tighter into his arms.

"Did you hear what I said?" I asked as I pulled away, turning to look him in the eyes.

He brushed the shaggy brown hair out of his face.

"Yes, I heard you. I'm just not surprised, that's all." He showed no emotion on his face at all.

"What do you mean by that? You knew it was going to happen?" I looked at him with a wrinkled brow, and dotted at my eyes again with the tissue.

"No, of course not. I just mean that everyone hates her. Except you, I guess. You have been talking to her a lot lately. Are you best friends now, or what?" He sounded almost accusatory.

"No. Not even close. I was just worried about her. I had a bad feeling that something was going to happen to her. That's all." There was no way that I could tell him what I knew.

"Where's your mom? Does she know what happened?" Carter asked me, looking around.

"No, she's up in her room. I haven't told her."

Both of us turned toward the front door when the doorbell rang. The visitor didn't wait for an answer and opened the door tentatively. It was Simon. When he saw the both of us sitting on the floor, with Carter's arm around me, he gave Carter a look. That look caused Carter to release his arm from around my shoulders. I saw every bit of what had happened during the silent exchange between the two boys.

"Hey, Baby, are you all right?" Simon walked slowly over to where we were sitting and sat down on the couch across from us. "Come over and sit with me." He patted the space on the couch next to him.

I hated that he called me 'Baby,' but had other things on my mind at that moment. It was the least of my worries right then.

Though I had just broken up with him less than an hour ago, I slowly got up, walked over, and sat down next to Simon. I knew why I did it. Regardless of the way he had treated me sometimes, in that previous life, I had once loved him. I had married him and had two beautiful children with him. He was once the love of my life. I couldn't completely forget all of that. Especially now. I craved the comfort that only a husband could provide.

I glanced guiltily over at Carter, who was looking at me incredulously. I could see the pain in his eyes and it just broke my heart. I turned back to Simon.

"You heard?" I asked him.

"Yeah, it's all over town. I'm so sorry. I know you two weren't really friends, but you had known her for a long time, right?" Simon asked me.

"Yes. Since Kindergarten. We actually used to be really good friends. I can't believe she's dead again," I told him.

"Again?" Simon asked.

Carter perked up also when I said that.

"Oh, I don't know why I said that." I flicked my hand in a dismissive manner. "You can't be dead more than once. That's stupid. Um, anyway, does anyone know how it happened?" I needed to deflect the conversation, so I didn't have to give a better answer.

I looked at both boys, hoping that the change of subject worked.

"No," Simon replied. "I heard there was a lot of blood though."

"Blood? She wasn't strang...?" I caught myself before I said 'strangled.' I couldn't believe all the stupid mistakes I was making. I needed to check myself before I started looking suspicious. "I mean...um...how did they find her?"

I bit my lower lip.

"I heard that someone was walking along the road, next to the forest, and she was just lying there. The killer didn't try very hard to hide her body," Simon explained.

"Oh, you know what?" Carter piped up, "I never did go change. You gonna be okay, Ivy?"

I nodded my head and Carter left me and Simon alone. I really wished he hadn't done that. Though I did appreciate everything Simon was doing for me, comforting me and all, I really didn't want to be left alone with him. I hadn't forgotten what he was capable of. Regardless of whether it was this Simon or a previous Simon, he probably never changed all that much.

There was something odd about the way Carter was acting. I couldn't quite pinpoint exactly what it was. And by his appearance, something was up. Though he was never going to be a fashionista, walking around town with sauce, or whatever it was, on his clothing, was not like Carter. I needed to get some answers.

CHAPTER 5

Once I shook Simon loose, I went to my room, where I stayed for the rest of the night. Josephine called me at some point, but I refused to take the phone call. I'm sure she just wanted to see how I was doing, after the news of Bernadette and all, but I just couldn't bring myself to talk to anyone. Not even Josie. I had failed again, and I needed to be alone to process that.

I had fallen asleep early that night. So the next morning I was awake long before anyone else. I got up and peered out my window. The sun had just started its ascent over the nearby mountains. It was going to be a dark, cloudy day, and I pulled my robe tightly around me in response.

I thought about Carter, and why he had been acting oddly the day before. Well, more than usual anyway. Was that really sauce on his pants? With Bernadette's body being found, and covered in blood, as I was told, was it possible that Carter had that same blood on his jeans?

Carter. My Carter. I just couldn't imagine him doing something so horrible to someone. No, he didn't like Bernadette, but that was no proof at all. And it certainly was not a motive for murder.

He also didn't like Simon, yet he was still alive and well. The whole thing had to be a coincidence. Perhaps Carter did spill sauce on himself, like he claimed he did. I wondered why he would go out like that though. He could have changed first.

I looked out my window again, and toward Carter's window, which was within sight of my room. His shades were mostly closed. I couldn't see a thing.

Then something caught my attention. A shadow. Movement. And it was behind Carter's window shades. Was that him? It seemed awfully early for him to be up and about. But it was his bedroom, so it had to be him. I needed to get a better look.

I quickly threw on some clothes and a sweatshirt, and tiptoed quietly downstairs.

I walked out the back door of my house, around to the side, and quietly opened the gate. I didn't latch it behind me, because it made a clanking sound when the latch engaged. Instead, I left it mostly closed and walked three feet over to the side gate at Carter's house. I pulled the string to release the latch and opened the gate without incident, but didn't close this gate behind me either.

I bent over and ducked as I walked past the windows in his house. The third window over was Carter's bedroom. I knew it well. Over all the years we had known each other, I had sneaked into his bedroom window many times. We just hung out and played games and had a great time. No funny business was going on between us. Ever. Though I wasn't so sure that Carter was entirely happy with that arrangement.

Looking up from my crouched position, I could see that Carter's bedroom shades were up about five inches. The window itself was just cracked open to let some of the cool early winter air in. I was thankful for that, afraid that if I made any noise, he might hear it if his window had been open wider.

Carter was wearing different clothing than the stained ones he had been wearing at my house. He had changed out of his jeans and into a pair of sweats. Well, of course he had. It was the next day. Now if I had found him still wearing those clothes, that would be super weird.

I noticed his dirty clothing in a heap on his floor. I watched as he walked over to the clothes on his floor, picked them up, and stuffed them in a trash bag. Then he tied the bag tightly and threw it on the floor next to his bedroom door.

The phone in is room rang at that moment and Carter picked it up. Since the window was barely cracked open, I could only hear a muffled conversation, with a few words drifting my way. I heard him tell the caller that it was a secret and to not tell 'her.' Who was he talking about? I wondered. And perhaps more importantly, who was he talking to so early in the morning?

As he appeared to be getting more agitated, Carter's voice got louder.

"No. And friend or not, 'you know who' would blab. Keep your mouth shut! Got it?"

I was surprised to hear Carter threatening whoever he was speaking to on the phone. That wasn't like him at all. He was usually a bit withdrawn around most people.

Could he be talking about Bernadette's murder? It had only happened a few hours ago and seemed like the likely topic of his conversation. No, it had to be something else.

My knees were beginning to ache as I crouched in that position, unmoving, for several minutes. Carter hung up the phone and headed for his bedroom door, grabbing the trash bag on his way out. I knew it was time to get out of there. And fast. I pivoted on my heels, stood straight up for a moment, then crouched back down to get back out under the windows of his house. As fast as I could move, I ran out the gate, and slipped inside the gate to my own backyard. Just as I closed it, I noticed movement between the vertical pickets of the wooden fence. I squeezed one eye shut and peered through one of the openings. It was Carter dumping the bag he had been carrying into one of the trash cans next to their house. Then he picked up the can and moved it to the curb for pick up.

I wondered what to do next. I couldn't exactly walk over to the trash can sitting on the street and start digging through it, right there in broad daylight. That might look a little suspicious. It would have to wait until dark. I walked back into the back sliding door of my house and to my bedroom.

An hour later, I heard the trash truck outside. Oh no, I had forgotten that it was trash pick up day. I ran outside, in my bare feet, and tried to get to the trash can first, but it was too late. They had already collected the bins in front of Carter's house and had moved on to the next one.

"Damnit, damnit, damnit!" I uttered out loud as I stood on the cold sidewalk. When I realized it was cold enough to see my breath, I ran inside to warm up.

I slept fitfully that night. I had a really bad feeling about Carter and his possible involvement in Bernadette's death. It was hard for me to imagine that he could be responsible, but he sure was acting strangely. Was that really sauce on his jeans? If it was sauce, and not blood as I suspected, why would he throw his jeans and t-shirt away? It all looked very incriminating to me. But it was Carter, my best friend for the last several years. I felt like I knew him better than anyone else on the planet. He could certainly be odd at times, but I had a very hard time wrapping my mind around the possibility that Carter could do something like that.

And what motive did he have? He barely knew Bernadette and she didn't give him the time of day. If he did do it, would it have something to do with me? In his mind, could he have been thinking that he was helping me deal with an enemy? No, that was preposterous. Even Carter was not that twisted. Was he?

The next morning was a rainy, dreary sort of day. I had a difficult time getting out of bed that morning. It seemed like the sunshine was the catalyst for getting out of bed, and being ready for a new day. There was no sunshine that day. It made me move slowly. Besides, my mind was on Bernadette, and my complete failure to save her. Once again. But, life went on for the rest of us.

Just as I finished getting dressed, the doorbell rang, and I ran to answer it. When I opened the door, I was surprised to find the sheriff standing there.

"Hi Sheriff, are you looking for my parents?"

"Actually, you are the one I want to speak with. Come on outside, will you?"

Sheriff Hayes stepped aside to allow me room to step out onto the front porch. He was a large man, about 45 years old, and just starting to gray around his temples.

It was chilly out, so I grabbed a sweatshirt off of the coat rack by the front door on my way out. It was a dark blue college sweatshirt that belonged to Parker. The sheriff waited patiently as I pulled it over my head and tied my long, red hair up into a ponytail. The sweatshirt was several sizes too big for me, but it was warm.

"Are your parents home?" Hayes was obligated to ask.

He knew it was protocol for him to question anyone underage in the presence of a parent, but the sheriff tended to do things his own way. He knew my parents weren't home and that teenagers were more likely to tell him things when their parents weren't there to shut them down.

"No, they left for work already." I stood and waited for the sheriff to explain why he was there.

"Okay then," Hayes began. "I want to talk to you about Bernadette James' death."

I nodded.

"What do you know about it?"

"Me?" I pointed to myself. "I don't know anything. I just heard about it from one of my friends," I told him.

THE MANY LIVES OF IVY WELLS

Hayes stood there for a moment, looking down the street, as he thought about his next question.

"Were you looking for her on the day she was killed?"

"Yeah."

I knew better than to lie. Red Lake was a small town and I had been asking around about Bernadette. I was certain that the sheriff knew that. Luckily for me, I had lived more than 30 years, and wasn't some dumb teenager that would have no idea how to handle being questioned by the sheriff.

"Why were you looking for her?"

"No reason, really. I just wanted to talk to her. That's all." I wasn't about to add any explanations other than what he asked. Stupid people did that.

"Talk to her about what?" he persisted.

"Nothing in particular. Just girl stuff." I crossed my arms over my chest. Mostly to keep warm. But I also hoped that my body language would give him the hint that I didn't want to talk.

"I see." He said that a lot.

Hayes stood on the front porch watching me for clues. My body language was closed off. His eyes told me that he thought I might be hiding something.

"Rumor has it that you had a big fight with Bernadette in the morning before she disappeared."

Oh yeah, I had forgotten about that. It apparently happened before I 'woke up' in this life. Josephine and Parker had told me about it, but I had no idea of the details involved. I just knew it was over Simon, because Bernadette had been flirting with him and I was upset by it.

"No, not a fight. Just a disagreement." I was trying to downplay what had happened, though I wasn't sure what that actually was.

"About what?"

"Just about her flirting with my boyfriend. We argued about it and that was that. Nothing more or less." Good idea, Ivy, throw in some cliches. That will make it sound more casual, I thought.

"Did you see her after your fight?" he continued.

"No, I went to the beach with my friend." I needed to remind myself: Don't answer more than he asks.

"Do you have an alibi for that afternoon?"

My eyebrows shot up. "Do I need an alibi, Sheriff? Am I a suspect?"

Sheriff Hayes ignored me. "Answer the question please."

"I don't know." I thought for a moment. "I was at home, and with my boyfriend, and my neighbor at different times. And my brother drove me and Josephine to the beach and back. You can check with them, if you want."

"Oh, I will."

I just nodded in response.

"I have a lot of investigating to do. You aren't planning on going anywhere anytime soon, are you?" he asked me.

"No, of course not."

"Good."

Sheriff Hayes turned and walked down the front porch steps and headed for his cruiser that was parked at the curb. "I'll be in touch," he told me over his right shoulder as he opened the door and climbed into the car. As soon as he got into his car I went back into my house. I didn't want to stand out there watching him any longer than I needed to.

CHAPTER 6

I made myself a bowl of cereal, kicked off my shoes, and plopped onto the dark brown couch in the living room. Looking around, I realized, perhaps for the first time, that the room was quite dark and gloomy. The couches were brown, the walls had paneling on them that must have been there since the 1970s, and even the carpet was a mixture of browns and tans. Though I had lived in the same house since I was born, I never spent much time in this room and hadn't really realized the oppression of it.

On this particular day, I felt that the gloomy weather and dark room was just what the doctor ordered. It gave me nothing to do or think about, except the case of Bernadette. Not that I could do anything more to help her at this point, but I could at least try to figure out who killed her. And why.

I needed time to think about everything that was going on. I was pretty sure that the sheriff thought I had something to do with Bernadette's death. Just because we got into an argument the morning that she died? That was crazy. Teenagers fought all the time and didn't kill each other. Most of the time that was the case anyway.

And why was Bernadette's death different this time? In her

previous two lifetimes, Bernadette was strangled and thrown into the sinkhole. At least I thought she was strangled and in the sinkhole the second time. I never did verify that. Either way, it was odd that Bernadette was killed differently this time. I realized then that I didn't know exactly how Bernadette died, only that there was a lot of blood. Was she stabbed? Shot? Bludgeoned?

Thump!

I jumped up off the couch at the sudden sound, knocking my bowl full of cereal onto the floor. I looked down briefly to see the carpet swallowing up the milk. Mom's not gonna be happy about that, I thought.

Thump!

There it was again, causing me to jump a second time. It sounded like it was coming from upstairs. I was alone in the house and was visibly shaking by then. I tiptoed across the carpeted floor, in my bare feet, and quietly removed the poker from the fireplace tool set. It clanked louder than I had intended it to, and I looked around guiltily.

If I had been smart, I would have hightailed it out of there. I could see the front door from where I was standing, though I did have to pass by the staircase to reach it. I could make a mad dash for the front door and probably be out before whoever, or whatever, was upstairs got to me.

Or I could run out the back door. I looked in that direction. Yeah, that was the safer choice. I could then run around the side of the house and out the side gate, to the front yard.

What would I do once I got outside? It was freezing, as well as raining out there. I wasn't dressed for this weather. I only had on shorts and a t-shirt. And I was barefoot. I wasn't going to last long outside, in November, dressed like that.

Standing there in the living room, holding the poker for a full three minutes listening for any noise, I found it was dead silent in the house. Had I imagined the thumping that I heard? Was I just being jumpy due to there being a serial killer somewhere in Red Lake?

I must have imagined it. Or perhaps a bird hit a window or something. Wait…two birds? How likely was that? I let out a deep breath and put the fireplace poker back into its home. Though I was indoors, I noticed that I was shivering. I crossed my arms in front of my chest and rubbed the opposite arms to warm them up. I needed to go change into something warmer.

Though I was pretty sure that I was completely alone, I hesitated at the bottom of the stairs. I looked up just in time to see the legs of someone running across the top of the stairs, toward my bedroom. The stair light was turned off and all I saw was a shadowy figure. Well, shadowy feet anyway.

Involuntarily, I let out a little shriek, and stood there immobilized.

When I heard footsteps leave my bedroom and run toward the stairs, I turned to run outside, to the safety of anywhere but in this house. It didn't matter how I was dressed. I would take freezing over being stabbed any day. Been there, done that.

"Hey, are you okay?"

My hand had just reached the front doorknob, when I heard the familiar voice and turned toward it.

"What the hell, Parker!" I yelled.

"What?" he answered, both palms facing up.

He started walking down the stairs calmly as he was speaking.

"You scared the life outta me. Have you been home all this time?" I asked my brother.

"Yeah, why? You don't mind if I hang out at my own house, do you?" Parker sneered, as he ran his hands through his short red hair.

"Whatever. I just thought you were at work and I was alone. What was that thumping up there?" I pointed toward the second floor.

"I was just moving some stuff around. Sheesh, Ives, don't be so paranoid."

Parker apparently was finished with our conversation. He left me standing there and walked to the kitchen. "I'm starving. Do we have anything to eat?"

I was not finished with our conversation and followed right behind him.

Parker began rummaging around in the refrigerator and pantry. "Somebody needs to go grocery shopping. It's slim pickings in here."

He had already forgotten about our conversation and the fact that he had scared his little sister. So typical of him, I thought.

"Did you hear about Bernadette James' murder?" I sat down at the kitchen table watching my brother forage.

"Yeah, who hasn't?" he responded, casually.

Parker finally settled on some sort of chocolaty cereal and reached into the refrigerator for milk. He sat down in the chair opposite of mine and constructed his meal in a bowl.

"Sheriff Hayes was here this morning questioning me about it," I told him.

Parker stopped mid-chew as he looked up at me. "Why was he questioning you? What do you know about it?"

"Nothing. But apparently she and I had an argument that morning, over Simon, and news of it got around. Well, you know about that. You were there." I pointed at him. "I don't know if he really thinks I had anything to do with it, or just needed to cross me off of his suspect list."

"You two aren't...weren't...friends?" Parker checked his tenses. Bernadette was certainly a past tense by then.

"No. I mean I didn't hate her. I did try to smooth things out with her. Not that it did any good. She still decided it was okay to flirt with my boyfriend."

I couldn't believe what I was saying. Simon was my boyfriend. Ugh. That needed to change. And quickly.

We both turned toward the front door when the doorbell rang. "Who in the world is here at this hour?" Parker looked up at the clock.

I shrugged my shoulders toward Parker and got up to answer it. He wasn't about to budge from his chair. I was less jumpy than earlier, knowing he was nearby. I felt a sense of comfort, knowing he was there to protect me.

"Hey, come on in," I said to Carter. "You're up early."

"I know. I couldn't sleep. I saw your lights on and figured you were up," he explained. "Want to walk to school together?"

"School? Oh shoot, I forgot today was Monday," I admitted.

"You forgot about school?" Carter looked at me with an odd expression as he spoke.

"There's been a lot going on these past few days," I answered. "Wouldn't you agree?"

"Well, yeah, I guess so. Are you ready to go?" Carter asked.

"You don't think I'm going to school in shorts and bare feet, do you?" I asked him, and we both looked down at my clothing.

Carter smiled in response and shrugged. "It's fine with me. Wear whatever you like."

"Ha ha. I don't think so," I laughed back. "Give me a minute to change."

I ran upstairs and was back down, ready to go in under two minutes. No makeup and fancy hair necessary. None of that mattered to me. I handed my books to Carter and pulled my red hair back into a ponytail as we headed out the door.

"Bye Parker!" I called out as the door slammed behind us.

"So," I began, taking my books back from Carter, "tell me the truth about those red stains on your pants the other night."

"What do you mean?" He had a confused look on his face.

"Was it really sauce, like you said? Come on, you can tell me the truth," I prodded.

"Yeah, it really was sauce. Seriously. What do you think it was?" Carter asked.

"Blood, maybe?"

"What?!" His eyes became huge saucers. "No, it wasn't blood. Oh my god. Is that what you really think? Does this have to do with Bernadette's murder?"

"Well...yeah. I mean, it's quite a coincidence that you came home with red stains on your clothes on the very night that Bernadette is killed."

I didn't know what else to do but be as straight forward with him as I possibly could. Carter was one of my best friends. I needed the truth, and I needed to hear it from him.

"That's exactly what it is. A coincidence. I can't believe you actually think I had something to do with her murder."

At that moment, I saw sorrow in Carter's face. Not anger. Not indignation at my accusations. Just sorrow.

Regardless, I had no choice but to press on.

"Then why did you throw away your clothes? That looks really suspicious, Carter."

His jaw dropped open. "How do you know that I threw them away?"

He stopped walking. I followed suit. Carter turned to face me.

"How do you know that, Ivy?"

"I..uh...well...I saw you throw them away." What else could I say? There was no other way for me to know.

"You were spying on me?" he asked. His clenched jaw told me that he was getting angry with me. I could understand why.

"Yeah, I guess I was. Look," I said, reaching for his arm, in an attempt to comfort him...or at least calm him down. "I'm really sorry. I had no right. I know that."

He pulled back from my touch. I understood.

"Even so," I continued, "I really would like to know why you threw them away, if they didn't have blood on them."

"Not that it's any of your business, but the sauce stained my clothes. Aunt Jean told me to just put them in with the laundry, but I didn't want to mess with it. I have other clothes. And that's the truth."

He looked me in the eyes as he spoke. Unblinking, and unwavering. For what it was worth, I believed him.

"You can ask my aunt, if you don't believe me," he added.

I just nodded.

"Then who were you talking to on the phone? The call sounded really intense. You were threatening someone." My eyes were downcast as I questioned him. I knew full well that I was crossing a line.

"Are you freaking kidding me? You were listening in on my phone call too?"

Carter began pacing and rubbing the back of his neck. He appeared to be thinking about what he was going to say to me.

"I'm sorry. I…" I was interrupted.

"You already said that! I can't believe this. I thought we were friends."

"We are friends. I'm sorry. Oh, sorry, I didn't mean to say that again." Aw geez, I was starting to sound like an idiot.

"If you must know, I am planning a birthday party for my aunt. I was talking to my cousin, who is helping me," he replied, though he didn't look happy about it.

"Really? You sounded like you were threatening them. You told them to keep their mouth shut and that someone would blab."

Before he had a chance to answer me, I realized what I had just said.

"Oh. I'm so sorry. I just realized that the call makes sense if you were planning a surprise party. I'm such an idiot."

At that moment, I felt like the world's biggest idiot. Once he put the phone call into perspective for me, it all made perfect sense. He wasn't actually threatening anyone. He was trying to keep the party quiet, so his Aunt Jean wouldn't find out.

I reached for his arm, once again, to comfort him. Or more

likely, to make me feel better. Carter let me that time and nodded in response.

"Are you agreeing that I'm an idiot?" I gave him a little half hearted smile, in a sad attempt at lightening the mood.

"Yeah, kind of." He smiled back.

"Carter, I'm really sorry. I mean it."

"I know."

We turned and resumed our walk to school together. Neither one of us said another word.

CHAPTER 7

A few days had gone by, and I had not heard back from Sheriff Hayes. That was a good thing, I figured. Yet, as far as I knew, no suspect had been arrested. That was a bad thing, and it meant that the killer was probably still wandering around Red Lake. I had the nagging suspicion that it was someone I knew. After all, he (I assumed it was a he) killed Bernadette, and would be killing Josephine in a few months. If history repeated itself at least. I imagined that the odds of both Bernadette and Josephine being killed by a complete stranger, was slim. So slim in fact, that I pushed that idea out of my head. It was someone I knew. I was almost sure of it.

But who in the world could it possibly be?

Now I was worried about Josephine. My sweet friend that was destined to die, unless I stopped it. Could I stop it? I didn't know. I had been unsuccessful in stopping Bernadette's murder. Twice I had been unsuccessful. Was I just wasting my time trying to stop the inevitable? Perhaps.

Since Bernadette's death had happened differently, Josephine's might also. It might not even be on the same day. That thought terrified me. The idea that I may not know the future like I thought I did was one of the worst things I could imagine. Everything could be in complete chaos this time, and there wasn't anything I could do to change that.

Was it possible that I was to blame for the change in the killer's method? I hadn't been here long, but this life was already shaping up to be different than the others. For starters, I didn't have a birthday party on Halloween, like last time. Therefore Bernadette, and perhaps the killer, were in completely different circumstances that night, in this life.

Whoa, I thought, was it possible that the killer was at my Halloween party during my last lifetime? Since most of the teenagers I knew had attended, yes, it was entirely possible. I ran through the guest list in my head thinking about each and every one of the partygoers. I dismissed the females for the time being, knowing that it was probably a male that did the killing. Statistics backed that up.

There really was no one on the list that stood out to me. Yes, I had suspected Carter might've had something to do with it. But in reality, I knew it was quite unlikely. It probably really was sauce on his pants and I was just jumping to conclusions. His explanation sounded quite plausible to me.

I jumped when the doorbell rang.

"You really need to stop being so jittery about everything." I was talking out loud.

I looked around the room nervously as I started walking toward the front door. I didn't want to have to explain to people why I was speaking out loud to myself. No one was around though.

I open the door to find Simon standing there and I smiled.

"Hey Baby, miss me?"

Simon took my head in his hands and planted a passionate kiss on my lips. I did not resist, because I had decided to give Simon another chance. This boy was not the same man that I married in my first life. It really wasn't fair to punish him for something someone else had done. Could I blame this guy for something he did in another lifetime? Or in another dimension? Or whatever it was. I just knew that it was all very confusing. Either way, this was not the exact same person and I needed to see where our relationship would go. I did love him once. And there was something about this Simon. He was so handsome, and so remote at the same time. I was beginning to have the same old feelings I had in the past. I wasn't nearly as strong, nor as immune to his charms, as I would have liked to be.

"Yeah, where have you been?"

"Oh, you know, here and there." Vague, as usual.

I wondered if I should marry Simon again. It would mean the world to me if I could get my kids back. Then I thought about that some more. I realized that would be an almost definite impossibility. I would have to conceive at the exact moment that I conceived the first time. And even if I knew exactly when that happened, which I didn't, the odds were certainly stacked against us.

Sure, we could have more children, but they wouldn't be the same children. Would that matter? I was sure that I would love any children that I had, but I would spend the rest of my life missing Hunter and Courtney. I just couldn't imagine never ever seeing them again. Though I was coming to realize that was probably going to be the case. Unless I just happened to wake up in my first life again, exactly where it left off. But I did not expect that would ever happen.

Over the next few months, Sheriff Hayes investigated Bernadette's death extensively. The coroner did determine that Bernadette had been stabbed to death, which was certainly not the same as the last time she was killed.

The sheriff questioned pretty much every resident of Red

Lake, and nothing came of it. It seemed to the citizens that Bernadette's killer would never be caught.

During the time that I was getting to know Simon all over again, Josephine started dating a nice young man. His name was Graham and I liked him very much. I felt that Graham was good for Josephine. He was just average looking, with dirty blond hair and glasses. Nothing really special about him. But he was a super nice guy, which was exactly what Josephine needed.

One day, in late April, which was a couple of months after Josephine and Graham started dating, Graham showed up on my front porch in tears.

"What's the matter?" I asked him as we sat down on the couch.

"Josie and I had a fight," he told me. He was trying to hold back his tears.

"About what?" I asked quietly. Graham and I weren't particularly close, so it was surprising that he came to me for advice.

"It was nothing, really. I tried to cancel a date we had so that I could go out on the lake with my friends. She got mad at me for that." He pulled off his glasses and dabbed at his eyes with his shirt sleeve.

"You know, I have to agree with Josie. You had a date set up and it's really not cool to cancel it to hang out with your friends. I would be upset also," I told him, truthfully. "Besides, the lake isn't going anywhere, and you have all summer to go out there."

He nodded slightly at me, in response.

"Yeah, I guess," Graham reluctantly agreed. "Hey, are you going to the water tower razing next week? It should be pretty cool to see."

"Oh my god, that's next week?"

I hadn't realized how fast the last few months had gone by. The day the water tower is demolished, is the day that Josephine is supposed to go missing. Or was during her first life at least. I had no reason to think that things would be any different this time. Even though Bernadette's death had changed, it was still on the same day.

"You forgot?" Graham was surprised. "It's the only thing happening right now in this podunk town of ours."

"That's true. I guess I've just been preoccupied," I explained. "I was wondering if I could ask you a favor?"

"Sure, what?" His eyebrows raised in anticipation.

"Can you make sure that you stay with Josie on that day? I mean all day. You can't let her out of your sight for even a second." I knew it was asking a lot, and that I wouldn't really be able explain why.

"Why?" Graham asked.

I knew that question was coming. Of course he would ask. It was a strange request on my part.

"I really can't explain it. It's just a bad feeling that I have about that day. I'm just worried about her. Can you please just make sure she is all right? Keep her safe for me? You can't let her out of your sight, even for a moment. Promise me." I gave him a stare so he would know that I meant business.

"Well, okay. I'll try. But you know Josie, she has a mind of her own. She may not be happy about me following her around."

"I know. Just do your best. It's just that after Bernadette was killed, I'm a bit jumpy," I tried to explain.

Simon walked in the front door of my house just as Graham was leaving. Simon gave Graham a look. An 'I don't like you hanging around my girlfriend' type of look. Graham didn't even notice. But I did.

"Hi Baby. What was he doing here?" Simon asked me once Graham was gone. His voice was upbeat, but I could hear a tiny bit of resentment squeezing its way through.

"He just wanted to talk about Josie." I had no desire to elaborate. It was none of Simon's business. Besides, it wasn't a lie. That's exactly why Graham showed up.

"That's all? You know, I think he has a crush on you. You

should keep your distance from him."

Simon tried his best to make it sound like a suggestion. It wasn't.

That was it. I had enough of Simon and his 'suggestions.' He made somewhat of an attempt to veil his orders to me, but I could see right through it. I was not his property and didn't need a repeat of that first life I had with him.

"Simon, we need to talk." No good conversation in the history of mankind ever started with those words.

"What?" It was as if he had no clue what was coming.

"I don't think we should see each other anymore." I took in a quick breath as I waited for his reaction.

"Why? Because of that dude?" Simon tilted his head toward the closed front door that Graham had just exited out of a minute prior.

"Graham? No, of course not. He's Josie's boyfriend. I'm not interested in him," I tried to explain. "It's just that I'm not interested in you either."

I hated being so blunt, but sometimes that was the only way to get through to him.

"Yes you are. Come on, don't be like that."

Simon reached for me. I anticipated his attempt to wrap his arms around my waist and backed up, leaving him grabbing the air in front of him instead.

"Ivy, please. I love you." He dropped his arms to his side.

"Simon, I just don't love you back. I'm really sorry. Please understand."

I didn't want it to be a bad breakup, with hard feelings. We did have to continue living in the same small town after all.

"No, I don't understand. Everything was fine yesterday. Then that guy showed up here. There is something you are not telling me."

Simon took two steps toward me. It was an intimidating gesture and I backed up just as far. He was starting to scare me.

"I told you, Graham has nothing to do with this, and everything wasn't fine yesterday. I've been feeling this way for a while now," I admitted.

"I don't believe you!" he yelled.

I backed up another step right into the wall opposite the front door, and next to the stairs.

"Please just go. Leave me alone."

It was all I could do to keep my voice from shaking. It was important that I didn't show fear. That was a weakness that Simon would exploit.

"No, I'm not going to do that. You need to listen to me!" Simon was still yelling.

Before I had time to register what was happening, Parker ran down the stairs and latched his right hand around Simon's throat.

"Did you hear what my sister said? She wants you to leave her alone." Parker was speaking slowly and deliberately. With that menacing tone in his voice, Parker would have no problem making his point.

Simon gagged. It was mostly him being dramatic though. Parker was not squeezing the air out of him. He was just holding Simon's throat tight enough to immobilize him. Simon was no match for Parker's size and strength.

"Answer me!" Parker was quite a bit louder that time.

Simon nodded his head as best he could and Parker let go. Simon bent over gagging and was breathing heavily. After a moment, he stood up, red in the face. He started to say something to me, but glanced at Parker and thought better of it. Simon turned and walked out the door without another word.

Well, that was that. I was done with Simon for good. It was a great feeling. But scary at the same time. Simon was not one for giving up so easily, as I found out in my other lives.

I thanked Parker for intervening.

"No worries." Parker smiled.

I knew my big brother would do anything to protect me.

CHAPTER 8

The day had finally come. It was one of the biggest things to hit Red Lake. The water tower was getting torn down. It hadn't been used in a lot of years and was slowly being eaten away by decades of rust and wind. The residents were worried that it would just fall over on its own, seriously hurting someone. They decided that it either needed to be repaired or torn down. Tearing it down was the cheaper way to go, and so it was decided.

I remembered the first time that I attended the razing of the water tower, and it was a huge party. The town really did the whole event up. They had music, food, and even a bonfire. I wouldn't have missed it. There were so few fun events going on in our small town that it was the funnest thing going on.

Parker and I arrived at the water tower gathering together. We had invited Carter to come along, but he told me that he would be by later. Though it was only a short walk over from our house, it was a muggy, hot day, and both of us were sweating by the time we arrived. We made our way to one of the tables, bought some lemonade, and stood under a big oak tree for some respite from the blazing sun. It seemed as if every single person in town was there. Parker and I spent several minutes saying hello to everyone, as several people walked over to stand in the shade as well.

I left my brother talking with some friends and weaved my way through the crowd to find Josephine. After several minutes of searching, I came to the conclusion that Josephine was not there. That was probably a good thing. Graham had done as he promised and was somewhere else with her, keeping her safe. I had made sure to call him that morning to remind him. I know he thought I was nuts, but he said he would do as I asked.

I walked back over to the oak tree to find Parker, and he was nowhere in sight, so I grabbed a plate of food and sat down at one of the long picnic tables that had been set up for the event. It had a white plastic table cloth with red, white, and blue patriotic decorations on it. The decorations looked suspiciously like the same ones that the city used for the annual Fourth of July picnic. It made me smile. Nothing wrong with recycling.

Simon, and some girl that I didn't recognize, sat down at my table with their plates of food. I did my best to ignore the fact that we had only been broken up for a few days and he had already found another girl to replace me. Was I so forgettable that he could replace me so easily? I wasn't sure why I even cared. After that unfortunate incident where Parker had to defend me from Simon, I was glad to be rid of him.

I caught myself looking at him and the girl without meaning to. Simon glanced up and caught me. That's when I lowered my eyes down to my plate as my face heated up. I didn't dare look up again. Whatever, good riddance.

The mayor walked up to the portable stage that had been brought in. He was a portly man, in his mid sixties, wearing a lime green shirt that was much too tight for his girth. He pulled a white handkerchief from his pants pocket and wiped the perspiration off of his forehead, before he began to speak.

He gave a long speech, much longer than what was warranted for a water tower being torn down. But really, he rarely got the chance to address the town. It was his chance to shine. When he finished, the entire crowd clapped and cheered. The mayor pulled out his handkerchief to wipe down his forehead again, as he walked down the steps. The band began playing then and many people got up to dance.

Though the entire event was based on the water tower being torn down, they weren't even going to actually tear it down until much later in the day. Probably long after most people left. We were told that they thought it was a bad idea to do it with so many people in attendance. I knew they were terrified that something might go wrong and crush some unsuspecting soul.

"Josie, come on. I want to go to the water tower party." Graham was at Josephine's house, trying to persuade her to go.

"It's gonna be lame. I just know it," she responded. "But, hang on. I need to get ready."

"You look fine the way you are. Come on, we are going to miss everything." Graham sounded a bit whiney to Josephine as he begged her to hurry.

"You go ahead. Ivy and Parker are there. You can hang out with them until I get there." Josephine turned and headed to her room to get ready.

"Okay, fine. I'll meet you there." Graham left, slamming the door. His promise to Ivy completely lost to anger.

A half hour later Josephine was ready to go. She looked into the mirror and smiled, happy with the results. Her wavy brown hair was perfect, her makeup was perfect, and her warm brown skin glowed. Once Graham got a look at her, she knew all would be forgiven. Her parents were already at the tower, so she figured she would just walk over alone. No big deal, it wasn't far.

When she opened the front door, Josephine was startled to see someone standing there. He looked like he was about to knock, knuckles in mid-air, when she interrupted him.

"Hey, what are you doing here?" she asked him. "Why aren't you at the water tower with everyone else?"

"Oh, I was running late. I figured I'd just walk over with you, if that's all right?"

"Sure, I guess," Josephine responded. "I was just heading over."

"It's really hot out there. Can I get some water first?" he asked her.

"Yeah, of course. Come on in. I'll get a glass."

Josephine turned toward the kitchen. The front door closed behind them.

"Do you want some ice in your gla...?"

Josephine never finished her sentence. She was grabbed from behind just as she pulled the glass out of the cupboard. A strong arm wrapped around her throat and she dropped the glass on the tile floor. It shattered as she gasped for breath.

Josephine started flailing her arms and legs in an attempt to get away. She gave it her all in the life and death struggle that ensued. Her attacker could tell that she was not going to go down easily, as Bernadette had. A few quick jabs with the knife, and it was all over for Bernadette. She never even got the chance to fight back. Josephine was turning out to be a whole different story. He didn't mind. A heart racing challenge once in a while would keep him on his toes.

He needed to get control of the situation, and quickly. Leaning back, he squeezed his forearm even tighter around her throat. Josephine was struggling to breathe. When he leaned back to get better leverage, her feet were lifted off the ground, and he was hanging onto her only by her throat.

This gave Josephine an advantage. She swung her feet up onto the kitchen counter and propped them against the ledge. Then with everything she had, she shoved her feet against the counter, in an attempt to launch off of it. This caused her attacker to lose his balance...and his grip on Josephine. As he was shoved backward, his feet went out from underneath him. He released his grip on her as his arms flew out instinctively to stop his fall. Time was not on his side though.

They landed in a heap on the hard tile floor. His arms never slowed the progress of their landing, and her attacker cried out as his head slammed hard into the refrigerator behind them. A large, round, head shaped dent now graced the refrigerator door, but neither of them noticed.

Josephine was gasping for breath, but knew she had no time to try and recover. Her attacker was lying on his back and she was on top of him, also on her back. She rolled off of him and scrambled to her feet before he had the chance to grasp what was happening. His head meeting the refrigerator door had slowed down his senses a bit.

As she took her first step toward the front door, he rolled over, reached out, and grabbed her right foot, all in one swift motion, tripping her. Her forehead hit the wooden threshold divider that separated the kitchen tile floor from the living room carpet. Josephine's vision turned to stars. She could no longer make sense of what was going on. For the moment, at least.

Though Josephine wasn't completely alert, she could feel the sensation of him grabbing her left arm and turning her over to face him. He climbed on top of her, in a sitting position, with one knee on either side of her hips. He was crazed by then and had only one thought going through his mind at that moment. Kill. There were no emotions available to him. No compassion. No regret. And no control. This thing in him was in charge. He could do nothing to stop it. He was almost unaware of his actions. Almost. Even so, it was too late now.

As her vision cleared, she looked him in the eyes. It was the first chance she had to think about what was happening to her. Her body started trembling, uncontrollably. She knew she was about to die. She could see it in his crazed eyes. Suddenly she knew that this was the person that had killed Bernadette only a few months prior, and she was no match for his strength.

"Please...no," Josephine choked out.

"I'm sorry," he responded. Though he didn't know why he had said that. He wasn't sorry. He felt no remorse. It just seemed like the appropriate response.

Her attacker wrapped both hands around her neck and began applying pressure with his thumbs. With no ability to breathe, Josephine's face began turning red. She made one last ditch effort to fight him, and to save her life, before her world turned black. Her father's face swam into her mind, out of nowhere, and she remembered him telling her many times that if she were ever attacked, to go for the eyes. Scratch them, gouge them out if she needed to. Get away. Whatever it took.

She reached for his eyes and swiped with her claws out. She missed though, and managed only to scratch the left side of his face. She had no idea that she had made contact, as her vision began to fade, and she resigned herself to the inevitable.

"You bitch!" he yelled, as he loosened his grip and reached up to touch his cheek. He pulled his hand back to reveal blood on his left fingertips. "Damnit! Now look what you've done."

Josephine gasped for breath and her head began clearing up when he released his grip. She began flailing aimlessly at him. It didn't last long though. He once again wrapped his hands around her neck and squeezed. For the last time.

Josephine didn't have a chance. She died there that day, on her kitchen floor. She knew the killer, and he knew her. That was a secret she took to her grave.

When it was all said and done, her killer lifted off of her lifeless body and sat down on the kitchen floor next to her, with his back leaning against the very refrigerator that now bore an indentation from his head.

He began to cry. He hated what he was. He didn't want to kill her...or anyone. He liked Josephine, but he just couldn't help himself. Josephine had been an easy target, one that satisfied his urge to kill. He had run into her boyfriend just as Graham had arrived at the water tower. When the killer asked about Josephine, Graham was nice enough to provide him with enough details about her whereabouts, and the fact that she was alone, to pique his interest. That was all he needed.

When he arrived at Josephine's house, everything went as planned. The entire kill took under five minutes from start to finish. Everything except the damned scratch that now graced his face. She was a fighter and the killer liked that. It was boring when they didn't give him a challenge.

After a minute, he calmed himself down enough to get up and find something for his face. He cleaned up in the hall bathroom and applied two bandages to his cheek. The wound had already stopped bleeding, as it was not very deep, but they were obvious scratches and he needed to hide them the best way he could. If anyone asked, he would say that he got scratched by some thorny bushes when hiking in the forest. No one would be the wiser.

CHAPTER 9

"Where's Josie?" I asked Graham when he found me at the water tower.

"She's home getting ready. She said she will meet us here," he explained.

I gasped. "What? I asked you to not let her out of your sight today! You promised!"

"Why are you yelling at me? She was taking forever. What's the big deal?" Graham asked me, calmly.

"Oh my god. What have you done? We need to get to her house. Right now!"

I looked around frantically for someone to drive us to her house. But, everyone looked like they were having way too much fun, and drinking heavily, to bother driving me anywhere. I would have to get there on my own.

I knew in my heart that it was too late. It was always too late.

I made Graham run most of the way to Josephine's house. We crisscrossed the streets in a panic, and were nearly run down by an elderly woman in an equally ancient car. I watched her eyes grow as huge as saucers, though she could barely see over the top of the steering wheel. At the last moment we leapt out of her path.

We ignored the screeching brakes as we continued our frantic race to Josephine's house.

"Ivy! Please...stop! Is this...really...necessary?!" I heard Graham yell behind me, his words coming out in gasps as he tried to catch his breath.

Ignoring him, I continued. Though I never looked back, I could hear Graham's staggering footsteps continuing behind me. They seemed to be trailing off. But I wasn't stopping for anyone. This was my one and only chance to save her. There was no way I would let myself fail. I had already done that twice with Bernadette. Josie was going to make it, or I was going to die trying.

Both of us were panting hard, with red faces and sweat dripping from our chins by the time we reached our destination. Graham could barely keep up. Not that I was in much better shape than him, but my determination, with probably some adrenaline mixed in, won out over the oppressive heat of the day.

Reaching Josephine's house, we found the large garage door was wide open. The garage had no vehicles in it.

"What the..." I heard Graham exclaim as I raced through the garage, without pausing to contemplate why it was wide open.

When I reached the door that led into the kitchen, it was also open, and I ran inside. It never dawned on me that there could be a killer inside. Josephine was the only thing on my mind at that moment.

I only paused for a moment when something crunched under my feet on the kitchen floor. I looked down to see shattered glass all over the floor. That was a bad sign. It seemed unlikely that someone in her family dropped something breakable and just left it there without cleaning it up.

"Josie!" I called out as I scoured the house. "Help me look for her," I ordered Graham, when he stepped into the kitchen. He also looked down at the floor in response to the crunch under his feet. He didn't say a word about it though.

Graham ran upstairs to search, and came back down a minute later.

"Nothing. She's not here. Maybe she's already at the water tower," he offered.

I sat down on the couch in the living room, covering my face in my hands and began to sob.

"She's not...at the...water tower. We are...too late," I managed to get out between sobs.

"What do you mean?" Graham sat next to me on the couch.

"She's gone. The person that killed Bernadette has now... killed...Josie," I wailed.

"No, you don't know that. I'm sure she's fine." Graham did his best to calm me down. "There's no evidence of any problems here. No blood." He looked around the room. "Nothing's even out of place. Have you noticed any problems here?"

"No," I barely choked out. "Except a broken glass, or whatever it was, on the kitchen floor. That's kind of strange."

"Maybe they were in a hurry to get to the water tower and planned to clean it up later. It could happen," Graham offered as an explanation.

I shrugged my shoulders. "Yeah, I guess. But that seems unlikely. Anyway, what about the garage doors? Why would she leave and not close the garage doors?" I looked up at him with tears dribbling down my face.

"I don't know. Maybe she was preoccupied with getting to the water tower, that she didn't think about it," Graham told me. "Come on, let's go to the water tower and look for her. I'll bet she's already there looking for us."

Graham stood up and reached out his hand to help me up. I took his hand and grabbed some tissues to wipe my face as I stood up.

"Maybe you're right. This could all be for nothing. Let's go look," I agreed. I wasn't convinced of my own words though. Dread coursed through my veins.

As we walked back to the party, I had my doubts. Things could certainly be different this time. They were for Bernadette. At least sort of. Maybe things would be different for Josephine too. I didn't believe it though. I knew in my heart that my best friend was gone. And I was to blame.

The two of us spent an hour looking for Josephine, while everyone around us was having a great time. Even Josephine's parents were there, drinking and laughing with their friends. I didn't know what to say to them. I certainly couldn't just go up to them and explain that Josie was missing and that I was pretty sure she was dead. How do you say that to someone's parents?

I had two children of my own. Or used to anyway. I couldn't imagine ever having that conversation with someone about one of my kids.

I spotted Sheriff Hayes talking to his wife and made a beeline for him. He was wearing shorts and a baby blue polo shirt. I almost didn't recognize him. In all the years I had lived in Red Lake I couldn't recall a single time that I had ever seen him out of uniform.

"Excuse me, Sheriff. Can I talk to you for a minute?" I looked over at his wife. "I'm really sorry, do you mind?" I asked her.

Mrs. Hayes saw the look on my face and nodded at her husband. "I'll go get some pie. Want some?" she asked him.

He shook his head at her and she walked away. She had been the sheriff's wife for a very long time and knew when she needed to walk away.

"What can I do for you, Ivy?" he asked me, taking a long pull on the beer he had been holding. I watched as the condensation dripped down onto his hand.

I waited until he was done.

"It's about my friend, Josephine. She's missing."

"What do you mean by missing?" He looked up. "Her parents are sitting right over there. They don't seem concerned."

I looked toward where the sheriff's eyes were pointing, then looked back at him.

"They don't know yet. I just found out myself," I announced.

"What makes you think she's missing?" he asked, narrowing his eyes at me.

"Well, she was supposed to meet me here and she didn't show up. So Graham and I went to her house and she's not there. We can't find her anywhere." Oh god, I could hear how lame that sounded the second the words left my lips.

"Sweetheart, she's a teenager. She's probably shopping or something. Why don't you start by asking her parents where she is?"

He turned away and started heading over to the pie section to join his wife. I grabbed his arm to stop him. When he looked down at the spot I was holding, I immediately let go of his arm. He turned once again to face me.

"Sorry," I told him. "But, Sheriff, you don't understand. This is not like her at all. She was getting ready to come here, not go shopping. Besides, most of the store owners are here. Is anything even open today?" I asked.

Sheriff Hayes ignored that last question.

"Young lady, you are wasting my time. If her parents tell me she is missing, then I'll take this seriously. Right now, she is just acting like a typical teenager."

"But, Sheriff…"

He walked away before I had a chance to finish my sentence. I watched him in utter disbelief. I couldn't believe that he was not taking me seriously. But what could I do? I couldn't force the sheriff to investigate a missing person, when no one even knew she was missing. Yet.

I searched the party for Parker, because I wanted to go home. But he was nowhere in sight. He probably went with his friends to find some beer somewhere. So typical.

I walked home alone. A failure. I hadn't been able to even

convince Graham that Josephine was missing. He figured that she would turn up, just like the sheriff said she would. I knew she wouldn't turn up. No one would ever see her alive again. I could feel it deep down in my core.

~

The next day, Sheriff Hayes showed up on my doorstep. I knew he would.

"You don't look surprised to see me," he said as I walked out on the front porch to speak with him.

"No, I'm not. I was dead serious yesterday when we talked. But you couldn't be bothered." I knew how I sounded. I sounded pissed off and sarcastic. I was both.

The sheriff scrunched up his face just enough for me to notice, but said nothing about my attitude.

"Ivy, your friend Josephine has been reported missing by her parents."

"I know. They called me looking for her." I spoke to him with a dead pan expression. I had already cried myself out over my friend.

"I would like to know what you know about her disappearance."

"Everything I told you yesterday is all I know. You wouldn't listen to me then. Why listen now?" I crossed my arms in front of my chest as I spoke.

I was tired of being ignored. None of it mattered anymore anyway. Josie was dead and I would never see my friend again.

"Why don't you tell me again. I'm listening."

Without actually coming out and saying it, I could tell that the sheriff regretted dismissing me at the water tower razing. His voice sounded a bit contrite. At least now he was sober and wanted to hear what I had to say. Not that any of it really mattered at this point. Or even when I spoke with him at the water tower yesterday. I was sure that Josephine was already dead by the time I tried to report her missing to him.

I obliged and repeated what I had told the sheriff the day before, leaving out the part about my time traveling and how that's why I knew Josephine was dead.

One week later, Josephine's purse was found in some bushes within a few yards of the sinkhole. Her mother identified it. Everyone in town, the sheriff included, surmised that her body was in the sinkhole. I knew it was.

As it always did, life went on.

I spent that summer in my bedroom. My depression was so deep that I hardly ate anything. My mother was beginning to worry about all the weight I was losing, but I didn't care. What was there to live for? I wasn't suicidal, I just didn't want to talk to anyone. Not even my other best friend, and the only one I had left, Carter. He had tried several times to get me up and out into the sunshine. He failed.

With all that had happened, much of my time was spent thinking about my children. Though it had been several years since I had seen them last, I couldn't get my mind off of them.

As I laid on my bed that summer, barely getting up for any reason, I actually found myself dialing my old phone number from the house I lived in with my children.

Of course, the number was disconnected, and it was like that every single time I dialed it. I don't know why I kept trying. It was a strange thing to do, I know. I just hoped...prayed really...that some how, some way, Hunter or Courtney would hear the ringing, somewhere in time. Maybe then, they would answer it, and I could hear their precious voices once again.

Tears dribbled down my cheeks as I hung up the phone, once again.

After three lifetimes, and two unsuccessful attempts to save Bernadette, and one unsuccessful attempt to save Josie, I knew that there was no point in it all. If there was a point, if there was a reason why I kept coming back, in the midst of all the tragedy, then why had nothing worked?

I felt defeated. Defeated by life, and by death, and all that entailed.

CHAPTER 10

About a week before school started, Graham came by to see me. My parents were not home and I was sitting on the living room couch, reading. I had finally ventured from my room. Initially, I ignored the knock at the door, figuring that whoever it was would go away.

"Ivy! I know you are home," he yelled through the door. "I'm not leaving until you answer the door!"

"Ugh, fine." I put down the book and walked to the front door.

"I really don't feel like talking right now," I told Graham.

"Well, I do."

Graham walked right past me and sat down on the chair opposite the couch. He pushed the glasses up on the bridge of his nose and gestured for me to sit on the couch. I obliged, with a huff. He noticed, but chose to ignore me.

"Look," he began, "I miss her too. But we are still here, and we need to get on with our lives."

I shrugged without speaking.

"That's it? You have nothing to say?" he asked me, tapping his foot as he spoke.

"What is there to say? I did my best to save her, and look where it got me."

I made a point of refraining from blaming him for her death. Somewhere inside, I felt that he was partially to blame though. He had promised me that he would not let her out of his sight that day. That horrible, fateful day. Yet, he did anyway. And she was killed. So, part of the blame landed right on his shoulders.

"You had no way of knowing what would happen. There was nothing you could do." He tried to comfort me with kind words and a soothing tone.

Of course Graham knew nothing of my super powers. The ability to die and come back to life in one giant leap. I felt there was no point in trying to explain it to him. He wouldn't believe me anyway. Besides, I couldn't really explain it. I had no idea how it happened. It just happened.

"Come on. I'm taking you to lunch." Graham reached out to take my hand as he stood up.

I didn't budge from the couch. "No, I don't feel like it. Besides, look at me, I can't go anywhere looking like this. I haven't even showered today. I'm a mess."

I looked down at my sweatpants and tank top. Neither had been washed recently. I wasn't exaggerating. I really was a mess.

"We can just make sandwiches here," I offered, as I left his hand hanging there without taking it. He dropped it down to his side.

"Yeah, you are kind of a mess." He smiled my way to lighten the mood. "But you need to get out of the house, and I'm not taking no for an answer. Go get a shower, change your clothes, whatever you need to do. And do something with that hair." He waved his arm in the direction of my head.

I smiled at him without meaning to.

"All right, fine. I'm going. I can't promise to offer any riveting conversation though." I stood up.

"Did I say anything about riveting conversation? You can sit silently, if that's what you want. You just need to get out of this house and into the world of the living."

The stern look on his face was enough to get me moving. I ran up the stairs, while he waited patiently for me.

Over the next few months, Graham and I saw each other every day. At first, we were just comforting each other over the mutual loss of Josephine. But then, something happened, and it became more than that. That's when we both realized that we had been dating and didn't even know it. At first, I felt some guilt. But that subsided with time. I understood then what my friend had seen in Graham. He was one of the good ones. I felt sure that Josie would be happy for the two of us.

Graham was so much better than Simon in a thousand different ways. I never regretted for a moment my decision to be rid of Simon. Except when I thought about my children. That's when my heart ached the most. I knew that I would never see them again. How could I? It was as if they had died with me on that fateful day that Simon killed me in our front yard.

I still saw Simon around school, and in town sometimes. There was no way to avoid him altogether. Red Lake was much too small of a town for that. When I did see him, he was usually with a pretty girl. It seemed like there were a lot of them these days. I didn't care. But, I could see that he did. He had a scowl pretty much every time I saw him. And more so, when Graham was with me. He usually didn't say anything to the two of us, but I could see the hatred in his eyes.

And then there was Carter. My best friend since we were 9 years old. He rarely came around anymore, and I was sure that Graham was the reason. When I did see Carter, he was cordial, but that was just about it. I figured that he didn't want to hang around the two of us together, so he avoided us. I so hoped that he would find a nice girl, one that would bring Carter out of his shell. It hadn't happened yet, but I had high hopes.

I had thought a lot about Josephine in the months since she had died. I knew in my heart that I hadn't done enough to save her. I had just pawned the job off on Graham, without revealing the reason why to him, and as a result, my friend had been murdered. I didn't know why, or who had done it, but I vowed that if I got another chance, I would stop at nothing to save Josephine. And Bernadette as well. They both deserved my help, and I would give it.

Graduation for me, Graham, Simon, Carter, and all of our class-mates, came and went. It was bittersweet without Bernadette, and most of all, without Josephine.

I was most excited about starting college in the fall. It was something I had never done before. I would be living in the dorms at the university four hours from home. Close enough that I could still drive up and visit my parents anytime I wanted to, but far enough away from Red Lake that I could put some emotional distance between me and everything that had happened.

One day in July, after graduation, I was cleaning up my room, organizing things and figuring out what I wanted to take with me to school in the fall. I was listening to 70s music, my all time favorite, when a newscast broke in. The newscaster said that they believe the Red Lake Slasher had struck again.

A third victim had been found in the woods. I'm not sure why he said that, because technically, Josephine had never been found. It was just assumed that she was killed by the Slasher and thrown into the sinkhole.

It devastated me to even say that. She was my best friend and life without her would never be the same.

He went on to say that the name of the victim was being withheld, pending notification to the families. I had heard nothing about it. But was sure that it was no one I knew, because there were only the two victims ever, until he struck again when I was 30 years old in my first life.

I forgot all about the newscast when I heard the doorbell ring. I lit up, expecting Graham. We had planned on spending the day at the beach together. My beach bag was ready to go, and I grabbed it on the way to the front door.

"Oh, Simon, it's you," I said, as I opened the door, disappointment dripping from my voice.

"Try not to sound so happy about it." He smiled. It was a joke, but I didn't smile back.

"I just wanted to make sure you were okay," he told me.

"Yeah, why?"

"Oh, no reason. Just checking in on a friend," he replied.

"Oh, okay. Well, I'm fine," I told him.

"I came to take you to breakfast. Just old friends. What do you say?"

"I can't." Not that I would anyway. "Graham is coming by any moment. We are going to the beach."

"Oh, I already talked to him this morning. We ran into each other at the coffee shop. He said he couldn't make it and asked me to let you know."

I tilted my head his way. "Why would he do that? He would call me himself," I replied.

"Something about his parents taking him out of town on a last minute trip. Come on, I'll take you to breakfast, then to the beach. You look all ready to go." Simon gestured for me to hurry up.

"I don't believe you. I'm calling him."

Before Simon could stop me, I picked up the living room phone and dialed Graham's home. No one answered. When the voicemail picked up, I left a message, but didn't expect a call back that day. I hung up. I hated that Simon was right.

It wasn't completely out of character for Graham's parents to do that. They took him out on last minute trips all the time. They were quite a spontaneous family. Graham told me one time about how his parents woke him up at 5 a.m. one Saturday morning and took him camping for the weekend. No advance plans. No warning at all. They just decided right then and there to go. So they went.

I figured there was no harm in having breakfast with an old friend, or past husband, or whatever he actually was. I no longer had plans, so why not?

It surprised me that I actually ended up having a nice time with him. He made me laugh, just like he used to when I first fell in love with him. When breakfast was over, he persuaded me to let him drive me to the beach. He had a swimsuit in the trunk of his car, just for 'emergencies' like this.

I had nothing better to do, and since I had planned on being at the beach that day anyway, I agreed. We had a great time, and a few hours later, he drove me home, like a perfect gentleman.

Sheriff Hayes was at my house, speaking with my mother when we drove up. I felt a jab in the pit of my stomach. Still sitting in the car, Simon asked me if he should stay and I told him no. I could see the relief in his face as he drove away.

"Miss Wells, we meet again." The sheriff nodded my way as I walked toward him.

"Hi," I replied, setting my beach bag down on the front porch next to me. I looked to the sheriff and my mother. "What's going on?"

"Sweetheart, maybe you better sit down." My mother gestured to the bench on the front porch.

"I don't want to sit down. What is going on?" I could feel the panic starting to rise up in me.

"Well okay. I don't know how to tell you this, but something has happened. It's about Graham," my mother began.

I took in a quick breath of air and held my breath, waiting for the bad news. It had to be bad news. Why else would my mother look so worried, and more importantly, why would the sheriff be at my house?

"What about Graham?" I asked. "What's going on?" I looked back and forth from my mother to the sheriff, and back again, trying to gauge the look on their faces.

"Graham has been killed," my mother told me before the sheriff had a chance to say anything.

I felt my head start to spin. Not again. I couldn't handle losing another person in my life. Not Graham. As my knees began to buckle, Sheriff Hayes sprung to action and caught me. He guided me into the chair on the porch, and and my mother ran inside to get some water.

Once I drank some of the refreshing water and had a few minutes to recover, Sheriff Hayes started battering me with questions. Where had I been? Who was I with? When was the last time I saw or talked to Graham? Did I know what happened to him?

I answered all of his questions calmly and accurately. The sheriff seemed satisfied with my answers. He told me to contact him if I thought of anything that could help them. I agreed.

As I watched the sheriff drive away, I suddenly realized that maybe there was a reason Simon had me distracted all day. He was the one that told me Graham was going out of town with his parents on a last minute trip. That was obviously a lie. Why would he lie about that?

It was Simon. I knew at that moment that Simon was the killer. It all made sense. He was never around whenever any of my friends went missing. Even that very morning, Simon could have done something to Graham before he showed up at my house. It all made sense. Simon was possessive and jealous. He hated that I had friends that weren't him. He probably hated even more that I was falling for Graham.

The problem was, what could I do about it? Would the sheriff even believe me if I told him my suspicions about Simon? I had no proof. It was all conjecture on my part. Bernadette, Josephine, and

Graham were all friends with lots of people in town, not just me. It could be anyone that didn't like them for some reason. It may have absolutely nothing to do with me, just a coincidence.

I knew that wasn't true though. I knew it had to do with me, and I knew it was Simon. It was the only thing that made sense.

CHAPTER 11

I never shared my theories with the sheriff. He had never been my biggest fan. Not in any of my lives.

He wouldn't believe me anyway. There was no reason for him to believe anything I said. I was the one that had all the friends that were dying. That alone was reason to be suspicious of me. I was actually surprised that he didn't suspect me. At least I didn't think he suspected me.

I needed to figure out who the killer was on my own. The sheriff didn't have the knowledge of the killings, and all the years of experience with these particular deaths, that I did. No one did. That was something that was unique to me. Wasn't I the lucky one.

I was the only one that knew what had happened to my friends. Well…I didn't actually know what happened. I still didn't know for a fact that Simon was the killer. That was just suspicion on my part. But, I did feel pretty confident that it was him. Simon was the most likely person. His odd behavior, his aggression, and all that. And, let's not forget the fact that he did stab me to death in my first life. That was something I did know for a fact.

So, maybe it was time I proved who the killer was. There was only one way that I could think of to do that. The sinkhole. I had to go there for myself. Again. And, to do that, I knew I was risking my life. Again. The last time I dared to venture to the sinkhole, alone, which was a stupid thing to do anyway, I was killed and left for dead. Would that happen again. God, I hoped not. Getting stabbed was a horrible way to go.

Without thinking any longer about it, mostly because I didn't want to talk myself out of going to the sinkhole, I grabbed my beach bag and ran inside to my room. I left my mother standing on the front porch. I could explain my actions to her later.

I quickly changed into jeans, a t-shirt, and tennis shoes. By the time I got back downstairs, I could hear my mother in the kitchen, preparing dinner. I yelled to her that I was going out for a little while and would be back by dinner.

I headed straight for the woods, and the sinkhole. That was where the killer's dumping grounds were and I needed to find something to prove my theory. There were clues there some-where, and I just knew it. I would be out there as long as it took to find them. Simon was going to go down for this, if it was the last thing I did. I prayed that it wasn't.

On my way there, it hit me that I wasn't torn to pieces by Graham's death. Don't get me wrong, it hurt, but not like you would expect it to. Had I been jaded by all the deaths I had been exposed to? Was this just another day, in another life, of Ivy Wells? A day where a friend dies and I barely notice it?

That was a horrible thought. I didn't want to barely notice when a friend of mine died. I wanted to be affected by it. I wanted to mourn them.

Perhaps it was all because in the back of my mind, I wondered if I would just die at some point and wake back up, to start all over again. If that happened, then these deaths didn't really happen, did they? At least in my reality they didn't. I had no idea if each reality, or dimension, or parallel universe maybe, continued after I died and started my new life.

THE MANY LIVES OF IVY WELLS

I really hoped that the reality I left when I died didn't continue on without me. Because if it did, then that meant my children were left motherless, and probably fatherless, in my first life. They may very well have come down those stairs at some point, and found both of their parents lying dead, on the grass in the front yard, having stabbed each other to death.

God, it hurt my soul just thinking about it.

Stop it, I told myself. I needed to focus on the task at hand, not on something that I couldn't control, and most definitely couldn't change.

I picked my way through the dense forest. In my previous life someone had put powder blue ribbons around the trees along the path to the sinkhole. That had been very helpful in the gloominess of the forest. Without the ribbons, it was slow going. I had to be careful where I stepped, and needed to make sure I stayed on the path, and didn't wander off and get myself lost. In this forest, that was entirely possible. There was a search and rescue team in town that made frequent visits to the forest to look for some poor lost soul. It was always someone that thought they knew where they were going, and didn't stick to the 'buddy system' as we were all taught in school.

Save for the victims of the Slasher, it had been decades since anyone had gotten lost and succumbed to the perils of the Red Lake Forest.

As soon as I found the sinkhole, I knew in my gut that it was a stupid thing to do. What was I thinking, going out there all alone? The sinkhole was a dangerous place for anyone, due to the Red Lake Slasher, and the perils of being near the sinkhole in general. But it was an especially dangerous place for me.

The last time I was at the sinkhole, I had been attacked, strangled, and stabbed. I would be on high alert this time. I didn't want to die again. At least not yet. And not here.

I kept one eye on the surrounding forest area, while looking for clues. I didn't want to be surprised again.

159

An hour into my search, I still had not turned up anything, and was beginning to feel like the whole thing was a fat waste of time. Besides, it was late afternoon and the sun was dipping lower and lower in the sky. I knew I should start heading out of the forest very soon. If I didn't, I would certainly get caught there, as night fell, not being able to find my way out. Damn, why hadn't I thought to bring a flashlight? Even with all my years of living, I still acted like a child with no sense in her head sometimes.

I had a few minutes left before it got too dark. I wanted to do everything I could while there. It was my goal to not have to ever, and I mean ever, in any lifetime, to have to see the sinkhole again.

I got as close to the sinkhole as I dared, but there was nothing to really see from the edge. It was just a dark, deep cavern in the ground that was not going to give up any of its secrets. I wondered how many people had lost their lives to this great chasm in front of me. No one really knew how long it had been there. Hundreds of years. Maybe even thousands. People disappeared all the time. Could this be their final resting place?

Standing there contemplating life and death, as it were, suddenly, there was a rustling in the bushes. When I jumped as a result, I realized I had been standing dangerously close to the edge of the sinkhole. The ground below me was slowly giving way, and I quickly moved to safer ground.

The rustling in the bushes gave me a sense of déjà vu. I needed to get out of there before it got dark. The forest was no place for me alone at night. I cursed myself for not bringing that flashlight with me. I needed to get out of there before whatever was in the bushes got any closer.

As the evening wind howled through the trees, I heard another noise. This time I knew it was not the killer. It was a wild animal...maybe a wolf. Probably a wolf. They didn't show up very often, but it was well known that wolves lived in the area. I had seen a few during the many years I had spent in Red Lake. They were bold, daring animals that usually ran in packs. I needed to get out of there fast.

If there was a showdown between me and the Slasher, or me and a pack of wolves, I would take my chances with the Slasher any day. At least with him, I would have a fighting chance.

As I turned to leave, I didn't see the large branch near my feet, and tripped over it before I realized what was happening. As I was falling, it felt like slow motion and I could see everything in the forest shake, with a loud rumbling accompanying it. My arms didn't have time to slow my downward progress.

When I hit the ground, I landed with a hard thud and cracked my head open on a large rock. I only had a moment of consciousness before everything went black.

My children were my last thought. Then everything stopped.

PART 3

CHAPTER 1

As I slowly regained consciousness, I shook my head, trying to clear the darkness, and the fog from my mind. I felt like I had been asleep for days, yet not long enough. Just let me sleep a little longer, I thought.

In those twilight moments, when I was not completely asleep, but still not fully awake either, I became aware somehow that I was still taking in those deep, slow breaths, that happened when I slept. Then memories squirmed their way into the recesses of my mind. In the darkness I could see shapes forming, and the trees moving. I could even feel the cool breeze on my skin.

Oh, I'm in the forest, that's right. It was coming back to me now. I reached up with my hand and felt the left side of my head, where I expected to find a lump forming. I remembered tripping over something and landing on the ground, just as my head thumped against a rock. My head hit so hard that I could have sworn that I heard my own skull crack in protest.

I remembered fading out and losing consciousness. I wondered to myself how long I had been lying here in the forest before waking. Had the sun gone down yet? It would be horrible to be caught in the forest alone after dark. I couldn't bring myself to open my eyes just yet. I would need another minute or two to get that task accomplished, as my head was still clearing the cobwebs.

On the side of my head, I felt no lump. That's odd. I felt around in that general area, and still nothing. With my eyes still closed, my head ached, and I knew it was from slamming it into the rock when I tripped in the forest. The pain seemed to radiate from that exact spot.

Wait, I could hear talking nearby, and something soft below me. Not forest-like at all. No pine needles sticking into my skin. No damp earth below me. What the...

I slowly opened my eyes, as flashes of light danced across my vision, causing my aching head to pound even harder.

"Ahhh, what is that noise? And that light," I said out loud, not expecting an answer, since I was lying in the forest, all alone. Had I been out here all night? Was the sun coming up?

"Honey, you fell asleep watching TV. You're dreaming."

I recognized the voice immediately and sat straight up, opening my eyes wide. Simon was sitting next to me, watching me with a curious look on his face. I looked around the room and realized that I was sitting on the couch in our living room. In our house. The one I shared with Simon all those years ago when we were married. The very house that I ran away from.

Suddenly I understood the situation. I was in a new life. And I was married to Simon. The skull cracking rock in the forest forgotten.

"Son of a bitch!...Oh, ow." I grabbed the side of my head again. Still no lump. So why was my head hurting so badly? Did I carry the pain over from my past life? Could that happen even without the lump?

"Shhh, you'll wake Hunter," Simon whispered to me, patting my knee in a gentle, loving manner.

I took in what he had just said to me, and gasped in response.

"Hunter?...Oh my god, Hunter. Where are they?" I looked

around the room frantically. No kids. "Simon! Where are they?"

"Who?" he asked me. "What do you mean by 'they'?"

"The kids. Are they in their rooms? Please, where are they? I need to see them." My heart started beating a mile a minute and I was on the verge of hyperventilating.

"Um, Honey, are you all right?" Simon picked up the TV remote and hit pause, turning toward me. When I looked at him, he had his head tilted and seemed genuinely concerned.

"What do you mean?" I asked. "You just said I was going to wake Hunter. Didn't you?"

"Yes. But we just have Hunter. So far anyway."

Simon gave me a crooked smile as he reached over and patted my belly gently.

That was when I looked down and realized that I was pregnant. And by the looks of things, our daughter would be here soon.

"Oh my god. Courtney. My sweet baby."

I burst into tears as I thought about my new reality. They were not tears of sorrow, but of joy. I rubbed my hands around my growing belly and smiled as tears ran down my face. My beautiful daughter was growing inside of me. After a moment, I wiped my face with the sleeve of my shirt, and looked up at Simon. Even seeing him couldn't put a damper on the magic of that moment.

I couldn't think of a single thing that would have made me any happier right then. Other than seeing my son, that is.

"I need to go see Hunter."

I struggled to get off the couch gently. It was not an easy task to do so gracefully. By my estimate, I was about six months along. I grimaced when I thought about going through childbirth again. And then it didn't matter at all. I would go through childbirth every single lifetime, if it meant I could get my babies back.

"I'm going to finish the movie, if you don't mind," Simon called after me, as I started climbing the stairs. I heard the TV unpause. "You were asleep and missed half of it anyway."

I barely heard him. When I reached the top of the stairs, I made a sharp right, and a beeline to Hunter's room. It had been several years since I had been inside this house, but I would never forget where my children's rooms were.

I opened the door gently, not wanting to startle him, and smiled at the glow in the dark stars on the ceiling. I had almost forgotten about those.

"Hi Mommy." Two year old Hunter reached for me as I walked over and sat down on the edge of his bed.

I took a deep breath and held back my true emotions. I wanted nothing more than to burst out crying tears of joy, but didn't want to frighten Hunter. I took my young son into my arms and held him tight. I closed my eyes and held him like I would never let him go.

It had been my only wish, my only dream, to be with my children again. Something I was sure would never happen. Yet here I was, hugging my son, and expecting my daughter. If a billion dollars rained down on me at that moment, I would not have cared. I had every single thing I ever wanted right there in that little blue bedroom.

Hunter started squirming out of my hug, and I released him.

"Oh, sorry Sweetheart. You okay?"

"Yeah. Water, Mommy."

I nodded and got up to get him a glass of water. As I walked out of his room, I turned back to look at him, and I couldn't help but smile. The last time I had seen my son, he was 9 years old, and doing his homework at the kitchen table in our other house. He was a talker too. It was hard to get him to be quiet long enough to get a word in.

Now, that same boy was only two years old and was just learning to talk. I was perfectly fine with that, and looked forward to getting to know my children all over again. The sweet little girl, on the way, that was Courtney. And the rambunctious yapper? That was Hunter.

CHAPTER 2

I spent that night tossing around on the bed I shared with Simon. My restlessness was partly because I was several months pregnant, and it was so very difficult to get comfortable in that condition. Though it had been a lot of years since I had last been pregnant with Courtney, I remembered it well. I couldn't sleep on my back. It put too much pressure on me. I couldn't sleep on my belly, because there was a baby there. I didn't want to smash her. So, sleeping on my side was my only choice. All night long it was sleep on my left side for a little while, then maneuver to the right side for a little while, and back again. It was not a pleasant thing at all.

In the grand scheme of things, I didn't mind much at all. I would do it over and over again, just to have my children back with me. I was ecstatic to be back with them again.

Simon was another story. I could see his isolating behavior already, and it had only been a few hours since I had shown up in this life. After I spent some time with Hunter, I went to the phone to call my mother. I just wanted to hear her voice and make sure my parents were all right. That's when Simon intervened.

"What are you doing?" he asked as I reached for the phone.

"I'm going to call my mother. Is that all right with you?" I wasn't asking permission. There was definitely some snark in my question.

He narrowed his eyes my way. "It's kind of late, don't you think?"

Simon reached over and put his hand on top of mine as I started to lift the receiver. He gently guided it back into its cradle.

I tried to size him up. I had no idea if he was just trying to be courteous to my mother, or was actually trying to keep me from talking to her. I decided that I would let him have his way this night. He was right about it being kind of late. Besides, I needed a bit of time to find out if he was kind and giving, or if he was the same man that I had lived with all those lifetimes ago. If he turned out to be the same type of man, I knew that I had a lot of work ahead of me. I wouldn't stay as long as I did last time, and would get out right away.

"You know, you're right. It is getting late and I'm tired. I think I'll go to bed," I yawned as I spoke. I was thankful that the headache that I had when I first 'woke up' was gone.

I had been so consumed the previous night with my son and soon-to-be daughter, that Bernadette, Josephine, and Graham hadn't even crossed my mind. The second I woke up that morning though, they were right there, front and center.

Simon was leaving for work early, much to my relief. I didn't have to talk much with him at all that morning. In fact, the moment I got up, I headed straight for Hunter's room. He was already up and playing on his floor. I scooped him up and carried him down the stairs for breakfast. He cried out with glee.

I put Hunter in his highchair, while I went about making him some breakfast. Simon was already sitting at the kitchen table, eating. Apparently he hadn't wanted to be bothered to take care of his son this morning.

That was very telling. Wouldn't most husbands, that had a pregnant wife and a 2 year old, want to help take care of the child, while his wife got some much needed sleep? Was I being unrealistic? I wasn't sure. Simon was my only experience with having a husband. Maybe they were all like him. No...I knew that wasn't true.

"What do you have planned for the day?" Simon asked me as he finished up his toast and kissed his son on the top of his head.

"Oh, I don't know. I'll probably go see my mom," I answered.

"I see." I watched as his eyes scanned the kitchen and living room. "Well there's a lot to do around here. Don't stay there all day."

It sounded a lot like an order to me. I thought about not rocking the boat, then thought better of that. His behavior wasn't going to fly with me at all. Husband or not. I had lived much too long, and had experienced so much already in life...and in death. Being the submissive wife was not my thing.

"I'll stay as long as I like." I gave him an icy glare.

Simon pursed his lips as he glared back at me. Without another word, he turned and walked out the front door.

"That's what I thought," I said out loud. Hunter laughed.

I had my hands full with Hunter that morning, having forgotten how demanding 2 year olds were. I didn't mind a bit though. After he ate his lunch, I put him down for his afternoon nap. When I got back downstairs, I promptly sat at the desk in the living room and started searching the internet. I needed to find out if everything I knew was still the same.

Within minutes, I found what I was looking for.

Bernadette and Josephine had indeed been killed in this lifetime. Their bodies were found in the sinkhole, and they had both been strangled. I wondered how they got them out? The authorities had never been able to recover any bodies from the sinkhole previously, because it was quite unstable.

I noticed a tear land on the computer keyboard as I sat their reading. I was too late to help anyone this time.

I searched for another half hour, but could find no mention of Graham disappearing or dying. That was great news. And it didn't look like anyone was using the term 'Red Lake Slasher' either. At least not yet.

I sat back in my chair for a few minutes to digest what I had just read. Apparently everything was exactly like it was in my first life. So those subsequent lives did absolutely nothing to change the events. Everything was a big fat waste of time. I could have just stayed in my original life in the first place. So, why did everything happen? Why did I keep dying and coming back to life? Was there no reason for it?

I had been certain that there was a reason all of it was happening to me. I thought that perhaps I was sent back to save everyone. But that didn't seem to be the case. So what the hell was it all about?!

I continued reading about the murders, hoping to glean some sort of information that would be helpful. Something to shed some light on why I was being put through this misery of doing it all over again and again.

I read that there had been a chain link fence around the sinkhole for years, with no trespassing signs. After the bodies were discovered, it was boarded up and steel bars installed over it. That was new. They never did that in any of my previous lifetimes. I wondered why things were different this time.

The story went on to say that no physical evidence of the killer was ever found at the scene. It was nearly impossible to gather evidence in a sink hole, due to the danger involved. During heavy rains, water collected in the sink hole, making it even worse. They used a crane to lower rescue workers in to retrieve the bodies. But, due to the tentative nature of the sink hole rim, investigators spent no more time than absolutely necessary to look around. After a short time, the search around the sink hole was abandoned altogether.

As I sat there engrossed in the stories about the murders, the phone rang, startling me. I was a bit apprehensive about answering the phone. What if it was someone that I knew in this life, but didn't know in any other lives? That would be an awkward conversation. While I was thinking, the ringing stopped and I let out a breath of relief.

Then, seconds later, the ringing started again, which was odd. I figured that I had better answer it this time. It might be important.

"Hello?" I said into the phone tentatively.

"Ivy, why didn't you answer the phone?" It was Simon.

"Oh, I...was busy." I didn't know how to answer his question. He had caught me off guard.

"Doing what?" His question sounded accusatory to me and I felt the hairs on the back of my neck stand up.

"I was on the computer, if you must know. I was reading about the murders of my friends." I didn't care that he knew.

"Why? That's old news. You don't have anything better to do around there?"

"Not right now, I don't. What do you want?" I was getting really tired of his attitude.

"I'm just checking in on you."

"Well, I'm just fine. I don't need you to check in on me." I was starting to get angry.

"Where's Hunter?" he asked me.

"He's taking a nap. Anything else, Boss?" I knew that snarky comment was not going to go over well.

There was a pause on the other end of the line. I just sat there and waited for him to respond. I could almost feel the steam rising from his ears, and I smiled.

"We'll talk later," was his only response. With that, the line went dead.

"I guess we will," I said out loud as I hung up the receiver.

Simon was the least of my problems, though I was totally discounting his ability to make my life miserable. I did know though, that if he kept it up, I, and the kids, wouldn't be around long. I looked down at my belly and smiled. I rubbed it gently. I couldn't wait to see my beautiful daughter again.

CHAPTER 3

The next day, just after Simon left for work, I got Hunter dressed, and the two of us headed for the grocery store. I wanted to make a nice lasagne to help smooth over the fight Simon and I had the night before. He was still angry with me for talking to him on the phone the way I did and we argued about it.

I did not give in though. Simon had no right to speak to me the way he did and I made it clear to him that I wouldn't put up with it. I could see the surprise on his face when I laid it all out for him. Apparently I had let him walk all over me before I 'came to' in this life. Well, I was here now, and things were going to change.

We had two children together. Well, as soon as baby Courtney was born, we would have two children together. If I could make things work with Simon, then that's what I wanted to do. My children deserved a mother and father that loved them, and each other. Maybe I could turn Simon and his controlling ways around. Maybe I couldn't. But, I really wanted to try.

Was Simon the Slasher? Good question. I was beginning to seriously doubt my previous belief that he was. I just wasn't sure, and had serious doubts. He didn't seem capable of such horrible crimes. Not this Simon anyway. I would be sure to keep a close eye on him either way.

While I was standing in the pasta aisle, reaching for the lasagne noodles, which were just beyond my reach, I heard a familiar voice and froze.

"Here, let me get those for you."

I didn't even have to look his way to know exactly who it was. Before I had a chance to respond, a hand reached up above mine and plucked the noodles off of the shelf for me. As I turned to look at him, I smiled.

Graham.

In my reality, it had only been a few days since I had seen him last. Right before he went missing, and was presumed dead. I just realized that I never did find out for sure if he was dead. I wondered how long it had really been, in this lifetime, since we had last seen each other.

"Hi Graham. How are you?"

I looked him in the eyes. He still had that dirty blond hair and glasses. Of course, he was several years older than he was when I last saw him. He hadn't changed much.

Something I did notice was the look in his eyes. It was a look of bewilderment, as if he had to search his memory for my name. It couldn't have been that long, I thought.

"Um, hi. I'm good. How are you?" His answer was tentative.

Oh no, he doesn't know who I am. I was devastated. I had been hoping that he could be an ally in this lifetime. I could tell immediately that was not to be.

"Ivy Wells," I announced, holding out my hand. "We went to high school together."

"Oh yes, of course." He shook my hand. "I'm sorry, it's just been so long since high school. I didn't recognize you at first. You haven't changed though."

"Oh, you're sweet. What's been going on in your….." Hunter

began wailing, interrupting me mid-sentence. "I'm sorry, I guess I need to go."

"Yeah, looks like you have your hands full."

Graham looked like he couldn't get away fast enough. I couldn't blame him. We were strangers. Since he didn't know me, then it was obvious that he hadn't dated Josephine either. Boy, I had a lot to catch up on in this lifetime.

Once we arrived home, and the two of us had eaten our lunch, it was nap time for Hunter. I remembered being a big fan of nap times. It was my chance to relax and unwind. Or sometimes I used that time to get things done around the house, that I had no time to do with a two year old in tow.

Besides, I was exhausted. Raising a toddler, and being almost seven months pregnant, was very draining on me. I needed Hunter's nap time to rest myself. I would have to get up soon to make dinner.

While sitting there on the couch, resting my weary body and thinking, I made a decision. As I reached for the address book sitting next to the phone, I desperately hoped that it was the right decision. I searched and dialed the phone number.

"Parker, can you come over? I want to talk to you about something." I didn't greet him when he picked up, I went right into what I wanted from my brother.

"I guess. I get off work in an hour. I'll come over then."

"Perfect, see you then."

I hung up the phone. I spent the next hour wondering exactly how I was going to have that conversation with Parker.

"I need to tell you something," I started, as he sat down at the dining room table. I handed a can of beer to my brother and sat down across from him.

"Okay, what's up?" He opened the can and took a long pull on the beer, wiping his mouth with his sleeve.

"Classy," I commented with a smile.

Parker just shrugged.

"So, what was so important that I had to come over right after work? You got any cake? I'm starving." Parker looked around the kitchen without budging from his chair.

"No, I don't have any cake. Listen to me please." I tapped on the table to get his attention.

It worked. Parker turned his attention back to me.

I took a deep breath. "Okay, here goes. I'm not really sure why I'm telling you this. I just need to tell someone."

Parker stared at me. "Would you get on with it already. Do you have any chips?" Parker's eyes wandered the room.

With a huff, I got up and walked over to the pantry and pulled out a bag of corn chips, tossing them to my brother. I knew if I didn't, I was never going to get his full attention. He smiled as he tore the bag open.

"Now Parker, can you please focus on what I want to say?" I queried, as I carefully maneuvered my ever growing frame back into the dining room chair.

"Yeah, sorry," he said as he crammed a handful of chips into his mouth.

"I know this will sound completely crazy, but please hear me out, okay?"

"Okay," he replied, mouth full. I looked down when some of it spilled out of his mouth and landed on my clean table.

"Oops, sorry." He gave me a sideways grin as he swiped the crumbs off the table and onto the floor in one quick motion.

"Are you serious here?" I glared at him. "You should have just left it on the table. Now I have to sweep the floor." Ugh, he was such a child.

"Sorry." He didn't smile that time.

I waved my hand dismissively in the air. "Whatever, never mind. I have more important things to worry about right now."

He swallowed the chips. "Like what?" he asked, reaching back into the bag.

I took a deep breath, inhaling courage.

"I have lived this life several times. I keep dying and waking up. And, I remember everything that has happened to me in the previous lives."

I bit on my lower lip as I watched Parker for a reaction. He had just pulled a handful of chips from the bag and stopped midway to his mouth, which hung there, wide open.

"What?" He put the chips back in the bag. "You are crazy."

"Believe me," I began, "I know how it sounds. But it's the truth. Every word."

Parker sat there for what seemed like ten full minutes just looking at me. He never said a word. I didn't say anything either. I wanted to give him time to process the story I had just told him.

"Prove it." That was all he said.

That was an odd reaction. I had almost expected him to get up and walk out, after hearing my ludicrous story. But that's not how it went at all.

"What? How can I do that? You won't remember anything that happened in any of my previous lives, so there's no way to prove anything I tell you. You just have to trust me," I responded. "I don't know what else to tell you."

"Okay, let me ask you something. You said you keep dying. How do you keep dying? Of old age?"

It was a valid question.

Parker had always been someone that had an open mind about things. He believed in ghosts and the paranormal, and all that stuff. Even so, I was still surprised how unaffected he was by my announcement. He was taking in all in stride, as if this was an everyday sort of conversation.

And it certainly wasn't that.

"Old age? I wish. That would be a lot easier. But no. In my first life, I was 30 years old and married to Simon. We got into a big fight and he stabbed me. In my second life, I was a teenager and someone stabbed me from behind. I don't know who. In my third life, I was a teenager again, and I tripped in the forest and cracked my head open on a rock. That's it so far."

"So, this is the fourth time you've lived your life, and you chose to marry Simon. Again. And have his babies. Again. Even after the way he treats you, and after he stabbed you?"

It was clear then that Parker was acquainted with my volatile relationship with Simon, and did not approve. I wondered how much of our relationship my previous self had divulged to my brother.

"Well, sort of. This time I just woke up a few days ago. I was already married. And we already had Hunter, and I'm clearly pregnant with Courtney. It was too late to avoid it." I looked down and rubbed my belly without thinking about it.

"What do you mean that you 'woke up?' I don't understand. Weren't you just born again? None of this makes any sense."

I could tell I was losing him, and had to think fast.

"In each of my lives, I don't remember being reborn and growing up again. I die, then I land in my next life at some point. Once I was 12 when I woke up, and once as a teenager. It was on my 15th birthday actually. This time it was just a few days ago. I call it 'waking up' because I don't really have a better word for it. It is the point in time that I become aware of being in a new life, and remembering my old one."

Parker was trying to reconcile everything I had just told him. I could almost see the wheels spinning in his head.

"Does any of this make sense now?" I looked at him expectantly.

"I suppose I get what you mean. I'm not quite sure I believe you. But, I've never known you to lie to me. I'll give you the benefit of the doubt for now. No promises though."

I jumped up and wrapped my arms around my brother's neck, squeezing a hug out of him.

"Thank you! It means a lot to me that you believe me. Or at least are trying to. I told Josephine about this a couple of times. In one life I believed me, and in another she thought I had lost my mind."

"Well, the jury is still out on that one," Parker teased.

CHAPTER 4

"So, why exactly are you telling me all of this?" Parker asked, cramming another handful of chips into his mouth. "And I'm still not saying I completely believe you. Or believe you at all really."

I mulled over his question for a moment. "You know...I just needed to tell someone. And I trust you. Someone in Red Lake killed two of my friends. It has happened in all of my lives, and I need to figure out who it is. I was hoping you would help me try to find out who the killer is. I could really use someone on my side." I gave him a cheesy grin. "Pleeeeeeease," I begged.

"Didn't the cops investigate the deaths thoroughly? I mean in your other lives? I know in this one they did. What makes you think we can find the killer, when the cops couldn't?"

Parker drained the rest of the beer in front of him. "Got anymore?" He held the can up in the air in front of my face.

Without comment, I got up and got him another beer. It annoyed me that he expected me to be his waitress. I thought about making some smart comment about the location of the refrigerator, and how he could see it from where he was sitting, but thought better of it. Apparently he didn't notice that I was struggling to get up from the chair just to fetch a beer for him.

I really needed him to be on my side, so I let it go. I needed an ally in this lifetime. Parker was the only one I could think of that could be that person. Bernadette and I weren't friends anyway, but with her gone, and with Josephine gone, I had no one else. I couldn't tell my parents. There was not a chance in hell that would work out in my favor.

Ditto with Simon. He was a realist. In a million years, and a million lifetimes, he would never believe that I had lived other lives. Not for a nanosecond. Hell, I had a hard time believing it myself, and I was the one it was happening to.

Besides, Simon might still be the Slasher. He wasn't ruled out just yet. It would be foolhardy for me to talk to him about my lives, and about the killer. If he was the guy, then I might be putting myself in danger by having that conversation with him.

I handed the beer to Parker and sat back down.

"I really don't know if we can figure out who the killer is, even though the cops couldn't. Maybe we can't," I explained. "But I can't help wondering if the reason I keep coming back to this life is to figure out who the Slasher is. And maybe stop him."

My brother's eyebrows shot up in response. "That's interesting," Parker replied. "You haven't stopped him before. Why do you think you can now? Is he the one that killed you? In the other lives I mean, after Simon stabbed you."

Even with that comment about Simon stabbing me, I smiled at my brother.

"See, I've been paying attention," he responded with his own smile.

"Well...to answer your question, I'm not sure. There was only one life that I was killed in by someone unknown. I'm assuming it was him. Though, I have no proof of that. For all I know, I could have surprised some drifter that had been camping out in the forest. I just don't know. I really have no answers for most of what has been going on."

"How do you know it was a man?" Parker seemed to be getting

into my story. He opened the beer and began drinking. "And I doubt it was a drifter. They seemed to want to stay in the shadows. You know, not do anything that will bring attention to them."

"Hmm, good point," I agreed. "But one thing I do know is that it was definitely a man. I was at the sinkhole and he grabbed me from behind. He was taller than me, and had strong arms…manly arms. Yes, I'm sure of it. It was a man. Besides, even if I didn't notice the muscular arms, I think it's unlikely that a woman was killing teenage girls. But, I guess you never know. It could happen. Just not this time. I know it wasn't a woman. As far as who the man was? I'm not ruling anyone out at this point," I told him.

"So…you think that if you figure out who the killer is in this life, that you can stop him in another life?" Parker asked me. "I mean, since he's already killed your friends this time, it's too late to stop him. Right?"

"Yeah, right," I answered. "If I wake up young enough next time." I paused for a moment. "You know, that's assuming I wake up at all. This life could be my last. And I might even just die of old age. There's no way to know, until it happens. I don't know if me being killed so young triggers the new life. Or if it is all just some random cosmic coincidence that made me the lucky one." I shrugged.

"I want to relive my life. It sounds kinda cool," Parker admitted. "You get to fix all your stupid mistakes from the last time. That might be worth getting stabbed for."

I shook my head. "No, it's really not. At least in my case, it's not worth it. It seems that no matter what I do, I can't change things. Not permanently anyway. In each life, Bernadette and Josephine both die. And I can't seem to figure out why, or how to stop it. No, I don't think it is worth it at all. Believe me when I tell you that it is my fondest wish to just live this life, and die a crusty old woman 70 years from now." I smiled as I pictured myself in my 90s.

"I don't know. I would still like to see what it's like. At least once anyway," Parker responded, drinking the last of his beer.

"Anyway," I changed the subject back to what was currently happening. "This time it was too late to do anything for my friends. At least he didn't get Graham this time," I added.

"Graham?" Parker widened his bloodshot eyes. It was probably time to stop the beer dispensary.

"Tell me about Graham." Parker leaned back in his chair, feet on the edge of the table. I watched him as he dangled there precariously.

"Oh, that's right. You don't know Graham this time." Trying to keep it all straight was starting to give me a headache.

Parker dropped his feet and the front of his chair hit the tile with a thud. He started speaking before I had a chance to tell him about Graham.

"Wait. That means I keep re-living my life too? Why don't I remember anything? What was I like before? Was I as handsome then as I am now?"

I chuckled and swatted my brother playfully on the arm. "Ha ha, very funny," I responded.

Parker laughed and swatted back at me.

"I'm not sure how it all works. I've thought about this a lot and I don't think the rest of you are re-living your lives though. I think only I am. For you, each and every time is the first time you've lived your life. Does that make sense?"

"No, not really. It seems that if we are in your lives each time, and things are changing each time, then we are all living our lives over again too," Parker added.

"You may be right. Maybe you are all living your lives over and over, but just not remembering it. I really don't know. I wish I knew, but I don't have any answers. So…will you help me find the killer?" I raised my eyebrows in anticipation of his answer.

"Yeah, sounds like fun."

I scowled. "I don't know if 'fun' is how I would describe it. But whatever works for you is fine with me."

Both of us turned toward the stairs when we heard Hunter crying. He usually woke up cranky and crying at the end of each nap. I remembered it well. I also remembered that Courtney usually woke up smiling and wanting to cuddle. I couldn't wait for my little girl to come into the world.

I looked up at the clock on the stove. "Simon's gonna be home soon. You should go."

"Yes, I should." Parker reached over and rubbed my growing belly as he stood up. "Take care of little Courtney for me. That's what you said her name was, right?"

"Right."

CHAPTER 5

"Where's dinner?" It was the first thing Simon said upon entering the house. He kicked off his shoes as he spoke.

"Hunter had an unusually long nap, and I was just about to get started on making dinner," I explained.

Simon looked at, then removed his wrist watch and placed it in the bowl next to the front door.

"Well, it seems to me that if Hunter was asleep so long, then you should have had plenty of time to have dinner ready."

I narrowed my eyes at him. "You do know that I don't work for you, right?"

I knew that I was treading on dangerous ground, but I couldn't help it. I was not going to live like I had the first time. That life was fraught with constant fear and timidness. Simon had been a drunk and he was a mean one. He liked to take it out on me, and occasionally he would smack one of the kids. Though hitting the kids was not his normal way of doing things. I was generally the one he took his frustrations out on.

This life was going to be different. I had a lot more experience with life, and with Simon, than I had the first time.

Simon stopped in his tracks. "What did you say?"

"I said that I don't work for you." I wasn't backing down. For a moment I wished that I hadn't started the impending argument. I should have just started dinner.

"What the hell did you do all day while our son was asleep? Watch TV?"

Simon was walking toward me as spoke. I didn't like his body language, and I started shaking without warning. It seems that no matter what came out of my mouth, I had no control over the rest of me.

I took a calming breath before I spoke. "No. Parker came over. We hung out and talked," I told him honestly.

Simon stopped walking toward me when he reached the kitchen, where I was standing.

"So, you spent the day hanging out with your brother, gossiping? And not making dinner? Or cleaning the house, by the looks of things." Simon's eyes were scanning the room. Sweat was beginning to bead on his forehead, and his face was turning red.

I decided not to poke the bear, and did not respond. Oh, there was so much I wanted to say.

"I don't want you hanging out with your brother when you have so much to do around here," he ordered.

"Simon, can we not argue in front of Hunter please? This can wait until later, after he goes to bed," I asked in the sweetest voice I could muster. It was mostly for my son's sake.

Simon looked over at his son sitting in his high chair watching the two of us intently. Simon didn't know how much Hunter actually understood, he was only two, but he shut up anyway.

Simon reached down and picked his shoes up off the floor and walked with them over to the couch. He sat down and began putting them back on.

"What are you doing?" I asked him.

"I'm going out to get some dinner, and maybe a couple of drinks. I'll be back when I'm back."

"Whatever," I muttered as the door slammed behind my husband.

The next morning I took Hunter to go see his grandparents. I needed some time away, and a chance to talk more with Parker. Even though he was three years older than I, he was living with our parents. He had gone away to college, right after high school, but he didn't have a lot of ambition as far as getting a good job to support himself. He was a pretty good guy, but he took advantage of our mother's desire to help out her son.

Parker and I decided to take a walk, away from prying ears. Besides, our mom was thrilled to spend some time alone with her only grandchild. From what I could glean from her, without sounding like I had no clue what had been going on, Hunter and I didn't see my family much. That was obviously Simon's doing.

Once we got away from the house, and anyone that might hear us, I started the conversation off.

"I've been thinking," I began. "I'm pretty sure that I know the killer."

Parker stopped mid-stride, turning to look at me. I stopped in response.

"Why do you say that?" he asked.

"Because I know all the victims. That can't be a coincidence, can it?" I looked up to my big brother for answers. "Is it possible that I'm partly to blame for all of this?"

"This is a small town, Ives. Everybody knew all the victims. You get that, right?"

"Yeah, I guess that's true," I agreed.

We turned and started walking again.

"But, they were all my age," I added. "Maybe it was just someone targeting teenagers, and since there is only one high school in town, of course they would all be people I knew," I answered honestly.

It was something I hadn't previously considered. Had I been so self centered to think that it was all about me? Perhaps none of it had anything to do with me at all. I just happened to be another teenager at a school full of teenagers. A school full of potential victims.

"Do you have any idea who might be responsible?" Parker asked as we turned a left corner, toward the lake.

"Yes. But it's just a complete guess at this point. I really have no proof whatsoever," I told him. "I'm working on that part."

"Who? Who do you think it is, Ives?" he asked me.

"Simon. I kinda think it's Simon. Is that a crazy idea? I mean, he's a jerk...but a killer? Am I crazy to think that?" I started to second guess it as soon as the words came out of my mouth.

I looked over at Parker for validation of my theory, and watched as his eyebrows raised in response.

"You know," he responded, running his fingers through his short red hair, "I hadn't really considered Simon as being the one. But, it makes sense. Honestly, I don't think that's crazy at all. Didn't you say he killed you in your first life?" Parker asked. "That proves he is capable of killing someone."

"Well...yes. But we were fighting. I picked up the knife first. I really don't know if he came to the house intending to kill me. I think it was more of a 'in the heat of passion' sort of thing."

I bit my lower lip as I thought about that incident. The incident that separated me from my children for several years. They were not bad years, really. Lonely, yes, but not bad. However, there was always the thought of my babies overshadowing everything I did. I had missed them terribly.

"And you said you don't know who killed you the second time, right? That could have been Simon too. It really makes a lot of sense," he told me.

"That's true, it does," I replied. "But, I have no way of knowing if it was him or not. I can't go back to find out. At least I don't think I can anyway. Who knows? All of this is so far out of the ordinary as it is. I don't know what is happening to me half the time," I admitted.

"Just because I keep reliving my life, doesn't necessarily mean that I can't go back to a specific place in time, and redo it. Such as when I was standing at the sinkhole and was grabbed from behind and stabbed," I added.

I took a deep breath. Having said all of that, I doubted it could be done. And even if it could, I didn't have the slightest clue how to make that happen. So, I just had to move on. I had to figure out how to flush the killer out from his hiding place and then had to somehow stop him once that happened.

Rant over. Back to the topic of Simon.

"It's just hard to think of my husband as being a serial killer. Why would he do it? What is his motivation?" It didn't seem to be an unrealistic question to ask.

"Because he's an awful human being," Parker answered. "It's as simple as that. I think we should put him at the top of the suspect list."

I nodded in agreement.

When the two of us reached the lake, we turned right and began walking along the shoreline, in a counterclockwise route around the lake.

"I was just thinking this morning, that you never did tell me about Graham. You said he was one of the victims of the killer?" Parker asked. "Who is he?"

"Oh yeah. That's right. I almost forgot. Graham was killed in my third life. Or at least I think he was. He disappeared one day, but I died before I got confirmation that his body was found. I think it's pretty safe to say that the killer got him."

"How did you know him? From school?" Parker asked.

"Yes, he went to school with me. But I know him mostly because he was dating Josie. Then after she died, I started dating him. And, he just disappeared one day, which wasn't like him at all. I know he would never have left town without telling anyone, especially his parents. He was a teenager. Where would he go anyway?" I added.

"Is he alive now?"

"Yes. In fact, I just saw him at the grocery store. He barely remembered me from high school. We obviously didn't date in this life. Probably because I stupidly started dating Simon while we were still in high school."

I shook my head, lamenting on the fact that I had found myself attached, once again, to Simon.

Parker stopped and picked up a couple of small, flat rocks and skipped one of them across the lake while I watched.

"I never could figure out how to do that," I chuckled. "My rocks go straight to the bottom of the lake. They drop like, well... rocks," I laughed. It felt good to laugh, even with all of the heartache and tragedy that I had witnessed.

"It's takes a special touch."

Parker skillfully skipped another rock across the smooth lake. There was no breeze that morning, and the lake was very calm. It looked like glass. As the two of us watched the rock hit its furthest point in the lake, and fall into the dark water, a fish jumped, disturbing the calmness.

"So, do you think Graham is in danger in this life?" Parker asked me, as we resumed our walk.

"No, I doubt it. Previously he was a teenager when he got killed. And, as far as I know, only teens have been targets. I have never heard of any adults being killed," I explained. "Of course, that doesn't mean it can't happen. But it's unlikely. Besides, I haven't heard of anyone being killed since I was in high school. Have you?" I asked him.

"No. I think it was just them. Here in Red Lake anyway," Parker told me.

"Hmmm...it's interesting that you said that. I hadn't even

thought about checking with other towns around here to see if people have been killed there. What do you think?" I asked my brother.

"Oh, I don't think that's necessary," Parker answered. "If there were any killings anywhere near Red Lake, we would have heard about them."

CHAPTER 6

That evening, I thought I would try to make nice with Simon. Getting along with him was the least I could do for our son.

I spent hours preparing a scrumptious dinner of pot roast, complete with carrots and potatoes. It was one of his favorite meals. I even opened a nice bottle of wine. I fed Hunter early and put him in his playpen to entertain himself, while we had dinner together, just the two of us.

Though Simon and I had not been getting along since I woke up in this life, I still wasn't entirely sure whether he was a good guy or a bad guy. Perhaps his bad behavior was due to my attitude toward him, rather than his own attitude. I needed to find out which it was. I would hate to think that most of our problems were my fault.

Of course, I wasn't naive enough to think that Simon was innocent in all of this. He was still Simon. He was cocky, bossy, and domineering. Three things that I hated about him. However, he had a lot of good traits too. For one, he loved our son. He treated Hunter like gold. At least for now, he did. I couldn't be sure how he would act in the future. I do remember that other

Simon smacking our kids once in a while. I would like to think that this Simon would never be that other guy.

For now, I needed to give him the benefit of the doubt. It was important to me that I stick around and see where all of this was heading. I wouldn't put up with it if he hit me or our kids though. Not this time. I had too much experience in life to ever allow that to happen again.

Even though I did want to try to make things work, it did terrify me to think that I might be living with a serial killer. I slept next to him every night and was vulnerable. But, I was his wife. I was bearing his children. Would he really hurt me? The old Simon did. But I didn't know if this Simon was capable of the horrible acts of his predecessor.

Simon walked in the door smiling. "Ooh, what smells so good?"

"I made pot roast. You still love it, don't you?" I stood there grinning, while wearing my silly apron with ducks adorning it. I thought it would make him laugh.

"Well…yes. I do love your pot roast. But I was hoping to take you out to dinner tonight. I even talked to your mother about babysitting. What do you say?" Simon seemed in an unusually good mood.

"What about the pot roast?" I looked at the nice spread on the dining table.

"Oh, it'll keep. Why don't you just put everything in the fridge and we can have it tomorrow? I'll go change."

Somehow it sounded like an order, rather than a question. Simon had made plans and that was that. I wasn't complaining about being taken out to dinner, but I had worked so hard in preparing the pot roast that evening that I was a bit hurt when he didn't even acknowledge what I had done for him.

"Ivy!" Simon yelled from our bedroom upstairs. "Hurry up, I'm starving!"

Thirty minutes later, Hunter had been dropped off at my parents' house and we were sitting at a nice table in the only steakhouse in town. It had a cozy feeling with its log cabin decor. I thought it looked like a hunting lodge, decorated in browns and reds. It was done very tastefully. But, the best part of the steakhouse was the view. It was right on the lake. It sat up high and from our table we could see almost the entire lake. It shimmered in the moonlight. At that moment I thought it was the most beautiful place on earth.

As I was gazing out the window, I felt a hand on mine. It momentarily startled me and I turned to look at Simon. He was smiling. It was a bit disconcerting.

"Hi Simon. Ivy," our waitress greeted us. It was a small town. "What can I get the two of you?"

Simon pulled his hand back from my hand. He looked up at the waitress, who had clearly interrupted whatever it was he was about to say, and he clenched his teeth. None of it went unnoticed by me.

After we ordered our steaks, Simon took my hand again. "I want to talk to you about something."

"Okay." I looked into his steel gray eyes.

"What do you think about moving to Chicago?"

"Chicago! What? Why do you want to move there?" I pulled my hand back and picked up my glass of water. I peered at him over the rim of my glass as I sipped slowly.

"I just want to get out of this one horse town. Chicago is a large, vibrant city. It's also on a lake, a much much larger lake." He turned toward the window and looked out on the lake as he spoke.

"Yeah, I know where it is. But Simon, I don't want to move." I sat my glass down on the table and looked him directly in the eyes. "What about your job?"

"I can get another job." Simon's eyes were pleading.

"My family is here. My friends are here. I'm not leaving.

Besides, doesn't Chicago have some hellish winters? No thank you." I shivered just thinking about the blizzards.

"I was really hoping this would go a lot easier. Why do you have to be like this?" Simon questioned me, with a pinched expression on his face.

"Like what?" I asked.

"Here you go." Our waitress showed up then and sat our drinks on the table. Water for me, beer for Simon. Neither of us said a word until she was out of earshot.

"You know what? We are moving. You are my wife, and I say we are moving." Simon picked up his beer glass and drained it in one try. He then stuck his arm up in the air to get the waitress's attention. When she turned toward him, he pointed at his glass and she headed to the kitchen to oblige.

"The hell we are. Well me anyway, you can do what you want. I'm staying, and the kids are staying here with me." I crossed my arms across my chest defiantly. "You aren't ordering me to move anywhere."

Our waitress looked at the two of us nervously as she picked up Simon's empty glass and sat a fresh glass of beer in front of him, and quickly walked away, without a word. I looked around the room and noticed a few eyeballs pointed our way.

I unfolded my arms. "Simon," I leaned forward and whispered, "people are looking at us."

His eyes never left mine as he picked up his beer and drained that one quicker than the first. He got the waitress's attention and she brought him another.

"Don't you think you need to slow down?" I asked him.

"Don't tell me what to do."

By the time our steaks arrived, Simon was slurring his words, and I had lost my appetite. I hoped that the dinner of steak, potatoes, and bread would help soak up some of the alcohol he had consumed.

The problem was that he kept drinking and the food did little good in alleviating his condition. We barely spoke for the rest of the dinner. Simon tried, but I refused to argue about it in public. I knew there would be a discussion about it later at home.

Thankfully, Simon did not argue with me when I demanded the car keys from him before we left the restaurant. I made sure to get them while still inside the building so I could enlist the help of the staff if necessary. It didn't come to that.

It was a busy night and the steakhouse parking lot was full, so we had parked two blocks away and walked over. As we walked down the dimly lit street, a young man, in his twenties, was walking toward us. As we passed, the man and Simon bumped shoulders. The man said nothing and continued his journey down the street.

Simon stopped and turned around. "Hey! Are you even going to say excuse me?" he called to the man.

The young man turned, shrugged his shoulders our way, and continued walking, having never said a word.

"Hey! Did you hear me?!" Simon yelled.

"Simon, just let it go. I want to go home." I reached for him and he jerked his arm away from me.

Simon wouldn't let it go. Couldn't let it go. It wasn't in his nature to allow someone so rude to get away with that behavior. It was compounded by the fact that he was drunk. Quite drunk.

Simon walked toward the man. Once again, I pulled on his jacket to stop him and he shook his arm until I released him. The man was unaware of Simon following him. Simon sped up until he was jogging and the man only realized what was happening at the moment Simon pounced on him. They both went down on the sidewalk hard, the man's head bounced once. Simon climbed on top of his back, grabbed his ears, one in each hand, and slammed the man's face into the concrete several times.

I screamed. "Stop it! Simon, stop it!"

Simon was in a drunken rage and didn't hear a word I said. It was quite dark out, and the man was making no sound, other than

THE MANY LIVES OF IVY WELLS

the thud, thud, thud of his skull meeting concrete. I had no choice but to work my way in between the two men. It was tricky in my condition. Six months of pregnancy was not conducive to breaking up a fight. Once I did get in between them, I shoved my husband as hard as I could, and Simon lost his grip on the man. Before he had a chance to recover, I yanked him off. That time it was Simon's head that hit the sidewalk.

"Damnit, what did you do that for?" he yelled at me, rubbing the side of his head where it had met the concrete.

"Simon, you hurt him pretty badly. We need to call an ambulance."

"No we don't." He jumped up and grabbed my hand, yanking me to my feet. "Let's go."

I planted my feet firmly. "Simon, we can't just leave him here. He could die." I turned toward the man, as Simon dragged me down the street. Stubborn feet or not, I was no match for Simon's strength.

There was blood. A lot of blood.

I knew my protests would get me nowhere. They wouldn't work if he was sober, and certainly wouldn't work in his current condition. Simon was furious. I felt it was better to give him his way, for the moment anyway, than to try to argue with him. I saw a group of people run up to the man just as we turned the corner around a building and disappeared into the night.

At least someone was there to help him, I thought.

We did not pick up our son that night. He didn't need to be around his father in the condition he was in. I felt that it was my duty as his mother to protect him from such things. As long as I could anyway.

I drove straight home. I wanted to get off the streets as quickly as possible.

Simon was passed out in the backseat by the time we arrived home. For a brief moment I considered just leaving him there for the night. He would find his way into the house in the morning.

But then I considered the foul mood he would be in when he discovered that I had just left him in the car all night, and I didn't need another thing to deal with in the morning. So, I managed to wake him up enough, so that he could walk into the house under his own power. No matter how determined I was, I would never be able to get him inside otherwise.

Once inside the house, I left Simon unconscious on the couch, for that was as far as I was going to get him. I then called my mother and arranged for Hunter to spend the night. I would pick him up in the morning. My mother couldn't have been happier with the arrangement.

CHAPTER 7

The next morning I called my mother and asked if it was all right if Hunter spent the day with her. I told my mother that Simon and I wanted to spend some time together, which couldn't be further from the truth. A little white lie wouldn't hurt. Of course it was all right with my mother, no matter the reason.

I turned on the kitchen radio and made myself some breakfast of poached eggs and dry toast. It wasn't much, but it was all my belly could handle that morning. It seemed that my pregnancy with Courtney this time was harder on me than I remembered it being in the past. Maybe I had just forgotten. It had been a lot of years since I was last pregnant.

As I sat down and poured some orange juice in a glass, I heard Simon stirring on the couch. I couldn't help but smile as he retched and sprinted to the bathroom. Even the sound of vomiting coming from down the hall didn't ruin my breakfast. "Serves you right," I said out loud, knowing he couldn't hear me.

"Get me some aspirin," Simon ordered. He shuffled to the kitchen and sat down at the table.

"A 'please' would be nice," I said.

Simon glared at me through glassy eyes. "And some coffee," he added.

I got up anyway and got the aspirin and a glass of water and set both of them down in front of him. He never did say please or thank you.

"Stay tuned for the news, after this short commercial break," I heard from the radio as I poured Simon some coffee and sat down across from him to finish my breakfast.

Simon drank the black coffee greedily. His eyes were squinty and bloodshot. He was in no mood for conversation that morning, after all the beer from the night before. We sat in silence

When I finished, I got up, picked up my plate and headed to the kitchen sink.

"Last night a 22 year old man was found beaten to death on Lake Street, in front of the pharmacy. His name is being withheld pending notification to the family. Witnesses said a man and woman were seen fleeing from the scene."

I stopped in my tracks and turned to look at Simon. He had heard it too and was suddenly much more alert than he had been a minute ago. He looked me straight in the eyes, but still said nothing.

"If anyone has any information on the perpetrators, please call the Red Lake Sheriff's Department. Stay tuned for the Dr. Stephen show coming up next."

I reached over and turned the radio dial to the off position.

"Oh my god, Simon, what do we do now?" I sat down across from my husband and finished off my orange juice.

"Nothing. That's exactly what we're going to do. We had nothing to do with that. Got it?" He watched me for a reaction.

I nervously fidgeted with my long red hair. "Simon, you killed that man. We can't just ignore that."

"No...We went to dinner and came straight home. That's all."

Simon leaned toward me as he spoke, pressing his lips together in a tight, straight line when finished. His body language was aggressive, causing me to lean back a bit. Being within striking distance of my husband was the last thing I needed right then. I absentmindedly rubbed my belly, protecting my Courtney from the man in front of me.

I could see that he was never going to admit to any wrongdoing. I glanced down at his hands. There was not a single mark on them. He had not hit the young man, he had just slammed his head into the concrete over and over. I knew right then and there that Simon was never going to pay for his rage. He would get away with it, just like he did with every despicable act of his life.

Even so, I couldn't just let it go. I thought of the poor man, and his family.

"Someone needs to know why this happened. He has parents that love him and will mourn him. And maybe even a wife or girlfriend, and maybe children. Don't you think they all have a right to know why he died?"

Simon leaned menacingly toward me once again, causing me to back up a few more inches. He was so close I could smell the previous night's beer still on his breath.

"If you say a word to anyone, and I mean any person whatsoever, I will kill you. Do you understand?" His words were slow and deliberate.

My body began shaking uncontrollably. I nodded my head slowly. I knew he meant every word.

"Perhaps Hunter and I should go stay with my parents for a while. Let's just give us all some time for this to die down." I grimaced at my unfortunate choice of words.

As I stood up, Simon grabbed me by the wrist and yanked me down close to his face. "You are not going anywhere. I'll kill you before I let you leave me. And I'll kill the kids."

He looked down at my growing belly and I put my free palm over it in a protective manner. That last sentence made my blood run cold.

~

From that moment on, I was more convinced than ever that Simon was the serial killer. I knew he was capable of killing in cold blood. What I witnessed the previous night was proof enough of that.

I knew what I needed to do. I needed to get out of there, with my son. I had done it once before, in my first life. So I knew I was capable of living on my own, and raising two children alone. I knew that I would have to be smarter this time though. Last time it took Simon two years to find us, but he did find us. That's when he killed me. I never did know if he died from his wounds that day. I certainly hoped so, for my children's sake. It pained me terribly to think that he survived and went on to raise Hunter and Courtney on his own. It would have been no life for two young children. Having both parents kill each other would have been bad enough for them, but to have their father kill their mother, then raise them, would have been worse. I knew that as fact.

It was time to put my exit plan into motion.

CHAPTER 8

Though I had definite plans to leave at some point, I couldn't just yet. I still needed to somehow confirm that Simon was the killer. If he turned out not to be, then I needed to find out who was. Since the murders had already taken place, several years prior, then there was no need for me to try to save anyone, which took up so much of my time in my previous lives. This one was different. I could focus on this one task of outing the serial killer once and for all.

If I left town, on the run from my husband, then there was no way I would be able to figure out who the serial killer was. So, for the foreseeable future, I would stay. I had work to do, and I needed to do it fast. Staying with Simon any longer than absolutely necessary was not on my agenda.

There was a good reason why it was so important to find out who the killer is as quick as possible. It was because if I finished this life early, and came back to life before the killings next time, I could stop him. At least that was the plan. Unfortunately I had absolutely no control over my lives. Or my deaths. They happened when they happened. Though I couldn't help but feel that they were happening for a reason. I had to be coming back over and over to stop the terrible injustice.

～

After that fateful night, Simon's controlling behavior seemed to multiply in intensity. I felt that he was watching everything I did. Even when he was at work, I felt watched. I just knew that he had people keeping an eye on me for him. It was unnerving.

Whenever I made plans with a friend, Simon always called me, needing something that would interfere with my plans. I always complied. I was biding my time until I was ready for my escape. There were plans to be made and money to be saved. But I would get it all done. It would just take a few months. I prayed that I could put up with him until then.

I considered, for a brief moment, moving in with my parents. They would have gladly taken us in. But, that would be the first place Simon looked. By doing that, I would be putting my parents and brother in danger. I couldn't have that on my conscience. My parents knew nothing of my troubles with Simon. They thought of him as a pretty decent husband for their daughter, and father to their grandchildren. They didn't know him though. Not really. All they saw was what Simon, and I for that matter, wanted to show them. He came across to them as a decent man, that provided a nice home for his family. I would never be able to bring myself to let them in on the reality of it all.

～

During the last two months of pregnancy, my brother, Parker, and I spent a lot of time trying to figure out who the serial killer was. We searched the woods near the sinkhole for evidence. Nothing. We questioned anyone that was close to Bernadette or Josephine, even their parents. Still nothing. The problem was that it had been several years since their deaths. Evidence had long since washed away, memories faded, and our brother-sister, crime fighting duo found absolutely nothing of any use to us.

"What are we going to do?" I whined one day to my brother. He had come over to the house to talk while Hunter was napping.

"I think that it's time we gave up. There's nothing here to find. There's no evidence still left and no one has been helpful at all," Parker told me. "I can see now why the sheriff has not been able to solve this. It's unsolvable." Parker was trying to be the voice of reason.

"Nothing is unsolvable. Even 50 year old cold cases sometimes get solved. Of course, we can't take that long. I don't know when this life will be done, and I have to start all over again." I sighed at the thought.

"I don't know, Ives," Parker responded, shaking his head slightly from side to side. "I just don't know where to go from here."

"We just haven't talked to the right people. Yet." I was having a difficult time letting go. "Let's go over our list of potential witnesses again."

I pulled the list out of my purse, unfolded it, and laid it out on the table in front of us. Parker gently pushed it back toward me without looking at it.

"There's no one left. We have talked to everyone. I'm sorry Ives, but I'm out."

"What? No, please don't do this. I need your help," I pleaded with my brother.

"What's going on here?"

Both Parker and I turned toward the voice. Simon had come home early.

"Nothing's going on," I told him. "We are just talking." I quickly folded up the list of witnesses and put it back in my purse. Simon didn't seem to notice.

"Well, you need to leave. Ivy has stuff to do." Simon was speaking directly to Parker.

Parker looked to me for confirmation. I nodded my head.

"Okay, fine. I'm going. Keep your hands off my sister. Got it?" Parker told his brother-in-law. "If I hear that you have hurt her, or Hunter, in any way, we are gonna have a problem."

Parker and Simon stood there for at least one full minute glaring at each other, while neither one spoke. Finally, Parker walked out the door.

"What have you told him?" Simon demanded the second the front door slammed shut.

"What? Nothing," I replied. "We don't talk about you."

"I don't believe you."

Simon took a step toward me and stumbled just a bit before righting himself.

"Are you drunk?" I asked him, instantly regretting it.

"No, I'm not drunk, and what I do is none of your damn business. But I could use a beer. Get me one."

Simon plopped down on the couch and turned on the TV. "And make dinner."

I was standing in the dining room and Simon had his back to me, so he could not see me. I rolled my eyes, but got him his beer. I could smell the alcohol on his breath as I leaned over and handed it to him. Before I had a chance to say anything, Hunter started crying and I headed for the stairs to retrieve him.

I placed Hunter in his high chair while I made dinner. Simon didn't even acknowledge his son until I called him in for dinner.

That night Simon got heavily drunk. When he was a bit drunk, Simon was in a great mood, laughing, and making a fool of himself. It was all in good fun. I actually enjoyed him then. But when he got really drunk, it was like day and night. That's when he became a nasty drunk. His mood went from goofy, directly to hateful. This was one of those nights.

I knew his moods well, and saw it coming. I knew it might mean trouble for me the next day, but I took our son and sneaked out of the house while Simon was asleep on the couch. Even though I would later live to regret it, especially since I was in my ninth month of pregnancy, I returned home after dropping Hunter off at his grandparents' house.

The reason I returned home was a simple one. Had I left Simon to his own devices, I knew that at some point he would wake up. If I was nowhere to be found, he would go looking for me. That could mean a lot more trouble out in the world than it would right there in our home. I could not unleash him, in that condition, on the world.

I thought about that poor young man that Simon had beaten to death out on Lake Street. I had been too terrified of my husband to tell anyone. If I got the chance, I would later make sure the family knew what had happened. And who had done it.

Just as I walked through the front door, it started. "Where the hell have you been?"

"I just took Hunter over to spend the night at my parents' house. They wanted to see him."

I tried my best to sound like it was just a normal night at my house. Simon didn't need to know that my intention was to get Hunter out of harm's way.

I put down my purse and keys and walked over to sit next to him on the couch. I desperately hoped to smooth things over before they got out of hand. If I were lucky, he would just want to go to bed and that would be that. But no, that's not how the night would go.

"I want to know what you and your brother have been up to." Simon appeared to have sobered up a bit.

I was taken aback. That question seemed to have come out of nowhere. He hadn't mentioned Parker since my brother left the house earlier that evening. I thought the whole incident had been forgotten.

"What do you mean?" I was stalling for time and I knew it.

"You two have had your heads together for months. Something's going on and I want to know what it is." His words were still somewhat slurry.

"Nothing is going on. We just like to hang out. Really." It didn't sound convincing, even to myself.

"I don't believe you. Tell me what it is. Right now." Simon was not backing down.

I contemplated my answer. Should I stick to my story that nothing was going on? Or should I tell him the truth? That we had been working on trying to figure out who the Red Lake Slasher was. And if it was Simon, then what?

Ooh, interesting. My mind whirled. What if I told Simon the truth and he confirmed that it was him? That would certainly clear things up for me, in a big way. But then he would know that I knew. Obviously. That could cause me to be in more danger than I already was. And in my current condition, I wasn't so sure I should go there.

"Answer me!"

Simon reached over and backhanded me across the face.

"What the hell?" My hand shot up to my mouth and I tasted blood on my lower lip. "That's it. I'm done."

I got up. I had every intention of grabbing only my purse and keys, and leaving that house for good. I didn't even care at that moment that I wouldn't be taking a single thing with me. That could all be dealt with later.

But it wasn't to be.

Simon's hand shot out and grabbed me tightly around the wrist, yanking me back down onto the couch.

"Where the hell do you think you're going?" he asked me through gritted teeth.

"I'm leaving, that's where I'm going."

I attempted to get up again, but Simon held onto my wrist. He was squeezing so tightly that it began to ache. I couldn't fight him too strenuously, in my current condition. I had Courtney to think about.

"Ouch, you're hurting me." I tried to wrench my arm loose, but that only made him squeeze tighter.

"You aren't going anywhere. I told you before that if you try to leave me, I will kill you. You won't live long enough for that baby to be born."

He looked down at my belly and I cringed.

He was speaking with such intensity and hatred, that I believed every word he said. It was in that moment that I began to hate every fiber of his being.

"Okay fine," I replied. "Whatever you say."

"Are you being a smart ass?"

Simon pulled his free arm back and slammed his fist into my face before I had a chance to react. I responded with a howl of pain. I was positive that my nose was broken. It was gushing blood.

"Dammit," I yelled. "I need to stop the bleeding," I added as I pinched the bridge of my aching nose. "Let me go to the bathroom."

I shook my wrist free from his grasp and jumped up off the couch. He let me go.

By the time I returned to the living room, Simon was fast asleep on the couch. I dared not wake him. I crept upstairs, quickly cleaned myself up, grabbed a suitcase from the closet, and hastily packed a few things of mine and Hunter's.

When I got back downstairs, I momentarily considered picking up a lamp and bashing the bastard over the head. But what good would that do? It would only land me in prison, and leave my children without any parents.

It would take the sheriff about two minutes to put it alto-gether. My blood on his knuckles and on the couch, and in the bathroom. And Simon with a high blood alcohol level and a lamp shaped indentation in his skull. The lamp would have my fingerprints all over it. Yeah, that would be a stellar idea.

Instead, I went to the refrigerator, took out the ketchup, and squirted it all over Simon as he slept. He didn't even stir. It was juvenile, I know. But it gave me a bit of satisfaction that he would be waking up to that mess, with me and Hunter long gone.

CHAPTER 9

"Oh my god, what happened to you?" My mother's hand flew to her mouth when she opened her front door and saw the condition I was in.

I couldn't help but start crying as she ushered me into the house.

I spent about ten minutes explaining to my mother, as best as I could, what had happened and that I had to leave town. For good.

I knew that I had no other choice but to leave. It was really important to me to stay and do my best to figure out who the Slasher was, yes. But it was more important to me to stay safe, and to keep my children safe. That would never be the case if we stayed in Red Lake. That's where Simon was, and we needed to get as far away from him as we could. And we needed to do it quickly.

I would just have to do my best with the investigation, from somewhere else. Though I knew that would be next to impossible, it was still something I had to do, no matter where I lived. I would be careful.

"Do you know where you are headed?" my mother asked me.

"Do you have an address? I need to know that you will be all right."

I could see the sadness in my mother's eyes and it just broke my heart. But there really was nothing I could do about it. I had to go.

I thought about reporting Simon to the sheriff. But I knew that would get me nowhere. Simon was well known in town. And well liked. His ways were smooth, and he would have little problem turning the entire situation around on me. By the time he was done with the sheriff's office, I would be the one that was in trouble. I was certain of it.

Besides, I already figured that he would have the sheriff after me the second he woke up and found us gone. That's why I called my brother on the way over to my parents' house. I asked him to keep a close eye on Simon and do his best to make sure that Simon didn't report me for kidnapping. Maybe have a man to man talk with him.

Parker could not stand Simon. And even in the beginning of our relationship, Parker was not much of a fan of Simon's. He was never shy about sharing his opinion on the matter either. So, Parker readily agreed.

I wasn't entirely sure that Simon could report me for kidnapping though. Hunter was my child too. Didn't I have the legal right to leave with him, even without Simon's consent? And, even though Courtney wasn't born yet, she was Simon's child. Did I have the right to leave with her?

Those were questions that I didn't know the answers to. I did know though, that I didn't have time to find them out.

"I'm sorry, Mom, but I can't tell you where we are going. If you don't know, it will be safer for you. Simon will be furious when he wakes up. I'm worried about what he will do when he finds us gone." I hugged my mother, for perhaps the last time.

I was right, of course. His in-laws' house would be the first place Simon would go to look for me, and his son.

"I understand. Let me just go get your father. He's asleep, but he will want to say good-bye."

As my mother turned to leave, I took her gently by the arm. "No, Mom, please don't. He will try to stop me. And he will want to go after Simon. That will just make things worse."

"But I…"

"Mom, please. Just do as I wish. Tell him I'm sorry and that I love him." A tear slid down my face.

"What about the baby?" My mother looked down at my huge belly. "You are due any day now."

My hand rubbed my belly protectively. "I know. I'll just have to do it alone. I have before." Oops, I hadn't meant to say that last part.

"What do you mean?" My mother's head tilted to the side as she asked the question.

"Oh, it's nothing. Mom I really have to go. I don't know when Simon will be waking up. I need to get a good head start. Can you go get Hunter for me?"

"Of course."

My mother ran off to the guest room to retrieve her grandson. I headed to the bathroom to collect myself. I didn't want to cry in front of Hunter. A couple of minutes later, the three of us met in the living room. Hunter was fast asleep in his grandmother's arms. I took him and laid him on the couch for a moment while I spoke with my mother.

"I have one more favor to ask of you," I told her.

"Anything. You know that," my mother replied, eyes wide.

"Can I borrow some money? I only have a few hundred dollars saved up. That won't get me far. I will get a job as soon as I can and promise to pay you back." I looked at her expectantly.

"Of course. Anything you need, Sweetheart. I'll be right back." She didn't even hesitate. I loved her so much for that.

My mother disappeared down the hall, while I peered out the front window. I was terrified that Simon would show up before

Hunter and I got out of there. My mother returned in under one minute with a handful of hundreds.

My eyes went wide. "Mom, where did you get all this money?"

"Oh, it's my rainy day money." She waved her hand and smiled. "I've had it hidden away for years. A girl never knows when an emergency will pop up. I think this qualifies."

Without counting, I leafed though the cash. There was at least five thousand dollars in my hand.

"Mom, it's too much. I can't take all of this." I tried handing back half of it.

"Don't be ridiculous. You are my daughter and I love you. You and Hunter, and that baby girl on the way, need it much more than I do. Now, go. I have no use for it anyway."

I hugged my mother tightly. I never wanted to let go, but knew we needed to hurry. I picked up Hunter and the two of us walked out into the darkness of the night. My mother cried behind us, not knowing if she would ever see her daughter and grandchildren again.

I wasn't so sure if it was the right thing to do or not, but I headed straight for the same mountain town I had fled to in my first life. Aspen Ridge. The best thing about it was that it was many states away from Red Lake. It was the cutest place, and I had loved living there and raising my children the first time. Of course, Simon had found us, and that I was wary about. I certainly didn't need a repeat of my encounter with him there.

But, I felt comfortable in Aspen Ridge. I knew it well. There would be no learning curve, like there was the first time. Of course, no one there would know me now, but I would make friends all over again. I was sure of that. And, I would be more careful this time. I would make sure that there was no way Simon could find me.

I wasn't positive, even now, how Simon found me the first time. But, I would figure it out. It took him two years back then, so I knew that I had time. At least I hoped that was the case.

CHAPTER 10

The first thing I did upon my arrival in Aspen Ridge was to change my name. Ivy was not a very common name, and if I kept it, Simon might have an easier time finding me. The internet made it a lot harder to hide these days. I was now known as Ellie Brown.

I spent some time at the library a couple of towns over researching last names before I chose one. Yeah, it may have been overkill for me to travel several miles away just to use the library, but I felt that I couldn't be too careful. What if someone at my local library was able to see what I had been researching? It might seem suspicious to them.

I couldn't take any chances. Not with the lives of my children. Not ever.

During my research of names, I found that Brown was in the top five on the list of the most common surnames in the United States. That would make it even harder to find me. It was perfect. So, Brown it was.

I thought long and hard about changing Hunter's name, but in the end decided against it. Hunter was a common enough name that he wouldn't stand out. Besides, it would be really confusing for a 2 year old to understand why his name was different. I figured that I could still name the baby Courtney, since that was a new name to everyone.

Within the first week of arriving in Aspen Ridge, I changed my name, got an apartment, got a job answering phones in an accountant's office, and had my baby.

My new job would not be demanding, as it was the off season for the accountant. Mostly answering the phones, doing some filing, and greeting the occasional walk-in client. The office had a spare room and my new boss said it was no problem if I wanted to set up a play room for Hunter in there, so I could bring him to work. He even put in a new crib, at his expense, so the baby would have a place to sleep while I worked. I could not have asked for a better place to work.

On my third day at my new job, I went into labor two hours in. My new boss drove me to the hospital himself. His wife said she would watch Hunter while I was in the hospital. That took a load off of my mind.

My new baby girl, Courtney, was born at 3:13 that afternoon. She was born a few days earlier than she had the first time. I chalked that up to the stress of my new situation.

Over the next few weeks, Hunter, Courtney, and I settled into life in Aspen Ridge. I had met and befriended a couple of my friends from my first life. Of course, they didn't remember me from before, but it certainly made it easier to get to know them this time. I knew everything about them. We hit it off immediately.

I had made no contact with my family and had no idea whatsoever about what was going on with Simon. I didn't know if he was looking for me or if he had just let me go and moved on with his life. I was pretty sure it was the former though. He was not the type to give up. Besides, I remembered well the day he found me the first time. That was they day we fought and stabbed each other. I died, I'm pretty sure, but had no idea if Simon did or not.

And, there was no one to ask. It was something I would never know.

Finally, about six weeks after fleeing Red Lake, I decided to contact my family. It wasn't fair to them to just leave them hanging, not knowing if I was dead or alive, if I had given birth yet, and just generally how we were doing. They deserved to know.

I couldn't call my parents, especially my mother. I loved the woman dearly, but my mother liked to talk, and she was a terrible gossip. Even if she swore to never utter a word about me, I knew that at some point, my mother would slip. She would never do it on purpose, but it would come out. Some little hint about my whereabouts to one of her friends, and that could be the end of me. More than one marriage in Red Lake had ended due to my mother's big mouth. I just couldn't, and wouldn't, take that chance.

I would call Parker instead. My brother did know how to keep his mouth shut. I trusted him with my life. Since Parker lived with our parents, I planned my call for a time that I was sure both of our parents would be out. I knew their schedules pretty well.

It was winter and I bundled up the children for the four hour journey to a payphone in a huge city in the neighboring state. I picked one right in the middle of downtown, on a bustling Saturday afternoon. The reason for this choice was twofold. First, in a big busy city, no one would even notice a young woman with two small children, talking on the phone. Second, it was far enough away from Aspen Ridge, that even if someone traced the phone call, they would never find me so far away. That big city is where they would be looking. Next time, I would pick another city to call from.

"Hi Brother," I said when Parker picked up the phone.

"Ives! Where the hell have you been?" He was genuinely happy to hear from his sister. I could hear the smile in his words.

"Oh, you know, here and there." I laughed in spite of it all. It was so great hearing his voice.

"Are you good? Did you have the baby? How's Hunter?" Parker was peppering me with questions.

"Whoa, slow down," I responded. "Everything is fine. Yes, I had the baby. Her name is Courtney. Please don't tell anyone that. I'm trying to make it as hard as possible for Simon to find us."

I instantly regretted telling him the baby's name. The fewer people who knew, the better. Of course, before we fled, I had told Parker what I was going to name her. I'm sure he remembered it. But, he didn't have to know what I actually ended up naming her. I could have made up a name, just for his benefit. But honestly, there was no reason to. I really did trust him completely.

"Understood. I won't divulge her top secret name," he laughed. "I'm glad everything is fine."

"Don't even tell Mom and Dad. Okay? Please Parker. It's important." I did my best to use my 'I'm extremely serious' voice on him.

"Yeah, yeah, got it. Don't tell anyone the baby's name. Cross my heart."

I pictured him doing the universal gesture over the phone.

"How are Mom and Dad?"

"They are good. They miss you and the kids terribly. They aren't home right now, so you can't talk to them," Parker explained. "They're gonna be sorry they missed you."

"That's okay. I probably shouldn't talk to them anyway. You know how Mom has a hard time with secrets."

"Yeah," Parker replied. "That's why I never tell her anything important about me. Not that I'm that interesting anyway, you know."

"Hey, what's the latest with Simon?" I dared ask, changing the subject.

"Oh boy. He is so pissed off at you. He came over here the morning you left, and looked really hungover. He was screaming at Mom and Dad to tell him where you were. Luckily they didn't know, so they were unable to give him any information, even if they wanted to," Parker explained.

"I'm so sorry you all have been dragged into this mess."

I meant it too. If I could have kept my family out of it, I would have done anything to make that happen. Unfortunately, due to my circumstances, that was impossible.

"It's not your fault, it's his." Parker sounded sincere.

"I know, but still...."

"He's been over here every few days since you left. We keep telling him that we don't have any idea where you are, and that we haven't heard from you, but he doesn't believe us. Don't worry though, I can handle Simon."

I could hear the determination in my brother's voice. He had never been afraid of Simon, and that worried me. Simon could be nastier than he looked. I had seen it first hand. Though Parker was physically larger than my husband, Simon was more of an aggressor. It worried me to think of the two of them getting into an altercation. I wasn't so sure that Parker would be the victor in that scenario.

I didn't want to admit to Parker that I was worried about him. He didn't need that added pressure, in addition to dealing with Simon. So, I agreed with him. For now, anyway.

"I know you can handle Simon," I told him. "Thank you for being there for me and my children. And mostly, thank you for being there for Mom and Dad." I could feel a single teardrop sliding down my right cheek.

"Mommy, wanna go."

Hunter was getting impatient with me. Both of the children were strapped into a stroller and had been waiting for me to get off of the phone. Thankfully they had been mostly quiet, giving me the chance to have a conversation with my brother without interruption. But that time was coming to an end.

I looked over at Courtney and she was fast asleep. Not Hunter.

He was squirming and straining against the restraints. When he started whining, I knew I needed to cut my conversation short.

"Parker, I need to go. The kids are getting fidgety," I told him honestly. I reached over and handed Hunter a cracker as I wound up our conversation.

"Can I come visit you?" he asked me.

"Oh, I don't know if that's a very good idea. What if Simon follows you?"

That was my biggest fear. I had done my very best to not give away our location to anyone. And to not divulge to anyone in Aspen Ridge any details about our circumstances. My story to them about just needing a fresh start with my kids seemed to alleviate their curiosities.

"I will make sure he doesn't follow me. I promise. I can follow him to work, before heading your way. He won't even know I've gone. Please, come on?"

I thought about it as I bent down to put the pacifier back into Courtney's mouth. She had awakened and was beginning to get fussy.

I could hear the desperation in his voice. My brother and I had always been close. Well, mostly anyway. We had issues during our teen years. Who didn't have issues with their siblings growing up? But overall, we were pretty good friends. And I really did miss him. It would be great to see his handsome face again. Besides, I would really love for the kids to know him. Since we hadn't been gone that long, Hunter would still remember him. But, he and Courtney had never met. Maybe it was time they did.

"You know, this is against my better judgment, and I hope I don't regret it, but okay. I would love to see you, and your niece and nephew would love to see you."

Oh boy, I desperately prayed that it was the right decision.

I gave Parker my address and made him swear to keep it hidden from everyone. We had no way of knowing who might be spying on my family for Simon. We made plans for him to be in Aspen Ridge in a few days.

"Oh, and my name is Ellie now. Never call me anything else when in town. Okay?"

This was important and I needed to make sure he understood how serious it was.

"Yeah, got it. See you in a few days, Ellie."

Parker hung up the phone. I smiled all the way home. I couldn't wait to see my big brother again. I had missed him so much.

CHAPTER 11

Over the next two years, Hunter, Courtney, and I thrived in Aspen Ridge. Hunter started Kindergarten, and Courtney went to work with me some days. On others, she stayed with the sitter.

I still worked for the same accountant that had hired me when I first showed up in town. I had been towing along a two year old and was nine months pregnant at the same time. The man was a saint.

Though I still sometimes found myself looking over my shoulder for Simon, I had mostly moved on. My only contact with my family was Parker. I felt terribly guilty about that, but my life, and the lives of my children were at stake.

Parker came to visit several times. I loved his visits, as did the children. Uncle Parker was their only link to my family. They had no contact with their father's side of the family. That was obvious.

Parker and I had many discussions about the identity of the Red Lake Slasher, but nothing ever came of it. I was beginning to feel as if all of it was a waste of time. In all of my lives, I had not saved a single person. In fact, I caused Graham to die because I began dating him. He hadn't been killed previously. I felt partly to blame for that. In my heart, I just knew that I was reliving my lives so that I could save these people. Save my friends. I just couldn't figure out how.

Though Parker tried to help, he didn't have the answers either. I know that he spent countless hours, at my pleading, following Simon around. He also kept a close eye on others that we suspected. Simon was at the top of the list though, as our main suspect. Unfortunately, Parker never once caught him doing anything suspicious. That made us re-think our entire strategy. Were we completely mistaken in our convictions about Simon?

One day, three years into my new life in Aspen Ridge, I came home to the worst thing I could ever imagine.

It was 5:20 pm when I walked in the front door of my house. The very first thing I noticed was how quiet it was. With two small children living there, it was never quiet. The silence was unnerving, and caused the hair on the back of my neck to stand up. I knew something was wrong. I could feel it deep in my core.

I laid my purse and keys on the table next to the front door and called to the kids. No answer. And the babysitter, Kylie, didn't answer either. I almost always found them either watching TV or playing in the backyard. Kylie was too young to drive, at only 14, so they never left the house.

I walked through the living room and out the back sliding door to an empty backyard. Where were they? Perhaps they had gone for a walk. I knew that was unlikely because Courtney's pink tennis shoes were lying in the entryway where she had kicked them off the night before. I thought about the fact that I had specifically told Courtney to pick them up that morning as I left the house. Something was up, I just didn't know what it was.

I continued to search the house. Perhaps they were all taking a nap, though I thought that was unlikely. As I opened the first bedroom I came to, my bedroom, I saw Kylie lying across my bed. I scrunched my face in confusion.

"Kylie?" I said quietly, not wanting to startle the girl. Why was she taking a nap when she should be watching my children?

No answer.

"Kylie," I said louder.

Still she did not stir.

I walked over and gently shook the teenager and got no response. That's when I noticed the blue color of Kylie's face.

"Oh my god."

I felt for a pulse and there was none, which is exactly what I expected after seeing the discoloration of the poor girl's skin. I immediately ran to Hunter's room, which was the next one in the hall. He was not there. I began to panic as I ran to Courtney's room and opened the door tentatively, afraid of what I might find.

There Courtney was, in her bed, with the covers pulled up to her chin. I held my breath as I walked the short distance from the door to the bed.

"Courtney?"

I was terrified.

"Mommy," Courtney replied, rubbing the sleep from her eyes.

"Oh my god, thank you. Are you all right sweetheart?" I tried to hide the panic from my voice.

"Yeah, I was sleeping," she answered in her soft, three year old voice.

"I know, Baby Girl." I looked around the room. "Do you know where your brother is?"

Courtney shook her head.

I picked up my daughter and walked into the living room. I called the sheriff's office to report Kylie's death and Hunter's disappearance. Just in case he was afraid and hiding, I searched the house from top to bottom while I waited for officers to arrive. There was no sign of my son.

I sat down on the couch, holding my sweet daughter, while

waiting for the authorities to show up. My body was shaking, almost as if I were freezing, and there was nothing I could do to stop it.

I was certainly affected by Kylie's death. The girl had been babysitting for me for months, and I just loved her. And more importantly, the kids loved her. Even so, I was terrified for my son. My first thoughts went straight to Simon. But why would Simon take Hunter and not Courtney? Perhaps because Hunter knew him, but Courtney did not? Hunter may have gone easily, it was his father after all. Courtney almost surely would not have. Simon was a stranger to her.

But then again, Hunter had not seen his father in three years. He had only been two when we left. Surely Hunter would not remember Simon. Would he?

The deputy entered my bedroom to check on Kylie. He returned a minute later with the bad news.

"It looks as if the young lady was strangled."

I gasped. Though I wasn't sure why I was so surprised. My son was missing. That was enough of a clue that Kylie didn't die of natural causes, or even an accident.

"What about my son?" I pleaded.

"Ma'am, we have already issued a county wide announcement. Every available law enforcement personnel is on the case. If he's in the area, we will find him."

I broke down crying, as I hugged my three year old daughter tight.

"What's going on here?"

It was Parker's voice that caused me to look up. I didn't even know he was in town. It wasn't Parker I saw though, it was Hunter that my gaze landed on first.

"Oh my god, Hunter!"

I sat Courtney on the couch next to where I was sitting and jumped up to greet my son. I dropped to my knees and wrapped my arms around him as I cried even harder.

"Ives, are you okay?" Parker tapped me on the shoulder. "Why are all these cops here? What's going on? Did 'you know who' find you?"

My brother looked at me with wide eyes. He was trying not to mention Simon in front of the cops. I appreciated the sentiment, but figured it was too late now for secrecy. That was all about to be blown wide open.

I released my son and stood up to face my brother. "Kylie is dead," I whispered, not wanting to alarm my children. "And Hunter was gone. We thought he was kidnapped."

"What? No. Hunter's fine. I asked Kylie if it was all right if I took him to get ice cream. She said it was fine. Courtney was asleep, and I didn't want to wake her up," Parker explained. "Did you say she's dead?" Parker's mouth was hanging open.

"Yeah, I came home from work and found her dead in my bedroom," I told him. "I haven't even had a chance to call her parents yet."

"We will take care of that, ma'am. No need to worry," the deputy told me. He looked at Parker. "Is everything okay here?"

"Oh yes, thank you. This is my brother. I didn't know he had Hunter. I'm sorry for the trouble," I told him.

"Not a problem, ma'am. You can never be too careful with small children." His gaze averted to the hallway leading to my bedroom. "But we still have the issue of the deceased young lady in your home."

I found it odd that someone barely older than I was, called me 'ma'am.'

"We were only gone maybe an hour," Parker told them. "Kylie was perfectly fine when we left. She was watching TV."

"Mind if I ask your son a couple of questions?" the deputy asked me.

"Go ahead."

The deputy knelt down so that he was face to face with Hunter. He was fairly young, about 30 years old, and clean shaven.

"Young man, I was hoping I could ask you something. Would that be all right with you?" he asked Hunter.

Hunter nodded shyly.

"When your uncle here picked you up," the deputy gestured toward Parker, "where did you go?" he asked gently.

"We got ice cream!" Hunter squealed. It made them all laugh, despite the dire circumstances we had found ourselves in.

"I see. And where was your babysitter when you left the house? Did you see her?"

"Yeah, she was there on the couch," he pointed, "watching TV."

"So you and your uncle left the house together and she was sitting right there?" The deputy pointed to the couch.

"Yeah," Hunter replied.

"You drove or walked to the ice cream parlor?" the deputy continued.

"Uncle Parker drove us. I remember that he forgot his keys, so he told me to wait by the car while he got them," my son told the officer.

"I see." The deputy looked up at Parker.

Parker's eyes grew wide. "I was gone like ten seconds. They were right there by the door." He turned and gestured to the table where I had a bowl for exactly that.

"Sir, Parker had nothing to do with this," I interjected. "But I have a good idea who did. Can we talk outside?" I looked down at my son. "Parker, can you take the kids into the backyard?"

"Sure. Come on buddy. Courtney, let's go out back and play."

The deputy and I stood and watched as Parker rounded up the kids and led them out the back door.

I turned and walked out the front door, while the deputy followed me dutifully. I walked until we were at the edge of the lawn, almost in the street, before I stopped and turned to him.

"Look, you are barking up the wrong tree with my brother. It's my ex that you should be talking to." Even though we were several yards from the nearest officer, I spoke in a whisper.

"Why is that? What reason would he have to strangle your babysitter?" the deputy asked.

"He's crazy, and a bastard. That's why. I witnessed him beating a man to death a few years ago. He beat me up and threatened to kill me and the kids if I ever told anyone."

I was terrified by the fact that I was telling someone about Simon. I knew they would look into it. I also knew that things were about to get very serious for me and my children. Simon would undoubtedly find out where we were. I was positive that the sheriff's department would investigate and tell him.

Unfortunately, with Kylie's murder in my home, there was absolutely nothing I could do about any of it.

Of course, it was entirely possible that Simon already knew where we were. Who else would have killed Kylie? Yep, he already knew. I was sure of it.

In addition, the fact that I just told them about the beating death was going to mean trouble. Simon might just carry out his threats against my little family. I began to visibly shake.

The deputy pulled out a notepad from his front pocket. "I'll need to get all of your ex-husband's information."

"I know."

CHAPTER 12

Two weeks later, we moved back to Red Lake.

I knew there was no point in staying in Aspen Ridge when Simon already knew where we were. The sheriff's department had investigated him and cleared him in Kylie's death. His girlfriend was his alibi. I didn't believe her for a minute. Either the woman was so deluded by his charm and good looks, that she would do anything for him, or more likely, he bullied her into giving him an airtight alibi. At least I felt safer being around family, instead of being a sitting duck in Aspen Ridge.

The reunion with my parents was one of the best days in my life. I had missed them with all my heart. Three years apart was way too long. We were all sobbing like little babies when we finally got to be together again. Then my parents, my mother specifically, saw the children.

"Oh my goodness, Hunter, look how big you've gotten!" She walked toward him and he hid shyly behind his Uncle Parker's legs.

"Come on sport." Parker scooped him up into his arms. "This is your grandma and grandpa. Don't you remember them?"

Hunter turned his head and planted his face into Parker's shoulder.

Of course he didn't remember my parents. Hunter had only been 2 years old when we moved away. It was going to take a bit of time before he warmed up. But it would happen. Hunter was a loving child. He just needed to get to know someone first.

"Well, let's give him a bit of time. We'll be best friends before you know it," my father added.

"Oh Ivy, look at this little beauty." My mother was in love with Courtney the second she laid eyes on her.

"Courtney," I introduced her, "this is your grandma...and your grandpa. Can you say hi?"

"Hi."

Courtney was not the shy one in the bunch. She would talk to anyone, anywhere. That sometimes worried me.

"Hello sweetheart." My mother bent over and touched the side of Courtney's cheek. Then to me, "I can't believe how much she looks like you."

I just smiled.

"Oh, come on. I made up a room for you. The three of you will have to share," my mother told me.

"That's just fine. Thank you, Mom. We really appreciate it."

"It's my pleasure. Really. To have you all here with us again, is all the thanks I need. You can stay as long as you need to." She turned to my father. "Right, Dear?"

"Absolutely. You are not going anywhere," my father replied.

Later that evening, I fed the kids their dinner early and sent them to the living room to watch some cartoons. It had been a long day, and they needed some downtime. Besides, us adults needed to talk about my ex-husband.

While my parents, Parker, and I all ate dinner together,

without the children, Parker told us all about how Simon had been investigated by the sheriff. It wasn't for Kylie's death, as he had already been cleared of that.

The new investigation was for the beating death of the man on the night that Simon and I had been walking home from dinner together. Unfortunately, it had been three years, and there was no proof, or eye witnesses. I was the only witness, and due to the volatile nature of our relationship, the sheriff had told me I wouldn't be a credible witness. Therefore they couldn't charge him with anything.

And with his girlfriend giving him an alibi for the day that Kylie had been strangled, it seemed that Simon was untouchable.

I very much wished that I had been strong enough to stand up to Simon back then. If I had told the sheriff right after the beating happened, then he might be in prison now. And I might never have had to go on the run. The last three years could have been spent in Red Lake, with my family, and my parents wouldn't be strangers to my children.

But, that was all in the past now. It was said and done. There was nothing that I could do to change any of it. I had to live with my decision and move on.

After dinner, I walked next door to talk to Carter's aunt. I knew from Parker that Carter didn't live there anymore, but I just wanted to get his contact information. I hadn't spoken with him in years.

"Hi Carter," I said when he answered the phone.

"Oh, hi. I wasn't expecting you to call." Carter seemed a bit perturbed, and certainly not excited to hear from me.

I was a bit taken aback by his reaction. "Um, is now a good time?" I asked.

"Yeah, I guess."

"Okay…I just wanted to let you know that I'm back in town and living with my parents for now," I explained.

"I know."

His answers were abrupt and I didn't know why.

"You do? How do you know?" I asked.

"My aunt said she saw you," he told me.

"Oh, I see." The whole conversation seemed stilted. "Do you want to come for a visit?" I asked him. "I'd really like to see you."

"Sure. I'll come over tomorrow."

He hung up the phone. I pulled the receiver away from my ear and looked at it. That whole conversation was perplexing.

The next morning, at precisely 9 a.m. Carter knocked on our door. I hugged him tightly. I had missed my best friend. We decided to take a short walk, while the kids hung out with their grandma.

"How come you never called?" Carter asked me.

"You know I couldn't. I didn't even call my own parents. It was just too dangerous," I admitted.

"Yeah, I guess," Carter responded. "How did you like living in Aspen Ridge?"

My head whipped around when he said that.

"What? How did you know I was living in Aspen Ridge? I haven't told anyone."

"It's a small town. I hear things," Carter replied. He was very casual about it.

"But I didn't tell anyone. How could you hear things?" I stopped walking and turned to face my friend.

"The sheriff was investigating Simon about that person that was killed at your house in Aspen Ridge, right? People in this town talk."

Carter didn't seemed fazed by the conversation at all. But I was suspicious. I doubted that the sheriff leaked information about the investigation and my whereabouts to the public. Something was amiss.

On the other hand, it was a small town. He was certainly right about that. It was also a very gossipy town, and I knew that. It was entirely possible that Simon or his girlfriend told someone. They would have to have known what town I was in. Either because Simon killed Kylie or because the sheriff's office investigated his whereabouts and would have told him what town he was accused of being in.

I didn't know what to think.

CHAPTER 13

"Well, well, well, look who we have here."

I had been grocery shopping alone and turned toward the voice to see Simon standing five feet from me. A chill ran up my spine.

"I heard you were back in town. You look good, Ivy."

I watched Simon as his eyes traveled from my eyes to my feet, and slowly back up again. It gave me the creeps, causing me to shudder in response.

I put my hands up, palms facing Simon. "You need to back up. I have filed a restraining order against you," I told him.

"Yeah, I know. I'm just here doing some grocery shopping. I've come here every week for many years. You can't keep me from grocery shopping," he stated matter-of-factly.

"If you are shopping in the same store as I am, and at the same time, then yes, I can keep you from grocery shopping," I retorted back.

I stared him right in the eyes as I spoke. It was important to me that I didn't show him any fear. I meant it too. I was no longer that same frightened young woman that cringed in fear whenever he was around. We had to live in the same town, and I would have to deal with that. But fear would not be part of my response.

"I don't care about that stupid restraining order. I want to see my kids."

Simon took a step closer to me and I moved the shopping cart in between us.

"I don't know..." I started to say.

"Don't you think the kids have a right to know their father?" he asked me.

I shrugged. He had a point. Maybe. He had been horrible to me, but really never did anything to Hunter. Courtney hadn't been born yet when I left, so she never experienced any issues with him.

I had thought long and hard over the matter. Simon was a bastard. That fact was never in dispute. But even with all he had put me through, and killing that man on the sidewalk a few years back, did I have the right to keep his kids from him?

If I tried, I might be able to keep him away. But, was that the best choice? How would my children feel about the matter? One day they would both be old enough to make that decision for themselves. They might want to have a relationship with him. If I kept them from him, would they eventually resent me? They might. Did I want to take that chance?

I didn't know the right answer. I had to think of someone other than myself though. And someone other than Simon. I had to think of the kids.

"I'll tell you what," I began, "I'll bring the kids to the park this afternoon at three. You can come to the park and see them then. That's the best I'm willing to do right now."

With a tight smile, Simon agreed. "Fine, I'll be there."

I walked away, leaving him standing there staring after me.

∼

At 3 p.m., Parker and I arrived at the park, kids in tow. As soon as I released them from their rolling prison, they bolted for the swing set. I couldn't help but laugh at their enthusiasm.

Simon arrived 15 minutes later. I did not comment on his tardiness. Simon stood at the edge of the playground and watched Hunter and Courtney for several minutes. And I watched him. He made no attempt to make any contact with them. I was thankful for that. I wasn't too keen on the idea of a stranger walking up to my children and talking to them. No, I needed to facilitate that meeting.

After watching the children, Simon walked over to the bench Parker and I were sitting on.

"Why did you bring him?" Simon sounded a bit irritated as he looked Parker directly in the eyes. "You need your brother to protect you from me?"

"Something like that," I responded. Parker said nothing.

"I would like to talk to the kids," Simon looked toward his children playing on the slide.

Parker looked at me and I nodded.

"I'll go get them." Parker jumped up and headed to the sandbox.

"Hey," Simon began once Parker was out of earshot, "I want to apologize to you for my behavior from before. You know, when I hit you and threatened you. And I threatened the kids. I'm really sorry." He sat down on the bench next to me. "I was drinking a lot back then, and I treated you badly."

"Yes you did." I wasn't ready to let him off the hook.

"Things are different now. I am going to meetings and haven't had a drink for over a year now. I know we can't be a family again. I have no illusions about that. But can we at least try to be friends? For the sake of the kids?"

"Well, it's going to take some time, but we can try getting along. I suppose we can be civil to each other for the sake of the kids," I replied. "But you and I are never going to be friends."

I had no idea why I was agreeing to anything that my ex-husband said. Actually, he was still technically my husband. I never got a divorce when I was on the run, because I was afraid he would be alerted to my whereabouts if I filed paperwork.

Parker and the kids walked up to us then.

"Daddy!" Hunter exclaimed and jumped into Simon's arms.

Simon, Parker, and I all looked at each other in amazement. None of us ever expected Hunter to remember his father. He had only been 2 years old when we left Red Lake.

"Hi Buddy," Simon said to him as he hugged his son for the first time in three years. I saw a single tear slide down Simon's cheek.

A couple of minutes later, Hunter climbed down off of his father's lap and asked me for some juice. I asked Parker to take care of it. While Hunter was engaged, I had something I needed to do.

"Courtney." I took her hand and guided her closer to Simon. "This is your daddy."

"Hi," Courtney said to him and reached out her hand to shake his.

"Hi Sweetheart. I'm very glad to meet you," Simon said, taking her hand into his.

Though I had hated Simon with every fiber of my being, this Simon wasn't so bad. He seemed genuinely happy to be there with his children. He was polite and friendly. Perhaps the fact that he had stopped drinking was making a huge difference in his personality. Even back in high school he seemed to drink a lot. Now he came across as a new person. He might be someone I could actually like.

"Ivy." Simon looked up at me. "I was wondering if I could come over tomorrow to visit? I really want to get to know my kids."

"Um, okay. I think that would be fine. I won't leave you alone with them though." There was no negotiating that.

"Understood."

THE MANY LIVES OF IVY WELLS

I was taken aback by Simon's willingness to agree to my terms. That wasn't like him at all. Maybe we could be friends. However, I wasn't just jumping headfirst into friendship with him. I still had my children to think about. They were the most important people in the world to me.

CHAPTER 14

A few days later, Simon showed up at our house, unannounced. No one was home, but me. Parker was at work, and my parents had taken the kids to some children's movie playing at the theater downtown. My parents loved spending time with their grandchildren. They had missed so much while we were away.

"What are you doing here?" I asked. "The kids aren't home."

It surprised me to see Simon standing at the door. We had an agreement that for now, we would schedule all visits in advance. I wanted my children on a regular schedule that they could count on. At some point, we might be able to loosen the reins a bit, but that was down the line. Not yet.

"I know. I just wanted to talk. Can I come in?"

I stood back and opened the door wider to allow Simon to walk in. The smell of beer wafted in with him, and I raised my eyebrows in response. I didn't say anything just yet though. I wanted to find out the reason for his visit. I closed the door behind him and followed him into the living room.

"Do you want something to drink? We have some cola. Or maybe water would be better," I asked him. "I can make you a sandwich."

At that point I didn't know if he was drunk or not. But I figured that getting some food and water into him wouldn't hurt either way.

"No thanks. I won't be long," he replied. "I came here to talk to you about something."

His mannerisms were odd. He wrung his hands nervously. That was a new one for me. Simon had always been the confident one. Nothing rattled him. I didn't know if he was sincere or just drunk.

"Okay. What do you want to talk about?"

I walked over to the kitchen and got myself a cola while he began speaking. He stood his ground in the living room, and didn't follow me.

"I was just wondering if you wanted to go out with me?" he called in to the kitchen. "I really want us to get along. And maybe be a family again someday."

I walked out of the kitchen, holding my glass of cola, and a little bit in shock. I looked at Simon just as he bit the inside of his cheek, waiting for me to answer.

"Have you been drinking?" I confronted him. I saw no other choice. He must have been out of his mind to ask me to go out with him. He had to know that that was never, ever, going to happen. Not in this lifetime anyway.

"What? Why would you ask me that?" Simon had a genuine look of surprise on his face.

"Because you smell like a brewery. Did you actually think I wouldn't notice? What happened to you going to meetings, and being sober for a year? Was that all a lie?" I was peppering him with questions faster than he could keep up.

"Whoa, hold on." Simon put up his right hand, palm toward me. "My drinking is really none of your business. None of it is your business." He was getting defensive.

"Actually it is my business. If you are going to be around my children, everything you do is my business." I put one hand on my hip in a state of defiance.

"*Your* children? I believe they are my children too."

"Yeah, but I have custody. And I have the say so on if you get to see them or not. And as long as you are drinking, I will make sure you never see them. Do I make myself clear?"

I didn't want to press the issue, but my children were my life and there was no way I was ever going to let Simon have them if he was still drinking. I had seen first hand what his drinking did to him. It was scary.

"Don't you dare threaten me. They are my children too and I will see them when I want to." Simon took a step toward me.

"We'll see about that," I responded. I set the glass of cola on the living room coffee table and folded my arms across my chest.

"You know, you haven't been as elusive these past few years as you think you have," Simon told me.

I cocked my head. "What? What is that supposed to mean?"

Simon shrugged in response.

"Simon! Answer me," I demanded.

"I've known where you were since not long after you moved to Aspen Ridge." He gave me a crooked smile.

"You're lying." I looked him square in those steel gray eyes. I couldn't tell if he was being truthful or just trying to scare me.

"I followed Parker there once. He led me right to you. He is such an idiot and had no idea I was there."

"If that's true, then why didn't you say anything?" I asked. I still didn't believe him.

"Because I thought that if you knew I knew where you were, you might run again. Then I might never find you. So, I stayed in the shadows watching you. Once I knew where you were, I made several trips out there to keep an eye on the three of you."

"No. You are making this all up. You are just trying to scare me." I hoped and prayed that I was right. I couldn't bear the thought of him watching us.

"I saw you taking my kids to work at that accountant's office, and the school Hunter attended. And I even watched when you took the kids to the park. For someone that was afraid for your life, you sure were oblivious to the world around you."

My hand flew to my mouth as I gasped.

"And that babysitter of yours. She was so stupid. I told her I was your ex, and she let me see the kids several times. I gave her a sob story about how I was so misunderstood and you wouldn't let me see the kids. She and I made my visits our little secret."

"What?" I was stunned and no words would come out. I fidgeted with my red hair nervously.

"That's why Hunter knew who I was when we met at the park the other day. I never told Courtney who I was. She thought I was just a friend of yours." Satisfaction dripped from his voice.

"Oh my god." It was all I could say. I couldn't believe what I was hearing.

Simon took another step toward me.

"You killed Kylie. It was you, wasn't it?" I was afraid to hear the answer.

Simon shrugged his shoulders. "Maybe I did. Maybe I didn't. Does it really matter anyway?"

Simon took another step toward me. I stepped back, bumping into the couch. As I looked down to where my heel hit, Simon lunged at me, and the fight was on. Unfortunately, Simon was larger and stronger than I was. I was no match for him. No matter how hard I fought, I wasn't going to win a one on one with my husband.

Simon slammed my head into the living room wall and I saw stars. As I tried to keep conscious, his hands wrapped around my throat. I swung and clawed, to no avail. My strength was draining away. My head started to swim as I fought off the blackness that was threatening me. I was getting no air at all and knew I would not be conscious much longer.

The moment before I passed out, I heard yelling and some

commotion coming from across the room. I couldn't see anything though. In the deep recesses of my mind, I thought it sounded like Parker. He was there to save me. I didn't even have time to smile as everything went black.

Parker wrapped his right forearm around Simon's neck and yanked him off of Ivy. Simon went sprawling as he was flung into the far wall. Parker was clearly the stronger of the two men.

Parker heard a bone snap as Simon hit the wall. He hit so hard that the sheetrock shattered in response, leaving a two foot diameter hole in its place.

Simon crumbled slowly to the floor. He landed in a heap, unconscious.

Parker took only a moment to study Simon. He wanted to make sure the man was not going to get up. He wasn't. Simon was out cold, and even if he managed to wake up, he would not be moving very easily. His shoulder had snapped upon impact.

Once Parker was satisfied that Simon would not be pouncing on him, he turned to his sister.

"Ivy, Honey, are you all right?" He rubbed her left shoulder gently to rouse her. He then placed his right hand on her neck and felt for a pulse.

PART 4

CHAPTER 1

I began flailing my arms and legs in an attempt to fight off my ex-husband, Simon, who had been strangling me. My throat felt like it was on fire. Yet I could breathe normally. Where's Parker, I thought. I know that I heard him in all the commotion. He was there to save me, I was sure about that.

My eyes flew open in a panic. Realizing that I was outside, lying in grass, with the sun blazing above me, I could see that Simon was no longer there.

"Oh no," I said quietly. "No, no, no, no, no!"

I jumped to my feet. I was wearing blue jeans and a pink sweatshirt. Even still, it was a rather cool day and I shivered as I wrapped my arms in front of me. I scanned the area. It was important that I got my bearings. I needed to know where I was and how old I was this time.

I recognized my surroundings immediately. I found myself again in Bernadette's backyard. I peered off in the distance and could see the water tower was still standing. I knew then that I was no more than 15 years old, as the old water tower had been torn down before my 16th birthday.

I turned when I heard the back sliding door of the house open, expecting to see Mrs. James coming out to investigate. I was not disappointed.

"Ivy? Why are you in my backyard?" Mrs. James asked me.

I held back my shock and remorse. I had lived enough lifetimes to see the woman's daughter, Bernadette, die four different times. No matter how hard I had tried, I just couldn't save the girl.

"What is the date?" I asked.

"It's Halloween. Why?" Mrs. James' eyes narrowed.

"How old is Bernadette? Fifteen?"

"Yes. What is going on Ivy? You're acting strangely."

I did not reply to her question, but asked another. "Is Bernadette here?"

"No, she's down at that burger place where you kids always hang out. Can I help you with something?"

I did not stick around long enough to answer Mrs. James' question. I bolted, running around to the side of the house, and out the side gate. I turned back once to see Mrs. James standing there, watching me. My actions were strange, to say the least, but so was everything I did. I would come up with an explanation for Bernadette's mother later, if I needed to. Right now, she wasn't important. Her daughter was.

Ten minutes later I burst through the front door of the diner. I was panting hard. I certainly wasn't in as good a shape as I usually was at this age. Several of the customers turned my way and went silent, as I made quite a commotion when I entered.

I looked around the room. There was no sign of Bernadette, or her friends, anywhere. I walked up to a table containing several students from the high school.

"Hi."

I tried to catch my breath as all four boys looked up at me and smiled. I ignored them.

"Have any of you seen Bernadette James today?" I raised my eyebrows as I looked around at each boy in front of me.

Ben, was the first one to respond in the negative. He was one of the popular boys in school. We had spoken a few times in one of my previous lives, but we had never been friends. I wasn't cool enough for him and his friends.

The next boy to respond was Steven. He was also popular. And a brain, as the other kids called him. I remembered him well. During our freshman year, we had been lab partners, and had to spend a lot of time together. He was really nice to me. I'm pretty sure he had a crush on me for a while, by the way he always seemed to bump into me at random times. He would start some awkward conversation that never went anywhere. I just wasn't interested. I also had no idea if any of that had happened in this lifetime.

"I saw her earlier today, walking around town with her friends," Steven answered. "But that was hours ago. Why are you looking for her?" By the look on his face, he no longer had that crush on me.

"I just need to talk to her. It's really important. Anyone have any idea where she is?" I looked around at each boy once again.

The last two boys just shook their heads no.

"Okay, if any of you see her, please tell her I'm looking for her. It's a matter of life and death."

I knew that the last sentence was a bit dramatic for four teen boys, but it wasn't a lie. If I didn't find her, Bernadette could very well end up dead. Tonight.

I left the boys staring after me and checked the bathroom. Still no Bernadette. I knew where to look next and turned and ran from the diner. The chatter in the diner wafted even louder as I exited, with me as the main topic of conversation, no doubt.

I took off running again. This time I headed straight for the forest and the sinkhole. I knew that in at least one previous life for sure, Bernadette's body was dumped into that sinkhole. It was the most obvious place to look for her.

I had no idea if it had already happened, or was even going to happen. Things were not always exactly the same, life to life. Once Bernadette was stabbed and left on the side of the road, which was different.

Still, I had to try. I could not imagine going through another lifetime and not giving it my all to save Bernadette.

Once I reached the edge of the forest, I hesitated. That's when I realized that I had come woefully unprepared. I had no back up and no weapons on me. What did I think I was going to be able to accomplish all by myself? I clearly hadn't thought any of this through.

I momentarily considered turning around and going to my house to get Parker. Or at the very least grabbing some sort of weapon. A knife, a pair of scissors, a crowbar perhaps.

Then I dismissed that idea from my mind, as it would take at least 30 minutes to do that and get back to where I was currently standing. And that was if I ran the entire way. Besides, I would have to explain the situation to Parker all over again. Would he even believe me this time? I didn't have the time to explain anyway. So, I forged ahead into the dark forest. It was the middle of the day, but the forest was so thick with trees that a lot of the sunlight was blocked out. It looked like dusk to me, making it very creepy. I had never been a fan of that part of the forest and avoided it whenever I could.

This time was different. I had no choice but to plod along toward the sinkhole. I had to see if Bernadette was there. I had to try to save her...if it wasn't already too late.

It was quite obvious to me that I woke up in Bernadette's backyard, on the day she is supposed to die, for a reason. I didn't know how it happened, but I knew the 'why' part. I had been chosen by someone, or something, to save Bernadette, and that was exactly what I was going to do. If I could. Failure was not an option this time.

When I reached the area with the sinkhole, I saw right away that it was uncovered and had no fence around it. That was a good sign. That meant that no one had fallen in, or been thrown in, during this lifetime. At least as far as I could tell. In my other lives, sometimes the sinkhole had a fence and metal bars on it, to keep people away.

There was no one in the general area that I could see or hear. Maybe I was too late. Or maybe it wasn't going to happen at the sinkhole at all. I had no way of knowing, and would probably not know until after Bernadette's death. I walked around, searching for clues for almost an hour, finding nothing. There didn't seem to be any disturbances on the edge of the sinkhole that would mean someone had been standing there recently. There were no recent footprints around the area either. I surmised that it must have rained rather recently for there to be no obvious footprints.

A twig snapped and I whipped my head around toward the source of the noise.

CHAPTER 2

I ducked and crept as quietly as I could toward a group of boulders about ten yards from my current position. Trying my best not to step on anything that would alert someone to my presence, was easier said than done. The forest was riddled with crunchy leaves and dried pine needles. Each step was noisier than the last. I was sure that I was alerting everyone within miles as to where my current location was.

I crouched down behind a medium sized boulder, picked up a rock, and peered around the side of the boulder. No one could see me there. Of that I was certain. I turned to look behind me, just in case. I peered into the dense forest. All clear.

Before I saw anyone, I heard a muffled sound and the crunch of more than one set of feet walking toward me. I began shaking.

I watched as two people burst forth from the dense forest, into the clearing, near the sinkhole. They were far enough from my current position that they didn't see me.

I recognized the person in front immediately. Bernadette. She was being prodded along by the man behind her. He had something in his hand that he was using to poke her in the back with.

Each time he did, she sped up her pace. I couldn't tell what it was that he was holding.

Bernadette was wearing jeans and a yellow t-shirt with a happy face on it. The irony was not lost on me. She had on no jacket and no shoes. She was walking tenderly and making a muffled painful cry each time she took a step. I looked at the girl's feet and saw why. They were bloody. There were many things on the forest floor that would pierce someone's tender, bare feet. Rocks, twigs, pine needles, and pine cones, just to name a few. No wonder she was crying out in pain.

But the state of Bernadette's feet was not the first thing I noticed. Bernadette had a blindfold over her eyes, and a gag over her mouth. The blindfold and gag were bright red in places, where she had been bleeding. Bernadette was too far away for me to see the source of the blood.

Poor Bernadette was rendered blind and mute by her captor. That explained the muffled sounds I heard as they were approaching. Bernadette was crying behind her gag.

Her pretty, straight blonde hair was a matted mess. It had blood in it, as well as other debris, from the forest probably. And with the blindfold and gag wrapping around her head, her hair was sticking out everywhere. The entire sight of Bernadette at that point in time was not a pretty one.

Unfortunately I could not identify the captor. He had on a black knit ski mask over his head and face. The man was wearing baggy sweats and a sweatshirt as well. Because of all those things, I couldn't see anything that would help me figure out who he was. I couldn't get an age or body type. I did know that he was a white man though. I could see his hands. That was it.

It wasn't much to go on, especially in the town of Red Lake, where we did not have much of a diverse population. I needed more than that.

The man began whispering to Bernadette, clearly disguising his voice. I found that odd due to the fact that they thought they were alone in the forest. Perhaps he didn't want her to know who he was, in case she escaped. That had to be the reason for the ski mask and the whispering. If he was certain that she would be dying that day, why not let her know who he was?

"Move. Hurry up!" the man whispered as loud as he could without actually speaking in his normal voice. They were too far away for me to recognize him.

"Ahhh," Bernadette cried out as she continued to gingerly walk on the debris of the forest floor.

"Shut up."

Bernadette stifled another cry. I couldn't see much of the girl's face, but I could certainly tell that Bernadette was terrified.

"This is all your fault, you know." He was still whispering. "If you had just left her alone, I wouldn't have to do this. But no, you had to become friends with her. I can't have that. She is mine, not yours."

The words were chilling. Not really what he said, but how he said it. It was slow and it was deliberate. Honestly, in the way he was speaking, he could have read a grocery list out loud and it would have given me the creeps.

After I got over the initial surprise regarding the way he was speaking, I wondered who he could be referring to. He was going to kill Bernadette because she was friends with someone? That was a strange reason to kill someone. Actually, when I thought about it, all reasons to kill someone were strange. Murder was not a natural phenomenon. It had to only be done by the deranged. Whether in a fit of rage, jealousy, or just plain evil, murder always had its own reasons.

Bernadette could not respond to the man. She had no way of speaking with the gag on. Instead, Bernadette began to scream from behind her gag. It came out as little more than a muffled cry. I knew that no one but me could hear the desperation in her voice.

She knew she was going to die today. Of course she knew.

There was no way that this man forced her to trudge all the way through the forest, barefoot, blind folded and gagged, just to release her. No, that was never going to happen. I knew it. The man knew it. And most of all, Bernadette knew it.

"I told you to shut up," he continued to whisper. Even though I was a ways away, I could still hear the anger in the man's voice.

Unfortunately for Bernadette, she did not heed the man's warning, and screamed again. I couldn't really blame her. She was terrified. Anyone would be. I was terrified for her.

Then I watched as the man walked up to Bernadette, pulled his fist back, and punched her hard in the face. Due to the blindfold, Bernadette never saw it coming. Therefore she had no time to duck or react in anyway. She experienced the full impact of his fist on her face.

She flew backward and hit the ground with a thud. From my hiding place, which was at least ten yards away, I heard the crunch of Bernadette's nose as the man's fist connected with it. Startled by the sudden chain of events, my natural reflex caused me to jump back. Then my foot caught and I fell over a log that had been lying behind me. An involuntary cry of pain escaped my lips as my hand landed on a sharp pine cone and pierced my palm.

I gasped in horror as I realized how much commotion I must have made.

The man and the girl had to have both heard me. How could they not? The forest had been eerily quiet, causing any sound that I made to echo and reverberate through the trees.

"Stupid, stupid, stupid," I whispered to myself. I wasn't going to help anyone, and was more likely going to get both Bernadette and myself killed if I kept up that kind of stupidity.

They both became deathly quiet, looking for the source of the sound, I'm sure. I couldn't see either one of them from where I landed on the ground, but I didn't dare move a muscle, for fear of being seen. Or heard.

Bernadette, knowing then that someone was nearby, began

screaming. During the cacophony she was creating, I dared to move and peek around the corner of the boulder to see what was happening. I saw that Bernadette was still lying on her back. Though I couldn't see the expression on her face, from the angle that she was at, I could see that she was shaking. Other than that, she wasn't moving at all. The poor girl must have been terrified beyond belief. I know that I would be. I know that I was terrified, even from where I was hiding.

The man must have been satisfied that no one was out in the forest, because he then turned back to Bernadette and knelt beside her. He picked up a rock as his knee hit the ground. He began to slowly lift the rock.

I knew at that moment that if I didn't do something, and quickly, that Bernadette was going to die. Her skull was going to be crushed and her body thrown into the sinkhole. I saw no other outcome.

I couldn't have that on my conscience in another lifetime. I didn't even think about it. No ramifications of my impending actions ran through my mind. I sprung into action. I leapt to my feet and sprinted toward the man and Bernadette. He was so engrossed in what he was about to do, with his hand and that rock high above his head at that point. He never heard my approach and didn't even realize I was about to pounce.

CHAPTER 3

As he lifted the rock high above his head, I leapt onto his back, throwing him off balance and we tumbled onto the ground together. He lost the rock in the ensuing struggle. The two of us were then in a life and death battle for our lives. I was not going to go down easily though. I had been attacked and killed by the best of them, and vowed that it was not going to happen this time.

I clawed, and scratched at the killer. The two of us spent what must have been a full ten minutes rolling around on the forest floor, in a knock down, drag out fight, that I feared would end in someone's death. I silently prayed that it wouldn't be mine.

During our battle, Bernadette was fighting a battle of her own. I couldn't focus on her. But, for a second, I could see out of the corner of my eye that she managed to locate a rock. It was the very same one that almost bashed her head in moments ago. She used that rock and rubbed her face on it to try and remove the blindfold and gag. She succeeded, though her face was scraped up pretty badly in the process. That was the least of her problems though.

Once the blindfold was off, that's when she saw that I was the one that the man was fighting with. I was sure that she didn't have a lot of faith in me being able to overpower a man that clearly outweighed me by 50 or more pounds.

Bernadette decided to keep her mouth shut. I don't think she wanted to distract me. So, she looked around for some way to get the zip ties off. There were rocks, of course, but as hard as she tried, she couldn't get the right angle to cut into the zip ties, as her hands were behind her back. But, there was something she could do to help me.

Bernadette stood up and pulled her right leg back, swinging it as hard as she possibly could, landing a hard square kick right into the man's ribs. He let out a howl that rattled throughout the forest and rolled off of me. It seemed that Bernadette did that just in the nick of time, because I laid there on the ground and did not get up. I was breathing heavily and just didn't have the strength to move.

The man carefully got up, and while he held the left side of his rib cage, he stumbled away from us and out of the clearing, toward the road. Even after our battle, he still had his ski mask on. Bernadette and I both watched him silently as he disappeared into the darkness of the trees. I was still lying face up on the ground, and hadn't moved from my spot.

"Ivy, are you okay?" Bernadette asked as she limped over and gingerly knelt next to me.

I knew that my face was bright red, as I could feel the heat and sweat emanating from it. I could also feel bruises that were probably already beginning to show through.

"I...I...think so," I stuttered out, trying to lift myself to a seated position. "Are you all right?"

I looked over at Bernadette and was shocked at what I saw. The poor girl's face was a mess. She had a broken nose, that was obvious. There was drying blood coming from her nose, down to her chin. She had a deep cut on her forehead that had also been bleeding. That one had been a deep one, and the blood traveled down her face and dripped onto the front of her shirt. There was mostly a void in the blood and dirt on her face where the blind-fold and gag had been. It gave her face an odd striped sort of look. And her feet were another matter entirely. She was barefoot, which was something I had noticed when she walked in with the killer. After that long walk in, and the ensuing fight and kick to his ribs, her feet were a bloodied, bruised mess. And with debris from the forest floor matted to her feet with the dried blood, the sight was just indescribable. I looked back up and into Bernadette's eyes.

Bernadette saw the look on my face as I studied her, and that's when it all hit her. Bernadette began to shudder from deep inside somewhere and it radiated out of her body. By the time she felt its full force, she was sobbing uncontrollably. Her hands were still tied behind her back, so her hysteric cries went unmuffled. Her cries and screams echoed throughout the forest.

I couldn't move very fast, but I got up and put my arms around Bernadette. We cried together. Though we hadn't been friends for several years, none of that mattered anymore. At that moment, we were two lost souls...injured and devastated by the circumstances that we had found ourselves in.

Both of us knew in our hearts that we had come very close to not making it out of there alive.

"Let me...see if I can...find something to get those ties...off." I did my best to take deep breaths as I was trying to compose myself.

I found a sharp rock and used it to cut the ties off of Bernadette, who immediately began rubbing her wrists. She cried out as her hands burned when the blood rushed into them.

"Come on." I helped Bernadette stand up. "We need to get out of here in case he comes back."

Bernadette and I decided to take an alternate route out of the forest, though we seriously doubted he would come back. At the very least he had a few broken ribs. There were more injuries too. I was sure of it. The two of us had been fighting for our lives. He was scratched, clawed, and bitten. All by me. It was a pretty safe bet that he was in no shape to come back and take both of us on that day.

We were both thankful for that, as neither of us had the strength for another fight.

As we veered off the path, and headed deeper into the forest, we held tight to each other. Partly for comfort, and partly for safety. We were both shaking so hard, it was astonishing that we could walk at all.

Poor Bernadette was stifling cry after cry with each step she took. Her bloodied, bare feet, were no match for the harsh forest floor.

"Wait, stop," I told her. She eagerly complied, relishing the momentary release of the pain radiating from the soles of her feet.

I tugged at the lower half of my shirt and tore it into two long strips. I was left with only half of a shirt, but I didn't care. This wasn't about me.

"Sit down," I ordered.

Bernadette could see what my plan was and sat down quickly. I knelt down in front of her and lifted her right foot. I balanced it on my knee as I went to work wrapping the cloth around her foot. I tied it off and tugged at it to test how well it would hold. I then duplicated the effort on her left foot.

"That should work, as well as can be expected at least," I told her as I took her hand and pulled Bernadette to a standing position.

She lifted both feet and walked around a bit to test it out.

"This should work fine. Thank you Ivy," she smiled my way.

We started walking again toward the road. Wincing occasionally, it was obvious that Bernadette was still in pain, which was expected. My torn shirt was not a miracle cure. But at least it helped.

We both ducked and cried out as a bird swooped and

squawked at us overhead. The damn thing apparently didn't like the fact that we were in his territory.

"Do you know the way out?" Bernadette asked me. "I've never been this way before."

We stopped and looked around at our surroundings.

"Sort of. I mean, I've never been this way either. But we are walking parallel to the path. At least I think we are."

I did my best to sound like I knew what I was talking about. Bernadette was traumatized. Really we both were. But she was having a harder time with it all then I was. My arm was starting to ache from how tightly she was hanging onto it. I was beginning to lose the feeling in it and had to shake myself loose from her grip. It was all I could do to not cry out from the pins and needles I felt once she let go.

"Come on, let's keep walking," I told her, as I took her hand and led her out the way we had come. She followed dutifully.

Snap!

We came to an immediate stop and both turned toward the sound.

"What was that?!" Bernadette said louder than I would have liked.

"Shhh." I held my index finger up to my lips. She nodded her compliance.

We stood, listening to the sounds of the forest for several minutes. The sound we had heard was not repeated.

"It was probably just a deer or something," I told her.

"Or something? Like what?" Bernadette's eyes widened as big as saucers, as she squeezed my hand even tighter.

"I…just mean…I'm sure it was a deer," I stuttered out in my attempt to calm the girl down. "Come on. If we keep stopping for every little noise, we are never going to get out of here."

I did not have to tell Bernadette twice. She started darting through the trees, pulling me along with her. There was no way she was going to let go of my hand. It seemed that she forgot all about her feet. Fear overcame the pain that day.

Thirty minutes later, we reached the edge of the forest. As we were walking alongside the road that led out of the forest, a car pulled over. After the ordeal that we had been through, we were as jumpy as one could expect us to be.

"Oh my god, it's him!" Bernadette yelled and started to take off running.

I dug in my heels and pulled her back to reality.

"Ow, why did you do that?" she asked me, rubbing the arm that I had just yanked to a stop. "We've got to get out of here."

I recognized the car immediately. I belonged to Jean, the woman who lived next door to me.

"No, it's fine. I know her," I told Bernadette. "She'll give us a ride."

We both walked up to the car, bent over, and peered into the passenger side window. It was not Jean, as I expected. It was Carter. He was technically not allowed to drive, due to only being 15 years old, but his aunt let him drive to run errands for her all the time. So I wasn't technically surprised to find him in the driver's seat.

The sheriff was well aware of Carter's driving. He had told Carter that he would be keeping an eye on him and put a stop to it the second he caught the boy speeding or running a stop sign. It was the kind of thing that only happened in a small town.

"Oh my god, what happened to the two of you?"

Carter climbed out of the car, ran around to the passenger side, and opened the back door for us to climb in.

"I'll tell you later. Take us to the hospital," I directed.

He drove there as fast as he could. Be damned the speed limit...and the sheriff.

CHAPTER 4

Surprisingly, Bernadette and I escaped the serial killer with only scrapes and bruises, for the most part. Bernadette did need stitches on her forehead. Her feet needed treatment too. They applied some medicine, and wrapped them in bandages. It was hard for her to walk, but she would be just fine.

The worst was her broken nose, which resulted in two black eyes, but it didn't need any treatment from the doctors. She just had to be very careful and it would heal on its own.

All the parents showed up to the hospital and we both gave our statements to the sheriff. Due to the ski mask, and the fact that he never said anything out loud, only whispered, neither of us could identify him.

"Bernadette, please explain to us exactly what happened. How you were abducted, up to the point that you arrived here at the hospital," Sheriff Hayes directed. "And don't leave any detail out, no matter how trivial you think it might be."

Bernadette nodded. Her mother reached over and took Bernadette's hand in her own as her daughter began to tell the story of her ordeal.

"Well...I was alone at home, just watching TV. I wasn't feeling good, so I didn't go out with my friends. Ow." Bernadette reached up with her free hand and touched her nose tenderly. "This thing really hurts."

She looked around at all of us standing near her, waiting for her story, and continued. "I never heard him come in. I still don't know how he got into the house. I just know that he walked up behind the couch and grabbed me, pulling me over the back of it. Then he threw me on the ground, and put zip ties around my wrists, so I couldn't fight him, I guess. I screamed, but no one was around to hear, so it obviously didn't do me any good. I couldn't tell who he was, because he had a ski mask on and never said a word to me. But he put a blindfold over my eyes anyway. And a gag over my mouth. Can I have some water?"

Her mother released Bernadette's hand and reached over to the pitcher and poured some water into the plastic cup on the tray next to the bed. She handed the cup to her daughter, and Bernadette thanked her, while we all watched, and waited patiently.

"Um, then he dragged me to the garage and forced me into the trunk of a car. I never saw the car. I don't know if it was his or not." She looked to her parents and the sheriff for confirmation, but no one responded.

"Before he shut the trunk, he tied zip ties around my ankles so tight that they hurt." Her voice was coming in shuddering breaths then, as she tried to hold back her sobs. "I was terrified," she admitted.

"Of course you were, Dear." Her mother comforted her by placing her hand on Bernadette's back and rubbing it gently. Bernadette smiled up at her, gratitude showing in her face.

I had never seen Bernadette look so vulnerable. She was usually the leader of the pack. The bully. The one everyone feared. Not that I would wish what happened to her on anyone, but perhaps this experience would soften her a bit.

"Go on," Sheriff Hayes prompted.

Bernadette looked up at him and continued. "We were only in the car for maybe five or ten minutes, so I knew that we hadn't gone far. Then when he opened the trunk, the sun blinded me, even from behind the blindfold. I tried pleading with him, but every word came out a gargled mess, because of the gag. All I could do was whimper."

"Oh Sweetheart," her father spoke for the first time. "We should have been home with you."

"No Daddy, it's not your fault. You can't be with me 24 hours a day." The look on her face when she looked at her father was admiration. I could come to no other conclusion.

"Please continue." The sheriff was doing his best to keep her story moving forward.

"Okay okay," Bernadette responded. "When we got to the forest, I figured it was the forest because of the smell and because I was barefoot and kept stepping on pine needles and stuff. Then when I got my blindfold off later, I knew for sure where we were. Anyway, when we got to the forest, he yanked me roughly out of the trunk and cut the zip ties from my ankles, so I could walk. I remember that my feet began to tingle as the blood rushed into them."

She paused and pulled some tissues from the table next to her. We waited as she wiped the tears from her face.

"I need to go to the bathroom."

No one said anything as Bernadette got up and hobbled toward the bathroom that was in her private room. She wasn't even staying the night, but I surmised that her parents got her a private room while she was there just because they could.

When she returned, Bernadette continued her story.

"At one point, I guess I wasn't walking fast enough for him, and he shoved me. I suddenly went forward and lost my balance. Since my hands were still zip tied, I had no arms to put out in front of me and cushion my fall. When I landed, my face hit some-

THE MANY LIVES OF IVY WELLS

thing hard and sharp. I'm assuming it was a rock. At least that's what I think it was. I know it hurt like hell."

Bernadette looked up at her parents and the sheriff to gauge their reactions to what she had just said. No one even flinched. I guess that her cursing was the least of their problems right now.

"Then I could feel the blood dripping down my face, and it was being soaked up by the blindfold and gag I had on."

"Did he say anything to you at all? Or was he silent the entire time?" Sheriff Hayes asked her.

"No...I don't...oh wait, yes he did say something," Bernadette replied tentatively. "He said that it was all my fault and I should have just left her alone and not become friends with her. And... that she was his, not mine. Or something like that anyway."

"What do you think he meant by that? And who was he talking about?" the sheriff asked her.

"I honestly have no idea. He didn't tell me," Bernadette answered.

"And then what happened?" he asked her, moving the story along.

Bernadette and I told the sheriff the rest of what happened, leaving nothing out. He took a lot of notes and said he would get to work on finding the perpetrator.

I followed Sheriff Hayes out the exit of the hospital and stopped him in the parking lot.

"Sheriff. Excuse me."

He stopped and turned around. "Yes? Do you have something to add?" he asked me.

"Yes. I didn't want to say this in front of everyone in there, but I need to tell you something. This won't be the last time this man is going to try to kill someone. He will do it again. And he may succeed next time."

I knew it was risky telling him that, but what else could I do? The sheriff needed to know that this man was a continuing danger. This wasn't just a one time thing for him. I watched the sheriff for a reaction.

"And how would you know that?" He lowered his head and looked up at me. I could see doubt written all over his face.

Yeah, that was a good question. How was I going to possibly explain how I knew what the killer planed to do? *Well, Sheriff, I have been living my life over and over. Time traveling. You know?* No, that would not go over well at all. Oh boy, I hadn't thought this through at all.

"I just...I just mean that...well, it seems unlikely that he would do this just once. We need to stop him before he hurts someone else." Smooth Ivy, I thought. You just stuttered your way through that one.

"We," he made the all inclusive gesture with his hand, "don't need to do anything. I will take care of it. You go home now." With that, he turned and walked to his car.

The next day, I walked over to Carter's house to thank him for rescuing us on the side of the road.

"I'm sorry, Ivy," his aunt told me, when she returned from Carter's bedroom. "He isn't feeling well. He said he'll call you in a few days. I heard about what happened to you. Are you all right Dear?"

"Yeah, I'll be fine. Just banged up. Please tell Carter I want to see him when he's feeling better."

"Damnit!" the killer exclaimed, as he put the icepack on his ribs.

His broken ribs were the most painful thing he had ever experienced. He had experienced a lot of injuries in his life, but this was far and beyond, the worst.

"I'm gonna kill that bitch for kicking me!"

He searched the basement for bandages and tape to wrap around his rib cage. He needed something to hold his ribs in place while they healed. He certainly couldn't go to the hospital. That was a dangerous place for a man such as himself. The doctors would ask him questions that he couldn't answer, questions about how his ribs got broken. Questions about his scratches. Questions about his bruises. No, he couldn't do that.

He opened the third drawer below the work bench and found some medical bandages left over from a previous injury. He winced as he slowly and carefully wrapped them around his torso, securing them with duct tape. Not the most efficient way of doing it, but it would work. He didn't want to be caught on some security camera at the pharmacy buying any medical supplies. He was much too smart for that. This wasn't his first injury, and certainly wouldn't be his last.

The man didn't know why he killed. He just knew that he had to. There was something deep inside of him, something that yearned for the kill. He smiled just thinking about it. Boys, girls, men, women, none of it mattered. He just needed the feeling of complete power he had over someone. And the ability to look them in the eyes, to see the fear in them, as they lay dying, was indescribable.

Ivy Wells was his ultimate target. Not to kill, but to hurt. Hurt emotionally, hurt deep in her soul. But to kill her? No, he had no desire to do that. He would though, without hesitation, if it came to that. He thought that was exactly what was going to happen in the forest that day. When Ivy attacked him, he would have fought to the death, if that's what it took to protect his identity. Once she or Bernadette saw his face, his identity known to them, it would be all over. He would not be able to hide from them, or anyone. And he would have had to kill her.

Ivy's friends were his main targets. It made him all warm and gooey inside to see her suffer when one of her friends was hurt.

He reached up to the wall and ran his hand down the photograph of Ivy's face, caressing it gently. He had taken the photograph himself, downtown, while she was eating lunch with some friends.

Ivy knew him. She just didn't know that she knew him. He hated that she ignored him, reaching out to her friends instead of him. His hatred for her radiated with time. It was an all encompassing hatred.

Anytime he and Ivy came across each other, he did his best to play the nice guy. He did not want to set off any alarms in her head. He felt that he had succeeded thus far. She had no idea of the true monster inside of him.

The next day, I walked over to Carter's house again.

"I'm sorry, but he's out," Carter's Aunt Jean told me. "You know, it was his mother's birthday yesterday, and he's been a bit out of sorts, spending a lot of time in the basement. I think he just wants to be alone."

"Oh, I'm sorry. He never did tell me how his parents died." It was my subtle way of trying to get information.

"Really? In all these years?" His aunt walked out the door and sat down on the step of the front porch, and patted the spot on the step next to her. "You know, you are the best friend Carter has ever had, and you deserve to know."

I sat down next to her.

"His mother was my sister, Candace." Jean looked off into the distance, bringing up a childhood memory that only she and Candace shared. She smiled to herself.

I waited.

"Not long before Carter came here to live with me, he was only 9 years old at the time. You remember that, right?"

I nodded.

"Right, of course you would. You two have been best friends ever since. Anyway, not long before he came to live with me, his house caught fire. They were all home. My sister and her husband, CJ, were both killed. Thankfully Carter was spared. He was able to get out of the house. His parents were in their room upstairs and were trapped. It was too late by the time the fire-fighters and paramedics arrived."

I put my hand on top of Jean's hand, in a comforting manner. "I'm so sorry. I didn't know. He just told me they died and he had to come live with you. That's all he ever said."

"There's actually more to the story," Jean continued.

I watched as she hesitated. I was sure that she was trying to decide whether to tell me the rest or not.

"The investigators suspected it was arson. And they suspected that it was Carter."

My hand flew to my mouth.

"He was only 9 years old!" I exclaimed. "How could they think that?"

"The reason that they suspected him was that it appeared the fire started in multiple spots, not just on the stove, or something common like that. And, the spots were all at the bottom and up the stairway. This meant that Candace and CJ couldn't get down the stairs. There was a concrete patio outside their bedroom window. I have to assume they didn't jump due to the fact that landing on concrete would surely have been fatal. Perhaps they just decided to wait for help to arrive. I really don't know. All I do know for sure is that my sister and her husband died that day. Carter had nowhere else to go, so I took him in." Jean looked over and gave me a sad sort of smile. "He can be a bit odd, I know, but I have a hard time believing that he would kill his parents on purpose."

I did not respond. I sat quietly and listened to the story.

"Due to his age, there were never any charges filed, and they just dropped it. What were they going to do? Lock up a 9 year old?

When I spoke with the investigators, they said that he was probably playing with matches, and didn't realize the devastating outcome of his actions. But honestly, we will never know. Carter won't talk to me about it."

"That explains why he never told me. Thank you for this. It really does explain a lot about his behavior. I can also understand why he never wanted to talk about it. I just thought his parents had a car accident or something. I just had no idea," I told her.

"He has a crush on you, you know."

"I know."

CHAPTER 5

Over the next few months, I felt that someone was watching me. I never could pinpoint who, or where, but I could feel it in my core. It made me a nervous wreck, always pausing when I walked into my empty house, listening for the smallest hint of an intruder. I would even go so far as to check in every closet and under every bed for that person I knew was going to kill me in my sleep. I never found anyone, or even any evidence that anyone had been in my house. That didn't make me feel any better though.

One Friday evening I headed out to walk over to Josephine's house to hang out for the night. I hated going out alone, and walking in the dusk alone, but no one was available to drive me. Every noise made me jump. I arrived at Josephine's house in half the time it usually took, because I ran most of the way.

"Why are you breathing hard? Are you all right?" Josephine asked me as she opened the front door.

I hurried inside. "Because I ran. Close the door, will you?"

I peered out into the darkness one last time as Josephine closed the door. She then turned and tilted her head at me.

"What is going on with you? You've been so jumpy lately."

"I think someone was following me." I leaned my back against

the closed front door, and shut my eyes. It was my way of trying
to calm back down.

"Who would be following you?" Josephine asked.

I opened my eyes to look directly into hers as I spoke. It was
important for me to see her reaction.

"I don't know for sure, but I think it's the killer. You know, the
one that attacked Bernadette and me," I replied.

"Weren't you the one that attacked him? That's the story I
heard," Josephine blurted out.

"Well…yeah, technically I was the one that jumped on him. But
you know what I mean." I gave her a look, to make sure she knew
I meant business.

With just the slightest shake of her head, the look on my
friend's face told me all I needed to know. She thought I was
losing my mind. You know, maybe I was.

"Why do you think he would be following you? I mean, he
hasn't been heard from in months. So…why now?" She narrowed
her eyes at me.

"Okay, but you can't tell anyone. Got it?" I gave her the wide
eyed 'I really mean it' look.

"Tell anyone what?" Josephine asked. "Ivy, if this is one of
your…"

I interrupted her mid-sentence, by taking her hand and pulling
her out of the foyer. "Come on, let's get go something to drink and
I'll explain."

Though it was Josephine's house, I led the way to the kitchen.
She followed close behind. We poured ourselves some sodas and
settled onto the living room couch. We both crossed our legs and
turned, facing each other. This was going to be a serious conversation and needed the full attention of both of us.

I went on to tell my friend all about the fact that I was living
and dying multiple times. I also told Josephine about the serial
killer I had been trying to stop. I left nothing out, including my
suspicions about Simon and Carter. Josephine sat quietly until I

finished. There was a long pause where I expected her to respond
to my story.

"Well?" I prompted.

"Are you out of your mind?" Josephine asked me calmly, her
eyes rolling heavenward.

"No, really. This is serious," I responded. "In fact, in my
previous lives you were one of the Red Lake Slasher's victims."

"The Red Lake Slasher? How come I've never heard of him?"
Josephine asked.

"Because he hasn't killed anyone yet...in this lifetime at least.
As far as I know of anyway. Later, people will start calling him by
that name."

I knew the whole thing sounded ridiculous to anyone not
living with my reality. But I had to try. She believed me when I
told her before. Maybe she would again. I desperately hoped so...

Josephine got up and walked to the kitchen, with me following
closely.

"Please believe me. You did before," I told her.

Josephine had just opened the refrigerator and stopped
abruptly, turning toward me. "What do you mean by that? Before?
Before when?"

"I mean that when I told you all of this last time, you believed
me. I want you to believe me again." I chewed on my lower lip.

"You are telling me that we've had this conversation before?"
Josephine continued standing with the refrigerator door wide
open.

"Yes?" I responded.

"Was that a question?" Josephine asked me. "Are you not sure?
Really, Ivy, this whole thing sounds like you are making it up as
you go along."

"Look, I know how it sounds. I probably wouldn't believe me
either. But it's all the truth. I swear it." I made the universal 'cross
my heart' gesture. I had a bad feeling.

"Like I told you, it's the same person that attacked me and

Bernadette by the sinkhole a few months ago," I added. "You know that happened. You saw Bernadette. And the story in the newspaper."

"Of course I believe you two were attacked. It's the re-living your lives thing that I just can't wrap my head around," Josephine admitted.

"Please just think about it. You know I wouldn't lie to you," I pleaded.

Josephine turned back toward the refrigerator, reached in and chose another cola. "You want one?" she asked me without turning to look at me.

"Sure."

Colas in hand, the two of us climbed back onto the sofa and crossed our legs as we sat down.

"You want to watch a movie?" Josephine asked.

It was clear to me that there was no point in continuing the conversation. Josephine was not buying my story.

"Sure."

I wrestled with the idea of talking to Josephine about Carter. I knew that it wasn't my business to be telling people what his aunt told me. It was Carter's story to tell. But, I needed to talk to someone. The whole story sounded fishy to me.

Sure, it was entirely possible that a 9 year old could have accidentally started a fire in his home, killing his parents. It wouldn't be the first time that ever happened, I was sure. But, the circumstances that Jean described, and the fact that he got out, but his parents did not, was strange. Plus, Carter had never told me about it in all the years I had known him. The two of us talked about everything. 'Two guppies in a pond,' my father used to call us. Was it possible that Carter was hiding something? I needed to find out.

And, if he did kill his parents on purpose, would it be out of the realm of possibility that he could also kill others? Perhaps it was time to do some investigating.

I couldn't concentrate on the movie. My mind was on other things. Good thing there was no quiz afterward, because I barely remembered the plot. After the movie was over, I said good-bye to Josephine and went home. I decided not to say anything to her about Carter. Maybe later. I saw no point in piling on another ridiculous story. She probably wouldn't believe me anyway.

Once home, I sat down at the computer in our living room. It was the one that everyone in the family shared. My parents refused to pay for an individual one for each of us. And, since I didn't have a job to buy my own computer, this was the one I was stuck with. I started by searching Carter's name, the town he lived in, and the words 'house fire.' Quite a few articles came up on the screen. I chose the first one and began to read.

The article just told the story of the fire, and of his parents dying, and that Carter survived. It said that arson was suspected, but could never be proven. The article did not say that Carter was a suspect. My theory is that due to the fact that Carter was a minor at the time, they were very careful in the wording of the article. No one wanted to point fingers at anyone.

I spent the next two hours searching and reading articles and found no more details than what I already knew. I finished my digging around and decided to pay Carter a visit.

CHAPTER 6

It was late April and the time was closing in on when Josephine was supposed to be killed. If my history held up anyway. The town was all in a buzz about the upcoming water tower razing. I had a plan in place to make sure that Josephine never left my sight that day. I had invited Josephine to the beach. We would hang out all day in the sun, and there would be no way the killer could get a hold of her. I would make sure of that. My brother even agreed to drive us.

"Hey Carter, how are you?" I asked when he answered the door. "I've barely seen you these last few months."

The look he gave me was unnerving. For a moment, he just stared straight at me. Unblinking. It almost felt like he was staring right through me. The hairs on my arms stood up.

"Carter?" I tried to break the silence.

"I know. Sorry. I guess I've just been busy," he finally responded. "Come on in."

The two of us walked through the living room, with its brown shag carpet and dark furniture, then through the kitchen. The entire house looked like it hadn't been updated since 1975, especially the kitchen. It had an avocado green refrigerator, dishwasher, and even the stove was that horrible color. What in the world were they thinking in those days? This is what passed for being cool back then? Or the 'in thing,' or whatever terminology they used?

I smiled to myself whenever I saw his kitchen. Carter opened the green refrigerator as we passed by and grabbed two colas.

Carter led the way out the back sliding door and we sat down at the patio table with the red umbrella. It was an unusually warm and bright day for April, and we were both thankful for the red umbrella.

"So, are you going to the water tower thing on Friday?" Carter asked, popping open the can and taking a draw.

"No, I'm actually not." I opened my cola also. It made the usual sucking sound as the air rushed into it. "Josie and I are going to the beach. The water tower being torn down is not that big of a deal. Been there done that."

"What do you mean by that?" Carter furrowed his brows.

"Oh…nothing. Just a joke." I needed to think before I spoke. "I just mean it's probably not that interesting. Someone will video it anyway. The beach will be much more fun. What about you? You going to be there?" I asked.

Carter shrugged his shoulders. "Yeah, I guess. It's probably the most interesting thing going on in this town all month."

"Yeah maybe," I agreed. Then, changing the subject, "Um, there's something I want to talk to you about," I began. "Something that's been bothering me and I hope you don't mind talking about it."

"What's that?" Carter asked.

"It's about your parents. I was wondering if you wouldn't mind telling me what happened to them?" I asked him.

"Why? What difference does it make now?" Carter's voice took on an edge to it that made me a bit nervous.

"You've just never talked about it. Or about them. Please tell me what happened," I begged.

"I think you already know. Don't you?" Carter narrowed his eyes at me.

"I...uh...well..."

"Yeah, that's what I thought. How did you find out? My aunt? The internet?"

I felt like he was grilling me at that point.

"I'm sorry. I didn't know it would bother you so much." I lowered my eyes and stared at the cola can on the table.

"No." Carter reached for my hand in a comforting manner. "I'm sorry. It's just a really sore subject for me. I lost both my parents that day and it seems like I've been getting grilled about it ever since. My aunt still wants to talk about it. I can't blame her. It was her sister that died. And I still get calls sometimes from the investigators. It seems they just don't want to let it go."

"Oh, I'm sorry. That must be really hard for you." I pulled my hand from his and patted him gently on the arm. "That's odd that they would still be investigating the fire after all this time," I added.

Carter shrugged his shoulders again. "I know what you want to ask me. You want to know if I started that fire on purpose. Right?" He looked at me with those deadpan eyes of his.

"No...I..." I had quite the way with words.

"It's okay. I'm used to it. That's what everyone wants to know."

His voice sounded sad. Or maybe it was resignation that crept through in his voice. He probably knew that he would never be free from the case, whether it was ever closed or not.

I nodded ever so slightly. There was no way I could ask my friend that question, even though that was why I was there. It was something I needed to know. I had to find out if Carter was capable of killing someone. And if he could kill his own parents, then it seemed quite likely that he could kill others.

"I was playing with matches. That part was true. My father smoked and I always thought it was really cool. I wanted to try it. They had gone to bed, and once they did, they never got up until morning. So I figured I could try it in the living room and they would never know. Remember, I was only 9 years old, and stupid, like 9 year olds are." Carter gave me a little embarrassed smile.

"Yeah, I remember being that age," I added. "You have no concept of the consequences of your actions."

"Yep. Anyway, I didn't want my parents to smell the cigarette smoke, so I lit a few candles and put them on the stairs. I figured the scent would mask the smoke. I sat down on the couch and lit up a match. It took a few tries with the matches before I got the hang of it, but once I did, I got the cigarette going. One puff and I was hacking away. That caused me to knock over the candle that was on the coffee table in front of me."

"Oh no," I said.

"Yeah, the wax spilled across the table and onto the carpet, catching it on fire. Then I panicked. All I could think of was that I was going to get into a lot of trouble for that fire. It never crossed my mind that the entire house could burn down, and what the final outcome of it all would be. Then I ran to blow out the candles on the stairs. I ran to the top of the stairs first to see if my parents had noticed anything. They were still in their room, and I heard nothing from them. So, I went to blow out the candle at the top of the stairs and in my haste, I kicked it by accident. It got knocked over and spilled down the stairs."

I gasped.

"Basically at that point it was all over. Everything went up in flames. I ran down the stairs, the fire wasn't huge yet at that point. I went to the kitchen to get a bucket of water, but it was too late. The fire was too much for me to handle. I ran outside and hid. I was terrified. I didn't even try to warn my parents."

Carter lowered his head, putting his elbows on his knees, and his hands over his face. I could see the shuddering movements in his shoulders as he began to cry.

"Carter." I put my hand on his shoulder in a comforting gesture. "I'm really sorry that I brought all of this up."

"No, it's okay," he told me as he took a deep breath and calmed himself down. "I've wanted to tell you for a long time, but didn't know how to bring it up. I'm glad you know."

"Me too."

The two of us sat there in silence for a bit, before I brought up another topic. One that I hoped would not upset Carter even further.

"Um, I wanted to ask you something. Do you know where Simon has been? I haven't seen him in ages."

"Simon? Who is Simon?...Oh, you mean the guy that was seeing Bernadette a while back?"

"He was?" I didn't expect that.

I had been afraid to ask anyone about Simon since I had been in this lifetime. It just seemed that so much had happened, and I was so worried about Bernadette and Josephine, that I had almost forgotten about Simon. It was now time to find out how he fit into all of this.

"Yeah, then right after you and Bernadette were attacked that day by the sinkhole, I heard that he moved out of town. Why do you ask? Did you even know him?" Carter looked at me with a tilt of his head.

"Not really, I guess. Did I ever date him?" I asked.

"What? You don't know if you dated Simon or not? How would you not know?" Carter gave me a strange look.

"I know it's a stupid question. I've been having some memory problems since that day. Maybe I got hit in the head during the struggle." It was the best I could come up with. "Do you know if I dated him or not?"

Carter paused, looking at me strangely. I wasn't sure if he believed me or not.

"I don't think you ever dated him. You never mentioned it to me if you did. Do you want to date him?"

"God no." I did not expand on that answer.

CHAPTER 7

I wondered about Simon. It was very strange that he would leave town right after the attack. Perhaps he needed to hide his injuries. I was sure that Bernadette had broken some of his ribs when she kicked him as hard as she did. If Simon did turn out to be the killer, it might be a good sign that he is not around now to kill Josephine. I wasn't taking any chances though.

On the morning of the water tower demolition party, Parker and I whisked Josephine out of town. I had previously tried telling Josephine about her many lives, but was met with disbelief. I decided to let it go. No need to stir that pot.

Our day at the beach crawled by, and was completely uneventful. I was thankful for that. By the time the sun started dipping down below the horizon, Josephine suggested that we leave. She was beginning to turn red. The three of us packed up and headed home.

It was after dark by the time we arrived back in Red Lake. Parker stopped at Josephine's house first and dropped her off. He and I watched her go into the house before we drove away. I felt that I did all that I could to stop her from being killed. Nothing would happen to her now that she was safe inside her house, along with her parents. I desperately hoped that was the case anyway.

I was a nervous wreck all night. Lying there wide awake, I was imagining all the horrible things that could be happening to Josephine. But, I also knew in my rational brain that it was all unlikely. She was home, safely in her own bed. Or at least I hoped so. It was the longest night of my life.

"Hi. Can I talk to Josie?" I asked the sleepy sounding voice that answered the phone the next morning.

"Ivy?" It was Josephine's mother and she didn't sound very happy. "Why are you calling so early?" She must have peered out the front window then. "The sun is not even up yet."

"I know. I'm sorry. It's really important. Can I talk to her?" I insisted.

"I'm not going to wake her up this early. I'll have her call you when she gets up."

With that, Josephine's mother hung up the phone. I was devastated. I hadn't slept all night, due to my intense worry about Josie. Now I had to wait even longer. I wondered how long I should wait before I called back.

For the next two hours I paced the living room. I didn't eat. I didn't drink. I didn't sleep. I paced. What if Josie wasn't even in her own bed sleeping? She could have been kidnapped in the middle of the night, for all anyone knew. Did her parents even care? I'm sure that they didn't bother checking her room when I called. Was she dead? Was she alive? I thought I was going to lose my mind with worry.

"Good grief, I'm being completely irrational," I said out loud, as I walked to the kitchen and pulled out a frying pan. Maybe some eggs and toast would calm me down.

Everyone in the house was still asleep when the toast popped up, just as my eggs were done frying. I buttered the toast, poured myself a glass of milk, and sat down at the dining table to eat. I could have really used some company right about then. As I sat there, lost in thought, something caught the very corner of my peripheral vision. I couldn't tell what it was and turned my head toward the window to get a better view. There was nothing there.

I thought I heard footsteps running along the side of the house, toward the front yard. No, I must be imagining it. Who would be in my backyard so early in the morning? In fact, who would be sneaking around in my backyard at any time of the day?

I stood up to get a better look, when I realized that my legs were shaking and unsteady. Placing one hand on the table, and the other on the chair I had been sitting in, while I steadied myself, helped a bit. I had to hurry though, if I was going to see who was outside the window.

Before I reached the window, though, I heard the unmistakable sound of the side gate clicking shut. That put me on the move. I ran toward the front of the house and yanked the front door open, just in time to see the back of someone running down the street. The person looked to be a male, wearing jeans and a sweatshirt, but I couldn't see his face. He had on a baseball cap, so I couldn't even see the color of his hair.

I stood shaking in the cool early morning air, watching the street where the man had just disappeared around a corner. What I was looking for, I wasn't sure. I was positive he wouldn't be back. The man had been seen and he knew it. After several minutes, I turned and walked back inside the warm house.

I contemplated calling the sheriff, but what would I say? I didn't see who it was and had no proof anyone was even there. He already thought I was crazy. No, I wouldn't call him this time. But if the man came back, I would report him.

Simon was the first person to come to mind. It kind of looked like him from the back, but it also could have been a thousand other men. I knew that I needed to do some research to find out where Simon was. And what if something did happen to Josephine last night? Was this man involved or was it an odd coincidence? I didn't even know if anything had happened to my friend or not, and was already trying to solve the crime in my mind.

Doing my best to put the man out of my mind, I decided that I was not going to wait one more minute to find out if Josie was okay or not.

"Hi. I'm sorry to call back so early, but it is really important that I talk to Josie," I said to Josephine's mother when she answered the phone for the second time that morning.

"All right, Ivy, I'll go get her." Josephine's mother sounded irritated. Of course she was. I could hear the phone's receiver as it made a clunking noise when it connected with the wooden table that the phone lived on.

It seemed like an eternity before someone finally picked up the phone. I held my breath, expecting the news that Josephine was not there and her bed had not been slept in.

"What is so important Ivy, that you had to get me up so early on a weekend?"

I let out a deep breath. I hadn't realized that I was also shaking.

"Thank god, Josie. I was so worried about you." I did my best not to cry tears of joy.

"Why? What's going on?" Josephine asked through a sleepy sounding voice.

"Well…remember when I told you about the Red Lake Slasher?" I was nervous even bringing him up to Josephine.

"Yeah, what about him?"

"Yesterday was the day he was supposed to kill you. At least he did in my other lives," I tried to explain.

"Really? Then why didn't he kill me?" Josephine didn't sound convinced at all.

"Because Parker and I were with you all day yesterday. The killer couldn't have gotten to you. But, I didn't know if it might've happened last night instead. So I was really worried about you. I just called to make sure you were okay."

I could almost hear Josephine's eyes rolling and her head shaking in disbelief over the phone line.

"Well, as you can tell, I'm fine. Can I go back to sleep now?"

"Yeah, sorry," I responded.

Josephine hung up the phone.

Though Josephine was clearly irritated with me for calling so early, I was happy. I had saved my friend from the clutches of the killer. At least I thought I had.

So far, this lifetime had been a success. I saved Bernadette months ago from the Slasher, and now Josephine. Unfortunately, a voice nagged me in the back of my mind. Was it all over? Was there any reason why he couldn't just come after them at a later date? I had no way of knowing. And I certainly couldn't watch the two of them every single minute of every single day. I just had to go on faith that I had done my duty, and saved the girls. And that would be that.

But, because of all the unanswered questions, I made the decision to find Simon anyway. I needed to talk to him and put my mind to rest about his possible guilt. I still couldn't figure out the 'why' part though.

It took a few days, but I found out that Simon was living in a nearby town. Apparently his father got a job there and they moved, explaining why Simon abruptly left town after the incident with Bernadette in the woods. It still didn't clear him of anything, but at least it was a good explanation.

"Um, hi." Simon gave me an odd look when he answered the door a few days later, and I was standing there. "I didn't expect to see you here," he told me.

"I know. I was wondering if we could talk." I gave him my best smile. I needed to get him to open up to me.

"About what?"

"Just stuff going on in Red Lake. Do you have some time right now?" I asked him.

"Yeah, I guess. No one's home, come on in."

Simon stepped aside to allow me to walk in. I hesitated.

"You know, can we just sit out here and talk?" I was a bit terrified of being alone in a house with Simon, and the fact that no one knew I was there. If he really was a killer, I would be an idiot to walk into that house. I was a lot of things, but not usually an idiot.

Simon walked out and we sat on the red decorative bench sitting on the front porch. I thought it was lovely and ran my hands along the carved out flowers on the back of the bench.

"Ivy, we really aren't friends, so I'm kind of confused why you would come all the way over here."

I wasn't sure how to respond. The day I woke up in this current life was the day Bernadette was attacked. I had no idea what my relationship with Simon was before that. Were we friends before he moved? Did we date? Did we even really know each other at all? Obviously he knew who I was, so we weren't complete strangers.

"We used to be friends though, right?" I was grasping at any information I could glean from him.

"Yeah, I guess. You knew I liked you, didn't you?" Simon asked me, point blank.

"Yes, I guess I did."

Based on his question, I guessed that we probably never dated.

"This may sound like a strange question, and bear with me please, but did we ever date?" I bit my lower lip.

"No, we never dated. Wouldn't you remember that?" He looked at me with an odd expression on his face.

"I've had some...memory problems. So I wasn't sure. I didn't think we had dated. I just wanted to make sure. Sorry, I know I sound crazy," I replied.

"No, it's okay. Is that what you came here to talk to me about?"

"Sort of, I guess. So, if you liked me, how come we never dated?" I asked.

Simon looked down at his hands and began rubbing them together in a sort of fidgety way.

"What is it?" I could see that he was nervous about something.

"I don't know if I should tell you or not. I mean, what's the point now? That's ancient history," Simon told me.

"Please just tell me," I pleaded.

Simon stood up and started pacing the front porch as I watched.

He stopped for a moment. "You want something to drink?"

"No thanks. So, how come you never asked me out?" I pressed.

"Okay, okay." Simon put his palms toward me in a stopping sort of motion. "It was because of your friend, Carter."

"What do mean?" My brows furrowed.

"I mean that Carter came to me one day and told me that if I didn't stay away from you, that he would kill me," Simon explained.

"He did what?" I was shocked. That didn't sound like Carter at all.

"Yeah, and the look on his face told me that he meant it too. It was like he was crazed. I don't scare easily, but that day he scared me. I decided to take his advice," Simon explained. "Besides, we were moving here soon anyway, so I figured I would just forget about you."

Though I was taken completely by surprise at Simon's explanation, I was also thankful for what Carter did. Without knowing it, he spared me heartache, and all that came along with that, by keeping Simon away from me. Wow, a life almost completely free of Simon. What would that turn out like?

CHAPTER 8

I thought long and hard about it, but in the end I decided not to confront Carter about him threatening Simon on my behalf. It was actually kind of nice that I didn't have the whole Simon thing to deal with this time. Simon was in my past, and that was where he would stay. He didn't seem like he wanted to be a part of my life at all anyway.

However, it didn't take long for me to get a creepy feeling that someone was stalking me. I never actually saw anyone lurking in the shadows, or anything like that, it was more of a feeling. Something deep down in my core ate at me. Several times it would seem like I saw something out of the corner of my eye, but no one was there when I turned my head. It started to feel like I was losing my mind.

Then something concrete did happen. It was when I was out shopping one day. When I walked through the parking lot, toward my car, I heard something that made me turn my head in search of the source of the sound. When I did, I saw the unmistakable figure of a person with dark hair duck behind a car several rows over. That's when I knew something was up. No one would hide behind a car unless they were up to no good.

I had reached my car at that point. So, without thinking about the consequences, I threw my bags into the backseat, and stormed in that direction. It was the middle of the day, so I felt fairly safe in the busy parking lot. When I reached the unfamiliar SUV, I walked around to the opposite side of it and found the person I was looking for.

"Simon, what the hell are you doing?!" I practically yelled. Then I looked around to make sure we weren't being watched.

"Oh hey," he said nonchalantly as he stood up, shaking out each of his legs in the process. "I was just looking for something I dropped, but I can't seem to find it."

He made a show of bending back down and looking under his car. I waited until he stood back up.

"Bullshit." I crossed my arms in front of me and narrowed my eyes in his direction.

"What? You don't believe me?" he asked innocently, giving me a crooked smile.

"Hell no, I don't believe you. I was way over there." I pointed in the direction of my car and we both looked toward it. "Then I noticed you over here and saw you duck behind your car. What was that all about?"

I was not beating around the bush with him. He needed to know that I saw him and he wasn't getting away with it.

"No, Ivy, you are mistaken. It was just a coincidence that I bent down right at that moment." He shrugged his shoulders. "It happens."

"No it doesn't. I don't believe you. I want to know why you are following me, or watching me, or whatever it is you are doing."

"You are being ridiculous and need to just calm down. This is a small town and we are bound to run into each other occasionally," he tried to explain.

"Don't call me ridiculous. I know what I saw. Besides, you don't even live in this town anymore." I said it louder than I meant to.

I watched as Simon's eyes scanned the parking lot. "Ivy, please, people are looking at us. Keep your voice down. Besides, I can still shop here, can't I?" His face was turning a light shade of pink.

I turned and saw the same thing. Though many of the heads turned toward their own business when they realized that I saw them. Good. None of their damn business anyway.

"Just leave me alone," I told him one last time and turned back toward my car. I had the unmistakable feeling of eyes boring into my back as I walked away.

As I drove off, I saw Simon get into his car and leave the parking lot in the opposite direction. I'm sure he wanted nothing more to do with me today. It hit me then that I had probably brought it upon myself by going to see him. That was probably stupid of me.

I flipped on the radio as I drove, hoping to hear some singable tunes for the drive home. At the last moment I made a quick right turn. I had one more stop I needed to make.

"Josephine! Ivy's here," her mother yelled when she saw me at the door. "Come on in." Her mother stepped aside to make room for me to enter.

"I'll just wait on the back patio, if that's okay with you?"

I didn't wait for a response, never needed to before, and walked straight through the living room and out the back door. I was there for probably five minutes before Josie showed up.

"Hi. What are you doing here?" she asked me.

That was an odd response. We had never needed a reason to see each other before.

"I just wanted to see how you were doing," I told her.

"I'm still alive, if that's what you came here to find out."

Her voice was oddly stilted, almost as if we were strangers, and not the best friends that we were. Or at least I thought we were.

"What's going on, Josie?" I asked as she sat down at the patio table across from me.

I watched as Josie took a deep breath. "Mmm okay," she started. "It's about this whole serial killer thing. I think you are losing your mind. I mean, no one has been killed in this town in… I don't know how many years."

"Yeah, I know," I responded. "But, it is supposed to happen. It happened…" I was cut off.

"I know, it happened in your previous lives," Josie told me. "That's the problem. That whole story is crazy. You can't live your life over and over. You need to talk to someone."

"I am talking to someone. I'm talking to you," I responded.

"No, that's not what I mean. You need to talk to a therapist, or someone like that. And figure out what's wrong with you."

Josie gave me a sad, pathetic sort of look, like she felt sorry for me.

"Wait. Hold on," I told her with my right palm facing her. "I'm not crazy, no matter what you think. You really don't believe me?"

It was odd how things changed so much from life to life. In the other life where I told Josie what was going on with me, she believed it and really didn't question it much at all. It was easy to convince her back then.

So why in the world were things so different this time? She's the same person. And I'm the same person. I guess I'm going to have to go this one alone. If she didn't believe me, I probably wouldn't be able to change her mind. I still needed to keep an eye on her though, whether she liked it or not.

"No, I really don't believe you. And I don't think we should hang out anymore," Josie told me point blank. She crossed her arms in front of her to show me that she was serious.

"What? You don't mean that." My heart was breaking.

"Yes, I really do," she responded. "I'd like to be alone now."

I figured that was her subtle way of telling me to get out. I left without another word. As I walked out onto the front porch, I turned to try to get her to listen to me, and the door slammed in my face.

Josephine stewed all afternoon, thinking about her conversation with Ivy. Sure, Ivy had been her best friend for many years, but that didn't change the fact that she thought Ivy was losing her mind. Time travel? Yeah, right, Josephine thought. This is not a movie. This is real life. Ivy was not time traveling. Why she thought she was, Josephine had no idea.

Josephine had enough in her life to deal with and certainly didn't need some crazy person yapping at her about reliving her life, and about how she was trying to save Josephine from some crazed killer, and all that crazy stuff.

She decided that she needed to move on, and spend more time with other friends, or make new friends. Ivy was not someone she needed in her life anymore.

Josephine called up her friend, Bridget. In reality they weren't really friends, more like acquaintances, having had several classes together over the years. But Bridget was the only one that Josephine could think of to call. She was someone that wasn't friends with Ivy, so Josephine felt fairly confident that Bridget would not go running to Ivy to blab about anything she told the girl. The two girls made plans to hang out that night at Bridget's house, since her parents were away for the weekend.

"Your parents just left you alone at home and went out of town for the weekend? Do they do that a lot?" Josephine asked the girl when she arrived at Bridget's house. "I can't imagine my parents ever doing that."

"Well, sort of. My sister is here and she's 18. So, technically there is an adult around. But what my parents don't know is that my sister won't even be here. She'll be at her boyfriend's apartment all weekend," Bridget explained with a smile.

"Nice," Josephine replied as Bridget gave her the the grand tour of their house. "Wow, this place is huge!"

Bridget shrugged her shoulders. "Yeah, I guess. Want something to drink?"

Josephine's ears perked up. "What do you have?"

The two girls walked to the recreation room, as they called it. The room had a pool table, ping pong table, and a bar. Bridget walked around behind the bar and reached into the mini fridge, pulling out a bottle of rum and some lime juice.

"How about a strawberry daiquiri?" Bridget asked.

"Ooh, sounds good," Josephine replied. "I've never had one before," she admitted.

"Well, you don't know what you are missing."

As Bridget gathered the rest of the ingredients and went about concocting the drinks, the girls talked a bit about school and their friends. After two drinks, Josephine became very chatty.

"So, how come you aren't with Ivy?" Bridget asked. "I thought you two were inseparable."

Josephine looked down into her mostly empty glass of the heavenly pink liquid. "Oh, I don't know. She's been acting kind of weird lately. I needed a change."

Josephine looked up into Bridget's large brown eyes.

"What do you mean that she's been acting weird lately? What has she been doing?" Bridget thrived on gossip. Her own life was not that exciting, so she loved hearing about others, especially the juicy stuff.

"Oh, I don't know if I should really tell you. It's crazy and I don't want you to think that I believe any of it," Josephine responded.

"Here, have some more." Bridgett poured the last of the blender's contents into Josephine's glass. "Now, tell me what's going on."

"Okay, but don't tell anyone. Promise." Josephine had a serious look on her face and Bridget nodded her head in agreement. "Um, Ivy thinks that she is re-living her life over and over." Josephine waited for a response.

"What do you mean? Like time travel?" Bridget tilted her head in confusion.

"Yeah, I guess. She said that she keeps dying and waking up at a different age than before. And, that some serial killer in town keeps killing me, while she tries to save me." Josephine was slurring her words by then.

"A serial killer? Here in Red Lake? No, that's crazy. No one's been killed around here in a long time," Bridget replied. "Like before I was even born."

"I know. That's what I told her. But she says that it hasn't happened yet in this life time. Then she told me that I was supposed to die on the day that the water tower was torn down, and that she saved me."

"Did you get attacked or something?" Bridget asked.

"No, that's the weird part. It was a normal day. We went to the beach and came back home. Nothing out of the ordinary at all," Josephine told the girl. "That's why I think she's crazy. If I had been attacked, at least her story would seem somewhat likely. Or maybe not. I don't know. The whole thing is stupid. People can't re-live their lives. It's not possible."

"Want me to make another batch?" Bridget asked.

"Yeah sure," Josephine said with a smile.

Bridget went about cutting the tops off of the strawberries.

"So, why do you think she would tell you that she re-lives her lives then?" Bridget asked. "I mean, what's in it for her? There has to be a reason. Don't you think?"

"I don't know. Maybe she likes the attention?" Josephine asked.

Bridget shrugged her shoulders. "I think I would stay away from her if I were you. She might be dangerous."

About an hour later, both girls were sufficiently drunk. They were laughing at everything and neither one of them could walk a straight line.

"If only Ivy could see us now!" Bridget laughed.

"You know, I really miss her." Josephine suddenly became melancholy. "She's my best friend."

"Well, I can be your best friend now," Bridget replied with a giggle.

"If she wasn't so stupid, with all of her stupid stories, we could all hang out," Josephine slurred.

"It's her loss," Bridget told her. "No one gets reborn and gets to live their lives again. There's no way she time traveled. She seriously needs to be in a loony bin."

"Hey! We should go see her. We can give her a piece of our minds!" Josephine practically yelled.

"Yeah, let's do that." Bridget had also begun slurring her words. "Wait…it's too far to walk."

"Don't your parents have another car? With this big house, they must have a bunch of them," Josephine commented.

"Well, yeah, they do. But I don't have a license. Neither do you," Bridget replied.

"Oh come on. We don't need a license. It's just a few miles. I'll drive!"

Josephine got up off the barstool and headed for the garage, with Bridget in tow.

"Where are the keys?" she asked, passing through the kitchen.

"Are these them?" Josephine grabbed a set of keys off of a key rack on the kitchen wall.

"Yes. I don't know if this is a good idea. You've been drinking," Bridget told her.

Josephine waved her hand wildly in the air. "Oh, I'm fine. Come on."

Josephine walked out the kitchen door that led to the garage. The first car she saw was a shiny red sports car. "This one will do."

Josephine pulled open the driver's door, losing her balance as she began to climb in. She landed on her backside on the garage floor, with one leg hanging out of the car.

"Oops," she laughed.

"Are you okay?" Bridget asked, laughing back at her friend.

"Yep, I'm fine. I just lost my balance. That car door was lighter than I expected and I pulled too hard, I guess."

Josephine pulled herself up and managed to get inside the car on her second try. Bridget climbed into the passenger seat and buckled her seat belt. She pushed the button on the garage door opener attached to the visor, as Josephine attempted to start the engine. It took her three tries to get the key into the slot. The engine purred to life once she turned the key.

"Woo, there you go!" Josephine yelled.

Bridget clapped in response.

The car was facing out, toward the driveway. Josephine struggled a bit, but managed to get the gear shift into drive and hit the gas. They were off.

As the two teens raced through the streets of Red Lake, they were laughing.

Until tragedy struck...

The girls were on their way to Ivy's house, but decided to cruise by the hamburger place to see if any of their friends were there. They wanted to show off their shiny red car. Turning onto the main street in town, Josephine hit the gas as she came out of the turn. In her inebriated state, she didn't see the blonde girl in the crosswalk, until it was too late.

Both girls screamed when the car hit the girl and she flew up and shattered the windshield, before rolling off, as Josephine slammed on the brakes. The whole incident happened so fast that what they hit hadn't even registered in their minds, before it was all over.

"What the hell was that?" Josephine asked, putting the gearshift into the park position and turning to her friend in the passenger seat.

"I..uh..I..think it was…a person," Bridget stammered out. "Oh my god, what have we done?"

"We need to go," Josephine announced.

She reached for the gearshift in an attempt to put it in drive. But Bridget reached over and pulled Josephine's hand off of the gear shift before she had a chance to switch it. Then Bridget leaned across, grabbed the keys, turned off the engine, and yanked the keys out of the ignition, all in one swift motion.

"We are not going anywhere," Bridget announced. "I'm not sure what you hit, or who you hit, but we need to find out. I'm sure we are going to be in some trouble, but I'm not adding felony hit and run to the list." Bridget was sobering up fast as the reality of their situation was closing in.

Both girls looked up to find a gathering crowd in front of the car. Even if they had both agreed to leave, it was too late now. People were looking at the ground, where neither girl could see, then looking back up through the windshield at the teens.

"Someone call an ambulance!" the girls both heard a man yell.

"Oh no," Josephine cried out, covering her face as the tears flowed.

"Come on, we need to find out who you hit," Bridget told her. "Get out of the car," she ordered.

Josephine complied. The girls got out and walked around to the front of the car, heads hanging low, as the crowd parted for them. When they saw the bloody and broken body lying in a heap on the road, both girls gasped in unison.

"Is that Bernadette James?" Bridget asked no one in particular.

"Yes," replied an unknown voice in the crowd.

"Is she...dead?" Josephine asked.

Someone was kneeling down on the ground, administering CPR on the girl. "She's not breathing," the man told the crowd.

Sirens wailed off in the distance and everyone looked up toward their direction.

CHAPTER 10

The sheriff of Red Lake drove up and parked across the street just as the ambulance pulled up beside the car and the crowd. As the paramedics attended to Bernadette, Sheriff Hayes climbed out of his car, walked over, and made his way through the large gathering of onlookers. He went mostly unnoticed until he began speaking.

"Everyone, please step back and give us all some room." The sheriff used his hands to motion to the crowd. "A little more please."

Once the crowd had moved back sufficiently, the sheriff looked down at the person lying in the street. He recognized her immediately. Hayes knew Bernadette's father well. Bernard James was one of the wealthiest people in town. Everyone knew who he was. Hayes knew that the man would not take the news of his daughter's accident very well. What parent would? he thought.

Looking up at the crowd, Sheriff Hayes continued.

"Who does this car belong to?" He turned toward the car, pointing with his thumb as he spoke.

All eyes turned to the two teenage girls.

"Um, it's mine," Bridget replied. "It's my dad's car actually," she added, looking down at the road below her.

The man looked at both of the girls. He knew them. He knew most of the residents of Red Lake. He had been Sheriff for a lot of years.

"Are you even old enough to drive?" Sheriff Hayes asked Bridget, already knowing the answer to his question.

"No. But I wasn't driving." Bridget looked at Josephine as she spoke.

Josephine's eyes grew large as everyone standing on the street looked her way. She had always hated being the center of attention. And this was the worst of the worst kind of attention to get. Her face turning crimson, she wanted to crawl into a hole and hide. Josephine knew that things were about to get very real for her.

"Josephine," Sheriff Hayes addressed her, "were you driving?"

Josephine looked off in the distance, unable to look the sheriff in the eyes. "Um, yes sir."

"Now I'll ask you the same question I just asked your cohort here. Are you old enough to drive? Do you have a license?" the sheriff asked.

"No sir. I'm 15," Josephine replied, her voice quivering.

Sheriff Hayes nodded his head ever so slightly. He looked down at Bernadette still lying in the road, still being attended to by the paramedics. But it wasn't Bernadette that was of the most interest that day, in front of the burger place. It was Josephine and Bridget. Bernadette was all but forgotten by the crowd.

"Have you girls been drinking?"

The crowd was eerily silent, listening to every word. No one paid a bit of attention to the paramedics while Bernadette was lifted onto a stretcher and then loaded into the ambulance. As the ambulance pulled away, sirens blazing, everyone turned to watch it disappear around a corner. Once out of sight, all eyes turned back to the scene unfolding before them.

Neither girl answered the sheriff's question about whether they had been drinking or not. It didn't matter though, he didn't need an answer. Sheriff Hayes could smell the alcohol on their breaths as they spoke. He took in the bloodshot eyes and the slightly slurred words produced by the teenagers.

"Follow me," Sheriff Hayes directed the girls.

Following dutifully, the three of them walked over to the sheriff's car.

"Now, I'm going to give you a breath test to see how intoxicated you two actually are," he declared as he pulled the device from his car. "Josephine, you are first."

"But Sheriff, shouldn't my parents be here?" Bridget interrupted.

She was no expert, but her parents had always told her to never answer questions when in trouble with the police. Let their attorney do all the talking.

Until this day, she had brushed off her parents' comments as something that would never happen to her. Bridget thought of herself as a good girl, definitely not a trouble maker that would need a lawyer to talk to the police for her. Now her father's words of warning were boring into her chest. She knew that she better listen to them. Though Bridget was not the one driving, they were in her parents' car and she was intoxicated. And someone had been hit by that car. Bridget began to visibly shake.

Hayes turned to Bridget. "Young lady, I don't think you understand the seriousness of what has happened here today. We will certainly contact your parents, that you can be sure of. But in the meantime, I have to test your alcohol level. It can't wait. Now get over here."

The sheriff's eyes narrowed as he spoke. Bridget took that as a warning and decided that she had better comply. Her father's words completely forgotten in the moment.

"Yes sir." Bridget answered meekly. She didn't have the strength in her to argue with the sheriff.

Once the test was administered, the sheriff gave them the results. "You two have high levels of alcohol in your system. Josephine, I'm placing you under arrest. Turn around."

Josephine never said a word as the sheriff put handcuffs on her and led her to the backseat of his car. Then he turned to Bridget.

"Bridget, get in the front seat of my car and I'll give you a ride home on the way. I need to have a discussion with your folks."

"They are out of town for the weekend, Sheriff," she replied.

"I see. Is someone staying with you or are you all alone?"

"My sister is 18 and she's in charge," Bridget explained, leaving out the part about her sister staying with her boyfriend all weekend.

Sheriff Hayes looked intently at Bridget for a moment, trying to gauge whether she was telling the truth or not. The girl was visibly shaking and looked terrified to him. He determined that she was telling the truth. Besides, he would find out soon enough if she was left home alone or not. He nodded his head in her direction.

"Well I will drop you off and call your parents once I get back to the station."

While everything had been going on with the sheriff, Josephine, and Bridget, the deputies had been taking photographs of the crime scene and had called the tow truck. Just as the tow truck arrived, Sheriff Hayes pulled his car out onto the road and drove off with the girls.

A few hours later, Sheriff Hayes received a phone call from the hospital letting him know that Bernadette had died from her injuries. By then, Josephine's parents had arrived at the station and had been informed about the accident. The sheriff released Josephine to her parents. She wasn't a flight risk. They could all deal with the courts on Monday.

As expected, the accident was the talk of the town. It didn't take long for Ivy to find out what had happened.

CHAPTER 11

All I heard was sobbing coming from the other end of the line when I answered the phone. The caller didn't say a word. It didn't matter, I knew exactly who it was. I sat patiently until the caller was able to collect herself enough to speak.

"Ivyyyyy....," Josephine wailed into the phone when she was finally able to get any words out. "I...killed...her," she said, gasping for breath between words.

I felt a prickly sensation on my arms. "What are you talking about? What do you mean that you killed her? Killed who?"

"Bernadette. I killed...Bernadette." I could hear Josephine take a deep shuddering breath after her announcement.

"What? You did not," I answered back. "Why are you being so dramatic? Is this your way of trying to get back at me for telling you what happened to me? Are you trying to shock me?" I let the annoyance shine through in my voice. It didn't matter anymore. Josephine and I were never going to be friends again. Not in this lifetime anyway. She had made that abundantly clear.

Josephine was being ridiculous. There was no way that she killed anyone. I wasn't buying her story.

"No, you don't understand," Josephine continued. "I really did kill her. I hit her with my car...and now she's dead!" Josephine began wailing into the phone again.

"What? Josie, please. You need to calm down and tell me exactly what happened." I sat down on the couch in my living room. "You don't even have a driver license. How could you hit her with your car? You don't have a car. Tell me the truth. What is going on?" Josephine was beginning to scare me.

The conversation was not going to go anywhere with Josephine blubbering into the phone. She was clearly quite upset. Was it possible that she was actually telling the truth?

Josephine took a moment to collect herself and I waited patiently on the phone, listening to her taking deep, calming breaths.

"Okay, I'm back. Sorry. It wasn't my car that I was driving. It was Bridget's. Or her parents' car actually," Josephine explained.

"Why on earth were you driving her parents' car?"

I still wasn't sure that I understood what she was trying to tell me. She hit Bernadette with Bridget's car? That couldn't be true. But why would she lie?

"Well, since we got into that fight and weren't talking to each other, I went over to Bridget's house to hang out with her. And her parents were gone for the weekend. And we decided to make daiquiris. The strawberry kind," Josephine told me.

"Oh no." The blood drained from my face.

"We got kind of drunk. Then we just wanted to go see you," Josephine told me.

"You did? Why?" I asked.

"Because I was mad at you for making up that stupid story and I wanted to confront you about it. Stupid, I know. But people do stupid things while drunk," Josephine explained.

"You mean like driving and hitting someone with their car?" I really didn't mean for it to come out the way it did. It wasn't my intention to be sarcastic. It just sounded that way, and I realized it the second it came out of my mouth.

"Yeah, like that." Josephine sounded angry.

"Okay, I'm sorry. I didn't mean that. Please tell me everything that happened," I instructed. "And is Bernadette really dead?" I asked, fearing the answer.

Josephine went on to tell me about how she didn't see Bernadette in the crosswalk and hit her, with the girl flying up and hitting the windshield of the car. I gasped as I pictured the event. Then she explained what happened when the sheriff arrived and arrested her.

I was in shock. I had tried desperately to save Bernadette in this lifetime. And had finally succeeded. Just to have someone kill her anyway. I wondered what that meant?

Was Bernadette destined to die, no matter what I did? Did I screw up the universe by saving her? Was there some bigger plan that I was unaware of? Did the universe really want her dead? And if so, why?

No, that can't be it. It just has to be a major coincidence that I saved Bernadette, then she ended up dying anyway. It was just an unfortunate accident. That had to be it.

"Ivy, did you hear me? Are you still there?" I heard Josephine raise her voice into the phone.

"Oh yes, I'm sorry. I was just thinking. But yeah, I heard you. What happens now?" I asked her.

"I don't know. The sheriff let me come home with my parents. He said there was no point in making me sit in a jail cell all weekend. Besides, since I'm a minor, he didn't want to keep me there, I guess," Josie explained.

"I'm glad you are not in jail," I answered, truthfully.

"But I have to go talk to the sheriff on Monday, and probably go see a judge. I'm not really sure. My parents have called a lawyer."

"I'm so sorry that happened. But Bernadette is dead, and that's worse than anything you have to go through," I told her. I couldn't hide the bluntness in my voice.

"Yeah, I know. I'm the stupid one and it's all my fault. No matter what, I can't bring Bernadette back," she admitted.

I might be able to though, I thought to myself. I wondered if there would be another lifetime to try to fix all of this mess. Thinking back to everything that had happened to me, it was a valid theory.

"Is there anything I can do?" I asked her.

"No, I don't think so," she paused. "Oh, someone is at the door. I gotta go. And Ivy? I really want us to try to be friends again." Josephine hung up the phone before I had a chance to respond.

As I put the phone back down on the table, something occurred to me. I wondered if Josephine was now in more danger also, since I saved her too? I mean, Bernadette died anyway, so now will Josie? Should I do something about it? But, what could I do? I couldn't move in with her and watch her every move. Even if I could keep an eye on her, I certainly couldn't do it for the rest of my life. How long would that be anyway? A month? A year? 75 years? I wish I knew.

CHAPTER 12

"Oh. Hi." Josephine eyes grew wide when she saw who was at her door. "My parents aren't home right now," she tried to explain.

"It's not your parents I'm here to see."

The man took a step closer to Josephine, breaking the plane of the doorway. She took a step back as he entered her personal space and things got really uncomfortable.

"You know why I'm here, don't you?" he asked, taking another menacing step toward her.

"No."

Josephine could feel herself shaking from the inside out, though she had no idea if the man had noticed. Josephine backed up two more steps, moving through the foyer and heading slowly with her back toward the living room.

"You killed my daughter." His eyes were unblinking.

The man matched Josephine's steps, taking two more toward her.

"I know. I'm so sorry, Mr. James. It was an accident, I swear."

She backed up again. Her breathing quickened as he followed.

"You were drunk, and she was in a crosswalk. That is no accident. You are completely responsible." He spoke slowly and deliberately. The anger in his voice was unmistakable.

"I know, and I feel horrible about it. I liked Bernadette. I would never hurt her on purpose," Josephine tried to explain.

"Shut up! You do not feel horrible. Everyone says you didn't like Bernadette. So don't tell me that you feel horrible, and don't act like she was your friend." He was fairly calm when he arrived, but was beginning to get agitated and began yelling.

He took another step forward, turned, and slammed the front door behind him.

"Please, Mr. James, it was an accident. I would never hurt her, or anyone, on purpose. I'm so sorry." Terrified, Josephine began to cry.

"I said shut up!"

He took another step. Josephine backed up, scanning the room for a weapon, in case she found herself needing one.

"What are you looking for?" he asked her, looking around the room himself.

"Nothing. I don't know," she replied.

Before Josephine had a chance to react, the man's arm shot out and his fist slammed into Josephine's face, breaking her nose instantly. She instinctively reached up to cover it with her hand, blood pouring down her chin and dripping onto her yellow blouse. She screamed out in pain.

While she was trying to recover, Bernard James lunged at the girl.

Josephine saw the lunge just in time to react. She backed up just far enough for him to go crashing down on the floor in front of her. She was a good 25 years younger than he was, and she was quicker. Josephine turned and ran toward the back door. Grabbing the handle, she yanked to open the sliding door. It didn't budge. Locked. "Dammit," she said out loud.

Those precious few seconds that she lost as she fought with the lever to unlock the door, were just enough for Bernard James to reach her. Josephine's head jerked back in response to him grabbing a handful of her short hair and yanking her away from the door.

She cried out in pain as he dragged her by the hair toward the kitchen. It was all she could do to stay on her feet, since he had her twisted at an almost impossible angle.

"Let me go! Please," she begged. "I want to talk about this."

Josephine was grasping for anything, any words at all, that would bring him back to the moment. He seemed like a crazed animal to her. She wasn't entirely sure he was even aware of his actions.

"Oh, you want to talk? Now? Why didn't you want to talk before you ran over my baby girl?" He screeched at her as they reached the kitchen.

That didn't even make any sense, Josephine thought.

"Please, Mr. James, you are hurting me!"

Josephine didn't see him pull the knife from the wood block on the kitchen counter. It was the nine inch chef's knife that happened to be the one that his hand landed on when he reached for the nearest weapon. She used it often when helping to prepare meals for the family.

He pressed it up against her throat. Josephine cried out, not in pain, but in fear. She had never been so frightened in her life.

"I said to shut the hell up!" he screamed at her.

Josephine nodded her head ever so slightly. Just enough to answer his demand, but not enough to cause the steel blade that was pressing against her throat to cut her. She stood as still as she possibly could. One wrong move, and the knife could easily penetrate the soft flesh of her throat.

"Why did you have to do it? She was my only daughter. You killed my baby."

He began sounding more like a father in distress, then one full of rage. Josephine prayed that he would realize what he was doing and let her go.

"I'm so sorry." Josephine sounded more like she was pleading, than apologizing.

"I don't believe you."

At that moment, the doorbell rang out. They both looked up, toward the front door, though it was around a couple of corners, and neither could actually see the door.

"I need to get out of here," Bernard James said, looking around for an escape route.

The person at the door knocked this time. It sounded more urgent.

"That's a good idea. Whoever is at the front door doesn't seem to be leaving," Josephine encouraged.

Bernard's eyes glazed over then. He pulled the knife away from the girl's throat, causing Josephine to let out a breath of relief. However, that was premature.

"I can't let you get away with murdering my daughter!" he yelled, plunging the knife into Josephine's back.

She was still bent over because he still had one hand firmly entrenched in her hair. With her back exposed, it was the perfect target.

Josephine's knees buckled as she watched her own blood stream onto the kitchen floor. Bernard released his grip on her hair and she slumped to the tiles. Josephine was unconscious before her body came to a rest, lying on her right side, with her back pressed against the kitchen counter, just below the sink.

I found the front door unlocked and entered Josephine's house tentatively. The house was eerily quiet. Perhaps no one was home and I was just being paranoid. Still…I needed to be sure that Josie was all right.

I didn't make a sound as I walked softly and entered the living room. The first thing I noticed was blood on the living room carpet, causing the hair on the back of my neck to stand up. It wasn't just a couple of drops. There was a good amount on the carpet. I followed the blood trail, walking around the corner, toward the kitchen.

I screamed as I entered Josephine's kitchen and took in the scene. She was lying there, on the floor, in a pool of her own blood. I looked up at her attacker. It was Bernadette's father, standing there, staring at the limp body on the floor before him. It was as if he didn't realize I was there. His face never registered any recognition.

"What did you do!" I screamed at him, with no regard for my own safety.

That apparently snapped him out of it and he looked me straight in the eyes, though he still said nothing.

When I looked over at the bloody knife he was holding, he promptly dropped it on the floor next to Josephine's head. It landed with a clank as we both watched it come to a rest.

Bernard James never said a word as he pushed past me and ran out the front door, tracking bloody footprints across the tan carpet.

He wouldn't be back...that I was sure of. I ran to my friend and felt for a pulse. She had a weak one, but there was definitely a pulse there.

"Hang in there, Sweetheart, I'm going to get you some help," I told her, but I wasn't sure she could hear me. Leaving her briefly, I ran to the phone.

While I waited for the ambulance to arrive, I grabbed some towels and pressed them against the single stab wound in Josie's back. It didn't seem to help though, as each white towel turned crimson almost immediately on making contact with her body. The wound appeared to be very deep, and had probably cut a major artery.

I did my best to stay calm, thinking of nothing but saving Josephine. I couldn't lose her. Not again. Not my best friend.

"Please don't let her die again." There was no one around to hear my desperate plea.

Sheriff Hayes called me outside to give a statement while the paramedics went to work on poor Josephine. I knew it was too late though. No one could lose that much blood and survive. I had lost my precious Josephine. Once again.

The manhunt for Bernard James lasted exactly six minutes. Just long enough to drive over to his house. He had gone straight home and was sitting at his kitchen table with his wife when the sheriff walked in. He hadn't bothered to even close the front door. He knew they were on their way.

Bernard knew that he would never get away with it. I had caught him, red handed, standing over Josephine with the knife in his hand. He still had her blood on him when Sheriff Hayes read him his rights. He went with the sheriff without incident.

Over the course of the next few days, Bernard James confessed to attacking Josephine over the death of his daughter and he was remanded to the state prison. I wasn't sure if there was going to be a trial or not, but it didn't matter either way.

My beautiful Josie never made it to the hospital. She bled out and died on her kitchen floor that day.

CHAPTER 13

"Why are you doing this to me?!" I stood in the graveyard yelling into the sky, my arms spread wide, after everyone had gone home.

Josephine's funeral was beautiful. Her parents were devastated, of course, and there was not a dry eye in attendance. After what Mr. James had done to my Josie, I had no desire to attend Bernadette's service.

I was tired of attending my friends' funeral services. I had done it countless times over my lives. It was all more than I should be expected to live through. I didn't want to do it anymore.

I just wanted to live this last life and be done with it. I didn't want to wake back up and start all over again. For what? For nothing, that's what. It was all for absolutely nothing. No matter what I did, they died. Bernadette and Josephine died every single time. Even in this life, when I actually saved them from their destined fate, they still died. Not from the serial killer, but it happened anyway.

None of it was worth it.

"Just stop! I don't want to do this anymore!" I yelled again.

There were a couple of people several yards away, standing

next to their own loved one's gravestone, and they looked up at me. I didn't care. It didn't matter. None of it mattered anymore.

"Am I going to just keep doing an endless loop for all of eternity?" I asked, quieter this time.

I sat down in the cool grass, next to Josephine's grave. She had already been lowered into the ground. There was a cloth of some sort over the casket, concealing it. I guessed that they would bring some sort of machinery out later to fill in the dirt, entombing my beautiful friend forever in darkness.

I sat there for over an hour, just staring at the spot where her casket rested. It still shook me to the core to think about her there. Dead and gone. Even after everything I did to save her.

I decided right there and then that I would no longer bother with it all. If I somehow found myself coming back, yet again, that I would just let things be. Why waste my energy on something that was never going to change? It was never going to be resolved. I just knew it.

Maybe if I was unwilling to do anything, it would stop happening. That was the only conclusion I could come up with. Nothing else seemed to work.

Finally, I got up and began walking. I didn't know where I was going, and paid very little attention. I just need to get away from the graveyard and be somewhere else. Anywhere else. I just wanted to walk, and to be alone.

Before I knew it, I found myself in the forest. I remember the feeling of darkness spreading over me that I always got when I entered the thick forest. But that didn't stop me. I remember the feeling of crunching under my feet as I made my way down the path. That didn't stop me. I didn't hear or see anything else on my way in. I didn't even realize what I was doing. It was as if something had a hold on me and I was going into that forest, whether I liked it or not.

When I turned to get my bearings, I realized that I was standing next to the sinkhole.

"What the…" I didn't finish that sentence. I just stood there in shock. "How did I get here?"

I heard the unmistakable sound of footsteps crunching on dry forest debris and I snapped my head in that direction.

"Who's there?" I asked, my voice barely above a whisper.

The footsteps stopped abruptly, with no reply to my question.

"Someone's there. I heard you. Answer me!" I said much louder this time. It was all I could do to keep the shakiness out of my voice.

A crunchy footstep.

I squinted my eyes, trying to see into the dark areas where the trees were close together. They formed a canopy that blocked out most of the sunlight and I couldn't see who was there. I could just make out a dark figure though. He stood perfectly still. It was unnerving and I began to shiver.

I rubbed my bare arms as I stood there deciding on my next move.

"You might as well speak up and let me know who you are. I'm going to find out anyway." I hoped that if I sounded sure of myself, and not like some terrified teenager, that I might actually get somewhere.

Still no response.

"Simon, is that you?" I took a shot. He seemed like the most likely candidate.

Another crunchy footstep. The figure moved toward me, very slowly.

Then it dawned on me. I lived my life over and over, right? Well then, what did I have to lose? If I confronted him, yes, I might die. If I did, then I would probably come back and start all over. Nothing lost.

But, I might also survive and find out who the killer is once and for all. If I caught him off guard, not expecting me to pounce, it might just work. Oh god, I hope this works.

"All right, if you are going to play these games, I'm going to play back!" I yelled.

Without giving it another thought, I sprinted. Not for the highway…but right at the figure standing at the edge of the trees. I couldn't see his face, he had it covered with a mask, but I registered his surprise anyway. It was in his body language.

Suddenly, his body stiffened up, straight as a board. The fact that he was caught off guard, caused a moment of indecision on his part. That was all I needed. I closed the gap between him and me in mere seconds, landing on him with all I had.

We both landed hard on the crunchy forest floor. Then we rolled, as he struggled to get the crazy girl off of him. I was swinging my fists as fast and furiously as I possibly could, aiming for his face. I didn't want to stop long enough to pull the mask off, as that might give him an advantage. I wanted him to put all of his energy into fighting me off.

He never said a word as I pummeled him. Though I did hear a few grunts and groans as my fists landed on his face, and again on his ribs.

Though I had gotten the best of him with my surprise attack, there was still one problem that I hadn't thought through.

He was still bigger and stronger than I was.

It was only a matter of time before he was able to gain control of the situation. That's when he pinned me down and slugged me hard in the face. Stars danced in my vision and my arms suddenly felt like they weighed 100 pounds each. I couldn't lift them. It was all I could do to stay conscious.

As I was trying to get my wits about me back, I realized that he had stood up and was dragging me by my feet. The crunchy forest floor had turned into prickly pine cones and rocks digging into my back as my shirt tore and my exposed flesh raked over them. It was one of the most painful things I had ever experienced. And that is saying a lot from someone who has been stabbed and left dying in a pool of her own blood.

I reached out grasping desperately for anything to stop me, and stop the pain. There was nothing.

Then clarity hit me. I realized exactly what was happening. I was being dragged toward the sinkhole. The horror of that thought was the scariest thing I had ever experienced in all of my lives. I gathered everything I had and let out a blood curdling scream.

Unfortunately, it was too late. I felt myself lifting from the ground and flying through the air, giving me temporary relief from the rocks and needles digging into my back. Once I realized that I was going over the edge of the sinkhole, my arms instinctively flailed, reaching for anything to stop my descent into the unknown. The attempt was futile.

It seemed like I dropped forever, down into the blackness, before I finally hit the bottom. Though I hit the bottom hard, I was not knocked unconscious as I expected. That would have been merciful. No, it didn't play out like that at all.

The bottom of the sinkhole was softer than I imagined it would be. It was wet and muddy. Perhaps that river or stream that everyone theorized caused the sinkhole was actually true.

I couldn't see a thing down inside, as it was pitch black. There was some light way above me, but it didn't reach down to where I laid.

The feeling didn't last long though. The sinkhole began to swallow me up, as the sides began collapsing in and debris piled on top of me. Within seconds, there was so much on top of me that I couldn't move and I couldn't breathe. I gasped for breath that would not come. I was suffocating and there was nothing I could do about it.

The last thing I saw before I was completely consumed and lost consciousness, was that dark figure standing on the edge of the sinkhole above, watching me.

PART 5

CHAPTER 1

Abruptly, I regained consciousness. I found myself still in the sinkhole. My arms began flailing about again, as I attempted to get out from under the crushing, heavy debris that had piled on top of me. I gasped for air. It felt thick and unyielding. I dared not open my eyes for fear that the dirt would get into them. I reached up to brush the muck from my face and eyes. But strangely, I felt nothing. My face was clean of debris. Still, I felt as though I couldn't breathe, with the crushing force on my chest. I once again gasped for more air. This time there was relief and I could breathe.

As the air filled my lungs, I screamed. It was a blood curdling sort of scream.

That's when I finally dared to open my eyes. There was no dirt and other forest rubble on top of me. I was no longer being held down by what felt like hundreds of pounds of dirt. All I could see was a clear, late afternoon sky. My eyes instinctively slammed shut as the bright light of the day assaulted my senses.

I didn't even take the time to figure out what had happened, as deep, shuddering sobs assaulted my body and I began to cry hysterically. In all my lives I have never experienced anything so frightening as falling into that sinkhole and being buried alive by tons of dirt. It was a desperate feeling of helplessness. And to know that I was suffocating, and dying, was the scariest thing to ever happen to me. Even in all the ways I had died, I wouldn't wish what I went through in that sinkhole on anyone.

When I finally calmed down a bit, I took a moment to look around and see where I was.

I found myself standing on someone's front lawn, next to some bushes that had been masterfully crafted into perfect squares. The street was lined with cute houses and manicured lawns. A boy of about 14, with what looked like his little sister, walked a tiny brown chihuahua, across the street from me. They were about a block away and had turned to look at me. It must have been my scream. I waved at them and smiled, as they turned and continued on down the street.

A red SUV drove past, slowing down to take a look at me as she did so. We made eye contact for just a moment, before she turned her attention back toward the road and continued on her way.

That was odd.

Oh! It just dawned on me that this was a new life for me. I guess dying such a traumatic death had really gotten to me, and I wasn't thinking about what was going on around me.

How old was I this time? I looked down at my body and I was tiny and skinny. Oh no. It was clear that I was very young. I looked up and saw a car parked on the street at the house next door. I walked over to it and looked at my reflection in the passenger window. Yes, I was very young. But how young? I then bent over and got a better look at my face in the passenger side mirror.

I took in a deep breath as I realized that I was not more than 8 or 9 years old.

"Oh my god, what am I going to do now?" I said out loud. I

quickly looked around to make sure no one heard me talking to myself.

"And where in the world am I? This doesn't look like Red Lake at all."

A breeze came out of nowhere, blowing my crazy red hair around in all sorts of directions. Ugh, this hair again. I did my best to smooth it down with my hands, but was getting nowhere. I really could have used some hair clips or something at that moment.

As I stood there, looking into the car window's reflection, trying to work with my hair, another car drove up the road toward me. Not wanting to call attention to myself, I ducked down next to the car. I was on the sidewalk, away from the road, and was pretty sure that they didn't see me.

I stayed bent over and almost crawled over to the bushes, so as not to be seen. Once I got to the bushes I was able to stand up straight and peer around them to the family in the blue sedan that had just pulled into the driveway of the house I had been standing in front of.

I watched a nice looking man and woman in their early thirties get out of the car. When the back door opened, and a young boy climbed out, I gasped. Then I covered my mouth quickly before anyone heard me cry out.

It was Carter. He looked about the age he was when we first met at 9 years old, all those years ago. All those lifetimes ago. The man and woman must be his parents. I had never met them because they died in that house fire that Carter accidentally set, right before he moved to Red Lake and in with his aunt.

"Come on Carter, hurry up. I have dinner to make and you need to clean your room," his mother told him.

Carter took his time walking into the house, paying no attention to his mother. His hair was too long and disheveled. He slumped when he walked. Some things never change, I thought.

Wow, I'm at Carter's house. I wracked my brain trying to remember what town that was in. Something Cove. I was sure Cove was in the name. Then I remembered doing research on Carter after his aunt told me about the fire, and Carter's parents dying. Sandy Cove, that was it. I was in Sandy Cove. Now, how in the world did a 9 year old girl get to a town several hours away all on her own?

And how was I going to get home? And why was I here? I had never woke up anywhere other than Red Lake before. Why here and why now?

I thought about my parents. They must be frantic. I figured I had better let them know that I was okay before they organize a statewide manhunt for me.

CHAPTER 2

Since I had no idea where anything was, I just picked a direction
and started walking down the street. I was glad to have a sweater
on because it was getting a bit chilly as the sun was going down.
Didn't I bring any clothes with me? A toothbrush? Anything at all?
I had no suitcase that I could find, or even a backpack. Was 9 year
old me that stupid, that I would just leave home with nothing
at all?

After walking for about 20 minutes I came across a small
outdoor shopping center, with a gas station on the corner. The
gas station had a payphone.

I walked up to it and took one look at the phone when I realized that yeah, I would need some money. It was called a
payphone after all. They weren't free.

I dug into the pocket of my jeans, hoping I was at least smart
enough to bring some money. I pulled out the contents and
perused them carefully. There were a few dollar bills and some
change. All good. But what I was most interested in was the bus
ticket. Apparently I had taken the bus to Sandy Cove. Okay, well
at least that was explained. Thank god I didn't hitchhike. And
thankfully, the ticket now in my hand was a return ticket to Red

Lake. I had a way home. I guess my 9 year old self was not so stupid after all.

The ticket had a date on it. Was that today? I needed to figure out what today's date was. So, I walked into the gas station convenience store and looked at the newspaper stack near the front door. Okay good. The ticket was for tomorrow. And I now had confirmation of my age. Nine years old. Oh boy, I was not looking forward to doing all those years over again.

I did find it odd that the return ticket was for tomorrow. So, I rode the bus for several hours to see Carter, I guess, just to go right back home the very next day? Why would I do that?

I didn't even know Carter yet. I don't think so anyway. In previous lives, I had always met him after his parents were killed and he moved in with his aunt, who lived next door to me. Well, his parents are still alive right now, so did I already know him in this life? Was he expecting me for a visit? Should I just go knock on his door? His parents, and mine, couldn't possibly have green-lighted a 9 year old riding a bus across the state alone.

So, if I didn't already know Carter in this life, then what in the world was I doing here? And just for one night, it seems. I didn't know any answers, and really couldn't just walk up to Carter and ask, especially if he had no idea who I was.

I walked back outside and over to the payphone. I dug the change back out of my pocket, careful not to drop the bus ticket. After dropping the required coins in the slot, I dialed my home number. Yes, the number was still the same for all the years my parents had lived in, or will live in, that house. Even after marrying, having both of my kids, and going into hiding, they still lived in that same house. Yes, I knew the number by heart.

"Hello?" my brother said into the other end of the line.

Wow, I thought, he's only 12 years old. It was funny to think of him so young. It had been so long, I almost forgot what he looked like back then.

"Parker, is Mom home?" I asked like nothing was amiss.

"What do you want, Brat," he responded. That part of him I did remember.

"I want to talk to Mom."

"She's not here. Call back later."

I knew he was about to hang up on me. "Wait! I have a favor to ask you," I yelled into the phone.

There was a slight pause. "I'm listening." I could hear the smile in his voice.

"Can you tell Mom that I'm spending the night at...um, that I'm spending the night at...Bernadette's house." I guess I hadn't thought through exactly what I was going to say before I called.

"I thought you two were fighting," he said.

"Um, not anymore. We're fine," I answered. "Can you just tell her?"

"I'm not your secretary," he blurted out.

"Parker, please, I..."

"Please deposit $1.00 into the phone." It was an automated voice that interrupted our call.

"Are you on a payphone? Where are you, Ives?" Parker asked me.

"Hold on."

I dug into my pocket and pulled out four quarters and deposited them, one at a time.

"Okay, I'm back," I told him when I was finished.

"Ives, why are you using a payphone? You aren't at Bernadette's house, so where are you?"

His 12 year old squeaky voice sounded concerned and that made me smile.

"I can't tell you."

"You are gonna have to tell me if you want me to lie to Mom and Dad," he explained.

I hesitated. How was I going to explain where I was and what I was doing, when I didn't even know why I was here? I had to try though. It was the only way he was going to give the message to my parents. If that didn't happen, they would call the cops for sure. And I would never be able to explain why I was in a town several hours away.

"Okay fine," I told him. "But you have to promise not to tell anyone. I mean anyone." I made sure that my voice conveyed the seriousness of my statement.

"Yeah, whatever. I won't tell anyone. Now what's going on?" he demanded.

"I'm in Sandy Cove," I said quietly.

"Sandy Cove! That's a really long way from here. What are you doing there? And how did you get there?"

"I...came to see a friend. On the bus." That's really all I wanted to tell him.

"What friend?"

"Um, his name is Carter." I knew there would be more questions.

"Who's Carter? I've never heard of him."

"His aunt lives next door to us. He's been there visiting. We became friends." It wasn't entirely a lie. It just hadn't happened yet in this life.

"Jean is his aunt? I've never seen any kids visiting her. What's really going on Ives?"

He didn't believe a word I said. I couldn't blame him. They sounded like something a 9 year old would say.

"Look, I promise to explain things when I get home tomorrow. Can you please just tell Mom that I'm spending the night at Bernadette's house?" I begged.

"If you do my chores for a month." There was that smile in his voice again.

"Ugh, fine. I gotta go before I have to put more money in here. Thanks."

I hung up without saying anything else. I was afraid of more questions that I couldn't come up with an answer for.

It was starting to get dark, and cold, as the sun dropped below the mountains off in the distance. I walked back into the convenience store and purchased some donuts and a hot chocolate. I really wanted a coffee, but figured they might find it odd that a 9 year old was buying coffee. I didn't want to draw any attention to myself, if I could help it. So, the hot chocolate would have to suffice.

I walked back the way I had come, having absolutely no idea what the plan was. I thought about knocking on their door, but what if Carter didn't know me? Or worse, one of his parents answered the door and started asking questions. No, that was a bad idea. I decided to lurk in the bushes for a while and see what was going on before making a decision.

When I reached his house, the lights were on in the living room. Since the curtains were pulled back I could see them clear as day. They really should close their curtains when the sun went down, instead of being there on display for anyone that walked or drove by. But, I was glad that they seemed oblivious to that fact.

I crawled in between two of the square bushes and sat down on the cool earth between them. I had already eaten my donuts on the walk back from the store, so I sipped on my hot chocolate, trying to make it last.

I wondered why I was here at all. There really was no need to wonder. When it came down to it, there was only one reason. The fire that killed both of Carter's parents. Carter's Aunt Jean had told me that they suspected arson, but no one could prove it.

Carter had told me it was an accident. He wanted to try smoking after his parents went to bed one night, and he lit candles to hide the smell. I wanted to believe him, but the truth was that I just didn't know. He was very young and the story sounded plausible. If it wasn't an accident, wouldn't he lie about it? Of course he would. We probably all would, for fear of going to jail.

I kept watch while the family watched TV for a while. Then they all got up, turned off the TV and began turning off lights. It must be bedtime, I thought, watching them walk upstairs. The last of the lights went off as they disappeared from my sight. No one bothered to close the curtains.

Now what? I just squat here in the bushes all night? What if someone sees me? I looked around at the neighboring houses, wondering if any of them were empty? The occupants could be on vacation, or maybe someone just moved out. I could maybe find an unlocked door or window and sneak in…No, that would be stupid. These days it seemed that everyone had either security cameras on their houses or an alarm. Or even both.

But wait. This is over 20 years earlier than the age I was in my first life. I was 30 then. Were there security cameras at houses back when I was 9? You know, I have no idea. Even if there were, it never occurred to me to even notice cameras at 9 years old. No, the best thing to do was to not take any chances. If the cops got me, then I would not be able to explain why I was here. That would just open up a big old mess of worms.

So, I wrapped my arms around myself the best I could, to try to stay warm, and settled in for the night. I'd figure out what to do tomorrow. An electric blanket would be really nice right about now, I thought as I closed my eyes.

CHAPTER 3

Something bright lit up beyond my eyelids, waking me up. It took just a moment for me to get my bearings. My legs ached from being folded in the cramped space between the hedges. As I stretched them out, I looked up to see that a light had been turned on in Carter's living room, and I perked up.

I had no idea what time it was, but it didn't seem too much later than when I fell asleep. The moon had only moved a little bit beyond the neighbor's house. I had been focusing on it when I fell asleep.

Other than that lamp in their living room, the neighborhood was eerily dark and quiet. I shivered in response. I had lived multiple lives and many decades, but dark streets still made me nervous. I lowered my head and tried to make myself as small as possible inside the hedges.

As I peered out from my hiding place, watching Carter, he got up and walked over to the window that opened up to the front yard. His eyes scanned the street just before he pulled the curtains closed.

"Oh that's just great," I said to myself.

I needed to get a look at what was going on, so I pulled myself up. As the blood rushed to my feet, I could feel the familiar pins and needles in them. I shook my feet around, one at a time, in an attempt to hasten the rush of blood to them. If anyone had been out, watching me, I would have looked ridiculous to them, all hopping around and such. But I was pretty sure it was after midnight. This was the type of neighborhood that shut down at dusk. It was quite unlikely that anyone would happen by at that moment.

Once I was able to walk, pain free, I slithered along the hedges, to the side of Carter's house. I didn't need to go into the backyard, because there was a side window to the living room that was before the gate. I ducked down under the window and peeked my head up, just barely enough to see into the living room. The curtains on the side window were also closed, but had a bit of a gap in them, which was all I needed.

I didn't need to wonder very long what Carter was up to at the late hour. I was pretty sure that I already knew. I watched as he picked up a pack of cigarettes that one of his parents had left on the coffee table. He carefully tapped the pack into his other hand, and pulled out a single cigarette. It was a maneuver that he had probably seen his parents do thousands of times over the years.

Then he put the cigarette in his mouth, picked up the lighter that had been lying next to the pack, and lit it. He coughed and spat out the cigarette after taking a deep pull on it. I watched as he then picked up the still burning item and put it in a nearby ashtray.

I saw that he still had the lighter in his hand, and stuffed it into the pocket of his pajamas. He walked over to a closet that was by the front door and opened it. He looked up at the top, but I couldn't make out what he was looking at. My eyes never left him as he walked to the dining room, grabbed a chair, and dragged it to the closet. He then carefully climbed onto the chair, reached to the top shelf of the closet, and pulled something down.

Candles. Oh no. He pulled down about ten of them, just a few at a time, dropping them on the carpet below him. When he decided that he had enough, he climbed down, dragged the chair back to its home, and walked back to the candles. Over the next few minutes, he carefully placed the candles on every other stair step leading to the second floor.

Once all the candles were in place, he lit each one of them with the lighter. When he was done, he stood back, at the bottom of the stairs, and admired his work.

Should I go knock on the door to stop what I thought was about to happen? I knew that if I did that, they would think I was crazy. They wouldn't know what to do about some little girl showing up at their house in the middle of the night to tell them that their son was about to accidentally burn their house down.

Of course, the candles were on the stairs, already lit. So there was that. But I had a feeling that they would be more focused on me. Of course they would.

I was conflicted. So I stood there, doing nothing. But that didn't last long, because Carter was on the move. He walked over and lit another candle on the coffee table. Then reached over and knocked the ashtray with the burning cigarette onto the floor. It was a deliberate move.

That was weird.

When done with that, he walked back to the stairs. I held my breath as he climbed them, carefully so as not to disturb the candles. I could see all the way up the stairs from my vantage point. Once Carter reached the top of the stairs, he spun around and looked down at the candles. I watched as his head turned and he looked down the hall of the top floor at something. I assumed it was his parents' bedroom door, but I'll never know for sure.

Then the unthinkable happened.

He stepped over to the top burning candle, pulled his leg back, and purposefully kicked it over. As it tumbled down the stairs, the spilled wax caught fire and there was a domino effect of candle hitting candle. Before it got to the bottom one, the left side of the stairs were all on fire and I saw Carter run down past the flames into the living room. He hesitated only long enough to knock over the candle on the coffee table and turn to the front door. He walked calmly out the front door, slamming it as the house burned behind him.

Pure shock overtook me for a moment. Almost everything that Carter told me had been a lie. Sure, he did try smoking, though that may have been a red herring for the purposefully set fire. And yes, he did light candles up the stair steps, like he told me. What he lied about was the fact that he walked up and deliberately kicked over the candles. He didn't accidentally knock over the candles when trying to blow them out, due to him being panicked his parents would find out. And he didn't accidentally knock over the candle on the coffee table while hacking away from smoking. And he never went into the kitchen to get a bucket of water for the fire, like he said he did.

He had deliberately deceived me, telling me half truths.

I now knew for certain exactly why I landed here in this town, on this front lawn, at this time. It was up to me to do something about the fire in front of me, and the pending deaths of Carter's parents.

As I stood there, my feet frozen into place, Carter walked to the edge of the lawn, near the street. If he had looked over, he would have seen me standing there. The oddest thing was though, that before he turned toward the house, I saw the smile on his face.

CHAPTER 4

"You lied to me!" I screamed at Carter, without thinking.

His head spun around and he looked at me, stiffening his posture and his mouth falling open. Then he tilted his head to the side and narrowed his eyes my way. I could see that he had no idea who I was or why I was there. Well, that question was answered. We had never met before. I wasn't sure if that made this harder or easier.

I didn't wait to explain to him the circumstances of my being there, and took off with a sprint in the direction of the next door neighbor's house. Carter watched me as I ran across his lawn, right past him, and up the steps of the house.

I began pounding on the front door.

"Get up!" I screamed. "Fire!" I yelled at the top of my lungs in an attempt to rouse the occupants from their slumber. I looked up when a light illuminated the window above where I was standing. A face peered out. I started screaming again.

"There's a fire next door! Call 911!"

I saw the man nod his head and leave the window. I hoped that he understood me and had obliged.

I turned to run back over to where Carter was still standing and noticed several people standing on their lawns in their pajamas watching the scene unfold.

One of the women called to me from across the street. "I already called the fire department!" she told me.

"Thank you!" I replied and headed to Carter.

"Can your parents get out?" I asked him.

"Who are you?" he replied, without answering my question.

"Nobody. I was just walking by." Was there any chance that he would buy that story?

"In the middle of the night? You were just walking by? Yeah right," he responded, calmly.

"Stop worrying about me!" I yelled. "Is there a way for your parents to get out?" I asked again.

Carter just shrugged his shoulders. His body language showed no sign of agitation or worry about his parents. What was wrong with this kid? He didn't seem like the boy that had been my best friend for all those years. Sure, he was a bit odd, but I never pegged him for a killer. And his own parents. I was in shock at his behavior.

I ran toward his house. I knew better than to run into a burning building, but I had to do something. I pounded on the front door and screamed. There was no response. His parents' bedroom was probably in the back of the house and they couldn't hear me. I ran to the side gate, but there was so much fire and smoke by then, I thought it would be suicide to get myself trapped in the backyard of a burning house.

I didn't even know his parents, yet I burst out crying when I realized there was nothing more that I could do. It must have been the stress of it all. I walked solemnly back to the sidewalk where the crowd had been gathering. Tears flowed freely down my face as we all waited.

Within approximately two minutes, sirens wailed up the street and we looked in that direction. The crowds moved to allow the fire truck to pull up to the curb right in front of the house. Within what seemed like only seconds, they were spraying water and asking questions.

"Is anyone in the house?" someone asked us.

Carter shrugged his shoulders. I couldn't believe what I was seeing.

"Yes. His parents are in there. On the second floor. Please hurry," I explained.

The firefighter took off like a flash. He spoke with a few others, and then two of them ran inside the house. I held my breath while I waited for the outcome.

Those brave men clearly had been trained well. Within a minute or so, they walked out, accompanying both of Carter's parents. They were disheveled and coughing, but alive. The firefighters led them directly to the waiting ambulance and left the paramedics to do their job.

I don't know for sure, but I could swear that I saw a look of disappointment on Carter's face.

It took a while longer for the fire to be extinguished, but they were able to get it out before the entire house was consumed. Though honestly, there wasn't really much left. It was unusable as it was, and would probably have to be torn down and rebuilt.

It was time for me to take my leave before people started asking me questions that I couldn't answer without sounding like a lunatic. The police had already pulled Carter to the side and were trying to get some information out of him. No one had really noticed yet that I was standing there alone.

I quietly, and deliberately, began walking toward town. I did my best to blend in with the neighbors still standing on their lawns and in the street, trying to get a better view.

Once I reached the same convenience store that I had been at a few hours earlier, I asked the clerk how to get to the bus station and he gave me directions. He didn't even seem a bit fazed that a 9 year old girl was asking for directions to the bus station at something like 1 a.m. Working the graveyard shift had probably shown him more about people than he ever wanted to see.

A half hour later, I was sitting at the bus station on an uncomfortable plastic chair that was being held together with duct tape. A sketchy looking man was sitting across from me, and a couple of chairs down. It was unnerving the way he kept staring at me, though I did my best to ignore him and not to look his way.

The entire bus station seemed to be in various shades of gray. The walls were a light gray, with some graffiti that no one bothered to paint over. The floors were a darker gray and didn't look like they had been mopped in months. The plastic chairs appeared to have been white at some point, but that was no longer the case. They were sort of gray and dirt colored. If I weren't wearing jeans, I would never have dared to sit down. God I hoped the bus was in better shape.

I dared to look up at the sketchy looking man again and he smiled my way. His gapped tooth grin and scraggly beard gave me the willies. For a moment, I considered finding another chair, facing away from the man. But then I thought better of it. I wanted to keep him in view. I would probably be even more nervous with my back to him. So there I sat.

I was dog tired, but refused to allow my drooping eyelids to shut completely. Not in this sketchy bus station. Yeah, I'm using the word 'sketchy' a lot, but there really is no other word in the english language to describe it. So 'sketchy' it is.

A few hours later, I was snuggled down in my bus seat for the long ride home. The bus driver had been nice enough to give me a blanket she kept up front for her own personal use when her legs got cold. I think she felt sorry for me.

"Girl, you are much too young to be traveling all that way on your own," she told me, handing me the blanket.

I thanked her and found a seat near the front, so she could keep an eye on me while I slept.

Sleep didn't come easily though. Too much had happened to

me in the last 24 hours. Not even 24 hours. It was late afternoon the day before, when I woke up from my plunge into the sinkhole. Now my mind was reeling from everything. And...I just realized that I was starving. The only thing I had eaten in this lifetime was a couple of donuts.

"Hey, Little One," the bus driver called to me.

"Me?" I looked around at some of the other passengers, who were all asleep.

"Yeah, you." She smiled my way. "You want the other half of my sandwich? I'm not gonna eat it all and you look hungry."

"I do?"

"Yeah, you are way too skinny. Now come here and take this sandwich before I give it to someone else." She held it up in the air like she had just awarded a prize to the winner of her sandwich trophy.

She didn't have to tell me twice. I jumped out of my seat, dropping the blanket on the floor as I did so. Her eyes followed it as it fell.

"Oh, sorry," I told her, quickly picking it up and laying it gently on the bus seat.

"Here you go. Made it myself," she said, handing me the sandwich. "Oh, reach over and open that compartment there." She pointed at the dashboard.

I did as I was told. I laughed out loud when I saw the contents.

"I keep a few things around for when I get the munchies. Help yourself."

Her 'few things' consisted of several bags of chips, some cookies, beef jerky, and an assortment of candy.

I reached in and took one bag of chips and a few cookies. I was starving and could probably have eaten half of the compartments contents, but I didn't want to be greedy and take too much of her stash.

She reached over and closed the compartment when I was

finished. "You know where it is if you want anymore. Have as much as you want," she told me.

Then I saw her look up into the mirror above her at the rest of the passengers. She didn't say a thing, but my guess was that she was hoping no one else would think that offer extended to them. No one said a word.

I sat and ate the tuna fish sandwich, which was not my favorite, but I was starving, so I was not gonna be picky. My mind drifted back to Sandy Cove. Now that Carter's parents were still alive, did that mean that Carter would not move in next door to me? Yeah, I guess it did. There would be no reason for him to move there. Hmm, that would be weird. I always had him there to be my best friend, no matter what. What would the rest of my life be like without him?

Another thing that jumped into my mind was that if Carter was the Red Lake Slasher, would everyone be safe if he stayed in Sandy Cove? I guess they would. It's not like he would be going all the way to Red Lake just to kill my friends. He doesn't even know me. Or them.

So, does that mean that some girls in Sandy Cove are now in danger? Girls that have never been in danger before? If he was the killer, wouldn't he just kill girls that were nearby? Oh god, what have I done? Have I put some innocent young girls in harm's way?

Carter has to be the killer, right? I mean, I saw what he deliberately did to try to kill his parents. There's something twisted in that mind of his. It seems really unlikely that this would be the one and only time in his entire life that he would do something like that. Yeah, there's going to be more. I was sure of it.

A few hours later, I thanked the nice bus driver, once again, and departed the bus. It wasn't that far of a walk home. When I walked in, my parents barely acknowledged me. Obviously Parker had done what I asked of him.

Later that evening, after dinner and while my parents were watching TV, Parker dragged me into the backyard.

"So spill," he demanded.

"What?" I pretended like I had no idea what he was talking about.

He wasn't buying it and gave me a crooked half smile, while glaring at me at the same time. He crossed his arms in front of his chest, waiting for my explanation.

"Okay, okay," I told him, holding my palms up in front of me. "I was out really late with my friends and we all told our parents that we were spending the night at each other's house."

"So, why were you on a payphone?" The look on his face said he didn't believe me. "And you told me that you were in Sandy Cove. What was that all about?"

"I lied about Sandy Cove. I just didn't want you to know where I really was. And I couldn't use the phone at anyone's house, which is why I used a payphone. We were all supposed to be somewhere else." I was making up the story as I went, trying my best to get it past Parker's 12 year old self.

"What were you all doing out so late? I mean, you are only 9 years old."

"Yeah, unfortunately, I know how old I am. We were...just goofing off. Nothing really. We eventually went over to Bernadette's and spent the night."

Maybe I shouldn't use words like 'unfortunately' and 'eventually' I thought. Those don't sound like words a little girl would be using. Tone it down, I told myself.

"We told her mother that Mom wasn't feeling well, so we went over to Bernadette's house. Her mother didn't seem to notice. It's none of your business anyway." I stuck out my tongue at him for emphasis. Now that was the behavior of a 9 year old. I hoped.

I looked at him to gauge his reaction and he shrugged in response.

"Whatever," is all he said.

CHAPTER 5

The very next day, I was sitting on the steps of my front porch reading a book. What else was I going to do? I was 9. As far as I knew, neither Bernadette nor Josephine were going to be in danger for at least six more years. I had to do something to kill the time. Okay, bad choice of words. But whatever. I'm 9.

While reading, and soaking in some of the midday warmth of the sun, a car drove past me and pulled into Jean's driveway. I froze. It was the same car that Carter and his family had been in the day before, at their house in Sandy Cove.

I watched intently as all three of them slowly climbed out. Carter was the first to exit the car, followed by his mother, then his father. Each of them looked deflated somehow. Like the weight of the world was on their shoulders. They all looked up at Jean as she burst out of her house and ran down her steps.

"Oh, my poor family!" she cried, hugging each of them, one at a time.

Not one of them smiled, and none of them hugged her back. She didn't seem to notice.

"I can't believe that your house burned down! You all can stay with me for as long as you need to."

She gave them a pathetic sort of look and ushered them in to the house. There were no suitcases. In fact, I just realized that they were all still wearing their pajamas. I guess it was kind of hard to go shopping in the middle of the night, with no money, and no real clothes to wear.

"Candy, I've got some clothes you can borrow for now. We can go shopping for CJ and Carter this afternoon," I heard Jean say right before she closed the front door behind them.

Oh wow, Carter is here. I saved his parents, but that didn't stop him from ending up in Red Lake anyway. I was sure their living situation was going to be temporary. It had to be. They couldn't possibly live there until we were teenagers. Could they?

Like a creepy little stalker, I did nothing over the next couple of days, except watch Jean's house. My mother even commented on it at one point, telling me to get outside and enjoy the summer. "Go walk the dog," she ordered.

"Ugh, fine."

I reluctantly removed myself from the living room couch, and my great view out the window to the house next door, and called the dog. He wasn't any happier about the walk than I was. Our dog, Midnight, reluctantly unfolded himself from the end of the couch and jumped down to the floor. I know, I know. Every black cat and dog is named Midnight. What can I say? I was 4 years old when I named him.

I squinted as we stepped outside. That's when I realized that I hadn't been out at all since Carter and his parents arrived two days ago. I really should get out more.

I turned to my right when we reached the sidewalk. I wanted to walk past the house to see if anything interesting was going on. It wasn't. But then, almost as if I willed it to happen, Carter came walking out just at that moment. He was wearing brown shorts and a tan t-shirt. It was exactly what I expected from him.

Carter took one look at me and stopped dead in his tracks. Then his face got all scrinchy.

"Hey, I know you," he called, picking up his pace and jogging to where I had stopped on the sidewalk in front of their house.

"What do you mean?"

I pretended not to know him, and did my best not to make eye contact. I was a terrible liar, and just knew that my expression would give me away. I fidgeted with my hair as I spoke.

"You were at my house the other night. Yeah," he paused a moment, looking at me from head to toe, "I'm sure that was you. In Sandy Cove. What were you doing all the way in Sandy Cove?"

"What? Where's Sandy Cove?" I didn't know if my stupid act was going to work or not.

"It was definitely you. I remember. You screamed at me."

It was clear that he wasn't going to leave it alone.

I shrugged in response. Kids do that all the time. Maybe it would seem normal to him.

"Why are you here? What's going on?" he continued.

Good grief, what's with all the questions, I thought. I needed a story. And quick. He wasn't going to believe that it wasn't me. He knew it was.

Midnight laid down on the cool grass next to us and closed his eyes. He knew instinctively that this was going to take a while.

"Um, well...I don't know what you are talking about. I've never been to Sandy Cove." Even I didn't believe what I was saying. How was I going to convince him of anything?

"I know it was you. I don't know what your problem is, and why you are lying to me, but it was you." He narrowed his eyes at me as he spoke.

Carter looked like he was beginning to get agitated. I didn't need him to stir up any trouble for me. And I certainly didn't need my parents, or his, hearing our conversation. They might ask questions. And they might actually require that I give some answers. I could probably fool a 9 year old boy, but adults were a different story. And if my mother started looking into my 'sleepover' at Bernadette's house from the other night, there really could be trouble then.

"I gotta go. Midnight needs a walk. Bye." I pulled on the leash to nudge the dog to get up and get moving. He obliged, albeit slowly.

I turned back once we got probably 50 feet away. Carter was standing there, arms crossed, glaring at me. I quickened my pace, daring not to turn back again.

Hoping to avoid another encounter with Carter, I took Midnight on an extra long walk, much to his chagrin. Carter was gone by the time we returned home.

For about two weeks, I managed to avoid Carter completely. It wasn't easy. Someone in that household seemed to be coming or going all the time. It seemed that Carter's parents must have gotten jobs, because their schedules became pretty regular, leaving in the morning, and arriving back home late in the afternoon.

That told me something interesting. If they had jobs, they must be planning on living there for a while. I guess it takes a long time to build a new house, if that's what was happening.

One beautiful, sunny afternoon, I decided that I couldn't hide out forever. I needed to get out into the world. Besides, my mother had been nagging me to go outside, make some friends, and enjoy life.

I grabbed a book and walked out to my front porch. I looked over at the house next door and all was quiet. I figured I had a bit of time to sit on the bench and read. Someone would have to go to some trouble to spot me sitting up there.

About a half hour into my reading, I heard the front door of Jean's house slam shut. It startled me, causing me to drop my book. Bending over to pick it up, I brushed off the cover as I straightened back up. The first thing I saw was Carter standing on the steps in front of me, staring.

"What is your deal? You live here?" He was direct, that was for sure. That was different. Carter never was the direct type when I knew him before.

"I don't have a deal," I responded, laying my book on the bench next to me. "And yes, I do live here."

"Then why were you in Sandy Cove?" he continued.

"I don't know what you're talking about," I lied.

"That's a lie and you know it. It was definitely you."

He stepped up one more step toward me, causing me to stand up in response. I wasn't about to get caught in a vulnerable position, just in case he turned violent. I now knew, without a doubt, what he was capable of.

"What did you see?" he asked, crossing his arms.

"When?" I was biding my time.

"Back in Sandy Cove, when my house accidentally caught on fire."

"Your house caught on fire?" I didn't know how else to respond.

"You know it did. You were there," he answered.

I said nothing in response.

"Why did you scream that I lied to you that night? What do you think I lied about?" he asked. "I've never talked to you before in my life."

Oh, if you only knew, I almost said out loud. I bit my lower lip.

"I told you already that it wasn't me," I responded, crossing my arms for emphasis.

The look on Carter's face told me that he didn't believe a word that came out of my mouth. But that was his problem. Not mine. I wasn't about to tell him the truth.

"How long are you all going to stay at Jean's house?" I asked, trying to change the subject.

Carter shrugged his shoulders. "Probably till next summer. Our house has to be rebuilt."

"I see." I reached down and picked up my book, hoping that would serve as notice that our conversation was over.

It didn't work.

"What's your name?" he asked me.

Oh yeah, I had almost forgotten that we didn't know each other yet in this life.

"Ivy."

"Like the plant?" he laughed.

"Yeah, just like that," I responded, mostly under my breath. I had heard all the jokes. They were old news.

I didn't like this Carter at all. Especially after I witnessed first hand what he was capable of. Now he was living next door to me, and he seemed quite confrontational. That wasn't like the old Carter at all. I wondered if he was looking for a friend. I didn't want to be that person.

But then again, maybe I should be his friend. It would be a lot easier to keep tabs on him if he thought we were friends. He would be more likely to let his guard down that way, and possibly open up with information about his parents.

"Carter!"

We both turned toward the voice coming from the house next door.

"I gotta go."

With that, he took off toward his new home. I watched him until he disappeared into the house.

"Ives, what are you doing?"

I jumped at Parker's voice. I hadn't heard our own front door open and close behind me. I had been focused on watching Carter.

"Nothing," I told my brother. "I'm just reading. See." I held up my book in front of me.

"Yeah, sounds fascinating. I saw you talking to that new boy next door. Are you friends now?" he asked me.

"No, not even close. He's kinda weird," I told him, trying my best to sound like a 9 year old.

"I noticed. Sometimes I see him in the backyard messing with bugs and stuff. Yeah, he's weird," Parker told me.

"You look over the fence and watch him?" I asked.

He shrugged. "Yeah, sometimes."

"Hey, tell mom I went over to Jake's house. K?" he asked.

"Why don't you tell her yourself?" I asked.

"Because she was on the phone. You know how she gets." He made the universal 'yapping' gesture with his hand. I thought it looked like a duck squawking.

"Ok fine. I'll tell her." I sat back down on the bench and opened my book.

CHAPTER 6

After that, life went on, as it tends to do.

Carter's family did stay with Jean next door for about a year. I made a bit of effort to be somewhat friendly to him, but he and I never did talk much. I did make a point to keep a close eye on him, just to be sure he wasn't up to anything suspicious.

He seemed to be an average kid. Nothing really out of place, that I could see.

One day he came over to my house.

"Guess what?" he questioned.

"What?" I asked.

"We are moving back to Sandy Cove this weekend."

"You are? I didn't know your house was ready," I told him.

"Yes, finally. Aunt Jean is okay, but her house is way too small for four people. I've been sleeping on the couch for a year. It sucks."

"Yeah, that would suck," I agreed.

"I gotta go pack. Bye Poison Ivy." He never turned back.

"Ha ha, very funny!" I called after him.

I was conflicted after hearing the news that Carter was moving out of Jean's house. On the one hand, he would be gone, out of

Red Lake for good. Or so I hoped. On the other hand, what did the future hold in the town of Sandy Cove, now that Carter would be back and growing up? Were there future teenagers in that town that would be in danger? Would that be partly my fault?

I was the one that changed the future by saving his parents, causing Carter to grow up in Sandy Cove, instead of Red Lake. But, did I have a choice in the matter? No, I didn't. I was sure of that. There was no possible way that I could stand on the lawn of that house and just watch it burn, knowing that his parents were inside, and in danger. I could never have done that.

I still didn't know for a fact that Carter was the Red Lake Slasher, but he sure seemed like the likely candidate. Being only 10 years old, there was nothing I could do, and really nothing that could be done yet. It was still years away before the Slasher would strike. I just had to wait.

Over the next five years, nothing significant happened. I half hoped someone would kill me off, so that I could start over as an adult. Starting over at 9 years old sucked beyond all imagination.

The only thing that I was thankful for was that I had gotten the chance to save Carter's parents. They never knew how dangerously close they got to dying that night. And they would never have known that it was their own son that did it.

But, having to go through all of those same years again, was not my idea of fun. That was the price I had to pay, I guess.

Carter did visit his Aunt Jean a few times over the years. Sometimes with his parents, and sometimes not. He always seemed to seek me out whenever he was in town. I think he had a crush on me. Actually, I was positive that he did. I was pretty sure that his visits to Aunt Jean were thinly veiled trips to see me.

The one good thing about it all, was that he never brought up the night of the house fire again. I guess he either decided that it wasn't me after all, or that I was never going to admit it. Either way, that was a win for me.

We got to know each other better over the years, but still not to the same degree as in my first lifetime, where we were the best of friends.

I just didn't trust him. I was pretty sure that Carter was not the Red Lake Slasher though. How could he be? He didn't even live in town. There was no way he would ride the bus all those hours just to kill someone. He could just kill in his own hometown. So, it had to be someone else. But who?

Or maybe it was Carter. And since he didn't live in Red Lake, then both of my friends would be safe, but others would be in danger. My head hurt just trying to fit all the pieces together. Nothing fit though.

My 15th birthday was fast approaching, and I was torn. It was the day that Bernadette always died. Well, except for last time. I actually did save her in my last life, but then Josephine got drunk and hit Bernadette with her car, so Bernadette ended up dying anyway.

That was my dilemma. Do I try to save Bernadette, knowing that she could very well die anyway, just differently? Do I not bother? No, that wasn't me. I couldn't just not try. No matter what happened to me, I couldn't sit back and just let it happen. I would never be able to forgive myself for doing something like that.

Bernadette and I barely knew each other in this life. Same with Josephine. I just didn't want to get too close to either girl, for fear that my relationship with them was the reason they died. And kept dying.

Bernadette still hated me though. That seemed to never change from lifetime to lifetime. I mostly avoided her, but she still found reasons to hate me.

I finally made the decision that I would have my normal Halloween Birthday Party. It was the perfect way to get both Bernadette and Josephine in my house, where I could keep an eye on them. Now...how to get them to come?

Just ask, I guess. It wasn't like the podunk town of Red Lake had a bunch of other things to do that night for the teens in town. I found Bernadette in the hall at school a few days before my birthday.

"Hi Bernadette," I said, approaching her and two of her friends. They were all gathered around her locker between classes.

Bernadette turned to look at me. "Oh hi." I could see on her face that she was genuinely surprised to see me standing there. Her friends said nothing.

"Um, I'm having a Halloween party at my house this weekend. It also happens to be my birthday. I'd love it if you came." I looked at her friends. "All of you are invited."

The three girls looked at each other, none of them knowing how to respond.

"We'll see," Bernadette finally spoke up. "I'm not sure what's going on that night."

"Parker will be there." I took a chance that she had a crush on my brother in this life also.

"Really?" Her eyebrows raised in response, as she wrapped her long blonde hair around her index finger and released it. I watched as it unwound and fell perfectly straight, once again.

"Yeah. Since it's my birthday, he wanted to come. My parents won't be there though." I hoped that the comment about my parents not being there would push her into accepting. No teenager wanted to attend a party where parents were chaperoning.

"We might be able to come. We'll see." She looked around to her friends as she spoke.

I figured she would probably be there, but didn't want to jump at it in front of her friends. That was probably the best I was going to get out of her.

"Okay. Well, you know where I live." What else could I say? I certainly couldn't beg her to come. I turned and walked to my next class.

Josephine was a bit easier. Though we weren't the best of friends, like we had been in previous lives, we were at least friendly to each other. She agreed readily. I made sure to enlist her help in setting up the party. She was happy to help.

I made sure to tell her, and anyone that would listen, that everyone was invited. I prayed that it wasn't a mistake, and that 400 people wouldn't show up. That many had never come in the past, so I felt fairly safe this time.

The day of my party, Josephine and I spent several hours setting everything up. I wanted...no, actually needed, everything to be perfect. Bernadette's life could depend on it. If she hated the party, and decided to leave early, that could be a really big problem. This party was for her. She just didn't know it.

An hour into the party, quite a few people had shown up. It was a nice turn out. Unfortunately, Bernadette was not one of them. I was beginning to get worried, and thought about calling her. That would be weird though, since she had no idea that her attendance was a matter of life and death.

Just as I seriously considered heading out to search for her, in she walked. Whew, thankfully. And then I noticed who walked in behind her.

Simon.

Oh man, I had almost completely forgotten Simon. He had rarely entered my thoughts over the last six years. That was probably because I was pretty sure that Carter was the Slasher, and not Simon.

Still…there he was. And I couldn't take my eyes off of him.

Images of my children suddenly slammed into my mind. I can't think of any other way to describe it. I still missed them horribly, and had tried my best to put them out of my mind. I knew that they would never exist again for me. Trying to get on with my life, and letting Hunter and Courtney go, was the only thing I could do to not go crazy with grief. And, I had done a pretty good job of it. Until Simon walked in…

"Hey Ivy," Bernadette slurred.

Oh great. She's drunk. Again. I wondered if it was necessary for her to get drunk every single Halloween, of every single lifetime.

"This is Simon," she announced, grabbing his arm and pulling him closer to herself.

"Um hi. Nice to meet you," I said to him, trying not to stare.

"Hi," he smiled at me.

"Do you have anything to drink around here?" Bernadette asked me.

"Yes, it's in the…"

I never got a chance to finish my sentence. Bernadette took Simon's hand and pulled him toward the kitchen. He looked back at me once more and shrugged.

Whatever. I really didn't care. My focus was on Bernadette for the night.

"Bernadette, maybe you should slow down a bit," I told her after walking into the kitchen and watching her chug some sort of mixed drink.

I had not provided the alcohol. I was only 15, and not that stupid. However, as was usual with teen parties, someone sneaked it in.

"What are you, my mother?" Bernadette was the only one that laughed at her joke.

"I just want to make sure you are okay. I can tell that you've had a lot to drink." I did my best to stay calm.

"Mind your own damn business," she slurred out.

"Whatever."

I turned and walked out of the kitchen. I didn't sign up for her abuse. All I needed to do was keep her at my house. I didn't have to actually talk to her. Or like her.

"How come no one told me we were having a party?" Parker said as he walked in the front door.

"It's just a bunch of teenagers," I told him. "I didn't think you'd be interested."

"Is there alcohol?" he asked me.

"Yeah, I guess. Someone brought some." I pointed toward the hub of activity.

"Then I'm interested," he replied, making a beeline for the kitchen.

By the time I made it to the kitchen, Bernadette was already all over Parker. She had grabbed his arm and pulled him close to her, not unlike what she had done with Simon when they walked in.

Simon looked pissed off. He had moved over to a corner and was holding a beer in his hand, glaring at Parker. He seemed to perk up when he noticed that I had entered the room.

By the look on Parker's face, he wanted to escape her clutches, but didn't know how to in a gentle way. He widened his eyes at me and then tilted his head toward her. I got the point.

"Hey Bernadette." I walked over and took her hand. "Why don't you help me carry some things in from the garage." I pulled her gently toward the living room.

Standing her ground, she jerked her hand out of mine. "I don't want to help you carry stuff. Get someone else to do it." She wrapped both of her arms back around Parker's arm.

"I'll help," Parker volunteered, unwrapping Bernadette from around his arm as he spoke.

The look on her face...

"Oh boy, thanks. I needed the help. I didn't know how to get away from her without causing a scene. She's pretty lit," he told me as we walked out.

"Yeah, I saw that. Can you go get some more chicken and egg salad from the garage? That's where we stored the extra till we need it."

"What? You were serious about me carrying stuff in? I thought that was just a tactic to get me away from Bernadette." He seemed genuinely shocked that I actually wanted him to do something.

"Well, she was part of it. But yeah, I really could use the help. It's just a couple of trays," I told him. "I'm sure you can handle it."

I stopped walking and waited for his response.

"Ugh, fine. I'll go get the food." He pointed at me. "You owe me."

I just nodded.

"Hey, Ivy."

I turned to see Simon standing behind me. I didn't respond.

"I, um, was wondering if you wanted to go out sometime?" He looked at me expectantly.

"With you?" I was stalling for time.

"Well yeah, with me."

"What the hell?"

It was Bernadette. She had walked up just in time. She looked at me, then at Simon.

"You came here with me, and you have the nerve to ask someone else out? With me right here?" She was slurring her words more than ever.

"Why did you even invite me here, Ivy? So you could steal my boyfriend!"

Her voice was getting louder and I looked around at the faces that were turned with great interest toward our conversation.

"I'm not your boyfriend," Simon told her. Then he turned to me. "I barely know her. I am definitely not her boyfriend."

Bernadette looked like she was about to cry.

"That's nice. Real nice," I told Simon. "Couldn't you just try to be a gentleman, for once?"

"What are you talking about? For once? You don't know anything about me. We just met tonight."

He tilted his head my way. He was confused. That was expected. But it didn't matter at the moment. I needed to deal with Bernadette, because she was already storming out the front door of my house.

"Now look what you've done!" I yelled at Simon, as I ran out the door after Bernadette.

CHAPTER 7

"Bernadette, wait!" I called after her.

Bernadette stopped and pivoted on her heels. "What the hell for? You invited me to your stupid party, then you try to steal my boyfriend. Or my date. Or whatever he is. He came with me. Not you."

"I know. I don't want Simon, I swear. I was just about to tell him that I don't want to go out with him, when you heard us talking and started yelling," I tried to explain.

"You always get everything, Ivy, and I'm sick of it. The boys always like you better than me. You do better in school that I do. You have a nicer family. I'm just over it. Leave me alone!" she practically screamed at me.

If only she knew how much I didn't have. I didn't have a nice boyfriend. I didn't have my kids. I didn't have a life. Not really. It could be pulled out from under me at any moment. I hated to admit it, but I envied Bernadette. Not at the moment, maybe, but yes, she at least had a fighting chance at a normal life. If I could save her, that is.

Bernadette started walking down the street again. I didn't know what to do. If I followed her, she wouldn't like that at all. If I just let her go, she might get killed. I couldn't just let her go. If she died, that would all be on me.

"Bernadette, wait!" I called after her.

"Can I help?"

"Oh, Carter, what are you doing here?" I asked him. "I didn't know you were even in town."

"I just got here a few hours ago. We are visiting Aunt Jean for the weekend. I heard all the commotion. What's going on with Bernadette?"

Carter being in town was a big problem. When he was several hours away in Sandy Cove, I felt pretty safe in the knowledge that he was not around to harm Bernadette. Because of that, I was pretty sure he was not the Slasher.

But there he was, standing right in front of me. That was a bad sign as far as I was concerned. If he is in town the night Bernadette is killed, that makes him a prime suspect.

"Um, she's drunk, and mad at me. I'm just trying to calm her down," I explained. "The best thing right now is for me to get her home."

Just great, now I have two people I have to keep an eye on.

"Can I help? I can walk her home, if you like," Carter volunteered.

That was odd. It wasn't like Carter at all to volunteer to help anyone. I found that quite suspicious. And there was no way on earth I was going to leave Bernadette alone with someone I suspected was the Red Lake Slasher.

"No, I, um, I'll take care of it. You can just go home. Don't worry about us, we'll be fine." I did my best to sound calm while I was talking to him.

"Are you sure? I'd really like to help. It looks like you have a party going on and a lot to deal with."

"No, really. Go on home." I thought for a moment. "You are welcome to come to the party if you want." That might make it easier for me to keep my eyes on him.

Carter shrugged at me. "If you say so, then I'll go to the party for a minute or two. I don't really know anyone there, so I won't stay long."

"Okay, fine. You can get something to eat, at least. I've got to go find Bernadette," I told him. "Oh hey, when you get to the party, can you send Parker this way? Tell him I need his help with something." I didn't wait for an answer as I took off down the street in the direction she had gone.

I was afraid to look back at Carter. He was probably confused, and maybe angry, that I refused his help, but asked him to send my brother to help me. Well, I couldn't worry about that. I had more pressing things to worry about. I could deal with Carter later.

Ten minutes later I found Bernadette walking down the street toward town. About the time I caught up with her, Parker came driving up next to us.

"Oh Parker, thank goodness," I exclaimed, when he rolled down his window.

"What's up? Carter said you needed my help with something. He looked pissed off at you." Parker told me.

"Yeah, I'm sure he was," I replied. Then I turned to Bernadette, who was still walking. "Bernadette, Parker is going to take you home. Is that all right with you?" I knew it would be.

She stopped in her tracks and turned to look at me. She smiled when she saw Parker stop the car and get out to help her in.

"Hi Parker," she slurred. "You are really cute, you know that?"

Parker laughed. "Yes, I know that." He opened the passenger door for her. "Now come on, get in, and I'll take you home."

Bernadette climbed in and I watched as they drove away.

I breathed a sigh of relief, knowing that she would be safe, for tonight anyway. I couldn't predict what might happen in the future.

When I got back to my party, Carter was not there. Not that I really expected him to be. He did say he was only going to stay for couple of minutes. That was fine. I really didn't want to have to deal with him anyway.

Another thing I noticed was that Simon was also gone. Even though he came with Bernadette, and we didn't know each other, I still thought he might have hung around for a while. But again, that was fine too. Since Bernadette was safe at home, it didn't really matter where Simon was. He couldn't get to her at her house. If he was even the killer at all.

After I had enjoyed my party for a while, which usually didn't happen, and things began winding down, I realized that Parker had not returned. Of course, he was an adult, and maybe had just gone off with his friends, but I thought it was odd that he did not call me after dropping off Bernadette at her house. So I gave him a call.

When he didn't answer the phone, I left a message, and began to worry just a bit. Had he gotten Bernadette home safely? Good question, as no one bothered to let me know. So, even though it was getting quite late, I called Bernadette's house.

"Hi, Mrs. James, this is Ivy Wells," I greeted when Bernadette's mother answered the phone. "Is Bernadette home?"

"Ivy, it's quite late. Why are you calling? I'm sure Bernadette is asleep," she answered, without directly addressing my question.

"I know. I'm really sorry. I'm just worried about her. She left my Halloween party in a huff, after getting mad about something that happened. I just wanted to make sure she got home okay. Can you please check?" I pleaded.

"Well, okay. Hang on."

I waited for what seemed like an eternity for Mrs. James to get back to the phone. I thanked some of the party attendees as they headed out the door. Everyone was gone, and I was completely alone in the house. I thought about the fact that my parents went out of town for the weekend, even though it was my birthday. But that was okay, we had celebrated it together a couple of days ago at a nice restaurant.

"Ivy, are you still there?" she asked when she returned to the phone.

"Yes, I'm still here. Is she all right?" I bit my lower lip, waiting for good news.

"No, she's not here. What time did you say she left your party?"

"I didn't say, but it's been a couple of hours. I'm sure everything is fine. She's probably at one of her friend's house. Let me check around. I'll get back to you." I tried my best to sound calm and casual to her mother. But the fact was, I was panicking on the inside.

"All right. I'll make some calls too. Please let me know when you find her," Mrs. James asked.

"Of course." I hung up the phone, grabbed the keys to my mother's car, and bolted out the door. It never crossed my mind at the time that I didn't even have a license to drive.

I drove frantically around town. I checked the burger place, where everybody seem to hang out, and it was conspicuously empty. It was pretty late though. I really didn't know where else to check, so I just drove aimlessly through the streets. Where in the world could they possibly be?

As I drove past the town park, I spotted Parker's car. That's weird. Why would they be at the park? It was dark and the lights in the park were sparse, so I couldn't see anyone. I parked and got out of my car, heading toward the playground area. That's when I spotted them.

Parker and Bernadette were sitting together on the table top part of a set of picnic benches. I heard laughter and saw Bernadette playfully slap Parker on the arm while she was giggling. Okay, well then, I guess everyone's all right. I stood back though, and watched the scene a little longer. Neither one of them had noticed me standing there.

Bernadette was yapping away, and Parker seemed to enjoy her company. Luckily, talking was all they were doing. At 18 years old, Parker was an adult, and needed to be careful around Bernadette, especially since she had a crush on him.

"Hey guys," I finally interrupted.

Both turned to look at me. The looks on their faces told me they had no idea I was there. Apparently, they had been so engrossed in their conversation, that they were completely oblivious to the world around them. That was a bad sign. Parker certainly did not need to get involved with the likes of Bernadette. She would be nothing but trouble.

"What are you doing here, Ivy?" Bernadette kind of snarled my way.

"I've been looking for the two of you. Where have you been all this time?"

"We've been here," Parker answered. "We're just hanging out. It's all good."

"No, it's not all good," I replied, trying unsuccessfully to mask the irritation in my voice. "Bernadette, your mother is worried. Why didn't you call her?"

Bernadette shrugged her shoulders in response. "I just figured my parents would be asleep, and I didn't want to wake them."

"That's no excuse. You need to call her when you will be out late," I replied.

"You aren't my mother, Ivy. So just mind your own business," she retorted. "What do you care what I do anyway? Parker and I are just fine here without you."

Bernadette gave me a look that told me all I needed to know about how she felt about me.

"Ives, I'll take her home soon," he told me. "But, I'm starving. Bernie, you wanna go get a burger first?" he asked her.

"That sounds great. I'm starving too," she replied, ignoring me.

"Whatever," I told them. "Bernadette, please just call your mother first, before she gets together a search party."

"Fine, okay. I'll call her. You can go now," she said, waving her hand in my direction, effectively dismissing me.

I turned and left. My work for the night was done. I knew Parker would get her fed and get her home safely. So there was nothing for me to worry about.

Since I wouldn't be able to sleep anyway, once I got home I started cleaning up after the party. I don't know why I kept having the parties every time. People come, people drink and eat, then everyone leaves and no one helps clean up. It always gets left to me. Even Parker doesn't help. Oh well, at least he is helping me by getting Bernadette home safely. I could rest easy now.

CHAPTER 8

The next morning, I hesitated only a moment before I called Bernadette's house again. I held my breath, hoping that Bernadette would answer this time. But no, it was her mother again. Did no one else in that house ever answer the phone?

"Hi. Can I speak to Bernadette please?" I figured it was probably not necessary to announce myself. Her mother would know my voice by then.

"Ivy, why are you calling so early? Bernadette's not even up yet."

Yep, she knew exactly who was calling. It was pretty obvious to me that Mrs. James was getting irritated. Who could blame her? I was calling their house super late at night and then again early in the morning. Her mother must have thought my behavior was odd. Bernadette and I weren't even friends. I quickly got to the point, before she hung up on me.

"I'm really sorry. I just wanted to make sure that she got home safely last night. I went looking, like I told you I would. When I found her, I told her to call you, but I'm not positive that she did that. Her behavior was odd, and I just wanted to be sure she's all right. So, she is definitely home, and asleep?" I asked, fearing the answer.

"Yes, Ivy, she is definitely home and asleep. I saw her come home last night, and I just checked on her. She's out like a light." I could hear the exasperation in her mother's voice. "Do you want me to have her call you when she gets up?" she added.

"No, that's okay. I was just checking," I answered.

"Is there something going on that I should know about?" Mrs. James asked me. "You are acting kind of odd, Ivy. Do you have something to tell me? I'm her mother and should know if there is a problem. Don't you think?"

"Well yeah, you should know. But no, there's no problem. Not really. Bernadette was just hanging out with people that she doesn't know well." I didn't mention Simon's name, or the fact that she had been drinking. "I just wanted to make sure she didn't get herself into any trouble. I'm just a worrier, I guess."

I hoped that was a plausible explanation and that her mother wouldn't ask for more details.

"I see. Well, Ivy, why don't you let me worry about my daughter, and you can worry about yourself. Okay?" It didn't really sound like a question. More like an order.

"Yeah, okay," I responded. "Sorry again to have bothered you. I won't call back anytime soon. I promise."

She hung up the phone without responding.

Relief spread over me. For now Bernadette was safe and that was all that mattered.

I had gotten most of the party cleaned up the night before, but still had several bags of trash I needed to take out to the curb. As I was carrying the second load of bags out, Carter walked out of his aunt's house.

Great, just what I need, I thought to myself.

"Do you need some help?" he asked.

"Sure, thanks," I responded. "There are a few more bags inside, by the front door." Might as well be nice. I knew what he was capable of.

He ran inside and grabbed all of the remaining bags and hefted them out to the curb while I watched.

"There you go, all done," he announced.

"Thanks, I appreciate the help. No one else bothered," I told him.

"Yeah, no problem."

"So, how long are you staying? Just for the weekend?" I asked him, making small talk for a moment, so I didn't come across as rude. I didn't want to just get his help and dismiss him.

"Well actually," he looked at me coyly, "my parents said I could stay. We talked this morning and I'm moving in with Aunt Jean."

My posture stiffened. "You're what?" I asked, incredulously.

"I'm staying. I don't like Sandy Cove, and I'm not doing that great in school. So, my parents said I could move here. My aunt is a teacher, so she can help me. Besides, living with my parents is not all it's cracked up to be," he explained.

"What do you mean by that?" I asked, remembering that fateful night six years ago, that almost killed his parents.

He shrugged only his left shoulder. "Nothing. We just don't get along that great."

"Why didn't you tell me you were moving in with her?" I said much more forcefully than I meant to.

"Why are you yelling at me? I thought you'd be happy if I moved in next door." He sounded so sincere when he said that.

Could it be that I had misjudged him? Was it possible that he was actually just a nice guy and not the horrible person that I imagined him to be? No, I was still pretty sure he was not the sweet boy next-door. I did witness his attempt to burn his parents alive six years ago. That is a movie playing in my head that I will never get over. I had no proof that he was the Slasher, but he certainly had the temperament and ability to do it. Because of that, I would never fully trust him.

"Ivy. Ivy." A hand waved in front of my face.

"Oh, sorry. I was just lost in thought. Um, what did you say?" I responded.

"I just wanted to know if you were happy that I was moving in next door. Aren't you?" he asked. He raised his eyebrows expectantly.

"Yeah, I guess. Oh, you know what? I've gotta go. We can talk later." I needed to get out of there as quickly as possible. I did my best not to sprint back to my house. It was all I could do to walk normally, as he stood watching me.

After Carter went back home and I went back inside the house, I sat down on the couch and begin shaking. Carter was staying. What the hell was I going to do now? I had just saved Bernadette and now Carter was going to be around every day. That put Bernadette and Josephine in danger. At least I thought it did.

This was going to make a lot more work for me. But I guess I had to do what I had to do. There was no way I was going to let Carter harm anyone in this lifetime. If I had to die to save those girls, then so be it. It certainly wouldn't be the first time.

CHAPTER 9

Carter stayed with his aunt Jean, as promised, and I watched his every move, as I promised myself. Or I watched as much as I possibly could anyway. There was still school and other obligations that happened when I could not watch Carter.

The truth was that he seemed perfectly normal. At least, normal for Carter. I never saw him treat anybody badly or even give a sideways glance to Bernadette or Josephine. I was beginning to wonder if I had completely gotten on the wrong track with Carter. He was a model citizen as far as I could tell.

Several months passed without a single incident. Bernadette was doing just fine. Josephine was doing great with her friends, which I was not one of. I purposefully stayed away from Josephine. And even if we had become friends, I would not have dared mention my time travel adventures. I had made a lot of mistakes over the years, but I was not stupid enough to repeat that mistake.

Even though she believed me in one of my lives, in the last life she thought I was a crazy lunatic and Bernadette ended up dying because of it. I could never let that happen again, no matter how many lives I had.

Once again, the day of the water tower razing had arrived. In my past, it was the day Josephine always died. Somehow I had succeeded in saving Bernadette, at least so far, and I was determined to do the same with Josephine. No matter what happened, I was going to save that girl this time.

I knocked on the blue door in front of me and stood patiently, waiting for an answer.

"Oh, hi Ivy. What are you doing here?"

I'm sure I was the last person on the planet that Josephine expected to see at her front door on this day. Or any day, for that matter.

"Hi Josephine." I didn't call her Josie in this life. We weren't that close. "I was wondering if you wanted to hang out at the tower thing today?"

"With you?" She tilted her head and looked at me.

"Yeah, with me. Look, I know we aren't friends. But I'd like to change that," I tried to explain. "So, what do you say?" I smiled a cheesy smile, hoping to get her to laugh.

It worked.

"Okay, I guess so. I was just going to go with my parents. It'll be more fun to go with you." She stepped aside and opened the door wider. "Come in. I'm almost ready."

I obliged.

"Mom, Dad, I'm going to the tower with Ivy!" she called out. I didn't see her parents, but they must have been around there somewhere.

"Okay, we'll see you there!" her mother's voice flowed from somewhere else in the house.

I followed Josephine up the stairs to her room. I plopped onto her bed, because that's what teenagers do. Though I tried to act like a teen, I really didn't feel like one. I had actually lived over 40 years. Forty years that I remembered anyway. If you counted all the years from the time I was born to the time I died in each life, it was over 100. Oh wow, I hadn't really considered that before. One hundred years. Damn I was old. I laughed to myself.

"What's so funny?" Josephine called from the bathroom, where she was expertly applying her makeup.

"Oh nothing. I was just thinking of something. You almost ready?" I changed the subject quickly.

"Oh, damn!" Josephine yelled.

"What happened?" I jumped up off the bed and ran to the bathroom. "Oh never mind, you smell like a perfume factory blew up in here." I pinched my nose for emphasis.

"I know. I spilled my perfume all over me. Ivy, I can't go smelling like this. I need to take a shower and start all over. Ugh."

"That's okay. I'll wait," I told her.

"No, you don't have to do that," she replied. "It's going to take a while. You go and I'll meet you there."

"No, really. I can wait. It's no big deal," I tried to explain. The last thing I wanted to do was let her out of my sight.

"I'm serious, Ivy. I can't make you wait for me. Go on. I'll be there as soon as I can. I promise."

She nudged me out of the bathroom, then out her bedroom door, down the stairs, and opened the front door for me. I guess she was serious about wanting me to leave. I couldn't blame her. She really didn't know me. We were practically strangers.

"Okay, okay, I'm going. Are you just going to ride with your parents then?" I raised my eyebrows in hopes that was her new plan.

"Yeah, probably. If they want to wait. If not, I'll just walk. It isn't that far."

"Oh, I don't think you should do that…"

The door closed in my face.

"Well…okay then," I said out loud. "I guess that's that."

Now what? I wondered if it would be completely unreasonable for me to stand outside of Josephine's house until she was ready.

That could be an hour or more, knowing teenage girls. No I couldn't really do that. It would be too strange and would definitely make Josephine think twice about hanging out with me.

I stood there, watching her house for a couple minutes more, before I decided to walk to the tower alone and wait for Josephine. I knew it was a really bad idea, but what could I do?

I made a plate of food and sat down to eat alone, barely noticing anything except the road leading to the tower. The one Josephine would undoubtedly be walking up if she were alone. If she rode in with her parents, then they would park nearby and still walk up that same road.

"Hey there, how are you?"

I looked up as Simon sat down at my table, right across from me.

"Hi. I'm fine. You?" I replied, trying to be nice, keeping one eye on the road.

"You here by yourself?" he asked.

"Looks like it." I really wasn't in the mood for conversation. Especially with Simon.

I looked up again, toward the road, hoping for a glimpse of Josephine. What I saw made my blood run cold. Her parents. Walking up from the parking area. Alone. No daughter in sight.

Without a word to Simon, I jumped up and ran over to Josie's parents.

"Um, hi. I'm Ivy, remember me?"

"Yes, of course Ivy," her mother answered. "How are you dear?"

"I'm good, thanks. Is Josie with you?"

"No, dear, sorry. She had some sort of mishap and was going to be a while longer. She said she'd walk. She'll probably be along in a half hour or so," her mother explained.

Oh god, what do I do now? If I go to her house, and all is fine, she'll think I'm a crazy person, and may never talk to me again. If I sit here and wait, she may never make it. Is she at home being attacked at this very second? I felt a tear slide down my cheek.

"Ivy, are you all right?" Josie's mother asked me.

"Oh, yes. Um, I'm fine. I've got to go." I turned around and walked back to my table without another word to her parents.

I stood at the end of the table and started speaking before I had a chance to talk myself out of it. With all my heart, I hoped I wasn't making a really stupid decision. But with Josie's life on the line, I needed to act. And fast. With no time to waste, I followed through with that decision.

"Simon, come on. I need your help," I ordered.

"Okay." He jumped up and followed me, without question. For the moment anyway.

When I began jogging down the road, he easily kept pace with me.

"Where are we going anyway?" he asked as his breathing became more labored. "And in such a hurry."

"It's Josephine. I think something has happened to her."

My pace quickened. Simon matched it.

"Why do you think that? Weren't those her parents that you were just talking to?" he asked. "Wouldn't they know if something was wrong?"

"No they wouldn't," I huffed out, trying to catch my breath.

By the time we reached her street I was in a full run. Even Simon was having trouble keeping up. I could barely breathe, but I didn't care. I needed to get there. There was no time to waste.

The garage door was wide open. Oh no. I had lived this scenario before. I tore into the house, with Simon on my heels. I ran through the house screaming her name. After a thorough search, Josephine was nowhere to be found.

I finally stopped for just a moment to catch my breath. I had been so frantic that I hadn't realized that I could barely breathe. My vision started to dim and I felt wobbly. A pair of arms reached out and caught me before I hit the ground.

Simon sat me down on the couch.

"Ivy, I'll get you some water. Just stay here and try to breathe evenly. I think you're having a panic attack."

He returned in under 30 seconds with a glass of cool water. It helped calm me down as I took slow sips between breaths. Finally, my racing heart slowed, my breathing slowed, and I could finally speak.

"Thank you," I told Simon. "I'm really glad you're here."

He smiled when I said that. I thought I might need to clarify, but that would have to wait until later.

"We need to find Josie. She could be in danger," I told him, as I tried to stand up.

Simon helped me up, as I was still a bit wobbly. "Why do you think she's in danger?"

"It's a really long story. Believe me when I say that I don't have the time right now to explain it to you. Can you please just help me find her?"

"Yeah, sure. Anything you need."

He was so agreeable. I remembered that Simon. It wouldn't last long. It never did.

I didn't have the time to think about why Simon was being so nice and helpful to me.

"Come on. I know where we should look," I ordered again.

I grabbed his hand and pulled him out the garage door that led out of the kitchen. I lifted the car keys from their hook as we passed the threshold, handing them to Simon.

"Here, you drive. I don't have a license," I told him as I ran around to the passenger seat of Josephine's mother's car.

Simon looked down at the keys in his hand. "Um, are you sure this is okay? We could get into a lot of trouble for stealing someone's car."

"This is a matter of life and death. We can deal with all of that later. I'll give you directions on the way."

Simon crawled into the drivers seat and started up the car. As he backed it out of the driveway I pointed in the direction that he needed to go. He obliged.

When we reach the edge of the forest, I directed him to pull over and we got out.

"Where are we?" he asked, following me up the path.

"The sinkhole," I told him, not turning around to speak. I needed to concentrate on where I was stepping. There were a lot of rocks and other things to trip over on the way there.

"Oh. I've heard about this place, but never been there. You think Josephine is at the sinkhole?" he asked. "Why would she be there?"

That statement of his about never having been to the sinkhole made me wonder. Was that the truth? Had he never been there? Maybe not in this lifetime, no. But perhaps in one of the other lifetimes he had been there. I still wasn't one hundred percent convinced that he wasn't the Slasher. And if he was, I was taking a super big chance walking to the sinkhole voluntarily with him. But I had no other choice. It was this or possibly leaving Josephine to perish. Once again.

"Shhh," I told him as we drew near, holding my index finger over my lips.

He nodded.

We both saw her at the same time. Josephine was tied to a tree about 20 feet from the sinkhole. Her mouth was not gagged. Her eyes got big when she saw us, but she didn't say a word. She was smarter than that. I saw her scan the area for someone.

The strange thing was that we didn't see anyone with her. Who had tied her to the tree? Where had he gone? Why would he leave her alone, to possibly be found, or to get away?

It was at that moment that I realized, once and for all, that Simon was not the Red Lake Slasher. There was no way that he could have gotten to Josephine, and taken her to the forest, since he was sitting at the water tower razing party with me. After all that time, and all my lives, I finally knew that for certain. A bit of relief washed over me, but it didn't last long.

That raised the ultimate question. If not Simon, then who was the Slasher? Carter? He was my only other suspect. I couldn't imagine anyone else that it could be.

We didn't have to wait long to find out the answer to that question. Josephine let out a blood curling scream just as I heard a thump and a groan behind me. I turned to see Simon slump to the ground. I looked up and there he was. The same man that had killed me in the past. He had a ski mask on, so I still wasn't sure of his identity. But it was him.

I didn't wait around to be the next person to be knocked unconscious. I sprinted toward Josephine and stopped in front of her. I turned and used my body as a human shield. I couldn't let Josephine be alone and vulnerable without trying to help her. She was still tied up and had no way to defend herself.

CHAPTER 10

I started yelling at the man standing next to Simon's body. He looked up at me.

"I told the sheriff where we were going. He is on his way with a lot of back up!"

He started walking toward us.

"Stop! I mean it. You need to go before they get here," I added.

"I don't believe you."

His voice was raspy, yet familiar. I couldn't tell if he was disguising his voice or if he had a cold and was actually on the verge of laryngitis.

"Do I know you?" I narrowed my eyes at him.

"You know me."

He continued walking toward us. He did so at a slow, even pace, like he had all the time in the world.

At least I knew for a fact, finally, that Simon was not the Slasher. And not my killer. Not after the very first time, that is. But we were fighting, and I did stab him first. He wasn't a cold blooded serial killer. That I was sure of.

The strange thing was that Carter was my only other suspect, and this guy didn't sound like Carter either. I watched the way he walked. That also wasn't Carter's walk. Yet, his walk was also familiar.

I was a bit frazzled from the events of the day. I knew this person. I was sure of it. I just couldn't place him.

The man didn't walk all the way to where I was standing, guarding Josephine. He turned and started circling the sinkhole. I never took my eyes off of him as I watched him stop once, bend over, and look in. He was careful not to get too close.

"You know," he kind of whispered in that raspy voice of his, "I could throw the two of you in there and no one would ever find you."

He was clearly trying to hide his voice. That was something that someone would do if they were afraid of being recognized. Ditto with the mask he was wearing. I wondered if he meant to let us go. I'd seen enough movies in my time to know that if they are trying to hide their identity, then they might not be planning to kill you.

That didn't seem the case here, though. Why trouble himself with all of this? He definitely intended to kill Josephine. Otherwise, why bring her here?

"You don't want to kill us. Just let us go. We won't tell anyone, we promise," Josephine finally spoke up.

"Shut up. I don't want to talk to you. I want to talk only to your friend here," he whispered.

"Me? Why?" I asked. "What does this have to do with me?"

"What doesn't it have to do with you? It's all about you," he replied.

"I don't understand," I told him.

"I wanted to thank you for all you've done over the years. You certainly made things interesting."

I narrowed my eyes at him. "I don't understand."

"I know you don't. But you will," he said.

He continued his walk around the sinkhole and stopped when

he had made a complete revolution. He didn't come near us though. It was as if he purposefully kept his distance.

"Remember that first time that I killed Bernadette? No one ever knew for sure, because she went into this sinkhole, never to be heard from again."

"What do you mean by the first time you killed Bernadette? She's still alive. Isn't she?"

I turned to Josephine for confirmation. She shrugged her shoulders.

"Oh, she's still alive this time. I'm talking about the first time. And then how I laughed after I stabbed you and you laid in a pool of your blood, slowly dying. Right there in that exact spot." He pointed to the ground in front of him.

That was all he said. No clarification.

"I don't understand..."

My voice trailed off as realization dawned on me.

It must have shown on my face.

"There it is. She finally figured it out," he continued whispering.

"You...you are...living your life over...also?" I barely stuttered out.

"That's what I hear," he replied. Even with him still trying to disguise it, I could hear the smile in his voice.

"How is that possible?" I asked.

"How is any of this possible? I have no clue. But it's happening. I haven't been dying though. As far as I know, I keep on living. But, whenever you die, I somehow jump into another lifetime with you. The first time was surreal. But now I just find it great fun."

"Oh my god. So you've been one step ahead of me this whole time?" I was in shock.

"Yeah, pretty much. At least after the first time I was."

"Who are you?" I asked boldly, reaching over to try removing the duct tape that was holding Josephine's hands together around a tree branch. He was too busy bragging to notice.

"I can't believe you haven't figured it out by now, Ives."

My head whipped around and I dropped my grip on the duct tape. No. This can't be happening.

"Parker? That's not possible," I proclaimed.

"Well, you got me," he replied, pulling the mask off of his head and speaking in his normal voice.

I started to feel lightheaded. My own brother was the Red Lake Slasher. The one that had killed me, as well as my friends, over and over. I reached for a nearby tree to steady myself.

"But you...you...why would you want to kill me?" I finally stuttered out.

"Isn't that obvious? From the moment you were born, you were the golden child. The one Mom and Dad doted on, and completely forgot that I existed."

"That's not true. They treated you exactly the same as me," I replied.

"Oh, you are so deluded. You can't even see it," he snarled at me.

He picked up a rock and threw it into the sinkhole. We all stood quietly for several seconds, expecting that inevitable plunk as it hit bottom, but that never came. I thought back to when he threw me in and it took an eternity to hit the bottom. Then the hole seemed to swallow me up. I shuddered in response.

He kept his eyes pointed at the sinkhole, giving me a few more seconds to work with the duct tape. He didn't seem to notice when the tape finally tore and Josephine pulled her arms from around the branch. She began rubbing them to get her circulation back. She kept silent as she did so.

"You are wrong, Parker. And even if that is partly true, how can you blame me? I loved you. I would have done anything for you. And you hurt me, over and over. How could you do that to me?" I couldn't help myself. I started sobbing as I spoke, and fell to my knees with my head in my hands.

When I looked up at my brother, he was grinning at me. He wasn't the same person I knew. It wasn't my brother standing there. Something had taken over. Something evil.

"Josephine," he looked up at her as he spoke, "was particularly fun to kill. Weren't you Honey?" he made a kissing noise in her direction.

I was sure that he had noticed the fact that she was no longer tied up, but didn't seem to care.

Josephine turned her head in disgust.

"This girl here, gave me a run for my money. Once in her kitchen, she shoved her legs so hard against the kitchen counter that my head drilled into the refrigerator. That one hurt." He smiled. I could tell he was thinking back to that day. "It's more fun when they put up a fight."

I didn't even know how to respond to what he was saying. My head hurt just thinking about all the lives I had led, and all the deaths that he caused. Over and over again. All the time knowing that I was reliving my life. He seemed to take great pleasure in hurting me. I couldn't believe what I was hearing.

"Oh, and that time you told me about reliving your lives over and over? That was the best one," he smirked. "You were so sincere and worried that I wouldn't believe you. You had no idea that I already knew. Right?" He looked at me for confirmation.

"You are right. I had no idea. What is going on with you Parker? This isn't like you at all," I told him, as I stood up. I resolved to cry no more over my brother, and my lost lives.

"You think you know me, but you don't. Bernadette and Josephine aren't the only two people I've ever killed, Ives. There have been others. Lots of others."

He sounded like he was bragging, and it broke my heart. I couldn't believe what I was hearing from my own brother. My only sibling. The boy that I thought would stand by me no matter what ever came in life.

"What? Who? I know about Graham, but who else?" I was incredulous.

"No one you know. I had to branch out to other cities. Even other states. Places where I would never be a suspect. I'm not an idiot," he proclaimed.

"I don't think you are an idiot, Parker. I just don't understand all of this," I told him honestly.

He ignored me. "Do you want to know why I grabbed Josephine this time, instead of just killing her outright, there at her house?" He looked directly at me.

I nodded.

"Because I knew it would get you here. She was the lure. I thought it would be fun to kill both of you at the same time. Remember that time that you and Bernadette and me got into the fight right here? And Bernadette kicked me hard in the ribs?"

I nodded again.

"Well that pissed me off. My ribs ached for weeks. I actually had to wrap them myself and secure them with duct tape. It wasn't pretty, but it worked."

"Oh, and that time Josephine scratched my face? That was another doozy. Believe me when I tell you that hiding your face from other people for a couple of weeks is not easy. Luckily, no one noticed that they only saw my profile." He burst out laughing.

We did not laugh. There was nothing funny about the situation at all.

There was a slight movement several feet away from me and I looked over in the direction of the sound.

CHAPTER 11

Parker didn't seem to notice that Simon was stirring. He was much too busy bragging about all the people he had killed. And he seemed especially pleased in the fact that he was tormenting me.

Josephine walked over and stood next to me, grabbing onto my arm for comfort. That was something that Parker did notice. When he lifted the gun, we both gasped. In all that had been going on, I hadn't noticed the gun at his side.

"Don't move! Either of you," he told us, pointing the gun right at our heads.

We both nodded.

"I find it interesting, Ives, that you haven't asked me why I killed Graham," he said.

Josephine leaned over and whispered in my ear. "Who's Graham?"

"I'll explain later," I told her.

"I'll explain now," Parker blurted out. "No need to whisper. I can hear you."

Josephine looked down at her feet. She wasn't about to say anything to Parker that might make him angrier than he already was.

"Graham was your boyfriend, Josephine."

She looked up at him in response.

"I've never had a boyfriend named Graham. You must be thinking of someone else," she replied.

"No, I'm not thinking of anyone else. It was definitely you. It just wasn't in this lifetime. It was three lifetimes ago, I think."

He looked up at the sky while trying to do the math of everything that had happened, and in which lifetime. Good luck, I thought. I had a hard time keeping it all straight myself.

Even after listening to everything Parker and I had been saying to each other, Josephine still hadn't reconciled the fact that we had been reliving our lives, and scrunched up her face in confusion.

"Well, he was your boyfriend for a little while. Once you died, Ivy took over that job. Didn't you, Ives?" He looked to me for an answer.

I shrugged my shoulders. Josephine looked at me for answers.

"Parker, let's just…"

I never got the rest of that sentence out. Josephine and I watched in horror as Simon sneaked up behind Parker and pounced. I had no idea how he managed that, there in the forest, where every step seemed to result in a loud crunching noise beneath our feet.

Since Parker had been standing there, holding out the gun toward us, it went off when Simon landed on his back. Josephine and I both instinctively ducked. Thankfully, neither of us was hit.

The fight was on.

The two of them were on the ground, rolling dangerously close to the mouth of the sinkhole. I held my breath for a moment, not knowing what to do. Then, out of the blue, Josephine sprang into action. I watched as she ran over and picked up the gun from where it had landed on the forest floor. It was partially covered in leaves. She brushed them off quickly.

Once she had steadied herself, she lifted the gun in the direction of the men, who were pummeling each other mercilessly.

"Stop!" she yelled.

No one responded.

"I said stop!" she screamed and lifted the gun in the air, pulling the trigger.

The blast got their attention. The fight stopped and they looked up at her, eyebrows raised.

"Get up!" she yelled.

They obliged. Neither one took their eyes off of the gun as they both got to their feet and stood next to each other, their backs to the sinkhole.

"Simon, you come over here and stand next to Ivy," she directed, waving the gun to motion him to walk over to us.

She didn't have to tell him twice. He was standing next to me in a flash.

"Hey now, Josephine." Parker put his palms up toward her. "I would never have hurt anyone. I was just venting. Really."

"Shut up! You are a liar. You were going to kill all of us. I'm not an idiot!" she screamed at him.

"No, of course not. You are definitely not an idiot. Come on, why don't you just put that gun down?"

I could see his hands shaking as he held them up in front of him.

"Back up," she told him calmly.

"What? Why?" He looked behind him and realized how dangerously close he was to the sinkhole.

"Because I said so!"

He took one step back.

"Another step," she told him.

"Josie," I interrupted. "What are you doing?"

"I'm taking care of this horrible person that was going to kill us," she explained.

"Come on Josie. You are not a killer. That's my brother, Parker. Let's just call the cops and let them deal with him." I was doing my best to calm down the situation. She wasn't listening to me though.

"No way. The cops won't do anything. He hasn't actually killed anyone. Anyone that we know of anyway. Anyone that we can prove. But he had every intention of killing us. I can't let him get away with that," Josephine explained.

She turned back to Parker. "I said take another step." She waved the gun a bit, indicating that he needed to move.

He took another, very small step back. He was standing right on the edge of the sinkhole by then. When I looked down, I could see the edge collapsing in around him. If he stood there much longer, he would be going down with it.

"Josephine, stop," I told her, trying to sound as calm as possible.

"What is going on here?"

All four of us turned to see Carter making his way from the trees and into the clearing.

Then we all turned back to Parker as he yelled. He had lost his balance, standing there on the very edge, and his arms were flailing wildly, as he tried to regain his balance.

Without thinking about the consequences, I ran toward my brother. No matter what he had done, and how many lives he had ruined, he was my brother. He deserved prison, yes, but I couldn't let him die. Not like this.

Unfortunately, I was too late. I stopped right before the edge and reached out to take his arm, but he was too far gone. I screamed as he fell. I never did hear him land in the bottom, but a ton of debris from the sinkhole began to cave in. I shuddered violently, remembering that feeling of suffocation that he had to be going through at that exact moment. Like I said previously, I would never wish that on anyone. Not even the Red Lake Slasher.

If I hadn't backed up several feet when I did, then I would have gone in with it. We all stood there and watched in horror as the sinkhole continued to collapse in on itself. It made a huge ruckus and dirt and dust were flying everywhere. All of us still standing above, backed way up, as the ground underneath us was all collapsing in.

After what seemed like several minutes, it all stopped. We looked around at each other as the forest suddenly became eerily quiet.

The sinkhole was gone. Or mostly gone anyway. There was no longer a huge, gaping hole in the ground, just a bit of an indentation in the earth where it previously was. Still, we didn't know how stable the ground was, and we kept our distance.

I began sobbing. My brother was down there, crushed by tons of dirt and rocks. There was no saving him now.

"What the hell just happened?" Carter finally spoke up.

"We'll explain it to you later. Let's get out of here," I told him.

CHAPTER 12

An hour later, Josephine, Simon, and I had explained everything that had happened to the sheriff. I conveniently left out the part about me and Parker reliving our lives. The sheriff could see how shook up we all were. He believed us, especially when Josephine produced the gun that Parker had brought to the forest with him.

My parents were devastated. They had lost a son. I did my best to explain what had happened and what Parker was about to do, and had already done. Though I couldn't prove any of it.

It broke my heart to tell them everything that I knew, but how could I not? If it had just been Parker and me there at that sinkhole, I might have been able to concoct a story that would have resulted in it all just being an unfortunate accident. But, we weren't alone. Simon and Josephine had witnessed the entire thing. And even Carter had seen that last bit of it. No, there was no way to cover any of that up and spare my parents the heartache that would undoubtedly be a large part of the rest of their lives. Their son was a serial killer. There was no way to hide that fact.

Simon and I parted friends. I went on to finish high school and then started dating Graham. Simon went on to someone else.

That was fine. There was much too much history between us to ever try to make something work. It would never work. I knew that. We didn't talk much over the years, but we were always cordial.

Josephine and I became the best of friends once again, and I couldn't be any happier about it. She listened whenever I needed to talk about Parker, which wasn't often. I tried to put him, and his reign of terror, behind me. It didn't always work, but I managed to go on to lead a fairly normal life.

I never once blamed Josie for Parker's death. How could I? She did what she had to do. It probably saved all of our lives, including Carter's.

Carter moved back home to Sandy Cove with his parents. After the scene he witnessed, and after I told him what had happened, he wanted nothing to do with any of us. I couldn't blame a guy for that.

Five years later, while in college, Graham and I married. He was the love of my life. It only took a few lifetimes for me to realize that. Over the next ten years, we had three beautiful children together. My life was complete. I knew that I would always mourn my beautiful children, Hunter and Courtney, but they just weren't meant to be in this lifetime.

I'm 31 years old now, and am still going strong. Bernadette and Josie both survived, and are living their own wonderful lives. And since Parker was no longer around to hurt anyone, it was my conclusion that all had been resolved and I was living my last life ever. That was perfectly fine with me.

THE END

AUTHOR NOTE

I hope you enjoyed reading The Many Lives of Ivy Wells. This was such a fun series to write.

If you liked this book, please leave a review. Your opinion matters to me, and makes me work harder to bring you entertaining stories!

You can find the review page by going to my website below and clicking on the book.

If you enjoyed this book and would like information on new releases, sign up for my newsletter here:

www.MichelleFiles.com

Thank you!
Michelle

Secrets of Wildflower Island
Wildflower Mystery Series - Book 1

When four teenage girls discover a body, badly beaten, a nice day at the beach goes horribly wrong. As they embark on a quest to solve the murder, they find themselves as the main suspects. The girls quickly turn on each other as they are blackmailed by an unknown person and harassed by others. Who killed the boy? Will the girls be next? This mesmerizing mystery, suspense novel will have you guessing until the end.

CHAPTER 1 Preview

"Where is your sister? We have something we want to talk to you about," Mary's father, Tim, asked her as the family sat down to have a nice lunch of fish and chips at the Wildflower Inn Cafe they owned.

"She went to the beach party," Mary replied, propping her bare feet up on the remaining empty chair.

"I'm here, I'm here," Piper said quickly as she ran up the wooden stairs from the beach onto the cafe's deck. "Can we make this quick? I want to go back down to the beach party. Mary, move," Piper said, pushing Mary's feet off of her chair. Piper sat down and began braiding her long hair while she waited for her parents to tell them whatever it was they wanted and she could go back to having fun with her friends.

The teenage waitress took their lunch orders immediately upon them sitting down at their usual table, which interrupted their conversation. She ignored the other customers who had arrived several minutes before and were still waiting for her to address them. She was receiving irritated looks from quite a few tables, of which she was completely oblivious to. This did not go unnoticed by Tim Carmichael, Piper and Mary's father. He ran the cafe and it was important to him that his customers were well taken care of.

"Frankie," Tim said to their waitress, "please go help all of these nice people before you put our order in," gesturing to the other tables. "Remember that they pay your salary. And mine." He smiled as he said it. Tim was a pretty easy going boss.

Frankie was just 16 years old and had a head full of wild red hair. With her curves and just a few freckles on her nose, she was very cute, and a favorite of the local boys that frequented the cafe. She didn't pay them much attention though, which drove them even crazier. Frankie smiled back at Tim and wandered off to help the rest of her customers.

Tim Carmichael watched her walk away. He was a man, and not completely immune to the little swish in her walk, especially since she was wearing nothing but cut off jean shorts, a bikini top, and flip flops. This was the standard wear at the outdoor cafe on the beach.

Once she was out of earshot, Tim turned back to his family. He noticed that his wife, Roxanne, was watching him as he was watching Frankie. She didn't say a word, but he could see the disapproval in her eyes. He knew that was a conversation they would be having later that night, when they were alone. He grimaced at the thought.

"As I was saying, we have something your mom and I want to talk to you about."

He looked over at his wife again and frowned, terrified of delivering the bad news to their daughters. He knew he couldn't avoid it though, and he knew it would hurt the girls terribly. It just broke his heart that he had to break theirs.

You can find purchase options for this novel at www.MichelleFiles.com.

CPSIA information can be obtained
at www.ICGtesting.com
Printed in the USA
LVHW080418080621
689675LV00016B/166